THE COPPER SKY

THE COPPER SKY

ABHIJIT GUPTA

NIYOGI BOOKS

Published by

NIYOGI BOOKS
D-78, Okhla Industrial Area, Phase-I
New Delhi-110 020, INDIA
Tel: 91-11-26816301, 49327000
Fax: 91-11-26810483, 26813830
email: niyogibooks@gmail.com
website: www.niyogibooks.com

Editor: Upama Biswas
Cover Design: Rabia Gupta
Layout: Sarojini Gosain

ISBN: 978-93-83098-63-7
Year of Publication: 2015

Printed at: Niyogi Offset Pvt. Ltd., New Delhi, India

To my mother and father to whom I owe so much but who are no longer here to read this offering

FOREWORD

I doubt whether there is any author who can claim that they have not allowed their experiences to influence their writings. I certainly can't. But, this is not an autobiographical novel. It is a work of fiction.

If anybody feels they recognise themselves in the host of characters who make their appearance, I would urge them to read further and see that this is a work of fiction. If they see resemblances it is because fragments have been borrowed from personalities to give characters verisimilitude. If anything, this reflects the indelible impression they have made by the strength of their personality.

This is not a historical or political treatise. What appears is what the young enquiring mind of the protagonist has garnered from all he has heard and read and then processed in his own mind. People may not agree with the views expressed, but that is their privilege and right. The same right of freedom I exercise as an author.

Not many people of this generation realise the bitterness that the pre-Independence generation carried within them as a result of their subject status under the British. Maybe this will help open a few eyes to the plight of the current generation of subjects across the world today.

PART ONE

London

The drone of the engine was making him drowsy. The shapely air hostess caught his eye as she swayed past and stopped. She wore a heavy perfume and a tightly wound sari. She smiled, "Would you like anything to drink, sir?"

Amar hesitated. His only experience with alcohol, in spite of being nineteen years of age, had been a beer offered rather patronisingly by one of his elder sister's aspiring boyfriends, in a cafe in Simla. He had not enjoyed it. Today, still knotted up by the emotional turmoil of the last few weeks, Amar decided there might be solace in a beer.

The air hostess returned with a full frothing glass and a warm smile, "Looking forward to London, sir?"

"My first trip."

"You'll love London. If you need a refill just give me a shout." She smiled again as she glided away. Heavily made-up but attractive, Amar decided, as he guiltily dragged his eyes away from her saucy retreating bottom. He had just left his girlfriend in Delhi, and could not believe that he was already enjoying ogling other women.

❖

Preeti had entered his life courtesy his dear college friend, philanderer and guide, Sudipto. Walking back from the Delhi University coffee house one afternoon, Sudipto, who had often ribbed Amar about his girlfriend-less existence, had adjusted his gold-rimmed glasses and said, "You are a fool, wasting opportunities like this." He was given to obscure pronouncements, but even for him this was a new high. Amar was baffled.

"What the hell are you talking about?" he asked, irritated.

"Don't you know that Tutu's sister is crazy about you?" Tutu was Sudipto's latest girlfriend and had an attractive sister, Preeti. She had a slender sari-clad body topped by a classically beautiful face—large eyes, straight nose and tremulous lips; very aloof. Also coveted by the university's young men.

"She doesn't even know me," said a surprised Amar.

"That doesn't matter—she thinks you're 'dashing' and 'handsome', Amar."

Amar had laughed to cover his embarrassment. "Desperate lady, I must say."

"No, don't laugh," said Sudipto seriously. "There are plenty of young men dying to be introduced to her. So if you want to get ahead of them, then come to the coffee house tomorrow at noon."

And so, a relationship had taken root—growing in the noisy clatter of the coffee house, sustained by walks in the tree-shaded university avenues, and flowering in a lonely corner of a park near Kashmiri Gate where they exchanged their first kiss one afternoon. It was a tentative meeting of two lips, and little more. He had built up such huge expectations about kissing that this cursory brushing of lips disappointed him. Until Preeti took the initiative and kissed him deeply, allowing her tongue to find his. She appeared to be more experienced than he was. This bothered him until the pleasure of the commingling of lip and tongue drove the thought away.

For Amar, a curtain had lifted onto a new world. He was important to someone, someone who—saw a missing button on the shirt and offered to stitch it on, waited for him expectantly at the coffee house, noticed when he was worried or tense. He mattered.

They would look for privacy whenever they met, but Delhi in the mid-1950s was an unkind place for courting couples. They ultimately would find refuge in the last resort in those days—the rear balcony seats in a cinema hall. The darkness would allow more liberties than a public park, and hands could roam freely. But even here, there were limitations to more adventurous exploration. Often, he would come out from the hall more frustrated than satisfied. They would then walk to Wenger's, in Connaught Place, where over a plate of pakodas and hot tea he would slowly get back his composure.

The news of his father's posting to London had turned their world upside down.

Preeti had taken the news stoically. A tear had rolled down her cheek when Amar had first broken the news, but she had quickly wiped it away, smiled, and reached for his hand. Neither talked about what the future held. A hollow ache of impending loss became his constant companion.

His family had left for Bombay to take the ship from there. He was flying on a later date and would join them in London.

On the evening of his departure, as light ebbed from a dying day, they sat holding hands in the back seat of the battered Ambassador taxi lumbering to Palam airport. But the warmth seemed to have fled from their hands. Today, it was cold flesh against cold flesh. Tears rolled down her cheek and she made no effort to wipe them away, in spite of Sudipto's presence in the front seat.

At the airport, Amar asked them not to linger. He saw little point in prolonging the agony. He watched the retreating figures, with Sudipto's arm protectively around Preeti's shoulder and felt a sudden twinge of jealousy. But dismissed it as unworthy. Sudipto was a friend he could trust.

In the hustle of the neon-lit busy airport, with people all around him, he felt more alone than he had ever before. A part of his life was over and a new life awaited him outside in the night, in the shape of the gleaming Super Constellation sitting on the runway.

❖

The beer tasted bitter. He did not accept the offer of a refill. Jasmine, the air hostess, got chatting with him after dinner was served, kneeling by his seat. A plump sari-clad lady, nourished by pure *ghee*, a big *bindi* on her forehead, couldn't take her eyes off the two of them. She kept glaring across the aisle, her face breaking into a grimace occasionally. Amar thought it was due to the flatulence from her normal tea-time *hing katchori*. Jasmine thought she was being censorious and whispered conspiratorially, "Just look at her. She's staring as if we're making love in public." Amar was shocked, but equally thrilled at being included in the adult world. Especially when she later wrote down her London contact number in his new diary, and brushed his shoulder with her thighs as she passed down the aisle.

There was a refuelling stop at Cairo, and then they were airborne again for Beirut. He dozed fitfully through the night and woke up with the pre-landing announcement at Beirut. Dawn had broken and as the plane banked, his sleepy eyes were startled by blinding blue pouring through the window. A sea of incredible blue was flanked by brown hills. He hadn't expected Beirut to be so beautiful. He did not believe that the blue of the sea was real, and put it down to an optical illusion. But, the colour was reconfirmed as they sat in the airport lounge sipping fresh orange juice, gazing at the dawn-fresh turquoise sea through the large plate glass windows.

There was to be one more stop before landing at London—Zurich. As they approached Zurich airport, the plane had to go through grey clouds before landing. For a few minutes the world outside went dark, but suddenly the plane broke through and they were over the airport. As they disembarked, Amar began to feel for the first time that he was in a different world. Cairo and Beirut had not seemed so alien—the same skin colour as the Indians, the same kind of confusion, the same dirty toilets, and the same warm weather. But now suddenly, he felt he was in an ordered, manicured space, a different piece of time and place. Everything seemed to be in its ordained position, the waiters and waitresses were white-skinned, the lounge immaculate, the manicured grass outside a fresh emerald, the air coldly invigorating, and the hills through the window a blue-grey, their tops disappearing into the clouds. And of course, the pastries—creamy and delicious!

It was evening by the time they landed in London. Jasmine whispered to him as he deplaned, "London can be lonely—give me a call if you need cheering ..."

An Indian colleague of his father's had come to receive him, to put him up for two nights until the family arrived. As he carried his heavy case to the coach, the cold hit him and he involuntarily shivered. He was glad to get into the shelter of the coach.

They started moving. The London which he had read about, dreamt about, fantasised about, was about to unfold in front of him. For travel-drugged Amar, however, London did not really register as they drove into the city. Through the foggy evening gloom he noticed the neon signs over shop fronts, the red telephone kiosks at street corners, and the red double-decker buses which were familiar from posters and picture postcards. The air smelt of petrol fumes and coal smoke, quite different from the damp earth and mouldering-leaves smell he would encounter when he took the dog for an after-dinner walk around their house in Delhi. The sky was an odd burnished copper, the roads very wide. But all this he saw through a haze of exhaustion. Nothing really made an impression. Except the foreignness. And the intimidating dimness, as if he was seeing everything through a haze of smoke. He would have to spend three years in this semi-darkness. There was not a soul he knew here. His sense of loneliness deepened.

A black London taxicab took them from the coach station to the block of flats where his host and his family lived on the top floor. Amar drowsed through dinner at the family table, barely able to make conversation. His host, considerately, took him to a small bedroom and showed him the common toilet in the corridor.

His final thought as he fell asleep on his first night in London at the end of a momentous journey—how would he cope with a shared toilet.

Native Rites

He awoke early next morning refreshed and eager to catch his first daytime glimpse of London. From his window he could see a dark grey sky edged with crimson. Serried ranks of dark sloping roofs stretched out to the horizon. Smoke curled up from some chimneys. A thin fog hung over the city, through which a tapestry of orange-lit windows gleamed. He could imagine sleepy people in their dressing gowns putting kettles on the stove for their first cup of tea. On the street below he heard the rattle of milk carts. The city stirred awake slowly to another sunless day.

After a breakfast of hot *parathas* and a spicy dry potato *subzi,* washed down with sweet hot tea, he set out with his host to buy an overcoat. He was excited since this was his first experience of London streets. The sky was slate, but the shops were brightly lit even though it was morning. The buses ground along as noisily as in Delhi. As they walked to the bus stop, Amar felt the damp cold penetrating his suit.

On the bus he witnessed a remarkable tableau, which started with the ticket collector, a plump lady in a dark uniform, who approached him with outstretched hand and a loud "Thank you". Amar looked up in alarm. What was he supposed to do? Be polite and say, "You're welcome"?

His host came to the rescue. Amar listened open-mouthed to the exchange which followed:

"Thank you"—ticket collector.

"Thank you"—Amar's host.

"Thank you"—ticket collector.

"Thank you"—Amar's host.

During this, money and tickets changed hands.

Amar realised that he had a lot of native rituals to learn.

❖

He went to receive his family the next day at Tilbury docks—a bleak, cold and cheerless place. As people came down the gangway, Amar looked for his mother's short round figure. At last he spotted her, looking different because of the dark coat over her sari. As he embraced her and nestled his face against her double chin, he smelt the familiar whiff of talcum powder which had always been the smell he associated with her. "You're looking thin—you haven't been eating properly," she said.

His sister and brother hugged him shyly. "What's that you're wearing?" his twelve-year-old brother asked, pointing to his overcoat. "An overcoat, *boka* (stupid)—you'll be wearing one soon too." His younger sister, who had begun to shed her puppy fat as she moved into her teens, asked, "Seen any films yet?" "Just been here two days, *gadha* (ass)," he replied cuffing her affectionately.

His father hugged him rather absentmindedly and asked, "The London School interview is tomorrow?"

"Yes," said Amar.

Back in London they drove to the Park West on Edgware Road, a serviced apartment block. It was just that—a block. A gloomy, red-bricked monument to tastelessness. Amar's heart sank at the thought of having to live there for the next two to three months. But once inside their third-floor apartment, he felt better. It had a warmth and cosiness, belied by the exterior starkness. The wall-to-wall beige carpeting was soft, the furniture modern and comfortable, the walls papered in a soft floral pattern, lit by cosy low table lamps, and the kitchenette neat and efficient-looking. The Venetian blind-covered windows looked onto similar brick buildings, built around a rectangular lawn, with no visual relief when one looked out. However, Hyde Park was a five-minute walk away, and in it there was relief available in the acres of green parkland.

Amar decided he needed some fresh air and left, promising to return for dinner. Pulling on his new grey overcoat as he walked down Kendal Street towards Edgware Road, he realised that this was the first time he was on his own since arriving in London. He took a deep breath of the cold air and felt invigorated by this sudden sense of freedom. The cold stung his nose and cheeks. A haze hung in the air and the night sky was that coppery hue that he would always associate with London. It was as if a curved copper pan had been upended over the city, with the centre of it glowing red. Except, there was no heat.

The shops lining the street were brightly lit; red double-decker buses lumbered down Edgware Road grinding gears; grey-faced people hurried to their destinations like an old film in jerky fast forward. He decided, perhaps not originally, to christen it the "Lambeth Trot" and felt pleased with his cleverness.

Walking down Oxford Street he passed the Cumberland Hotel, after which the stores began. Most of the buildings looked massive from the pavement. They were of a grey stone which looked grimy because of the pollution and the traffic fumes. In spite of this, they had a certain dignity, lent by their huge size and proportions.

The shop windows were bright and well-decorated and helped to relieve the evening gloom. The women's dresses in shades of red, blue and beige, bathed in bright spotlights, were islands of colour in the otherwise drab street. Walking along the crowded pavement, feeling the energy of this big city, Amar realised that his spirits had lifted. He thought, guiltily, that it was helped by the young woman in front of him, in a tight red dress, swaying her hips as she walked. Realising that he had been staring at her for some time, Amar quickly looked away.

Yet, he had to admit, he enjoyed the buttocks bouncing cheekily in front of him. He had, initially, been shocked by the permissiveness he saw around him. Couples locked in tight embrace—a common sight with nobody seeming the least bothered. This was not the London he had expected. Not this permissive London, not this London of not-so-genteel depravity, where darkened doorways sheltered couples kissing passionately, where parks were littered with couples in varying stages of intimacy.

He decided he had to make a start on accepting these new norms sometime. Why not now?

He walked back admiring the passing sexy-bottoms and jouncing-breasts, though still guiltily, humming "*Yeh hai London, meri jaan*", a variant of a current Hindi film song. He suddenly remembered the phone number given to him by Jasmine on the plane. His mood had definitely improved by the time he reached home.

Admission

Amar did not sleep well that night, with the interview anxiety gnawing away. His eyes felt gritty and his mind fuzzy when he woke up. This was not the best preparation for an important interview, but he tried not to worry about it as he sipped his tea and glanced at the *Times* which had been slipped under the front door.

After a quick breakfast of cornflakes and toast, he got out the directions he had written down for getting to the London School of Economics. He had to go to the Marble Arch Tube station and take the Central line to Holborn. From there he would have to walk a short distance.

At the ticket counter he made sure to pronounce Holborn as "Ho'burn" and asked for a return ticket. He felt that he sounded like a regular and walked away from the counter with his self-confidence boosted.

Climbing up the staircase at Holborn, Amar found himself in a road called Kingsway along which he walked a little uncertainly. At the top of the road, he turned left and left again into a narrower lane with tall buildings looming over him and shutting off the light. Had he lost his way? Where was the LSE? He was looking for a grand building with a pillared entrance and wide steps sweeping up to imposing doors. But all he saw were grimy grey stone buildings on either side in what was almost a dark alley. Finally, he noticed some steps leading up to an unobtrusive door under an archway. This led him, rather anti-climactically, into the world-famous institution.

His interview was even more of an anti-climax, and was over in what seemed like five minutes.

"Now, let me formally welcome you to the LSE. We are very happy to have students from India and they have an enviable record here. We hope you will enjoy your stay with us."

He had been admitted.

He could not initially understand his easy passage. Later he realised that it was due, in large measure, to the BA Honours degree which he had from Delhi University. These degrees, unfortunately, were not recognised by London University, and as a result people like Amar had to do a second degree rather than a postgraduate course. So, actually, he came in better qualified than any of the local candidates who were coming in fresh from school. That must have swung the balance.

Amar collected his coat and emerged onto the street with a great weight lifted from his shoulders. He was now a student of the LSE!

❖

That evening Amar decided to go for a walk in Hyde Park. At Marble Arch, he crossed over to the vast green expanse and walked along one of the paths which criss-crossed it, as the weak rays of the setting sun died away in the dark trees.

The air was cold, and although his nose and ears were chilled, Amar felt stimulated. A young man sat on a bench reading a book in the fading light. Here and there couples lay locked in embrace. Nobody paid any heed to them. Amar thought back to his furtive encounters with Preeti in the rear seats of taxis and the balconies of cinema houses and recalled the constant fear of detection which had plagued them. Why had something so natural and spontaneous acquired this overlay of guilt and secretiveness in his country?

The euphoria generated by his admission to the LSE had not worn off. He strode along in the gathering darkness on the springy turf, feeling a surge of energy. There was so much to do, so much to explore, so much to experience in this new world. In his innocence he saw the future spread before him—full of promise, full of excitement, full of hidden delights—a treasure chest to pluck the wonders from at his will.

As he walked, his thoughts took on a more sombre turn. Preeti and the unresolved question. Was it fair to her—and him—to keep this relationship in cold storage for three years? Could he say that he would not look at other women over this period? Could he expect her to stay steadfast? The answer seemed to be no on all counts.

❖

The day finally arrived. Amar entered the LSE, rather self-conscious in his new clothes. The tweed sports jacket seemed to pinch under his armpits. Amar wasn't at all sure that the sports jacket design and colours were appropriate. But as he walked into the crowded lobby, he realised he had little to worry about. Most of the young men were dressed in shabby worn jackets and baggy grey flannel trousers. A number of them looked as if they had slept in their clothes, their dishevelled hair strengthening this impression. The women were uniformly drab in beiges and greys. The only splash of colour came from the Indian and African women. In his spotless white shirt, well-ironed trousers and clean jacket, Amar began to feel overdressed.

The crowded lobby led on to a passage which in turn connected to the library. The passage was lined with tables and hand-painted posters advertising the various societies and clubs. There were young women and men behind each of the tables trying to interest the newcomers in joining their respective societies. The whole scene had a carnival kind of air.

In those early days Amar was an apolitical animal, so the Conservative, Liberal and Labour societies did not interest him. He enrolled enthusiastically in the Rambler's Club because it promised country walks. He turned to the sports section. Cricket was his passion. The Cricket Club was his first target.

It turned out that the cricket field was at New Malden, some distance from London. The cost of the coach to New Malden and back seemed excessive. The cost of kitting himself would also be high if the prices of clothes and shoes in London were any guide. He would need sweaters, flannels and cricket boots—at the very minimum. No, there was no way he could afford it. He sadly turned away from the counter, his dreams of earning the cricket colours for LSE in tatters.

As he turned away, he noticed a cheerful young man smiling at him from the next table. “Come and learn the sport which tests your mind and body—come and exercise your muscles and your brain—come and experience what has been described as playing chess at high speed—come and learn to fence.” Fencing? Amar had always been fascinated by fencing on the screen—Errol Flynn, Stewart Granger, and other swashbucklers. The idea of learning fencing began to appear worth exploring.

Without appearing to be too money conscious (since the cost of anything was the first thing that a student asked about it was a totally unnecessary apprehension as Amar was to soon find out), Amar found out that the classes were held in the adjoining gym twice a week, and apart from a modest joining fee there were no other expenses involved. “All you will need in the way of kit will be plimsolls—we provide the rest,” said the young man behind the counter. Amar wasn’t quite sure what “plimsolls” meant but nodded sagely. “That sounds fair,” he said and signed up. He found out later, to his relief, that plimsolls were nothing more than tennis shoes.

None of the other societies were of interest to Amar who was already worrying about the money commitments he had made. However, he wandered around in the milling crowd enjoying the carnival feel.

❖

Amar’s first lecture on Economic Theory was in what was called the “Old Theatre”. It was something like a small theatre with seats going down in steps, and a stage from which the lecture was delivered. Amar chose a seat near the rear, and watched the freshers trooping in carrying briefcases. They were used for carrying papers, stationery, newspapers and even sandwiches and clothes.

When the lecture was over it was time to get some lunch and Amar followed the crowd going up to the refectory on the third floor. Amar joined the queue which had formed in the corridor. As he moved forward with the queue, he smelled boiled cabbage and heard the babble of voices and the clatter of crockery coming from inside. The refectory was a large neon-lit hall with chairs and Formica tables arranged around the room. As he got to the serving counter, Amar carefully watched the drill. One had to pick up a brown tray and then choose from the food laid out in a line of rectangular metal dishes. The prices were indicated on a board on the wall. The only thing which looked even remotely edible was the plaice, fried to a golden brown. Amar took the fish, a helping of chips and, rather hesitantly, boiled cabbage. For dessert, he chose the treacle tart.

He found an empty table in the vast room and sat down with his tray. As he was emptying his tray, he heard an Indian voice say, "Can I join you?" He looked up and found, to his dismay, that it was someone from his college in Delhi—a bespectacled, studious and earnest individual who Amar had not been friendly with. He had no idea that Pramod Sharma had also applied to the LSE. "Hey—this is a surprise, Pramod. Do join me. I had no idea that you were coming to the LSE."

"Actually, not many people knew about it. And I was not sure I would get a call from the LSE. But things worked out—and here we are," Pramod said in the deliberate way that characterised his speech.

"Well, that's good—that's good," Amar mumbled, not comfortable with the idea of sharing the lunch table with a stranger from his old college.

"You don't mind my saying this, I hope, but you don't say that with much conviction," Pramod said looking at Amar down his prominent nose. Confronted by this directness, Amar was at a loss for a reply. Then he surprised himself by deciding to answer back with the same bluntness.

"Well—since we are being honest, let me say that I really don't know you, although we are from the same college," Amar replied. What a way to start my first lunch at the LSE, Amar thought, as he busied himself with the food.

He looked up expecting an angry retort, but found Pramod smiling. "I am glad that we have started off with openness and honesty. Maybe this will help us be friends."

"Yeah—sure," Amar said chewing.

"You know, I wanted to get to know you in Delhi, but you were quite unapproachable, surrounded as you were by your Bengali friends," Pramod continued, spearing a piece of sausage.

"I had non-Bengali friends too, Pramod," Amar countered, recognising that he was being forced into defensiveness, and not liking it.

"Yes, yes, you did—I may sound as if I am blaming you, but I am not. All I am trying to say is that there were few opportunities for us to get to know each other. Here the circumstances are different, maybe we will get to know each other. But I don't want to force my friendship upon you. So if you feel otherwise you just have to say so."

By now Amar was getting quite exasperated. "Look, Pramod—why are you making such a big issue out of it? We have a certain common background, we are in the same college, we will be here for three years, we are bound to keep meeting—if things work out we will be friends, if not, we will not. We don't have to sign an agreement that we will be friends."

"I can see that you are angry, but calm down. We will not discuss friendship anymore. OK?" Pramod said with an appeasing smile. Now the fellow is trying to be patronising, Amar said to himself. He said little as he hurriedly finished his meal. Making an excuse that he had to see somebody, he left Pramod to finish his lunch on his own.

Amar was fuming as he went downstairs. He didn't like being blunt and hurtful and he had been forced to be both. Nor did he like being manoeuvred into swearing to a friendship he was not sure he wanted to pursue. What kind of a fellow was this, forcing himself on others?

He fished out his timetable and found that he did not have any more lectures after lunch and decided to call it a day.

❖

Back at Park West, Pori and Samir were very keen to hear how his first day at the LSE had gone. "Well, we all had to stand in a line and our nails were inspected, and then those whose socks were not matching their trousers had to take one step forward, and then because my right sock did not match my left one I had to take two steps forward ..."

"Ma-a-a, Chhorda is not being serious with us ..." Pori wailed in mock anguish.

Their rotund mother appeared in the doorway. "*Kee hocche* (What's hapenning)? Can't I have a little peace?"

"Chhorda refuses to tell us what went on in college," Pori pouted.

"I really don't know what to do with you three," their mother said and marched away to the kitchen.

Amar quickly followed and put his arms around her shoulders and nestled his face next to her soft plump face, "Really, Ma, I was only telling them how I was punished for wearing mismatched socks."

She didn't say anything but the beginnings of a smile lit her face. "That's enough of your nonsense, now let me get on with the mutton curry for tonight." Amar nudged her face with his once more and breathed in her odour. She had a very special "Ma smell", which he loved.

"All right," he said releasing her. Then continued in a sorrow-laden voice, "If your son being made to stand in the corner doesn't bother you, then I'll go back and continue to unburden my distress on my brother and sister."

"Oh ho, Amu, try and be a little serious with them. They'll never grow up otherwise."

The Letter

After the next morning's lecture, Amar decided to explore the library for the first time.

Settled with his book, Amar found that his mind was not really on history. It was back in Delhi, with Preeti. He missed her. He missed her not with passion and longing, but with a gentle fondness—an ache and a sadness. Again, the same unanswered questions floated to the surface. The tired old arguments kept circulating like a broken record.

He was not getting anywhere. He wondered how, in novels, the protagonists always thought logically and clearly. For the moment what he needed though was a break—and the English remedy for all ills, a cup of tea.

Walking up the stairs towards the library, he caught himself wondering why an institution like the LSE could not afford another lift. British parsimony?

Standing in the queue, he reflected that ever since he had landed in England, his ambivalent feelings towards the British had started surfacing more frequently. He was constantly measuring and weighing Britain and his own country. And he was constantly trying to pick faults with the natives—precisely as the average Englishman had done when he went to India. Was the concept of a nation state all about nitpicking and divisiveness?

His attention switched to an attractive young woman in the queue ahead of him. He noticed that the English boy in front of him was equally taken up by this woman. Here was the universal language which brooked no geographical boundaries. So, at the end of the day, what do we need to develop oneness in the world? More women with sexy bottoms. Amar had stumbled onto one of the eternal verities of life, while standing in a queue for tea. He was pleased.

❖

Amar sat entranced throughout the next lecture on Political Thought. The professor spoke slowly, as if he was polishing and chiselling each word as it came out. Not one word seemed superfluous—he spoke simply. Yet he spoke about profound thoughts which had changed mankind. Earlier, it had seemed inconceivable to Amar that philosophers like Aristotle, Plato and others from this distinguished pantheon could be made so accessible and interesting to the lay person. Yet this was exactly what the professor was able to do. Amar couldn't wait to get to the library to explore further.

He returned home, still exhilarated, wanting to share with someone his excitement at being at, what was for him, a new intellectual frontier. So he sat and wrote a long letter to Sudipto, recounting his experience. He enjoyed writing it, and when finished, remembered that he had not written to Preeti as yet. His mood changed. Somehow he was reluctant to pick up the pen.

That night, after dinner, he lay in bed with a novel he had bought in Delhi as travel reading. He looked at the book, felt the glossy cover in his hand, remembered the shop he had bought it in, the late-afternoon sun which had created a pattern on the floor, and began to think about Delhi, again, with nostalgia. Preeti was a recurrent theme in these thoughts.

Late night brings with it its own magic, softening the harsher outlines of memory, stirring the strings of a dormant, sweet melancholy. He lay in this kind of pleasant stupor letting the waves of sadness sweep over him. Reliving memories of their time together. He suddenly sat up.

This was self-indulgence. Worse, crass hypocrisy. He was happily ogling women during the day, and then at night wallowing in sentimentality about the woman he had left behind.

Amar tried to consider, as dispassionately as he could, what his feelings for Preeti really amounted to.

He wasn't sure, he had to admit, what he really felt for her. He had felt sexually attracted. He had felt happy to be seen with her. He had felt bigger in her company—his personality seemed to expand. He had missed her when she was not there. He enjoyed talking to her. And—he enjoyed the way she cared for him.

We're back to that again, he thought wearily. Her liking *me*, caring for *me*, valuing *me*. Me, Me, Me. Was that what so-called love was all about? Seeing yourself in a mirror that glorified and magnified you?

Was this enough to help him live through three years? An ascetic for three years? Considering that he was already feeling sexually repressed, this was hardly likely. Even less likely when looking at the permissive environment he was in. So did he have any right to ask her to wait for him while he enjoyed himself in London?

Disturbed, he got up and sat down at the table by the window and gazed out. He sat for a long while. The London night sank into slumber, dreaming its dreams. The lights winked out in the neighbouring apartments. The rumble of a late night bus drifted up from the main road.

Amar picked up his pen, and began writing. He felt breathless. He felt panicky.

> My very dear Preeti,
>
> I wanted to tell you how much I feel the lack of you. There is a yawning gap in my life since leaving you. You never seem to leave my thoughts. In spite of this, and maybe also because of this, I've begun to give serious thought to the wonderful thing between us.
>
> Preeti, both of us are young and swamped by needs and urges which adulthood brings. I have to admit that while my mind is occupied with your thoughts, another part of me is admiring the attractive women around me.

This is a dichotomy which I find very painful because of the guilt it brings. Can I truthfully say that someday this distant admiration may not lead me into something which will cause me even more guilt? No, I have to confess that I'm not impervious to these desires. This will make you think less of me, I know. But there are three long years ahead of me, and there will be temptations. And, Preeti, I'm not a saint.

There are three long years for you also. And it would be stupid of me to believe that you will not find yourself besieged by desire and temptation too. Whether you will succumb, I do not know. Maybe you are made of stronger metal.

It is night outside. The darkness through the window reflects the darkness in my soul. But I have to go on, though I'm being torn inside. Preeti, I do not believe that what is between us can take the stress of three years of separation. It is best to end it now, rather than wait for guilt to destroy it. So, it would be best if we do not write to each other. Maybe … no, let there be no maybes. Let the future take its course.

Preeti, you will never know the agony with which I write this. My prayer is that you will have a wonderful life filled with joy.

Forgive me …

As he wrote he felt the ache intensify inside him. Then a deeper sense of panic. What was he doing? Had he gone mad—throwing away what any sane person would cherish and preserve?

An insistent voice said—love comes unasked—and leaves unbidden when its time is done. Who gave you the right to play God? What about her feelings—her emotions? Have you even thought about them? All this cruelty just to buy a licence to philander?

While these thoughts swirled and raged in his mind, and tears stung his cheek, Amar's pen, driven by a capricious will, continued inexorably to destroy his bond with somebody who had come to mean more than anyone else to him. So while the city slept, Amar put to permanent sleep a tender dream that had just started budding. A part of him wept, a part stayed aloof.

Closure

The next morning he awoke with an unpleasant foreboding that something was wrong. Then remembered the letter he had written. It was lying on the table like a mute reproach and Amar shoved it brusquely into his briefcase. In the grey light of a cold autumn morning, what he had done last night seemed to be even more extreme. There was still time to tear up the letter.

But he did not. He posted the letter at the first post office he passed on his way to college, and as it slid in he could not help thinking in panic—there goes a part of my life.

As the day wore on, Amar's mind kept going back to Preeti. She was no longer there for him. Her memory, which he had hugged to himself every morning as he woke up, was no longer there to be treasured. Instead there was a fearsome void. And there was nobody he could blame, but himself.

❖

Five o'clock came with a welcome distraction. He would be attending his first fencing class. He had bought his plimsolls from Lilywhite, and with these under his arms he crossed the street to the opposite building which housed the gymnasium in the basement. The porter at the desk asked him whether he wanted a towel, and he declined, but was anyway given a long piece of wood with a number on it and a key at the end. He had no idea what it was for, but walked down the stairs and entered the gymnasium. There were benches on the sides to keep equipment. In one corner, the three people he had met on the first day when he enrolled, stood chatting. They were dressed in white canvas jackets and britches which ended just below the knee. On the benches lay wire-mesh helmets and foils. "Oh, hello," one of them said and picked up a piece of paper. "Right, now let's see … Das? I'm sorry I don't quite know how to pronounce your first name …"

"It's pronounced Uh-mur, but call me Am for short."

"Right, that's much easier—Am, I am John … this is Peter … and this is Mark." Amar shook hands all around. "The others have not arrived yet, but let me introduce you to our instructor, Bert". A short middle-aged man in a blue track suit and a white fencing jacket came up and shook hands.

"As soon as you get your plimsolls on, we can start," he said in what Amar had begun to recognise as a cockney accent. And so began Amar's introduction to fencing.

The lesson started with footwork. By the time the class ended Amar was stiff, tired and bored. This was very different to the glamorous stuff he had imagined fencing would be. This was more like a ballet class he thought. And without the attraction of half-clad girls prancing around! The women around him were clad in baggy trousers which totally de-sexed them.

John came up to have a chat with the freshers.

"Not quite as exciting as you thought it would be, was it?" he grinned. "Don't worry, we all went through this let-down when we started. As you get into it, you begin to realise that it's not all boring exercises. There's a great deal of subtlety and skill in fencing, and you need to use your mind as much as your body. That's what you'll find fascinating—how to outwit your opponent—how to out-think him. So don't go home disappointed, there's a great deal of satisfaction to be got in this sport—you just have to be a bit patient."

Somewhat comforted, Amar turned to go, and then realised he was holding the piece of wood that the porter had given him. "Er, John," he asked, rather embarrassed, "I'm not sure what I am supposed to do with this?"

"Oh, that's the key to a locker in the changing room upstairs. Come on, I'll show you." They went up some stairs and through a door into a white-tiled room with lockers along one wall and showers and toilets beyond. "Those are the lockers for you to leave your clothes, watch and wallet in. Carry the key with you when you go down to the gym," said John.

The smell of sweat and dirty socks hit Amar. And then he was startled to see a naked man emerging from one of the shower stalls towelling himself vigorously, quite unconcerned about his nudity. There was someone in one of the other shower cubicles he was talking to. "Thanks, John," he said hurriedly, "I'll find my way out. See you on Friday."

On his way home in the bus, Amar wondered if joining the Fencing Club had been such a great idea.

Betrayal

The days passed and Amar found that a rhythm had been established—lectures, library, lunch, lectures, library, home.

At the library he discovered the unexpected joy of reading Plato and Aristotle. A barrier to a new world had been lifted. It was like going on a journey to an unknown destination, each corner presenting something new with the promise of thrilling vistas up ahead. Most wonderful of all, he no longer felt apprehension in approaching the work of such great thinkers, since what they said seemed surprisingly accessible to ordinary intellects such as him.

Park West continued to be home, although some progress had been made in locating suitable houses. One evening, Amar returned from college to find a letter from Sudipto awaiting him. He was driven by opposing emotions. Nervousness about what it might contain, since this was the first news from Delhi after his letter to Preeti. And at the same time, an eagerness to find out what was happening in Delhi. At the back of his mind may have been lurking the hope that Preeti had not accepted what he had said and was prepared to wait for him, come what may.

He took the letter to his room and opened it. It started off in the usual banal way letters do. But midway came the bombshell, which was to have a far-reaching effect on his life. Sudipto wrote:

> I believe you have written to Preeti breaking off your friendship with her. Naturally she is upset. I don't want to comment on your decision. I am just glad that I did not write earlier, because then I would have felt responsible for the break-up. But in all fairness, I must tell you something.

> On the way back from the airport after seeing you off, Preeti was very upset and was weeping. I put my arm around her to console her, and she put her head on my chest. I am afraid it ended up with us kissing each other. I am not going to try and justify what I did. It just happened, and I am sorry that it did. To be fair to her, we must remember that grief sometimes leads to irrational behaviour. So don't blame her ...

Amar crumpled the letter and hurled it into the waste-paper basket. He felt numb. Anger was slow in coming. When it did, it was directed at Preeti more than Sudipto. "Bitch—bitch—bitch," he hissed between clenched teeth. Hers was the real betrayal. Between him and Sudipto there was a friendship—between him and Preeti there had been something more. She was the one who had let him down. Within minutes of leaving him with tears in her eyes she had sought comfort in another man's arms. Loyalty? Devotion? Caring? The single-minded love which poets down the ages wrote about? Lies. Lies.

He slumped into a chair to collect himself. He was breathing heavily and his head seemed to be bursting. He did not want his family to see him in this agitated state. Slowly, his breathing eased. He waited for a while. Then bent and picked up the crumpled letter from the bin. No need for his mother to know.

"Ma, I'm going for a walk." His voice sounded different—harsh and strident.

"But you've only just come back—you haven't even had a cup of tea as yet ..."

"Don't feel like a cup of tea—need some exercise—will be back by dinner time." Amar closed the door on his puzzled and worried mother.

He had no idea where he was going. After a time, he realised he was in Hyde Park. He had no memory of his walk to the park. He found a bench and sat down. It was bleak and dark and a fine drizzle had started. But he was oblivious to the droplets of rain.

The tiny drops, soundless and weightless, collected on his hair and trickled down his nose, the back of his neck.

After a while, he started feeling the cold and decided to get up and walk. His feet, of their own volition, took him towards the crowded Oxford Street. Life surged on. People laughed, shopped, bought evening papers, went about their business. He desperately wanted someone to heed his pain—share his sorrow. He wanted someone to tell him that they had been through all this too. There was no one. The world didn't give a damn.

Amar wept inside as he stumbled on, but the tears in his eyes would not flow.

Pain

After a restless night, his mind was sluggish. As it awoke he began to be more intensely aware of his loneliness. His elder sister was the only one in the family he could have talked to, but she was an ocean away. Friends? Sudipto, the only real one he had, was the one who had betrayed him. He was on his own.

❖

The wave of emotion from Preeti's betrayal receded slowly. He tried to set about the slow process of readjustment. He tried reason. After all, he was the one who had rejected Preeti in the first place—so where was the justification for all this rage? And wasn't a separation what he was looking for, anyway?

However, reason was too weak a force to tackle the fury of a wounded ego. The anger would not subside.

He realised that, ultimately, nature and time would have to rebuild the edifice which had been damaged by the destructive letter. Was this what most of life was about? Reconstructing your ego every time it was damaged? This futile exercise of building an edifice on sand when you knew that the ebb and flow of life would keep knocking it down?

❖

He was also trying to come to terms with something else which was threatening to knock the fragile support foundation from under him.

He had enjoyed scepticism as a part of the excitement of approaching adulthood—rejecting traditions, challenging conventions, defying customs. Yet, in this nihilism there was still need to have an anchoring to provide stability—the anchoring provided by a few core beliefs, a few immutable truths. For Amar, one of the core beliefs which had remained uneroded and constant was that of friendship. That there could be a relationship with another, which had concern, caring, compassion in it and which asked for nothing in return but trust. He had believed that this existed between him and Sudipto—but now that belief lay shattered. Sudipto had turned out to be a lesser being. The mooring provided by friendship was no more.

❖

As the days passed and the turmoil quietened, Amar told himself that he was now free, not bound by even a tenuous link to a woman. The thread had been snapped. Yet he felt no sense of release. He felt, instead, a lingering sadness and a weariness. Inside him battles seemed to continue—was he at fault or was she? Was she the guilty one or was Sudipto? Had he been wrong in writing that letter or was he right? And on, and on, ripping the wound open further and increasing the anguish.

Suddenly, a startling revelation came to him. That the debate that went on in his mind was entirely of his own creation, since he had discussed the matter with no one. Nobody was responsible for the turmoil in his mind but himself. No outside agency. Nobody had put these ideas into his head. He was responsible for his own pain.

It was, to him, an astounding discovery. It bred another amazing thought. If he created his own pain, then he could also uncreate it. Could the mind really have so much power? He felt he was on the verge of something important. But could not go on. He felt blocked. He needed someone to help him develop this thought towards further discovery. There was no one.

Suez Crisis

A house had been located at Willesden Green in the north of London.

It was a two-storey building, one of a long row of monotonously similar houses along Teignmouth Road. There was a tiny patch of garden in front with a monkey puzzle tree growing on it, and a larger garden at the back with a solitary apple tree. Unpainted, grey, weathered wooden fences separated the house from its neighbours on three sides, while a dusty hedge protected it from the road in front. Amar found the whole area depressing. All he saw along the road were red brick buildings of a dreary sameness, and bare trees sticking out of the concrete pavement with branches pointing like dead fingers towards the grey sky. The slate-grey road seemed to reflect the leaden sky. There was little green to be seen, with even the hedges looking stale and tired.

❖

At college he kept to himself—went for his coffee alone, discouraged people joining him at lunch, and sat with a newspaper in the canteen at tea time. But external events were taking place which soon pulled him into their vortex. The Suez conflict was one of them.

Following King Farouk's overthrow by officers in the Egyptian army in 1952, the Egyptian government had started becoming more assertive and nationalistic. This resulted in conflict with Israeli and European powers over the Suez Canal. Until India achieved independence in 1947, Britain had sought to justify control of the Suez Canal on the grounds that it was essential to the defence of

India and the Empire. However, with Indian independence and the gradual erosion of the Empire, this argument could no longer be used. In truth, the Suez Canal had acquired a different importance for Europe, since two-thirds of its oil now passed through the canal. Suez had now become a major factor in the oil industry's strategic map. If it was not allowed to use the canal, Persian Gulf oil would have to travel round the Cape adding the cost of 4,500 extra miles to the journey. For Israel too, its selfish interests required the availability of the canal for its own shipping.

Throughout 1956, tension between Israel and Egypt had been building, with each raiding the other's territory. On 26 July 1956, Egypt, under the leadership of President Nasser, blockaded the Gulf of Aqaba, closed the Suez Canal to Israeli shipping and announced the nationalisation of the canal. Shortly after the nationalisation—and these facts emerged many years later—a secret meeting took place between Israel, France and Britain outside Paris. It was agreed that Israel would attack Egypt, Britain and France would intervene, instruct the Israeli and Egyptian armies to withdraw from either side of the canal and then place an Anglo-French force in the Canal Zone around Port Said. The plan was codenamed, "Operation Musketeer".

On 29 October 1956, Israel invaded the Gaza strip and the Sinai Peninsula. As per the script, Britain and France offered to reoccupy the area and separate the warring armies. Nasser refused and this gave the pretext for these two nations to launch a joint invasion with the aim of regaining control of the canal and toppling Nasser's regime. Bombing of Egypt began on 31 October. Nasser's response was to sink the 40 ships which were in the canal, thus closing it.

These were days of turmoil. LSE was seething with arguments and raised voices. On the one hand were the Conservatives who supported the British government's action, and on the other, the Labour supporters with their numbers being augmented by a large proportion of the foreign students. For the latter, this action of Britain's was yet another act of imperialistic arrogance. For the government supporters, however, this was a timely reminder to the former colonies and the world at large that Britain could still flex its muscles when its own interests were involved.

Nehru, the Indian prime minister had come out against the action. The Indian students believed this was an opportunity for all those who had felt the burden of imperial rule to stand up and make their voices heard. So, for a lot of the young men and women excitedly talking in the corridors in the LSE, this was a delayed protest for the years of subjugation and humiliation they had suffered as subjects.

As Amar put down his lunch tray on a table in the refectory, Pramod joined him. Amar had not had much to do with him since their last encounter and did not particularly relish his presence across the table. But, he did not want to appear downright rude and smiled as he sat down. "So, lots happening around us, Pramod."

Pramod looked grave and nodded, "Yes, the perfidy of the British surpasses understanding."

Amar looked a little startled at this ponderous pronouncement, but had no time to react because an English student came and joined their table. Amar did not know him, but had seen him in the corridors. He looked the muscle-bound, thick-necked rugby type and Amar wondered why he had chosen their table. "Hello, I'm Christopher. May I join you?" His accent sounded public school. "Not many people concentrating on their books these days."

"No—understandably so," Amar replied. "The Suez business has touched a raw nerve in many of us."

"I wonder why," said Christopher. Patronising, Amar said to himself.

"Well, the answer is not far to seek," Pramod started, "Firstly, it's a revival of Britain's imperialistic past, and none of us enjoy it. Secondly, it's the action of a bully, and we enjoy that even less. Thirdly, it smacks of superpower ganging up, which is distasteful." Rhetoric, but effective, thought Amar and raised a silent cheer.

Christopher was not provoked and replied in a mild voice. "But surely you must see that Britain had to protect its own interests?

What would you do when somebody blocks off the road leading to your home? You would certainly act, wouldn't you? Britain has done no more than that—so why is there so much outrage?"

"Well, first of all, the road has not been blocked—Egypt had blocked the canal only to Israeli shipping. British ships were not blocked," Amar said. "It was only when Britain and France attacked Egypt that Nasser decided to sink all the ships and block the canal. What Egypt did was an act of defence by a country attacked by three nations."

"Again, taking up your analogy," he continued, "What would you have done if the road leading up to your house was blocked off? Got together a band of thugs and attacked the person blocking it? Or gone to the police? The latter I should think, since we live in law-abiding England. So why did this law-abiding England not go to the police—the United Nations?"

"You surely can't be serious. The United Nations is the refuge of the weak—those who don't have any clout in the world. Britain and France are powerful countries—they don't need to go crying for help to an international body! They're quite capable of sorting out their own problems. And, that is precisely what they have done."

Pramod intervened, "Are you a student of history?"

Christopher looked a little surprised. "No, my area is economics."

"But you must know a little about history?" Pramod continued. "And, you must know that when the United Nations was formed in 1945 Britain was a signatory. Also, that the main difference between the League of Nations, which had become an impotent body, and the United Nations was the stronger executive powers assumed by the Security Council and the requirement that member states should make available armed forces to serve as peacekeepers or to repel an aggressor. Britain was and continues to be one of the five members of the Security Council. So, don't you think Britain had an obligation to take the matter to the UN to deal with Israel, which was the attacker, instead of itself becoming the aggressor? Or do you believe that the members of the Security Council are above the law which only applies to the lesser nations?"

"Your knowledge of history is impressive," Christopher said with a smile. "But, you're not suggesting that if a country is threatened it does not have the right to defend itself? Egypt threatened Britain's lifeline—the Suez Canal—and Britain retaliated. I don't see where the United Nations comes in."

"Let's not dramatise things by calling the canal Britain's lifeline," Amar said. "Britain existed before the canal was built, and will continue to exist if the canal is closed for good. Yes, the canal reduces the cost of shipping, but its closure does not threaten Britain's existence. Why don't we call a spade a spade? Your oil interests have a major stake in the canal remaining open, because they save money by bringing in the Persian Gulf oil through the canal. So it all boils down to protecting the profitability of the oil industry. We are back to the days of the Empire. The highly successful Indian textile industry, known the world over for its quality, was destroyed by the British to protect its own mills producing very average-quality fabric. And now, to protect the oil industry's profits, Britain goes to war against Egypt. And, the tragedy is that Egypt had not banned British shipping from the canal."

"You know, all of you are overlooking the basic fact that Britain owned the canal and had a right to protect its ability to use it. You surely can't be saying that it is wrong to protect what is yours?"

"But the Suez Canal is located in Egypt—a sovereign country," Amar retorted. "You know, I am sure that originally the canal was built in the 19th century BC—mark my words, BC—and Britain had nothing to do with it. It fell into disrepair and the modern canal was designed and completed by the French engineer Lesseps around 1870. You may not be aware, but the British were against the building of this modern canal. Some years later the British became shareholders by buying the shares of the Egyptian Khedive." Amar blessed the newspaper reports he had been reading. "So yes, Britain owned shares in the Suez Canal Company. The nationalisation of the canal has come in 1956. And this nationalisation, according to legal experts, is within the law. Nationalisation of a company is a country's sovereign right—international law only requires that appropriate compensation is provided. At no time has Egypt said it would not compensate the shareholders."

"I am sorry, but the legality of nationalisation has not been accepted. It was an illegal act and Britain's response was an appropriate way to deal with the illegal act."

"All right, we can argue the finer nuances of legality till the cows come home," said Pramod.

"Let's use common sense to address the situation. Assume there is a company operating on British soil which has the majority of its shares held by a foreign investor. Suppose now, that the British government feels that such a holding is inimical to British interests and decides to nationalise the company, paying a fair compensation. Would you say that was an illegal action?"

"This is too hypothetical a question for me to answer," Christopher said.

"But would you consider it a possible option for the British government when faced with such a situation?"

"How on earth do you expect me to reply to a totally theoretical question? It depends on the situation. The British are educated people and would take a decision appropriate to the situation."

Amar jumped in. "So, by implication the Egyptians are not an educated people? My friend, Egypt existed as an entity in 3000 BC. It had a national administration at that time. The Great Pyramid is an example of technical perfection which even today's science finds difficult to explain. And you imply that the Egyptians are not educated?"

By now Christopher's face was a little redder than when they started the discussion. But Amar had to admire his restraint in the face of this onslaught from the two Indians. He had not once lost his temper. Although, Amar realised that he himself had, in his excitement, been raising his voice.

"Please don't put words into my mouth," he said. "I have not made any remarks about the lack of education in Egypt. I was merely responding to a totally theoretical and, if I might say, absurd question." Ah, thought Amar, the cracks are appearing.

Christopher managed a smile and said, "Well—I would have liked to have continued this discussion, but I have a class to attend. We'll talk again sometime. Your views were interesting but, I am afraid, not convincing." He gathered his tray and left.

Amar should have felt a great sense of satisfaction at having, together with Pramod, successfully dealt with a dyed-in-the-wool conservative Englishman on a difficult subject. But there was no elation. Pramod must have noticed it, "We've just demolished an imperialist, yet you don't look too happy, Amar?"

"I was just thinking that the arguments that I used were second-hand, culled from magazines and newspapers. They were not really mine. It's just lucky that I had read on this subject over the weekend. If I hadn't, you would have had to carry all the arguments. I would have been mute. So I can't really feel that I was a great fount of knowledge."

"Oh, come on, Amar. You're being unrealistic. How many people in the world are capable of creating new knowledge? A handful maybe? For most of us the challenge is to absorb knowledge and use it where it can be applied. Be happy that you were able to do it so effectively today."

"Well, you were pretty effective yourself," Amar said, beginning to feel embarrassed at this exchange of compliments. "I agree with what you say, but then think of this. We are, whether we like it or not, an elite few, lucky enough to be at this great place of learning. Right? So, are we to be content with just being absorbers of knowledge which we can spew out at the press of a button? Is our role no more than being just accumulators of knowledge? Should we not be aiming to push back the frontiers of knowledge? Otherwise—what are we doing here?"

"Pushing back the frontiers of knowledge is the big league," Pramod countered. "I am not sure how many people are really capable of doing that. Even if we can't do this, I think, for us, there is still a big role to play. Knowledge, after all, is collecting information through observation and then finding a meaningful relationship between them through intuition and reasoning.

We are here primarily to develop our skills of reasoning and information gathering. I am not sure whether intuition can be developed. But even if we can develop the other two skills—collecting information and using reasoning to process it—then we have a chance of doing what you call 'pushing back the frontiers of knowledge'. And even if we can't do that, we can use these skills to lead a more meaningful life."

"Going back to the discussion we had with Christopher—what do you think we really achieved through that long argument we had, apart from making him feel a bit silly?" asked Amar. "I enjoyed the cut and thrust, but did we really have any impact on his thinking? I mean, did he go away with his thinking cap on, pondering what we had said? I don't think so. I don't think we made the slightest dent on his views. All he will be doing now is thinking about what he could have said to counter our arguments. Nothing more."

"Does it really matter? We have the satisfaction of having knocked down every argument he put up. And the pleasure of showing him that we were no pushovers in spite of our skins being brown. And who knows, we might have opened a window or two in his mind."

Hungary

Around this period, the world was witness to another international tragedy, this time in Hungary. The Hungarians, a patriotic and proud nation, hated the Russian control they had been subject to. This control included censorship, a vicious secret police and an imposed school syllabus. Much of the food and industrial products produced in Hungary, and badly needed in the country, were being sent to Russia. Religion was banned in an essentially religious country and the leader of the Catholic Church was imprisoned. Matters came to a head and on 23 October 1956, rioting broke out amongst students and workers on one side and soldiers on the other. The next day, Imre Nagy took over as prime minister and asked Russia to withdraw its troops. To the surprise of many, Krushchev agreed and pulled out troops from Budapest.

The new Hungarian government started dismantling the controls. Democracy was ushered in together with freedom of speech and freedom of religion. Nagy announced that Hungary would leave the Warsaw Pact.

Sadly, freedom was short-lived. At dawn, on 4 November, 1,000 Russian tanks rolled into Budapest. The army was overcome and the Hungarian radio was taken over, with the last words being, "Help! Help! Help!" 4,000 Hungarians were killed fighting the Russian forces. These included children. One journalist found a 12-year-old girl lying dead clutching a machine gun.

No help came from the self-styled guardians of democracy, the western nations. 2,00,000 refugees fled into Austria, and some filtered into Britain.

Amar shared in the outrage felt by students who were horrified at the pusillanimity of the western powers. But his expression of indignation was muted by the Indian government's failure to condemn Russia. At the United Nations meeting to pass a resolution calling upon the Soviet Union to withdraw all its troops from Hungary, India abstained. Amar found it impossible to defend India's position when fellow English students questioned him. How could anyone deny the double standards that were being followed by India?

A number of his Indian friends tried to defend India's position. This anguished Amar almost even more than the Russian brutality. "Can't you see that we are tarred by the same brush? Why couldn't Nehru stand up for his much-vaunted principles and denounce the Russian action? How does Russia's action become acceptable when we are shouting ourselves hoarse over what happened in Egypt?"

"You must remember, Amar, that India's bulwark against the West is Russia," said Manpreet, an avowed socialist. "What military strength does India have on the world stage? Russia provides India that support. What Russia has done has to be seen in the wider backdrop of the Cold War. What's keeping the Americans from rampaging all over Europe? It's the Iron Curtain. And to keep that Iron Curtain in place, Russia sometimes has to take unpopular steps. India has taken a wider historical perspective and has thus been muted in its condemnation of Russia."

"Oh, come on! If Communism is such an attractive proposition, why does Russia have to use armed might to keep countries within the Iron Curtain? The attraction of the Communist theology should have them queuing up. Yet, Russia's repeatedly having to use crushing force to keep countries wedded to Communism. Look at what they did in Poland. And now in Hungary. Your defence of Nehru is based on the simplistic proposition that if country A can support me against country B then I must at all times clutch on to country A's coat-tails. In other words, realpolitik in its crudest form. Is this what our new country is all about? Fall into line behind the strongest bully, because then other bullies can't get to us? Somehow, I don't quite believe that this is what our leaders had in mind when they fought the British for freedom."

Amar's voice was in the minority amongst the Indian students. While this disappointed Amar, what upset him more was the ambivalent stand of Nehru who had been something of a cult figure in Amar's Delhi days. He was the person who had put India on the international stage through his non-alignment policy and his principled stand on important issues. Yet he had failed dismally now.

More and more, feet of clay were becoming visible to Amar as the days passed. First Preeti, then Sudipto, and now on a world scale, an iconic figure like Nehru. Innocence had begun to be stolen away from Amar.

❖

These momentous international events had taken Amar's mind off Sudipto's letter. But the betrayal kept bobbing to the surface of his mind like a rotting carcass in a stagnant pool.

Walking back home from the Willesden Green Tube station in the late evening on a deserted road, in the darkness intensified by the feeble light from the street lamps, his loneliness assailed him once again. He sighed—at least he had a home to go back to. He wondered what he would have done if he was returning to a tiny, cold and lonely room as so many other students had to. The suicide rate among foreign students peaked during the dark English winter. Amar was not surprised. The dismal sunless days; leaden skies; grey surroundings; close-faced people who passed silently by; a language which did not resonate within you; an absence of the sounds, sights and smells you had grown up with and now yearned for; a dark, dingy empty room to return to—was it any surprise that you switched on the gas fire without lighting it?

Christmas

December crept by with frost on the pavements and cold shortened days, darkness descending almost before the day settled in. The sky was perennially overcast, the bare branches of trees stretched up to the sky with skeletal arms, the soot-smelling air—damp, cold and raw— wrapped around the body like a clammy blanket. It was uncomfortable to be out with the chilly wind freezing the extremities. It was uncomfortable to be in, because the heating in most buildings was inadequate. Amar longed for a glimpse of the sun and the bright crispness of a Delhi winter. But instead got a constant twilight, a blanket of greyness all day.

Then, suddenly, things changed. Fairy lights started to come up in shops. Decorations appeared in shop windows—holly, mistletoe, reindeer, glinting stars, little bells and other glittering baubles. Some windows had tableau of Mary, infant Jesus and the wise men with plenty of chalk snow and silver tinsel in the background. Carol singers materialised on the streets and the gloom of winter was shred by vibrant young voices. Decorated Christmas trees were visible through the brightly lit curtained windows of houses. Oxford Street was gaily lit and bunting bedecked. The very air seemed charged with gaiety. The city of gloom had been transformed overnight.

Nature decided to do its bit. On Christmas day, Amar noticed feathers floating in the air. London was having its first Christmas snowfall in years. Chotku, Pori and Amar ran out into the garden as the snowflakes came drifting down. The overcast sky seemed to change colour and mood, becoming a purplish sky, smiling at the joy it was creating with its bounty. Very soon, the surroundings were transformed into a picture-postcard rendering—white snow covering everything around, trees and branches powdered with white, a few birds hopping about and creating patterns on the virgin snow, rectangles of golden light spilling over from windows onto the pristine blue-white surface. Amar felt a sense of elation. Life was suddenly beautiful.

❖

He wondered at this Christmas transformation. What had changed to bring about this alteration? The buildings were the same—dull, grimy brick under a dreary sky. The air was unchanged—cold, gritty, oily and dense. The same naked trees stretched out to the sky begging for benediction. So how did the conversion take place? How had a sense of joy coalesced from thin air—how had a feeling of goodwill become palpable?

Was it a benevolent God who had decreed that his subjects could take a small vacation from suffering, and waved a wand to bring to life a fairy tale? No. There had to be a more logical explanation to this transformation.

He set to work on it with enthusiasm.

Appropriate music has an uplifting effect on people. And, of course, over the centuries the mandarins had identified the music which would be appropriate.

Equally, light in a period of darkness would bring about a mood change. And December was a period of darkness all over Europe. The 25th of December was not the date on which Christ was born. It was just a day in the period of darkness and depression during the winter solstice. Between 20th and 23rd December, the northern hemisphere has the shortest day. So, the bright-coloured lights, and the decision to link it with a religious figure.

And sugar was a recognised mood uplifter, hence the sugary cakes, the mince pies, the sweet wine.

Finally the conditioned reflex—from childhood associating certain music, food, drink, sights with a feeling of joy and merriment. At the right time bring them on—and Pavlov's dog would begin to salivate. The bottom line was an inspired bit of marketing and manipulation, and a season of joy was born.

This assuaged Amar's need for a logical explanation. But simultaneously, he found, to his utter surprise, that the sense of joy he had been experiencing had evaporated. He felt a desolating sense of loss.

A deeper question had also begun to exercise him. Given all this—that humans were just responding to certain external stimuli and nothing more—given all this, there was still the inescapable fact that humans were capable of responding with joy and elation to some external factors—may it be music, light, colour or food and drink. This meant that there were these springs of joy and happiness inside a human being which could be tapped. These were all internal, although the stimulus to bring them to the surface may be external. Human beings therefore had this inherent ability to experience pleasure, enjoyment, and happiness—however momentary—and the source was *within* them. What immense possibilities this opened up! If only humans were able to recognise how to tap this eternal fountain of joy lying quiescent within them! What were the secret buttons to be pressed to unleash this tremendous force, this surging ocean of joy, contentment and bliss which was every human being's inheritance? He felt a momentary exultation—felt he had made a discovery of some importance. But, again, his concentration slipped and he could not follow through with his thinking. He realised that he had missed out on something of significance.

He suddenly felt the need to be out in the open. He wanted to feel the snowflakes on his face, to drink in the transformed landscape, to breathe in deep draughts of the energising cold air. To hell with logic and rationality. Now was the time to enjoy the primeval sense of being one with nature, of feeling the mystery of creation. He grabbed his overcoat and a woollen muffler and stepped out.

There was a hush in the world. His footsteps did not sound on the snow-padded pavement. The bare branches of the plane trees still stretched out to the dark sky, but now they were white and joyous, not naked and pleading. The snowflakes fell soundlessly—so different from rain. The street looked altered now. The soulless stretch of grey was transformed into a fresh river of white; the dreary brick houses had become magical sugar loafs with windows shining warm and gold; the flat metallic grey sky was now a misty violet twilight. Amar felt a resurgence of his earlier joy and marvelled at the power of nature, sweeping him away into a different world.

Bottle Party

Amar had been invited to a bottle party. On the day of the party he wandered uncertainly into the off-licence next to the Tube station and bought a bottle of Spanish Sauterne. He had no knowledge of wines, but thought the white bottle with the golden wine looked impressive enough. Moreover, it was just within his budget of five shillings.

This was his first student party and he was nervous as he walked to the flat, in St. John's Wood, shared by three English boys. While he missed female company desperately, he was apprehensive about being closeted with them in a party setting. Would he find the right things to talk about? Would he be able to converse intelligently? Would his limited experience with women become obvious? … and on and on—all the self-doubt, which adolescence brings and adulthood nourishes.

At the same time there was the ever-present hope of meeting an attractive woman at the party. It was not that he did not know any women at college. Just that he felt out of depth with them. Recently, he had gone up with a group of them to the "Shaw Library" on the top floor of the LSE. This was a very large room, quite luxuriously appointed in sharp contrast to the functional simplicity of the rest of the college. There was expensive-looking carpeting on the floor, and settees scattered around for students to relax on and browse through Shaw's works by the warm glow of the table lamps. Along the walls were glass cabinets with neatly arranged volumes. The ambience was warm, cosy and hushed.

The conversation had turned to one of the Indian girls they thought attractive, and Amar, as the only male in the group, decided he had to make a contribution. "Yes, she is rather attractive, with her hair growing below her waist," referring to the luxuriant black hair which she left undone. Justine, a gaunt but friendly Belgian girl, grinned and said, "But we all have hair below our waist, Amar." There were giggles all around while Amar blushed and tried, unsuccessfully, to find a repartee. This had not done much for his self-confidence.

Bottle in hand, he rang the bell. The door was opened by one of his hosts and Amar found himself in a dimly lit, high-ceilinged living room which had been cleared of furniture on one side to allow dancing space. A few table lamps provided the little illumination there was. A dining table against one wall contained bottles and glasses, some bowls of crisps and plates of rolls and sandwiches. He could make out a few figures on the couches with glasses in their hands. His host took the bottle from his hands and said, "Thanks. The drinks are on the table over there—make yourself at home. Oh, dump your coat in the room on the right." Amar saw the door and opened it.

The room was in darkness, but there was some light from the street lamps coming in through a window. He could make out the bed strewn with coats and scarves and added his own to the pile. He jumped back with alarm when he saw the pile move. He thought his eyes were playing tricks. Then, as his eyes got accustomed to the dark he saw two figures under the coats, moving rhythmically. He almost leapt out of the room, quickly closing the door behind him.

The semi-darkness helped hide his shock. His mind was reeling. He suddenly felt he was in a different adult world for which he was ill-prepared. He had never been even close to a naked woman, nor had he more than a vague idea of what the physical act of love entailed. And here he had been standing right next to a couple making love. The thought shook him and he found his heart beating wildly. He stood for a while, drew a few deep breaths and then walked as casually as possible towards the drinks table.

Nobody else seemed in the least bothered by what was going on in the room a few yards from them. Amar found an open bottle of wine among the clutter of beer bottles, and poured himself a drink into a thick glass tumbler. This would be his first alcoholic drink since his arrival in this country. He took a large gulp and grimaced. It was a dry wine. For him, it was a sour-tasting liquid which caught at his throat. Stuffing some potato crisps into his mouth, he looked around. There were couples lounging in various stages of entwinement, oblivious to anything around them. Soft music played in the background. There were a couple of groups of men engaged in conversation. But, there were no unattached women.

Taking a gentler sip of his wine, he found that it tasted less unpleasant, as long as he did not gulp it down. Nobody seemed to notice his presence. He decided to take advantage of this and compose himself. Seeing a couple in an advanced state of intimacy was enough shock. What added to it was the acceptance by everybody. For Amar, this was a window onto a new world. In Delhi, he and his friends had talked enough about sex, most of it jokingly, to hide their own ignorance and lack of experience. What was going on in the other room, had been a subject of fantasy for most of them—something longed for, but unattainable. And here were these people treating this as just another day at office! Sex was something casually to be had like a cup of coffee. And then the cup that had provided the pleasure was reused by someone else. As simple as that. Amar's worldly education had begun.

After a few more sips of wine he felt restored enough to make conversation. He strolled over to the nearest group. They were discussing the failings of the Eden government and he immediately felt at home.

❖

Much later, and after a few more glasses of wine, Amar began to feel a sense of contentment. The world appeared a pleasanter place. He felt he was seeing everything from a distance and with great detachment. The wisdom of the world was his. He even found himself engaging effortlessly in the conversation around him.

There had been some desultory dancing. One of the attractive girls from college was on the floor kissing her companion passionately. Again, shocking Amar. Women did not take the initiative in sexual encounters in Amar's world.

By now, the couple from the bedroom had emerged. Each went their own way. The curvaceous blonde in a tight-fitting maroon dress, whom Amar recalled having seen in the corridors at college, did not have a hair out of place. She had joined some people on one of the sofas. The man, smoothing his ruffled hair, made his way to another group.

A glass of wine and some half-hearted conversation later, he concluded that he had had enough of the evening. He said his goodbyes to his bleary-eyed hosts and walked into the chilly night.

❖

So this was the undergrad social life he had been missing out on. Aside from the lack of female company, something else seemed to have been lacking, although there had been the usual laughter and banter. Enjoyment. That was it. He had not sensed any great feeling of enjoyment among the group.

He thought back to his Delhi days and the sessions at the college cafe with his friends, laughing and joking over endless cups of tea and *samosas*. There had been enjoyment in that experience. There had been a feeling of community, a bond, among the group. At this party that sense of community had seemed lacking. Maybe they did not have shared experiences to bind them together. Then the truth hit him. He ... *did not* have any shared experiences with them. He was the outsider.

What's new? He had felt an outsider since childhood. He remembered sitting alone on an overcast day, as a ten-year-old, on the hill sloping down from their house in Shillong, feeling terribly alone. He was convinced that he was not his parents' child. He was adopted. And one day his real parents would come to take him away. In this isolation, he had finally decided, in his childhood wisdom, that God had chosen him as a friend. That he was one of the privileged ones who were entitled to carry on a conversation with God. So he did, sitting under the pear tree.

It was as good a protection against loneliness as he could get. But that was then. His relationship with God had become somewhat tenuous since. Standing alone on this cold gritty London night, the feeling of loneliness immersed him like black ocean waves.

He, unaccountably, remembered Jasmine, the air hostess. Fumbling in his pocket with numbed fingers for his diary, he found her number. He hesitated, then made his way to the red phone booth on the pavement. It really wasn't very late, he told himself. The alcohol inside him gave him the courage to pick up the receiver. It took her sometime to answer and his courage ebbed, tempting him to disconnect. Just then he heard her voice. It took her a little while to place him, but after that her voice warmed up.

"I know it's late, but I remembered you saying that I should call if London's loneliness started getting to me." He explained that he had walked out of a party because he wasn't enjoying himself. Could he come and see her? Though he would understand if she said it was too late.

She laughed throatily. For an air hostess time became meaningless. Of course he could come.

It turned out that she lived in a flat in Kilburn, the station before Willesden Green. Fortunately, it was in one of the more salubrious areas of Kilburn. All this time his wine-induced courage was seeing Amar through. But when he was finally facing her flat door, he almost turned around and made for the stairs.

She was wearing off-white slacks and a tight-fitting blouse. Her hair was pinned back. She welcomed him warmly. "Come in, come in. Sorry, I must be looking like an old hag without my make-up, but I like to give my skin a rest."

Her skin did look coarse and spotty, though her lips looked full with recently applied lipstick. This was a different Jasmine, yet her full bottom and thighs were still in evidence, and he felt a stirring within himself.

"A woman as attractive as you needing make-up?" said Amar, nervously groping for a gallant answer.

"Oh, you are sweet! Come and sit by me on the couch."

The living room was small, but cluttered with bric-a-brac. Little statuettes, candle stands, framed photos, a model Eiffel tower, picture postcards of forgotten beaches. On the wall were framed prints from calendars.

Over a cup of instant coffee, which he chose over a drink, they chatted about this and that. When there was a gap in the conversation she got up and said gaily, "Why don't we have some music." When she came back she positioned herself closer to Amar, so that if either one leant forward a little his arm would touch her breast. And they did lean, whether from accident or design, who was to know. Over the sticky sweetness of Mantovani on the record player, Amar kissed her. She responded and they drew closer with his hand creeping to her breasts.

The inevitable happened. They moved to the bedroom and undressed each other. She opened a bedside drawer, took out a condom and put it on him. She guided him in and tutored him. It was over almost before it started. As he recovered his breath a sense of shame overtook him. At his own inexperience, at his inability to satisfy her, at this soulless mating.

Adding to the melange was an overriding feeling of guilt. He had come with a motive. Not out of friendship. Not out of liking. But for sex.

All because a woman had, out of compassion and loneliness, given him her phone number.

He had used a decent young woman as an unpaid whore. He hadn't even had the courage to go looking for a real whore.

His head was throbbing. He wanted to weep. He had to escape.

He looked at his watch. "Oh God, I'll miss my last train. I hadn't realised how late it was. Sorry, Jasmine, I'll have to go … Sorry. So sorry …"

Jasmine seemed to flinch as if from a lash. She managed a forlorn smile, but he could see the pain of rejection in the eyes which had dimmed with the memories of other rejections.

He almost ran to the Tube station, as if the hounds of hell were chasing him. But it was worse—these were the relentless hounds of conscience in pursuit. More ruthless, more cruel.

Not only had he abused her kindness, he had also caused her hurt, and allowed his basest instincts to rule. Three unforgivable sins in his youthful lexicon. He had never felt smaller.

❖

The next day he wrote her a letter of apology for having left in an unseemly hurry. There was never any reply.

Pub

The Lent term began in January, and with it the round of activities which helped alleviate the sense of restlessness that Amar had begun feeling. Lectures, classes, library and fencing was the routine. Relations with Pramod were now on an even keel. Amar had decided to be a little more tolerant of his idiosyncrasies and Pramod had begun to be careful not to overstep boundaries.

After college, one evening, they had gone to a nearby pub for a pub initiation. They were nervous but excited, like children about to go on the giant wheel. It was smoky, crowded and noisy, and it took them a while to get to the bar to order their drink. Amar, by virtue of the party he had been to, was in charge as a newly anointed man of the world. He said with as much confidence as he could muster, "Two halves of bitter, please." It did not come out as smoothly as he would have liked. However, two glasses of beer were slid onto the counter wet with spillages, and Amar and Pramod said "Cheers". With great expectations, they took their first sip of English beer. The magical new experience they had so looked forward to.

Amar almost spat out his mouthful. He managed to swallow it, with some effort, and then in the approved fashion, nodded his head.

Pramod had been a bit more circumspect in his first sip, so the effect of the bitter taste was somewhat diluted. Even then he grimaced and glanced at Amar. "*Bahut karwa hai, yaar—karela jaise* (It's really bitter, mate, like bitter gourd)," he finally said in Hindi. Amar, the man of the world, nodded and said, "Takes a bit of getting used to." But then he had the problem of finishing his half pint, without tarnishing his newfound urbane image. Finding a corner to sit, he said, "Be back in a second," and went looking for a bag of crisps. A mouthful of potato crisps helped clear his mouth of the bitter taste and strangely enough the next sip did not taste so bad. He knowledgeably told Pramod, "The palate has to be cleared, you know."

Pramod by now had had enough, and said with a scowl, "Come off it, Amar, you don't have to put on this act. Next you'll be saying 'Good drop o' barley juice, innit?' Go on. Admit it. You're finding this beer as undrinkable as I am!"

Amar looked embarrassed. "Well, it did taste a little bitter. But …" Then he couldn't keep it up any longer and decided to come clean. "Actually, you're right—the first swallow was awful. Tasted …"

"Like *karela*?"

"Worse!"

They both laughed.

❖

The beer appeared to grow on them. Gradually, the mouth got used to the bitterness and the taste, if not enjoyable, was tolerable. To a system unused to alcohol, even a half pint of beer was like water on parched desert soil. The plant of well-being grew with miraculous rapidity. By the end of the half pint both were feeling a marked sense of wellness. "So, it wasn't too difficult to finish then, was it, Pramod?"

"No."

"I almost enjoyed it—what about another one?"

"Yes—why not."

Raising his full glass Amar was about to say "Cheers", but then changed his mind. Instead he said, "*Karela*". Pramod solemnly lifted his glass and repeated, "*Karela*". Both nodded gravely. A little later Amar found, rising to the surface of his mind, the local name for *karela* in Bangalore—*hagalakayi*. It was more euphonious, so he raised his glass and said "*Hagalakayi*", to Pramod's bewilderment. Amar explained.

From the euphoria of the second drink emerged the plan for a hitch-hiking holiday to the Lake District over Easter. Neither had much money, so the youth hostel and hitch-hiking option seemed perfect. The youth hostels would cost 2sh6d per night, and breakfast and dinner would be available at a reasonable price. Lunch could be sandwiches and coffee en route. The idea acquired added gloss as the evening progressed.

"Green hills among the daffodils—away from this fog and bleakness."

"Feet in the cold running brooks, breathing in the smell of wild flowers."

"Lying on the grass munching an apple—looking up at the clear blue sky."

"Nubile young women in hiking shorts sitting around the fire with us."

"Well yes, but remember, Amar, the women will be in separate dormitories!"

"No worry—there are meadows outside to frolic in."

And so the fantasies continued to flourish, fuelled by the brown liquid in their glass. By the end of the evening they had decided that English beer had some merit after all, and that arrangements for the holiday should be put in motion on the morrow.

Hitch-hiking, as a concept, was totally foreign to the Indian. In the harsh light of the day it did not appear a very promising route to follow. But acquaintances at college, who had some experience, reassured them saying it was "A piece of cake". They were given various tips, the most oft-repeated one being that they should not dress scruffily, or be unshaven, but should look like well-mannered sober students. Rucksacks were borrowed, routes planned, youth hostels identified.

Amar's parents were not very enthusiastic about the venture, but did not offer too much opposition. Amar's mother was all set to give him packed food for a week, but Amar, remembering the tiffin carriers and cartons of provisions and food which normally accompanied them on their holidays in India, hastily declined. "Ma, I'm carrying only that rucksack which has to accommodate my clothes, a spare pair of shoes, a bottle of water and my toilet articles. There just is no place for food." Finally, a packet of sandwiches was compromised on.

The Lake District

Shortly after the Easter vacations began, they left early one cold morning while it was still dark and took the tube to the end of the Bakerloo line. They got off at Stanmore station and stopped at a counter selling coffee, knowing that it could be a while before they managed to get a hot drink again.

The dark sky was getting lighter by the time they got to the main road and positioned themselves on the side. It was still chilly, but the air felt fresh. Their spirits were high and though a bit nervous, both were looking forward to this little adventure. A steady stream of traffic was building up as they stood on the grass verge with one thumb raised. None of the cars or trucks seemed to notice and half an hour went by without any result. "Well, patience was one of the things we were told we would need ..." Amar remarked as Pramod looked up the road to see if any other place would be more suitable.

"I was wondering if we needed to move up the road."

"Let's give it another few minutes," Amar said. And sure enough, after another fifteen minutes a large truck drew up. "Can take you lads, some of the way—get in," the driver said after they had explained where they were going. They got into the cab next to him and were off.

They drove for the next two hours with a brief loo stop at a service station. The driver was big, raw boned, and ruddy faced, not too talkative, though pleasant enough. Which suited them fine, because the engine drone and the driving made them drowsy. The driver stopped just before a road junction, "Right lads, this is it—I won't be going in your direction any more. Walk up and take the road on the left. You should be able to get a ride there."

Muttering their thanks both of them got out, glad to be able to stretch themselves and breathe some fresh air after the stuffy, petrol-reeking cab ride enlivened by the driver's emanations. Eggs, bacon and sausages did not make for good digestion.

They did not have to wait long for the next lift, again a truck. This ride was over three hours and as they got off they spotted a grassy bank by the roadside, where they stretched out.

"Amazing how sitting in one place for a few hours can make you hungry," Amar said opening their lunch packet. There were cheese and ham sandwiches which disappeared in a jiffy.

"Please tell Mashima that her sandwiches were delicious," Pramod mumbled through a full mouth. Munching on apples as a follow-up, they calculated that they would enter the Lake District by evening if all went well.

❖

As it happened, they were not far wrong as they stiffly dismounted from a truck at Kendal a little after eight in the evening. "Sorry, I can't take you to Windermere, mate," the driver said to Pramod, "But at least you're in the Lake area. Get yourselves a kip 'ere and you c'n get to your destination tomorrow—not far from 'ere."

The two weary travellers found a bench at the bus station where they had got off, and took out their youth hostel guidebook.

The light was fading and a cold breeze had begun to pick up. The street lights had started coming on. "We can spend the night at the Kendal hostel—let's give them a ring for directions," Pramod said. He wandered to the red telephone booth nearby and came back a few minutes later looking crestfallen. "They're full up".

"Oh, shit," was Amar's reaction. "Anyway, let's get something to eat at the cafe across the street, and discuss this over a meal."

They attacked their plates of sausage and mash with gusto. As they ate their mood lightened, and by the time they had finished the sweet milky tea served in thick cups, they were ready to face the world again. As they paid at the counter, they enquired whether there was any cheap accommodation available nearby. "Sorry, lads, but the few hotels we have are likely to be full. I can give you their phone numbers if you like. Or you can try at the next village—but are you sure you want to spend money on a hotel? You know, I seem to remember a nephew of mine telling me that the police station allows you a night's sleep, if their cells are unoccupied. No, I'm not joking. You'll find young Bert on the beat outside—just ask him." Amar and Pramod thanked the old man and went out wondering whether to take him seriously.

"Let's sit down at the bus station and work out our plan," Pramod said.

The bus station was an open space with three waiting areas around an empty parking area. The waiting areas were open on all sides but had a roof and a long bench in each of them. At this time there was no one around and they guessed that the last bus had gone. "Don't much fancy the idea of asking the policeman for place in the jail," Amar said.

"Me neither. Well, what about spending the night here on these benches? We have our coat and scarf to protect us from the cold?" asked Pramod.

Amar looked a bit dubious, but then agreed. "I can't see much option. We can't afford hotels. So rough it out, we will have to," Amar said with not much enthusiasm.

They settled in with the rucksacks for support, their coats on and their long woollen college scarf wrapped snugly around their necks. As the night progressed and a freezing wind scythed through them, their protective clothing felt totally inadequate. It was past Easter, and by rights winter should have been over. However, it did not feel like that at all. To keep warm they took to walking around the parking area. As they walked in the half-light cast by the street lamps, they saw a shadowy figure approaching. It turned out to be Bert, the policeman. "Good evening, sir, a bit nippy isn't it?" he said to Amar.

"You can say that again, officer," Amar replied. "The youth hostel was full up, so we decided to rough it out on the benches here. But it's turned out to be colder than we expected." And then he decided to take the plunge, "Tell me, officer, is it true that we can use the cells for the night if we are stranded—the gentleman at the cafe told us that it was possible."

The policeman had a cheerful young face, "Sorry sir, but the only way you can spend the night in the cell would be by punching me," he said with a straight face.

Amar looked up at the six-feet-plus figure in front of him and hurriedly said, "Thanks for the invitation, officer, but I think I'll pass."

"Only trying to help, sir," he replied with a grin. "What I would suggest, though, is for you to keep your heads covered—helps conserve the warmth. And if you're desperate, use newspapers under your coat—they're very good insulators. Don't worry, the night will pass in a jiffy, and you can have a nice cup of tea in the caff at six, when they open. Good night."

They both felt cheered by the civility of the policeman and for some time this kept away thoughts of the cold as they walked and chatted about the difference between the British enforcers of law and their rude Indian counterparts. Amar realised for the first time that the air smelt so much fresher here, with a hint of pine in it. The wind rustled the leaves of the nearby trees. A few lights twinkled on the dark hills nearby, a sight which never failed to stir Amar.

As the night advanced, the wind became brisker and Amar wrapped his scarf around his head while Pramod took out a woollen cap he had thoughtfully brought along. They huddled on the bench, and then when that did not help, marched around the courtyard. They foraged around in the litter bins and rescued some sheets of newspaper. The newspaper insulation did help a little, though Amar had to admit he had never been colder in his life. His fingers felt frozen despite the gloves, his ears and nose were like lumps of ice. After a while, Pramod had a brainwave, "Why don't we use the phone booth to shelter from the wind?"

"Brilliant," said Amar. Soon each of them was ensconced in a red telephone booth shutting the door to protect himself. There was only space to stand, and the interior of the booth smelt of stale cigarette smoke. But it provided relief from the biting wind. When they tired of standing they would sit huddled on the bench outside. Once the cold got too much they would again seek the refuge of the booth. Life seemed to have come down to basics—survival against the elements. The night appeared never-ending and the morning cup of tea at the cafe, a long way off.

By the time they saw the first signs of life on the street they were exhausted, cold and irritable. Traffic began to appear and after a while a light came on in the bus station's office. This was a signal for them that the toilets would also now be open. They used the facilities, brushed their teeth, splashed some freezing water on their faces and began to feel a little more human. Their spirits were further uplifted by the lights coming on in the cafe. They walked into a blissfully warm environment and realised suddenly how they tend to take the basic comforts of life for granted. Sitting there in the grease-smelling room, lit by a cheerless fluorescent light, with their hands wrapped around a thick china cup of tea, they still felt a great suffusion of well-being.

After a breakfast of fried eggs and bacon, toast and marmalade, they decided to have another cup of the thick sweet tea. The food and rest brought back their spirits and made them forget their exhaustion. "*Chal, puttar* (Let's move, son)," Amar said lapsing into his limited Punjabi, to get a rise out of Pramod, "Let's get the show on the road."

Pramod, who normally did not have a sense of humour when it came to his language, actually smiled and said, " Your Punjabi is as bad as your American."

"*Koi gal nai, badsho, seek lange* (No problem, revered one, I will learn)."

The sun was out as they walked up the road to a junction. They did not have to wait long for a car to stop. The elderly gentleman driving, called out, “Where are you bound?” “To Windermere, if you’re going that way?”

“Hop in. I am going that way—got a bit of shopping to do and have to visit an old friend.”

It turned out that the portly gentleman had spent a brief time in India during the War, and remembered Poona well. Questions about India occupied most of the journey into Windermere.

Amar had shrewdly taken the back seat, so Pramod had to do most of the talking. Amar sat back and enjoyed the view. The road was undulating and he caught glimpses of green glades through the trees, of wooded hills sweeping up to the horizon, of fat sheep munching grass in the meadows, of tiled cottages perched on the hillside. “You didn’t get around to seeing Sizergh castle at Kendal, did you?” Pramod had to admit that they had not. “But you must have visited Levens Hall and seen the topiary gardens?” Amar scrunched himself into a corner of the seat, in case Pramod looked at him for help—he had no idea what a “topiary” was. But Pramod was equal to the task. “Oh, what was that bird that flew across the road? Is it something native to the Lakes?” The old gentleman had to confess he had missed Pramod’s imagination-conjured bird.

At Windermere they were staggered by the size of the lake. “This looks like part of the sea—it’s so huge!” Pramod said, pleasing the old gent no end.

“Yes, well, it is large—though we don’t have any monsters lurking in the deep like our Scottish friends fancifully believe they have at Loch Ness. You don’t have any such frightening creatures do you?”

“We have, actually—it’s called *Kumro Potash*,” Amar said seriously. Pramod looked mystified.

“That’s interesting,” said the old gentleman. “Do many people claim to have seen it?”

“Yes, though only in the state of Bengal. And strangely, it’s been seen by only those who are literate,” Amar continued warming to the theme. By now Pramod had sensed something amiss, noticing

Amar's attempts to hold back his laughter, and stuck his hand out to shake the old gentleman's. "Many thanks, sir, we enjoyed talking to you."

"Sorry, I can't take you to the youth hostel. It's not too far from here, you can get a bus. Enjoy your trip."

As they walked to the bus stop Pramod asked, "What was all that nonsense about *Kumro* something?"

Amar collapsed into paroxysms of laughter. It took him a while to restrain himself, irritating Pramod even further. Wiping away his tears, he said "All true, my friend, no nonsense at all. *Kumro Potash* is accessible only to literate Bengalis." Amar spoke with a straight face.

"I hadn't realised chauvinism was one of your attributes," Pramod replied stiffly.

Amar started laughing again. When he finally succeeded in bringing his laughter under control he said, "Pramod, I swear I'm not being chauvinistic." Pramod looked away with a snort of irritation.

After letting Pramod simmer for some time, Amar sighed and said, "Well, maybe I need to educate you about this. *Kumro Potash* happens to be a pumpkin-based comical character in *Abol Tabol*, one of the most outstanding collection of nonsense verse ever written. I thought the old man was putting down the Scots, who I rather like. So I decided to introduce another monster, to show that the Scots were not alone. Except that in thinking of gentle rotund *Kumro Potash* as a terror figure, I found it difficult to control my laughter. But you do realise I was within the boundaries of truth, don't you? *Kumro Potash* can't be appreciated unless you are a literate Bengali."

"It still smacks of provincialism," said an unplacated Pramod.

"Hey, Pramod, don't get so huffy. Look, I was well within the bounds of truth. The verses are written in Bengali, so you have to be literate and a Bengali. I know we Bengalis have a reputation for being snobbish about our intellectual achievements, well-deserved I have to say, but we do recognise a few outsiders who come close to our level. So let's make you an honorary member. But all good Bengalis must have a nickname. We have to find you one, let's see—what about Keshto? Yes, that rolls over the tongue well. So, what about Keshto?"

Pramod said coldly, "Thank you for the signal honour. But I think I'll forego the nickname."

❖

That evening, after dinner, they decided that following the hardships of the previous night, they deserved an evening in town. They located a pub, not far from the hostel, and happily sat down with their beers. Amar raised his glass and gravely said "*Hag-ala-kayi*". Pramod repeated it solemnly. There was a group of youngsters sitting next to them and one of them asked whether this was the Indian word for "Cheers".

"Yes," Amar said seriously. Raising his glass he said, "*Hag-ala-kayi*" to the stranger, who smiled and responded. The others in the group joined in. Never had the humble bitter gourd received such respect.

Fog in the Mountain

On the third day they reached Buttermere. The youth hostel was a charming building set back from the road and overlooking Buttermere Lake, a small but delightful stretch of water with no habitation around it, and even better—no people.

They decided to spend two nights at Buttermere. The youth hostel was relatively small, and sufficiently off the beaten track to be only semi-occupied. The couple that ran the hostel were gentle and friendly. And sitting by the lake, feet dipped in the icy water with the silence broken only by the plop of fish, was a healing experience. The surrounding hills provided plenty of opportunities for treks, when they felt energetic enough. And occasionally the mountain winds carried two tuneless Indian voices singing Hindustani songs, which carried more than a little yearning for their birth country.

The next couple of youth hostels they stayed at were pleasant, but not memorable. They woke early in the morning on the day they were to take a slightly difficult trek to the next hostel. That it might pose some problems only came home to them when the hostel warden asked them where they were going. He then made them write down their destination and the time they were expecting to reach the hostel. "Is that really necessary?" Pramod asked.

The warden smiled and said, "Well, walking over these hills can be a little difficult because you never know when a mist suddenly engulfs you. It's easy to lose your way then. So if you don't reach by the appointed time, they'll organise search parties. It can get cold up in the hills—not a place to spend a night in."

"That's comforting to know," Amar said with a confident smile, "But I don't see much possibility of mist," pointing to the sun-dappled garden outside. The warden shrugged and smiled.

"The English and their obsession with safety," Amar said contemptuously to Pramod as they left. "The next thing we'll hear about is a registration process in public toilets."

Pramod looked bemused. "Public toilets?"

"Yeah. If you're not out of the loo within a certain time, alarm bells will ring, and the door will be forced open."

"I still don't follow."

"Think of the huge risk of getting stuck in the toilet seat. There has to be some protection."

"Sick sense of humour," Pramod said disgustedly.

They set off confidently, knowing that the walk should not take more than two to three hours and it was only ten in the morning—a long way to sunset. In addition, they had a map and a compass.

The path led along a valley with a narrow river meandering through it. The sun shone brightly and the river, which at places was narrow enough to be called a stream, gurgled as it sped crystal clear over the rocks. There were sheep grazing on the hillside, and their bells tinkled in the quiet morning. "Just follow the river, and you can't go wrong," the warden had said. They did this for some time. The river zigzagged and was obviously not the shortest way between the two points. They took out the map and spread it on a rock. Using the compass, they worked out that the shortest way lay over the hills to the point where the river again turned. It seemed a waste of energy to follow the river when a couple of miles could be lopped off by taking to the hills. It was a risk because there was no single path to follow, but as long as they followed the compass they could not go wrong. Also, there was the urge to explore the unknown.

"The spirit of misadventure is not dead in us," Amar proudly proclaimed, to a surprisingly superstitious Pramod's disapproval.

"These things can be prophetic," he muttered.

They started up the hill. Amar had been pleasantly surprised at the not-so-athletic Pramod agreeing to this somewhat strenuous venture. The way was uneven and rocky, and they had to watch their step. After about ten minutes of climbing up the sharp gradient they decided to stop for breath. It felt steeper than they had thought, made worse by the weight of the rucksacks. But their youthful confidence in their abilities would not allow them to accept that it had been a mistake to take to the hills.

As they climbed, it seemed to grow perceptibly colder. Squeezing between two rocks, they were amazed to see, a patch of white on the slope ahead. Snow at this time of the year? It seemed unbelievable. But there it was—a small patch of snow. In the hurry to get to the snow, Amar slipped on the loose shale. It was not a bad fall, but he found his palm bleeding from a small gash. He walked up the steep slope to the snow, picked some up, put it in his handkerchief, made a ball of it and held it against the gash. Pramod had caught up by now. "Are you hurt?" he asked.

Amar, though inwardly still shaken from the fall, waved it off and said nonchalantly, "Oh, just a scratch—and I've used some snow to staunch the bleeding." It seemed quite dramatic to Amar, using snow to stop the bleeding—shades of Scott!

"Let's rest for a while," Pramod said. There was not much of a view there, surrounded as they were by rock. After a rest they decided to keep climbing until they got to the top—where they would have some of the sandwiches they were carrying from the hostel.

They puffed and panted up the steep slope, stopping every now and again for breath. The compass showed that they were going in the right direction. When they finally got to the top, they undid their rucksacks and collapsed on the ground to rest their weary legs. "It's been tougher than I thought it would be," Amar finally admitted. The view from there was impressive, but bleak. There was not much greenery visible, just rocky mountains fading into a misty background.

The sandwiches as well as the prospects of going downhill, restored their spirits. However, as they went around a rock and started downhill they realised that there was another hill to climb once they got to the base of this one. Fortunately, it was not a big one. By the time they got to the top of the hill the light had diminished as clouds darkened the sky. They rechecked their compass and confirmed that they were on the right route. But there was another hill they would have to cross. And this brought home the realisation that the river path would have been a better option.

As they climbed the next hill it grew darker and a mist began to move in. When they reached the top it had become quite dark and visibility was down to a few yards. A little frisson of fear stirred inside Amar. Pramod, also, looked worried. They decided to review the situation. Amar was in favour of trying to find the river. Pramod, oddly the more adventurous at this moment, felt that they would be very near the point they had been aiming for and even if it meant climbing another hill they should go on. Any movement, however, became inadvisable as visibility became almost zero. They were surrounded by a greyish mist and could just about see each other. They decided to wait for a little while before moving, and sat down on the damp rocky floor. "We still have a long while to sunset, and not all that far to go," Amar said reassuringly.

"Yes, I reckon we don't have more than a couple of miles to go to reach the hostel" added Pramod in the same strain.

It was quite eerie sitting in the mist which kept swirling around them. They had lost all sense of direction in this grey world. The mist brought with it a little dampness, but oddly, it felt a little less cold. But, it was cold enough, and would get colder. All they had to protect themselves were half-sleeve sweaters and tweed jackets worn under their coats. While more than adequate for London at this time of the year, they were proving insufficient now. In a little while, it did become chillier. Amar wrapped his scarf around his neck a little more tightly.

Neither was in a talkative mood. Each one was trying to keep a sense of panic in check. Amar thought to himself—what's the worst that can happen, we may have to spend the night here. And we have some sandwiches left, plus a couple of apples and enough drinking water. But this did not reassure him very much and he decided not to articulate his thoughts.

Newspaper reports, which he thought he had forgotten, surfaced in his mind—lost hikers being finally found, half-frozen to death on hillsides. And they would have had better protective gear than tweed jackets and city overcoats. He remembered reading about—what was it—hyper … no … hypothermia—that's it, hypothermia. It was a condition caused by lowered body temperatures which led to impeded body functioning. One of the first signs being numbness of hands and extremities. Just as his were. In spite of his gloves, his fingers were numb, and his feet felt frozen. It was both the cold and the damp which was affecting him. He tried to dismiss the growing fears by reminding himself that even in London his fingers sometimes felt numb. It was just his poor blood circulation. Yes, but in London he could seek refuge in a heated room. His morbid thoughts continued. He seemed to remember that after a stage, hypothermia led to a lack of mobility and impaired muscle coordination. Was it wise then to continue sitting? This was ridiculous. They were not in the Arctic Circle, for God's sake! They were just in the Lake District during Easter—not even winter.

He willed himself to start thinking about getting out of this predicament. He tried to peer through the fog to see if it was reducing. At one moment the curtain of fog would lift, allowing them to see a few yards ahead. The next moment it would come swirling back to obscure everything. This seemed to go on for ages. Amar lost his sense of time. Checking his watch, he found that almost an hour had elapsed. "Seems to be clearing a little," Pramod said. And sure enough the mist had lifted a little. They could see almost twenty yards ahead. But then, relentlessly, the mist came back again.

They had to wait another half hour before the mist lightened. By now the anxiety was clear on both their faces. "Let's try going over the next hill—I think we will arrive at the right place." Amar agreed, particularly because movement would generate some body heat. They laboriously got up only to find themselves stiff and ungainly in their movements. This increased Amar's panic. Was this a hypothermia symptom? But he did not voice his fears. Gingerly and carefully, they began making their way down the hillside. They didn't get far before the same story was repeated. A white swirling curtain enveloped them again and they had to stop because visibility was zero and they knew that one misstep could send them hurtling down a cliff side. They could now no longer ignore the possibility of a prolonged stay on the hill and decided to discuss it openly.

"If it comes to a pinch," Amar said, "We will have to find a sheltered spot to seek refuge in."

"Yes, in some sort of niche created by the rocks."

"And maybe we could look for some wood to light a fire," said Amar, blessing his mother for having secretly packed, without his knowledge, a candle and a box of matches in the pocket of his rucksack.

"Yes, if there is enough light for us to look for wood."

"Well, we have a torch."

This planning helped to raise their spirits a little. At least they were not sitting back helplessly waiting for something to happen, though both knew that the possibility of finding firewood was negligible and locating a shelter would involve some luck.

"Also, remember, that if we don't reach the youth hostel by a cut-off time, they will start a search for us."

"Right. I'd quite forgotten," said Amar. "Maybe we need to save up the torch battery to signal to the search party."

After discussing their plans for a while they fell silent again, as the mist around them seemed to thicken. They were now getting reconciled to the idea of having to camp there for the night. Though the numbing fear did not leave Amar's mind. The fear of the cold, the physical discomfort and chilling darkness that would descend. This was at one level. At a deeper level was a sort of primeval response to danger, an internal voice screaming that they needed to get out from here—get out—get out—get out ...

They sat on the damp rocks while the daylight seemed to be ebbing away. In reality it was still some way to sunset, and in their rational mind they knew that. But sitting marooned in a cold, grey-white world with nothing else visible, destroys rationality. They would occasionally get up and stomp about to get their circulation going. It might have helped the circulation but it didn't help them get any warmer. It was definitely getting colder gradually.

They had lost track of time and didn't want to look at the watch, because it was distressing to see the minutes tick by inexorably, eating away at daylight. They didn't know how long they had been sitting there before they saw a small chink appearing in the mist. It widened enough for them to see a few yards ahead. They stumbled to their feet and hitched the rucksacks to their backs. They didn't want to waste any time and started walking before their limbs had recovered from their stiffness. They paid for their mistake as first Pramod, and then Amar slipped on the loose rocks and slid down the hillside. Fortunately, they landed on a small patch of open ground, and suffered no more than bruises and scraped skin. They dusted themselves off and decided that their objective had to be to get to the river by the shortest route. They set off downhill, somewhat more cautiously this time.

It felt good to be moving again and to have an objective in view. It made them feel a little more in control. It was slow-going because of the visibility, but at least they were going downhill. They paused for breath and waited for the mist to clear enough for them to try and spot the river, which by their calculation should now be below them. A gust of wind did lift the curtain briefly, only for them to be met with the sight of yet another hill ahead. "Let's turn left, because that seems the only way we will get to the river," Amar said. Pramod did not object, and they changed direction and started going down at a right angle to the direction they had been travelling in. It was a fairly steep slope and they slid and stumbled down it, often having to use their cold numbed hands to steady themselves.

"Look there seems to be a faint path going downhill. Let's take it," Pramod said excitedly. In a few minutes they saw another path crossing it, and they were faced with the prospect of deciding which one to take.

"Which one do you think we should take—maybe we should try and listen for the sound of the river before deciding?"

"Good idea," said Amar. They stood still and tried to hear the gurgling of the river. But to no avail. They resumed their slipping and sliding descent on the path they had been originally following, taking the skin off their palms as they tried to grab for support. Again, they came to yet another track going off to their left. And once again they stood and listened. There had been noise as they slipped and stumbled down the rocky slope. Now, as they stood still, there was silence. There was still no sound of the river. Suddenly, Amar put his hand up. "Wait a minute," he whispered, "I think I heard something."

"Yes, there it is—can you hear the sound of sheep bells, Pramod?"

Pramod listened but shook his head. "No, turn this way—there—did you hear the faint tinkling?"

"Yes, I think I heard something—but not clearly."

"Let's move toward the sound, because if there are sheep, there will be somebody looking after the sheep."

They moved in the direction that Amar indicated and sure enough, after a few steps, they both heard the tinkling. Amar's feeling of relief was huge. Suddenly, the hostile, lonely, forbidding hillside was transformed into a friendly space by the simple sound of sheep bells. The mist still swirled but it did not seem so threatening anymore. But, it certainly made it difficult for them to follow the sound. They would move one way and then suddenly have to change direction because the sound of bells came from another direction. "There are obviously a number of sheep around us".

"The more the merrier," Amar yelled in his excitement. As they walked down, the mist abruptly lifted—and there in front of them was what they had been looking for—the river.

As the mist kept lifting more of the river became visible and, together with it, the herd of sheep grazing quietly on the hillside. The sun was out from behind the clouds and shone on an idyllic setting—a bubbling brook, sun-dappled grassy banks dotted with wild flowers, grazing sheep—a far cry from the menacing environment of some minutes ago. Amar felt cheated in a sense—this surely was not what had scared the wits out of him just a short while ago? The scenery should have been more austere, bleak and intimidating than this. Who would now believe what they had gone through? Amar himself found it difficult to believe. To think that up in the hill, in the darkness of the mist, he had wondered if they would be found semi-frozen on the morrow after having spent a horrific night amongst the snow and rocks! It seemed downright embarrassing to think of it now.

They followed the river in high spirits. Their chilling experience seemed to have heightened their enjoyment of everything around them. The grass seemed a sparkling emerald, the sky a vivid cerulean, the river water a dazzling crystal—all the colours seemed enhanced, all the senses more open to receive. Amar went back to his recollection of the first snowfall he had experienced. Then, also, he had felt a similar exhilaration, the same sort of intensity of sensation.

They reached the youth hostel about a half an hour later than their scheduled arrival. By now the sky had darkened again and a few drops of cold rain started spattering against the tiled roof. The warden welcomed them with, "Good to see you—another half hour and we would have alerted the search parties."

Pramod explained what had happened. The warden was sympathetic. Amar could not restrain himself and burst out, "You know, when we managed to find the river and the sun came out everything seemed so normal and the hills looked so benign—I felt embarrassed at the fact that we had been so scared. I don't think I've been more scared in my life."

"Let me tell you, young man, up at the top at night it gets frighteningly cold. Frost bite for those not properly equipped is not uncommon—you can even get snow as late as now. And you were certainly not properly clad for a hike through the hills. So you were sensible to have got alarmed. I wish more people did so instead of trying to be ultra-macho. We would have less damage done."

This was reassuring to Amar's ego. "Thank you. I feel less of a coward now."

Kanika

By now Amar's parents had established themselves in the Indian community, and friends would drop in over the weekend. Collapsible garden chairs would be set out in the garden and the driver, who had arrived from India, would function as a part-time cook serving up hot *pakodas*, while Pori or Amar made the tea. They would sit and chat through the long summer evening while the sun refused to surrender to night, with *pakodas* and tea being regularly replenished. Sometimes Amar's father would offer a special guest a drink—and it was only on one of these evenings that Amar realised that alcohol was actually being stocked in the house.

One of the families was a young couple and their little daughter. The husband, Sanjay, worked as an engineer with some organisation while the wife, Kanika, worked as a teacher. The girl, nicknamed Buri, was about eight and formed an immediate attachment to Amar from the first evening they met. Kanika was an attractive, bubbly woman with mischievous eyes, and reminded Amar of Lucille Ball. Her husband was the opposite—a staid, phlegmatic man who said little. They would visit fairly often and Kanika's infectious enthusiasm would bring life into the house on a dull Sunday afternoon. After a while, Sanjay got a posting to the north of England and Kanika decided to stay on because of her job and Buri's schooling. Sanjay would visit over some weekends, but it was a lonely life for Kanika.

One evening when Kanika was visiting, Buri refused to return home because she wanted to hear more stories from Amar. She was placated by the promise that Amar would come on Friday after his fencing lesson. "*Thahole tui khey jash* (Stay on for dinner, then)," said Kanika. So began a routine which froze into permanence. Amar would visit after his fencing lesson every Friday, sit and tell Buri stories until it was time for her bed, and then chat with Kay *di*, as he called her, while she heated up dinner. They would eat together and Amar would leave for home soon after.

Initially, Amar was not very enthusiastic about this arrangement. But after a time when Buri's devotion to him became clear, he realised that it would be churlish to break the routine. It was only one evening a week, and did not use up more than two to three hours. He also had to admit that the prospect of spending the evening with the effervescent Kanika was not unwelcome. She seemed to look forward to his visits too. She would regale him with stories from her school—about the various affairs that were going on between married members of the staff, about the male teacher on whom most of the girls had a crush, about how she had been propositioned by an ageing teacher of English.

"So what was your reaction to the proposition, Kay *di*?" Amar asked innocently.

She held his eyes for a moment, then grinned. "You want to embarrass your aged Kay *di*, do you?"

"What's wrong with a bit of innocent flirtation? And in any case you are not old, Kay *di*, you are in the prime of your life—you're at the age when women are supposed to start really living," said the man of the world.

She blushed. "You're being naughty, Amar. But you're right—a little bit of innocent flirtation never does anyone any harm. So you see, your Kay *di* is quite liberal. But I have to find the right man to flirt with ..." she said with a sigh.

Amar nervously realised that he had ventured onto rocky ground. He quickly changed the subject, "Are you going to send me home hungry, Kay *di*—my stomach is crying for food!"

She was perceptive. "Getting embarrassed to talk about flirtations are you? Don't be—your Kay *di* doesn't mind. And maybe you can tell me something about your flirtations while I heat the food up. You must be having any number of girlfriends."

She got up and lit the gas in the kitchen alcove at the side. He followed her. "No, no such luck, Kay *di*—all the girls I could be interested in have boyfriends. I suspect they're paired off at birth."

"I don't believe that—a good-looking young man like you not having a girlfriend? Go on with you." The cooking area was small and Amar suddenly sensed her closeness.

"What am I to do, Kay *di*, all the attractive women like you are married," Amar was desperately trying to bring some levity into the conversation, but realised with alarm that what he had said bordered on the flirtatious.

She turned with a pan in her hand, her eyes sparkling, brushed against him and gave him a kiss on his cheek. "That is for saying such a nice thing."

Amar did not know how to react. Just then Buri's voice came from the partitioned area used as a sleeping space. "Ma, I can't sleep."

The sudden change in Kanika's expression took Amar by surprise. She scowled fiercely and shouted, "For heaven's sake, Buri, you're old enough to sleep without your mother fussing over you. Stop bothering me, now!" The last sentence was almost a shriek. "Really, Amar, you don't know what a misery she makes of my life sometimes. I just don't have any time to lead a life of my own, having her constantly around me. Do you think I can ever meet any friends socially? Not a chance. Working, cooking, cleaning and looking after my daughter. That is the sum total of my existence. At least other wives have their husbands to share the chores with them. But not me. My dear husband is happily sitting some hundreds of miles away, drinking with his cronies at the pub while I slave here. Marriage. I tell you, Amar, think a hundred times before you decide to get married. Go and live with someone but don't get married. It's the modern name for slavery." She paused, and continued in a lower voice. "Look at me, burdening you with all my woes and frustrations when you are the one person who takes time off to be with me. Sorry, sorry. I just got carried away. What were we talking about?"

By now, the original spell had been broken and their conversation just limped along over dinner. Amar had never before been exposed to the sense of bitterness which marriage seemed to engender, and was shocked. His parents always sorted out their differences behind closed doors. So, to Amar, this was a revelation.

He made his escape as soon as it seemed appropriate. As he was leaving, Kanika said, "I hope this won't mean the end of your visits. I would be heartbroken if it did." Her eyes seemed to fill up.

"No, Kay *di*, it won't. I enjoy my visits too much," he said, not completely sincerely.

She said, "Thank you," and closed the door.

Fencing Club Surprise

The end of term approached. It had sped by and Amar realised that he had almost spent a year in England. Nearly one-third of his stay was over.

Following fencing lessons one evening, Amar was towelling himself after a hot shower when John called out to him from across the room, "Join us for a drink at the Three Tuns, Amar?"

"Would be glad to. Thanks." Having got over his squeamishness about nudity, he took his time getting dry wondering why he had been called to the Three Tuns by the seniors.

When he got there he found them well into their first drink. "What'll you have, Amar?" John asked.

"A half of bitter, thanks," Amar replied.

Handing Amar his drink, John said, "As you know, Amar, we'll be leaving the LSE at the end of this term. We've naturally been thinking about our successors. Rod is the senior most amongst those left, and we've decided he will take my place as the president and captain. He has been fencing for a long time, and though, between you and me, I would not call him the best fencer in the group, we feel his age and experience will help the team. We have no doubt who the best is amongst the group—and that's you. So we would like to appoint you the vice president and by virtue of that, the vice captain. It is also clearly understood by Rod that next year you will be the president. How do you feel about the whole arrangement?"

Amar stared at John, flabbergasted and lost for words. Finally, he managed to find his voice. "How do I feel? Absolutely stunned! But delighted!" He paused, still trying to absorb the news. "I just can't thank all of you enough for this wonderful gesture. But, in all fairness, I need to ask you—are you sure? I haven't fired a shot in anger as yet—meaning I've not fenced competitively as yet, so is it appropriate?"

"Sure, it's appropriate—we've all discussed it. And don't worry about your experience—you've had enough experience in the gym with us to be able to take on any of the opposition you will be meeting. My only anxiety is about your equation with Rod. Is that good enough to take the strain both of you will be under from time to time? Have you any reservations about having him as your captain?"

"None whatsoever. I don't know Rod well personally, but I've always found him to be friendly and helpful."

"Excellent, in that case it's settled! Let's drink to that."

After another round they left and Amar sat with his drink, his head buzzing. How did this happen? He knew nothing about fencing a year ago and now he was vice captain of the team? There were others who had more experience, who had been fencing longer.

❖

The next day Amar bumped into Rod in the corridor. He was tall, thin and lanky, and was given to sporting a beard when the mood struck him. This was a beard phase. His bony face was saved from severity by his twinkling eyes and ever-ready smile. "Hiya, Amar, my friend! Congratulations! I am delighted that we will be working together. And to celebrate the occasion, how about the two of us sharing a jar?"

"You're the one to be congratulated, Rod! I look forward to working with you as president. Sure, let's discuss things over a drink."

The next day they met under the clock at the entrance. "Let me take you to a favourite watering hole of mine."

They walked down to the Yates Wine Lodge on the Strand. It was a long narrow room with the bar along the length of the wall. "The first round is mine," Rod said, "You're alright with wine, aren't you? Right. This is one of the few places where you can get wine by the glass which is not vinegar—and it's inexpensive too."

Amar tasted his glass of chilled white wine and said, "Very nice too, Rod. I'm not knowledgeable about wines, but I like this."

"There are not too many wine bars in London, I'm afraid, but this is one which is frequented by those who enjoy good wine at a reasonable price. It suits us students, but not too many people know about it. Actually not many people drink wine in England."

After spending some time talking about wine they got down to discussing the Fencing Club.

Going home that night Amar felt glad that Rod was an easy person to get on with. One of his worries was over.

❖

At home there was muted excitement because their father was going on a tour of Europe. Over dinner Pori asked excitedly, "Baba, which are the countries you will be visiting?"

He continued chewing for a little while. Then, he said unenthusiastically, "What is all this excitement about? It's almost as if I'm going to the moon."

Pori looked crushed and went back to her meal and ate with her head down. Amar could not contain himself. Yet, he held his feelings back and said gingerly, "Baba, all she asked was where you were going. She's naturally excited, as we all are. Why don't you just tell her?"

The expected explosion followed. Their father's face grew dark, his brows furrowed. "Are you going to tell me how to talk to my daughter?" he shouted. "All this exposure to the West is making you get above yourself. Concentrate more on your studies instead of telling me what to do." He continued muttering angrily, "I am to be taught by my son how to treat my own daughter!"

Amar pushed his plate back, got up and left the dining room. Upstairs, sitting at his table he felt a great sense of despair. This was not the first time Pori had been humiliated by his parents. What was this doing to her self-esteem, her self-confidence? And what had he, as her elder brother, really done about it?

Confrontation

The opportunity to talk to his parents came sooner than he wanted. He hated the idea of this confrontation. He knew his father's temper, and it still scared him, though the days of fearing a slap from him had gone.

That weekend Pori had gone to visit a friend in the morning and Chotku had gone swimming with his school group. His father was in the sitting room reading while his mother was in the kitchen. The morning outside was sunny and the French windows were open allowing the sunlight to pour in. Amar was reluctant to spoil such a lovely morning, but knew that if he did not have the talk now, he would not be able to summon the courage again.

He called his mother from the kitchen and she immediately sensed something was amiss. Her face paled. He walked in to the living room, wishing he did not have to, and told his father, "Baba, there is something I want to talk about." He looked up through his spectacles, his face expressionless.

Amar felt as he had when as a child he would be called for disciplining by his father. He took a deep breath and said, "Baba, I wanted to talk to both of you about something that's been worrying me. It concerns Pori and Chotku. I've noticed for a long time that you differentiate in the way you treat the two. Chotku is always treated leniently while Pori gets it in the neck for the smallest infraction. Now, I don't know why this is so, and I am sure you don't do it consciously. But to a third person like me, it is visible. And I believe it is doing damage to both of them. It is damaging Chotku's personality, because he feels that he is above the rules which apply to all of us. He's become a bully with Pori. As for Pori, she seems to be shrinking into herself more every day, because she feels she has no recourse. Who is she to turn to, if neither of you help her? I'm not just pleading for Pori. I'm appealing for Chotku too. I don't want him to grow into a twisted soul who feels he is above all law and discipline. And I am very much afraid that will happen unless something is done soon."

His father did not say anything for a brief while. Then, he glared at Amar and said in a low voice, "You've grown rather fond of lecturing your parents, haven't you? We've brought up six children—and you're presuming to tell us how we should behave with them? Let me tell you," and his voice became louder, "We treat all children equally. I'm not going to have you lecture me on that." He picked up his book as if to dismiss Amar.

His mother said gently, "Amar, we appreciate your concern. But don't you think we have enough experience in bringing up children? Both Pori and Chotku are treated equally by us as you should know."

Amar's anger had taken over. "No, they are not. I'm sorry to say this, but they are not treated equally. Let me ask both of you—when have either of you ever asked Chotku to do the washing up or at least help with the washing up? Pori and I are doing it all the time. When have you ever asked him?"

His mother looked a bit flustered and said, "But he is still so young, Amar. Let him get a bit older and he will do his share of work."

"Ma, he is over thirteen years of age. He travels around on his own. He goes to school on his own. You think he cannot wash a plate? How can you even suggest that he is too young to do housework?"

His mother put on a resigned expression. "Alright, if you insist, I will ask him to start helping with the housework. But it must not be at the expense of his studies."

Amar's indignation grew. "And what about Pori's studies or my studies? Do you ever think of that?"

"But you must remember, Amar, that he has not been doing well at school. So he needs more time with his books," his mother replied.

"Wonderful," said Amar. "So, Pori now has to do badly at school to be excused housework. I'll tell her that."

His father now intervened in support of his beleaguered wife. "That's enough of your sarcasm," he said sharply. "Both the children are treated equally by us. So now, instead of arguing with your elders, I suggest you do some studying of your own. All I see you involved with is your wretched fencing. Go and do some real work."

Amar had by now reached the point of no return. "Baba, you have no idea of how much studying I do—so how do you make these judgments? Do you even know the names of the books I am supposed to read? If you did, and you could point out which ones I had not read, I would accept what you say. So please, don't lecture me on that. And about treating both children equally, let me now tell you a few truths. In this house today Chotku enjoys a special status as compared to Pori and myself. And I'm sorry to say, that even before Chotku was born you were unequal in your treatment of your children."

"You think I'm being unfair? Let me give you an example. How come that even when I went to college in Delhi, I did not get a pocket allowance while your three elder college-going children all did? All I received was a lunch allowance, which would just about cover lunch costs. So if I wanted to see a movie with my friends I would have to forego lunch. Did either of you ever think of that? That there was inequality being practised? Let me give you another example. Did my elder siblings wear watches? Yes, they did. I am holding out my hands now—can you see a watch? I am now twenty years of age—and I have never been given a watch to wear. Can you see what I mean by inequality?" Close to tears now, Amar rushed out of the room.

He marched up the stairs to his room and banged the door shut. He was not in the mood to let his mother come in to placate him. All he wanted at the moment was to be away from this household and its pettiness.

He felt demeaned by his outburst. He did not believe in asking for things from people. And he had done just that. He had long ago decided that he would demand nothing from his parents—and he had broken that resolve. He had brought family relationships down to the street level. He may have managed to get his message across, but holding up his wounds for viewing and gaining sympathy had not been part of his plan. His intention of fighting for his sister had ended up in fighting for himself. His anger at his parents now turned to anger at himself.

Gift

The next few days were not easy at home. He was in no mood to be conciliatory. He barely met his father, because he made sure he had breakfast either before or after him. And he would come home late from college, by which time the family would have had dinner and would be watching television.

Finally, the day arrived for his father to leave for his tour of Europe. Amar mumbled a goodbye as his father left and guiltily felt a sense of relief when the car drove off to the airport.

❖

At college, the term was winding down. Students were busy making plans for the holidays.

Sitting idly in the library Amar began to consider a trip to Europe. Summer was the best time for a trip to the Continent, and there would only be two summers left after this one. Money, as usual, was the main deterrent. However, after the last experience on the Lake District trip, he was quite confident about hitch-hiking as a means of travel. Europe could be a viable option.

He sat down with pencil and paper and did some quick budgeting. Yes, it might be feasible if he could overcome his reluctance to ask his father for money for the trip. However, he had no intention of asking. So Europe would remain another unrealised dream.

Fencing Club matters took up the afternoon. Beverly, one of the girls in the club, was willing to prepare the posters for the stall to be put up at the beginning of the next term. Amar sat with her and worked out the wording and design over a cup of coffee.

"Thanks, Beverly. Both Rod and I need your support to keep up the tempo of activity in the club. We want to get a larger number to enrol—and for that I would like to ask you to actually help out at the stall on the first day of term. We need to get charming girls like you to attract the moths to the flame. Will you be able to spare the time?"

"Sure. Do we need to come in skimpy clothes?" She asked, grinning coquettishly.

"No, just a bikini would do!" Amar laughed.

❖

On the day of his father's return, another grey drizzly one, Amar deliberately stayed on longer in the library than he normally would. When he got home he found the family still up. With great excitement, Pori said, "Come and see what he's got for you." Amar took his time in leaving his briefcase in his room and having a wash.

When he came down, the family was in the dining room. Amar asked his father the polite routine questions about the trip. His mother intervened, "Amar, your father has got you something from Switzerland." Amar smiled and waited for the mystery gift to be unveiled. It turned out to be a small narrow box. "Open it, open it," Pori cried. He opened it and found a watch.

He went up to where his father was sitting, put his arm around him and said, "Thank you, Baba." His father looked embarrassed and muttered something inaudible.

"Baba has got a watch for me too," Pori said. At this Amar's spirits rose. "And for Chotku," Pori continued.

He smiled and said, "Now you two can fight over whose watch is more accurate."

After dinner, Amar sat at his desk in his room feeling a sense of sadness. The aggressive voice seemed to have won again. Rewards seemed to come only to those who demanded.

Surprise Offer

There appeared to be a change in his father following his return. He now seemed to be less peremptory in his approach to Amar. He also seemed to smile a little bit more if somebody cracked a joke at the dinner table.

One evening, after Pori and Chotku had gone to bed, Amar and his parents sat watching the late news. His mother, who managed the feat of stitching and simultaneously watching TV with considerable aplomb, said to Amar, "You know you've been looking a little tired of late, Amu. Your father and I thought a small holiday would do you good."

Amar tried not to show his astonishment. This was unprecedented. He tried to hide his surprise and said, "Thank you."

"So, decide where you want to go," his mother said, busy with her stitching.

"Look, I know that money is tight. I don't want to add to the expenses. Just the fact that you've made the offer is enough for me. It's very thoughtful of both of you."

"No, no, Amu, we've considered all that. Baba has some savings which have matured, so don't worry about that." She bit off a piece of thread from her stitching.

"Well … I had been wanting to go on a short trip to Europe. Only, the question of cost was discouraging me. But I've been talking to people, and if I hitch-hike the overall cost shouldn't be too much."

His father spoke up, "Where were you thinking of going?"

Amar looked a bit sheepish. "Well, I wanted to do Paris, and then Switzerland, and then return through Germany." This sounded a long trip and a lot of money, so he quickly added, "I'll stay at youth hostels all the way—to save money."

His father's face continued to be expressionless as he stared at the TV screen, while his mother continued to concentrate on her stitching. Finally, his father said, "All right. I'll take care of your ticket up to Geneva—and your channel crossing and return to London. Can you cover the rest through your hitch-hiking?"

Amar was overjoyed. This was more than he had expected. "Yes, yes, that should not be a problem."

"And how much would you need for the other expenses?"

Amar had done some calculations, "I think ten pounds should do."

"What? Are you sure?" his father asked in surprise.

"Yes, I think so." Amar knew that this would mean cutting it very fine, but he did not want to ask for any more.

"Then you had better arrange for your tickets," said his father and got up.

In his room, Amar sat down and wondered whether he should feel happy or despondent. What he had been offered by his parents was wonderful—and a break from the past. But he could not escape the nagging thought that it was related to his angry outburst the other day. He had been able to make his parents feel guilty, and this gift was the compensation. This was not the way he would have liked it to happen. This was not what he had intended.

Perhaps, he was being unjust. Damning them if they did and damning them if they did not. This reasoning was enough to mollify his conscience for the time being, though a discomfort remained. The thought of Pori being left out of the equation kept bothering him.

❖

He had told Pramod about his plans. He knew that he was not in a position to make this trip with him. This suited Amar because he wanted to do it on his own. He needed to challenge himself—face the unfamiliar—cope in a foreign country without knowledge of the language and without network support—manage within a shoestring budget.

Europe

Amar took the train to Dover feeling a great sense of freedom. It was exhilarating as long as he was able to suppress the anxiety which welled up now and then. However, once on the deck of the ferry to Calais, the cool wind whipping around him swept away any misgivings. It was thrilling to feel the invigorating sea air on his face; to see the unending ocean heaving around him like a giant live presence, hiding its wonders under its emerald waters. His imagination took flight. What richness of life swam unseen below the surface—colours more vivid than the eye could bear, shapes more mysterious than even dreams could bring, underwater forests swaying with the tide, creatures unseen by man.

❖

Having reached Paris, he was taken charge of by his host, an old family friend from India. He and his family decided to take Amar on a sightseeing tour in their car. All Amar saw was the frontage of buildings as they whizzed by. "And that is the great Louvre …", "And there you have the Arc de Triomphe …", "There's your Eiffel Tower …" was all that registered.

This, in a sense, seemed to set the tenor for his entire trip. A breathless rushing from one point to another with no time to linger, driven by the anxiety to manage within the tight budget of money and time. Tumbling exhausted into bed at the youth hostel after an insipid dinner.

Yet there were some pleasant interludes. Like the day he spent on his own in Paris. Walking in the streets he felt an exultation, a floating of the spirit, a sense of freedom. Paris seemed to be a city of air and light. The apartments had large open windows, through which light and air could pour in, in contrast to the English homes which lay marooned in their dampness and gloom.

Mistakenly allowing himself to be driven by the tourist's compulsion to cover as much as possible, he visited the Louvre, the Place de la Concorde, Champs-Élysées and the Eiffel Tower. At the end, he was a tired and dissatisfied tourist. It had been a site collector's outing. He had lost out on the magic of the city. He swore he would come back.

❖

The harsh realities of hitch-hiking in Europe were brought home to him during the days of travel through Switzerland and Germany.

It was a dreary routine. Up early, a big breakfast to minimise lunch expenditure, heart-breaking hours by the roadside waiting for a lift, and finally a weary collapse into bed after a barely digestible dinner.

On occasions when a lift did not materialise he would walk, initially with energy and enthusiasm. After a while his enthusiasm would wane. A little while longer and his rucksack would start to feel heavier. The back of his shirt would be soaked with sweat. But he would refuse to do what his common sense told him—take a bus into town. He would treat this as a test for himself. As exhaustion took over, he would concentrate on putting one foot down followed by the next. Finally, exhausted, he would give in to better sense and take a bus.

His final destination, before Calais was Koln. It would provide him the last and most pleasant interlude.

❖

It was early evening when he arrived, and for the first time on this journey Amar had the leisure to check into the hostel and wander around before dinner. He did not go far because of his fatigue, but walked to the embankment by the river and sat on the wall. There was a grey light since the sky was still overcast, and sunset was a little while away. The river looked like a wavy strip of brown satin, with buildings lining both banks. Not quite the vision of a blue Rhine that he had conjured up in his mind. But he was content to sit and relax while a needle-fine rain peppered his face.

Returning to the hostel he found that a group of cyclists had just checked in. Some of them seemed American and responded to his greeting with a "Hi". He chatted half-heartedly with them and then decided that he was ready for bed.

The next day he woke refreshed and in good spirits. He ate a large breakfast of eggs, sausages and toast, washed down with two mugs of coffee. Then, decided to visit the Dom, the Gothic stone cathedral which was *de rigueur* for all tourists.

❖

On his way back to the hostel, he found one of the girls from the American group walking towards him. She was petite and pretty with a fresh face which dimpled when she smiled. Unsure whether she recognised him, Amar essayed a tentative smile. She smiled back. "Hello," Amar said, "Out for a walk?"

"Hi. No, just looking for a drugstore where I can buy an English newspaper."

"I think I saw one just down the road—I'll show you where it is," and Amar fell in step beside her. He learnt that she was on her own on a cycling holiday in Europe and had joined this group only a couple of days ago.

"I met them at a hostel in Switzerland and decided to accompany them. Makes me feel a little more secure, since I don't speak any of the European languages, and they do."

Her name was Eleina and she was in college, in San Francisco. She seemed impressed to hear that Amar was at the LSE, surprising Amar, since he did not think many people in the US had heard of the institution.

She bought a copy of the *New York Times* and they strolled back. He told her of his visit to the Dom. "I am afraid I am a philistine when it comes to architecture," Amar confessed. "So, rather than spend time inside, I went up the tower and enjoyed a wonderful view. Do go up and take in the view if you have the time."

"Thanks, I will." Then looked at her watch. "Sorry, I wish we could continue chatting but I had promised my friends that we would go out together at lunch time." Amar mentally recoiled, at what felt like a brush-off. But she continued.

"Maybe," and she paused, a little uncertain "Maybe … we could meet later … that is if you're not busy …"

Amar's mood changed to one of delight. "I would enjoy that. Why don't we take a stroll after dinner tonight? It's still light and the riverside is quite pleasant."

"That would be great, Amar. Till this evening then—bye."

Amar came away happy. He was not yet used to women taking the initiative, but quite liked it. He had, impulsively, almost invited her out for a meal, but stopped himself when he remembered his stretched financial resources. However, a drink should be manageable.

❖

When dinner time came Amar put on his only remaining clean shirt, feeling like a school boy on his first date, and embarrassed by it. Yet, the fact was, this was the first occasion he was going out with a woman since leaving India.

When, after dinner, he met Eleina, he noticed with pleasure that she too had taken some trouble over her grooming. Her grubby and stained jeans had been replaced by a miraculously clean lemon cotton dress. Her hair also looked freshly washed.

"Hello, Eleina."

"Hi, Amar."

There was an awkward silence.

Amar took the plunge, nervously.

"Eleina, you should be saying in amazement—'Hi, Amar, you're almost smelling clean!'—'Your shirt only has three stains.'—'There's no dandruff in your hair' …"

Eleina looked momentarily shocked, then burst out laughing. Equal to the task she responded, "And you should have said, 'Hello, Eleina, your hair doesn't look greasy'—'What did you do with your filthy jeans?'—'Why isn't your nose oily?' …"

Amar joined her laughter.

"I have to confess—I was trying to think of something suave to say, but failed. So can I just say—you're looking nice?"

"That is the nicest thing you could have said. Thank you kindly, sir," and she made a mock curtsy.

As they walked to the embankment, the light was slowly fading, and the western sky had begun to change to a purplish orange. Amar spoke quietly. "I keep reading in England, that twilight is a time of depression. But, not in India. In our country, it is a time of great beauty. In Bengal, where I come from—one of the states in India—we call this the time of *godhuli*. It is the time when the cows are returning home. The setting sun, seen through the dust created by their hooves, acquires a magical colour. The mysterious aura created by the cattle—that is *godhuli*. If you're lucky, you can sometimes hear the haunting strains of a flute, played by the cowherd, adding further magic to the fading light. It is a time of enchantment."

They walked in silence for a while. Amar remembered the time, once in the flat countryside of Bengal, where he had actually experienced all of it. He was reliving the event, feeling the same sense of joy. The silence, therefore, was not a burden. His mood seemed to have been transmitted to Eleina, who walked along without breaking the stillness of the moment.

After a while, Eleina broke the silence. "You create a beautiful picture, Amar. I can almost see the dusk light and hear the music."

"I am glad," said Amar.

They walked a while longer before Amar said, "I wish more people could experience the beauty that is India. Maybe the West will stumble onto its treasures someday."

He paused. "Sorry—I had no intention of singing hosannas to my country. It all suddenly welled up. Memories of home seem so much more vivid and poignant when you are in a foreign land." Eleina did not say anything but took hold of his arm. They walked on companionably, with the Rhine sliding by, silently, beside them.

The night crept in, and lights began to twinkle on the banks of the river. The air was cool, the noise of the traffic was present only as a drone in the background. Amar was surprised at the silence of his American companion. Where was the garrulous, raucous American woman in her tight jeans walking roughshod over people's sensibilities? The shrillness, the insensitivity? The tacky nylon-ness?

"You're very quiet, Eleina?" Amar said after a while.

She looked up with a gentle smile and said in a quiet voice, "I've just been thinking about what you said." She paused. "We Americans really know very little about your country. We are an extremely insular nation, as you probably know. The news that we get from our local rags, will be about the birth of a kitten with tiger stripes, or the size of the prize-winning pumpkin. The outside world does not exist."

"You'll be surprised at the opposition I had to overcome, to make this trip," she continued. "Opposition from my family—from my social circle. 'What could you want to experience that you cannot see in your own country? Where else will you get this intermingling of cultures? Where else will you see such a varied and diverse landscape—from the cactus and desert in one part of the country to the lakes and snow-clad mountains in another? Where else will you experience such a diversity of flora and fauna? Why do you need to go across the ocean when you have it all here? You gotta be kidding.' That was what I had to respond to."

"And, your answer?" Amar asked.

"I didn't have difficulty with the answer. I told them that the intermingling of cultures was remarkable—but we still had segregation in our country. That the landscape which the whites rave about was land stolen from the native Indians who were now dying in their prisons—also called reservations—dying of the wonder medicine that the whites had introduced them to, alcohol. That the fauna was being brutally exterminated by overweight white hunters—using guns made with the latest technology—because they needed to feel that they were men. No, I did not have any trouble with my answer. But they had trouble receiving my message."

Amar was delighted. "Bravo! May there be more like you."

"No, Amar, may there be more people who do something about these injustices. I sound off on these issues. But I am not sure how much I do about them."

"Yet, you're creating an awareness, creating waves. This is as much a part of bringing about change as manning the barricades."

"Thank you. You're good for my soul. But I really want to do more."

Amar sighed. "Yes, isn't that the problem so many of us are facing? Is it enough to sit in coffee houses solving the world's problems? We are lucky that we are blessed with the privilege of time and space to think. Very few are. But are we making a difference? And at night when sleep is eluding you, this is the question which plays in your mind over and over again. I know what you mean."

They walked on in silence. Amar broke it after a while. "What do you say to the two world reformers shoring up the German economy by having a drink at the pavement cafe we just passed?"

She laughed. "Yes, why not—the German economy would welcome a little help."

They found a table and sat down. The cafe had a view of the river and was obviously quite popular. "Shall we try the beer this city is famous for? It's called Kolsch. Kolsch is also the name of the local dialect. And I believe this is the only language you can drink!"

Eleina giggled. "Yes, let's get word-drunk—but only on the tender words."

"Then I'll ask for *liebe* Kolsch."

They chatted, drank and laughed into the night like old friends. Neither paused to think this unusual. Yet both were aware of a mysterious chemistry which had built up between them.

"I'm usually struck dumb when I have to talk to a woman, particularly an attractive one," Amar said. "Yet here I am, jabbering away with you."

She blushed. "Flatterer."

"No, honest. You seem to have this capacity for listening which has opened the gates for me. You're a dangerous combination, lady. Looks, intelligence and receptivity. Oh lord—now see what you've gone and made me do. Actually say what I'm feeling—a considerable crime in polite society!"

She smiled. "You have a cute way with compliments. I like!"

She remained silent for a while then continued. "Anyway, I enjoy people who have the courage to be open."

"Courage of conviction? Very appropriate to talk about it here. Let me tell you a little story. Before the last war, there were 20,000 Jews in Koln. By 1945, they had almost all been annihilated. The only crime these people had committed was to live as Jews, and not hide their Jewishness. I'm not sure I would have been able to show that courage."

"At least the Allies avenged that crime."

"Yes ... yes," Amar replied moodily, toying with his glass. "Sadly, there is the other side of it that we forget. The loss of innocent German lives in the process. The Allies launched 262 air raids on Koln over the war period, and killed about 20,000 civilians. They also almost totally destroyed the city. So it's not only the Germans who showed their disdain for their fellow men. How do we decide which of the two acts was the more reprehensible?"

The conversation was turning dark, and to lighten the mood Amar added with a grin, "Incidentally, this is all newly acquired knowledge brought on by an afternoon of ennui, and a pile of available pamphlets. So don't get taken in by my scholarship!"

"Oh Amar, you shouldn't have told me," she pouted. "And here was I, all set to tell my friends about this vastly erudite Indian philosopher I had met. You've spoilt it now!" She looked glum. "What do I tell my friends about the mystical Indian I met?"

"Tell them that you met this amazing individual who spoke in riddles and parables, like any self-respecting wise man. And he asked you—what was the relation between Glockengasse and water."

Eleina looked bewildered. "Say again?"

"What is the link between Glockengasse and water? Come on, the clock is ticking."

"I—do—not—have—a—clue, oh wise man!"

"Deliver me lord, from the Developed World's ignorance! You must at least know that the Eau de Cologne this city is famous for, translates to 'Water of Cologne'? Yes? Well, an Italian expat called Farina developed and sold this cologne in the 18th century. It became hugely popular and Farina became a byword. Many years later, as a result of litigation, a new name had to be chosen for the product. The factory was at 4711 Glockengasse. So 4711 was the name chosen. Enough wisdom for the evening?"

Eleina bowed her head. "I'm so much the wiser, oh master!"

They chatted away as the tables gradually emptied around them. After a while, reluctantly, Eleina looked at her watch and said, "We'll be locked out of the hostel, if we don't get back soon."

Amar grinned. "Think of the story the Indian newspapers would make of it. 'Female CIA agent spends night on the pavement trying to recruit Indian student.' How does that sound? Our papers see a CIA agent in every American."

"Hmmm … a night out with a crazy Indian … doesn't seem too bad an idea. Except the pavement sounds a bit uncomfortable—maybe the park? The grass will be softer to lie on?" she said with a straight face.

Amar was embarrassed by the sexual implication, and must have shown it. She laughed and then took his hand and squeezed it fondly, as if to say—only joking, stupid.

In the ensuing silence Amar heard a bus roll by, its gears grinding. A group of youngsters passed by on the road, laughing loudly. She kept holding his hand in her warm grasp, and her expression seemed to slowly change to a serious one. She seemed to be lost in thought, but her fingers kept caressing his palm.

Amar didn't want to break this spell. Her fingers on his palm were strangely arousing. Finally, she said almost in a whisper, "Oh, I wish the evening could go on. I wish—I wish … you could come with me on my bicycle tour … sorry, I know I'm not being practical."

Amar did not know what to say. The bill came and he had to let go of her hand. They got up and he took her hand again. She did not resist.

As they slowly walked down the road, she said, "You must be thinking of me as another American caricature. A woman who meets a man for only a couple of hours and speaks so brazenly …" she paused. "Believe what you will. But as God is my witness, I've never done this before."

"I dearly wish I could accompany you …" She interrupted him by putting her finger on his lip.

"Hush. No more. It can't happen—so no more."

Her walk had got slower and slower as they approached the hostel.

Amar remained silent. He was overcome by sadness, but had no words to express it. As they neared the hostel, his heart sank because he knew that he would not see her again. He would leave early the next morning.

Eleina stopped. She turned around and was about to kiss his cheek. But somehow, with Amar trying to do the same, their lips brushed. They both hesitated and then put their lips together for a long kiss. They broke, and kissed again. Finally, Eleina broke away, and said holding him at arms-length, "Goodbye, Amar. May life treat you well." He hugged her again and with his face in her hair said, "Goodbye, Eleina. Keep a little fragment of this evening in your memory."

He watched her figure grow smaller as she walked down the corridor, and then turned to go to his dormitory.

Illusion

"You know, what worries me is that I was all set to convince myself that I was beginning to fall in love with her. Think of it—just after one evening with her. So, a nice shared evening over some excellent beer with a lovely girl, and lo—there was love!" Amar said to Pramod, over lunch at the refectory.

He speared a piece of sausage and continued. "Is love just most part a chemical reaction between two people and for the rest, self-delusion? If the settings are right, if strings are playing in the background, if the sun is setting gloriously on the horizon—isn't it possible to believe you are in love with any woman you find attractive? Just consider—if you spend six such evenings with different women the chances are you would have fallen in love six times over? Surely there must be something wrong with this thing called love—are we just programmed to build fantasies around it? Or is it that we just don't understand this phantasm?"

Pramod cleaned up his plate, and appeared to be thinking. He pushed his plate away and sat back. "You're asking the blind to lead the blind, Amar."

"Come on, don't be so modest. You've got Sushma."

"Sushma. Yes, Sushma. Well, her interest in me seemed to switch on and off like one of those party lights. She would show interest for some time and then would switch off. And then the cycle would begin again. I don't know the reason for the ups and downs. I couldn't figure out where I stood with her. So, we finally decided to close the chapter."

"I am sorry to hear that. But don't torture yourself, Pramod. There are other women," Amar said reassuringly.

Pramod was still hurting from Sushma's rejection, "It's a futile exercise. So much of it is fantasy, as you said. If it's just a physical urge that drives men to women, then why don't we also recognise a woman's sexual drive and let these respective sexual drives push a man and woman towards one another and be done with it. Why all these fripperies like courting a woman, bringing her flowers, buying her gifts, declaring undying love, before. And after? Uttering tender nothings and promising marriage, to show that it's not only sex you were interested in. All a facade, all dishonest, all part of the theatre of the absurd."

This was stronger stuff than Amar's tentative explorations of love. But he let it rest, seeing his friend's distress.

PART TWO

Second Year

The new term had begun. Being his second year in college, Amar discovered that he had to take two additional subjects, which need not be economics related. He chose Psychology and Logic and Scientific Method. Psychology because it had always interested him. Logic and Scientific Method because of its focus on reason.

His first lecture on Logic left him uninvolved and his mind wandered absently around various subjects unrelated to what he was hearing. He was relieved when it was over and they were given a reading list to be completed before the next lecture.

At the next lecture, the professor asked whether the group, which was a small one, had managed to do the prescribed reading. There were hesitant nods. "Any comments?" he asked. There was a prolonged silence. "Amazing—truly amazing." He paused and came to the front of the table and leant on it. Finally, he broke the unnerving silence. "Because what I said in class that day was at variance with what you would have read. And I was waiting for you to pick that up and challenge me. But I did not hear a single voice. That can only lead to three conclusions—that you did not listen to what I said that day, or that you did not read what you were supposed to, or both."

"Now, that is not what is important. We are not in school any more. We are adults, with the freedom of choice. You are free to read or not read. That is something you have to decide. No, my objective was not to trap you about your reading. My aim was a more serious one—it was to awaken in you the need to question everything you hear, spare no one. I may be the person lecturing you, but for God's sake don't put a halo around my head and say this is the source of all wisdom. Don't treat me as the source of unimpeachable knowledge just because I have been placed in a position of authority. Question me. Question authority. Question the unimpeachable. Do not accept whatever is fed to you. Because it is only through the process of challenging, the process of questioning, the process of testing that you will be able to get closer to the truth. Listen to people who have knowledge, read matter which has been published—but do not accept everything you hear or read. Question, ask, challenge. I do not propose to say anything more today. If my message has got through to you, I will be happy. That is the biggest learning I can give you today."

"Now that we have been through all this—can I ask you to read the material I had asked you to read last time?" Nods all around. "Thank you. We will meet next week and discuss what you have read." And with that he ambled out.

This was the shortest lecture he had ever attended. Yet Amar walked out profoundly affected.

He had always been in awe of authority. At the same time he had resented the expected subservience. At home the credo had been that the elders were the source of all wisdom and must not be questioned. In school and college it had metamorphosed to—authority must not be questioned. You could ask your teacher for information, but not challenge the pronouncements he had made.

What he had heard this morning was like a breath of oxygen, even if it was not something entirely new. What was new was hearing it from the pulpit, so to speak. Here was someone in a position of authority actually inviting, no—even entreating you to challenge him. He felt a bond break. He felt free and revitalised.

Angela

The days had begun to feel colder, the trees had started shedding their leaves, the light had started fading earlier—autumn had arrived. It was a time of some melancholy, but Amar found a strange enchantment in it. There seemed to be a pathos in the air, a sadness at the decline of the ageing year, the inexorable passing of time. It was also a period of softness and stillness.

❖

The Fencing Club had received a fair enrolment on the term opening day fair and classes had begun with gusto. Casting an eye over the female entrants, Amar had sadly concluded that there were no sexy starlet types among them.

However, as classes progressed, there was a girl who caught his eye. A slim, well-proportioned body with a face which was half-mischief and half-innocence. An enticing cocktail which was enhanced by the dancing hazel eyes. Her name was Angela and she was definitely attractive.

❖

Coming out of the library one afternoon, he found Angela at the notice board. Bumping into her when she was on her own was unexpected luck. She was normally accompanied by a friend called Jane, a short, squarely built, aggressive young woman.

He said, "Hello, Angela. Found something interesting there?"

She looked around and her face lit up with a shy smile, "Oh hello, Am. No, not really. I am not even sure I was reading anything!

I was just trying to psyche myself up to go into the library, though I don't particularly want to."

"A malady I too am suffering from. Our ancient sages believed that tea was the remedy in such situations. Will you join me in taking the cure?"

She laughed, "Your ancient sages must have discovered tea very early—because tea, as it's known to the modern world, is a fairly recent discovery. But I'd love to join you in taking the cure."

"Let me tell you, young lady, that tea is not a modern drink. Although I'd like to claim that we Indians discovered this wonderful leaf, in truth, it was the Chinese. Legend goes that about 5,000 years ago there was a Chinese emperor with a scientific bent of mind. He had given instructions to his subjects to always boil their water so as to ensure its purity. One day, in the course of his wanderings in the countryside, he and his party had halted to rest and as per instruction, water was being boiled for drinking. Some leaves from a tree fell into the water and it changed colour. The emperor was intrigued and decided to taste the water. He found it very refreshing and drank some more. And that is how tea came to be discovered."

"You're not pulling my leg, are you?"

"No—truly I'm not. From China, tea went to Japan and finally arrived in Europe sometime in the 17th century. Initially, all the tea was imported from China. In the 19th century the British decided to plant Chinese seeds on Indian soil. But interestingly, by this time, a native Indian tea was found growing in Assam in the north-east of India. Commercial cultivation of both types of tea was started, and today of course good tea is synonymous with Indian tea."

"That's very impressive, Am. How on earth did you pick all this up? I wouldn't be able to tell you the origin of roast beef and Yorkshire pudding or beer if you paid me a million pounds! Was this a subject you studied?"

"Briefly," Amar grinned. "At the India Tea Centre in London last week, over a cup of aromatic Darjeeling tea and hot *samosas.* There were some pamphlets on tea lying around and having no pretty girls to ogle, I decided to read one of them. So, that is the source of my knowledge. Though, really, to impress you I should have said that I am an honorary consultant with the Indian Tea Board."

She shook her head. "I would have seen through the fib straightaway. You don't wear glasses, you're not bald, and you don't have hair growing out of your ears. These are essential for a consultant."

Amar laughed, "Of course—I'd forgotten these basic requirements. But you've forgotten the other characteristics—they've got to say 'Actually' through their nose at the start of every sentence, and recite 'Humpty Dumpty' backwards at every opportunity."

They both laughed. "We're sounding like characters from *Alice in Wonderland*," Angela said.

"You do know, of course, that Lewis Carroll used to smoke cannabis, don't you? And probably wrote under its influence."

"Get off with you, Am. I don't believe a word of that."

"It's true, though. Anyway, what's the big deal even if he did? Which reminds me, I thought we came here in search of the miracle cure. What will you have?"

"Coffee for me please, Am."

Amar stood stock-still. "I don't believe this—I really don't," he expostulated. "Here I give her a 5,000-year history of tea—and what does she order? Coffee!" He shook his head, muttered, "Women," and walked to the counter.

He got himself a cup of copper-coloured tea in a thick china cup along with Angela's coffee.

He took a sip, grimaced, and said, "Like Alice, I'm drinking this because it's got 'Drink Me' written on it."

Angela peered closely at the cup "Ah! Of course the writing's not visible to everybody, is it?"

"No. Only to those who have seen a white rabbit with pink eyes taking a watch out of his waistcoat pocket."

"Careful, though, you might start shrinking like Alice," responded Angela.

"Ah, but Alice did not have an angel next to her to come to the rescue," he said solemnly.

"And what does the angel have to do?" Angela seemed to be enjoying the game.

"All will be revealed when you play croquet with the Queen of Hearts."

Angela started giggling. "Oh, Am, if anybody overhears us we'll be sent to the resident psychiatrist."

"Worry not, we shall make him drink this cup of tea. It will render him speechless."

"You don't really like our English tea, do you?"

"I don't, though I will deny in court that I ever said that," he said breaking into a smile. "No, I can't offend my host nation. The tea is hot. There—that's a compliment. Seriously, though, there are so many things I like about Britain, but when it comes to the tea I throw up my hands in despair."

The banter continued until Angela looked at her watch and exclaimed, "My goodness, look at the time. I'd better get to the library before I give in to the impulse to go home. Thanks, Amar, I enjoyed our chat. We must do it again."

❖

Amar sat in the library with the book open in front of him, although his mind was on other things. He felt happy at having been able to set up some sort of equation with Angela. It was a beginning. To what, he did not yet know.

The India Society

With winter came the damp coldness which seemed to permeate through wool and fabric. It was bad enough outdoors when the trousers stuck coldly and clammily to the legs. Indoors too, it was uncomfortable—a dampness seeping into the clothes, taking away the comfort of garment sitting softly on skin. It was almost as bad as wearing damp clothes. The central heating did little to eradicate this clamminess. The only relief came from sticking close to the warmth of the radiators. In the morning, while dressing, Amar would spread the trousers on the radiator to make them more wearable.

The fencing matches were going reasonably well. The outstation ones involved trips to cities like Leicester, Bristol, Birmingham and others which were within easy reach, so that a return was possible the same day. Their team did not have a series of runaway victories, nor were they at the receiving end all the time. In total they seemed to be winning more matches than they lost. Amar, to his surprise, found that his tally of wins was higher than the team average.

Over lunch, at the refectory, Amar began to tell Pramod about Angela. However, before he could start, an Indian called Nitin Parekh put his tray down at their table. "I thought I would join you," he said sitting down. Amar nodded an unwelcoming hello. Nitin was from Gujarat, and was one of its earnest but self-important representatives. His hair was always heavily oiled, his clothes always immaculate, a tie always around his thin neck. Amar thought he saw traces of powder on his face, but Pramod accused him of prejudice. Neither of them liked Nitin, but could not bring themselves to tell him to find another table.

As Amar glumly toyed with his shepherd pie, Nitin brightly asked, "So Amar, your *faincing* going well?"

"Yes, thanks, going well," and quickly took a mouthful so that he would not have to continue with the conversation. But Nitin was not to be deterred.

"I did not see either of you at the India Society meeting?"

Pramod answered, "No, both of us had other things to do."

"Which is a great pity. If Indians do not support the India Society, who will?"

Amar could not restrain himself. "Nitin, we haven't come all the way to England to spend our time with the India Society. We could have done that in India. Don't you think there is some merit in getting to know the non-Indians?"

Nitin looked grave. "Yes, yes—you should get to know non-Indians. But you also have a responsibility towards your country."

Pramod butted in. "And how exactly does attending India Society meetings, eating cold *samosas* and drinking bad tea, further the Indian cause? Can you name one thing that the India Society has done in the last year which contributed something to the Indian cause?"

Nitin bristled. "What are you saying? That the India Society does not do anything but eat *samosas*? It organises cultural get-togethers, it arranges talks by eminent Indians. Why, Professor Mahalanobis from the Indian Planning Commission was here to give a talk. How can you say that the Society does nothing?"

"Come on, Mahalanobis' visit was arranged by the LSE Union, not by the India Society," Pramod replied angrily. "And what great cultural get-togethers have been arranged—can you tell me? Apart from Indian students getting together to listen to some tinny Indian music on the tape recorder, I can't recollect any other great cultural festival."

By this time Amar was feeling sorry for the beleaguered Nitin. He decided to turn to lighter topics. "Oh, let's forget about the India Society. Let's talk about more interesting things. Tell me Nitin, have you managed to date one of the English girls as yet?"

Nitin looked even more upset. "I cannot believe what you are saying, Amar—as an Indian, would *you* like to date one of these white girls? I would not. They are licentious pleasure seekers, interested only in *pope* music, and *dayncing*. I, coming from the rich heritage of India, would not dream of going out with whites."

"Bravo," Amar said, "We need more Indians like you. Do you wear khadi underwear too?"

Now Nitin looked really angry. "I will not answer such a question. What I wear as underwear is between me and myself. "

Amar realised that he had provoked the poor man. So he tried to lighten the conversation again.

"Sorry, I was being a bit facetious. Forget about underwear. You will agree though that there are some very attractive English women. What happens if you find yourself falling in love with one of them? You know, the heart recognises no boundaries … etc., etc."

"*Chhi-chhi-chhi*! How can you even think of that, Amar? Fall in love with an Englishwoman? *Chhi-chhi-chhi* … I think you are only trying to pull my leg. But I will tell you seriously that I do not believe in this business of falling in love. What is this falling? Are you falling into a ditch? Tch, tch."

Amar tried to look astonished, "What—are you telling me, you—do—not—believe—in—love?"

Nitin smiled for the first time. "No, I am not saying that … I believe in love. But it has to be arranged love." And he sat back looking smug.

Pramod, looking bewildered, broke in. "Arranged love? Arranged love? You don't see any contradiction here?"

Nitin again smiled in a superior way. "No. There is no contradiction. When I go back to India, my parents will look around for a good bride. Once they find someone, they will get her horoscope and take it to our pandit. He will compare her horoscope with mine and decide whether it is a suitable fit. If he says yes, then I will meet her and take her out socially. We will meet a few times and a love will grow. That is arranged love," he ended triumphantly, and then leant back beaming.

Amar asked, "Tell me Nitin, why did you come to England since your views are so much at odds with the values here?"

Nitin smiled again. He leaned forward and said in a low voice, "A foreign degree is important in getting jobs. Also, it is highly regarded in marriage market. So, two good reasons!"

There was not much conversation after that.

❖

They realised that they had not escaped from the India Society when they met the next day for a cup of tea at the cafeteria. Barely had they sat down when a middle-aged Bengali came and joined them at their table. "*Arre*, Amar—*kothai thako bhai* (where do you disappear, brother)? Did not see you at India Society—never see you at Bengali get-togethers—what is matter?" And he took a long slurping sip of his tea.

"Oh hello, Dipak *da* (*da* standing for elder brother). You haven't met my friend Pramod. Pramod, this is Dipak *da*—one of the pillars of the Indian community at the LSE. How long have you been here Dipak *da*—quite a while, haven't you?" Dipak was doing some postgraduate course and looked older than most students. He had a face that looked like polished old wood, with the skin stretched taut over the bones. His face always managed to look calm and untroubled and Amar admired his equanimity. He was something of a father figure among Indian students, though a libidinous one, with a constant procession of girls on his arm, most of them English.

"Hello, hello, Pramod—I *hab* seen you around. Y-e-e-s, I *hab* been here long time—long time. I know *ebheryone* here—and I meet them oftentimes. Except your friend here, Amar. No—*baba*—it is too difficult to meet him. *Kano theek balchi na* (Am I not right), Amar? *Arre baba*—it is easier to meet queen—you understand? Queen." And with his hand he sketched a crown over his head. "What for you avoid us, Amar? Have we got leprosy or what? I don't understand," he said in a pained voice. Taking a deep puff of his cigarette and exhaling luxuriously, he repeated, "I don't understand."

"Dipak *da*, between the undergraduates and the postgraduates there are almost 400 Indians here. How is it possible to keep up with all of them? Not everyone has your social skills."

Dipak seemed mollified. "It is true—it is true. You know Pramod, I get on with *ebheryone*—from the porter to the professor. They all say—if all Indians like you, India should lead United Nations. But I am modest fellah. I say—no, no, do not say so much about me—it will bring me bad luck. I am just humble person. All I want is good friends around me, a good smoke and a good glass of whisky! Ha-ha," and he leant back to take another deep puff, holding the cigarette between his ring finger and his little finger and using his clenched fist as a smoking tube.

"But tell me, Dipak *da,* why are you suddenly so concerned about my not attending the India Society meeting? There are plenty of other Indians who must have attended?"

"*Arre baba,* Amar, you do not understand. Very few people comes. Very few. And those of us there, we are asked to get more people to come. So I see you and your friend and I say—*Arre* here are two people—right here who can add to quorum next time. And for me this is special responsibility—very special. Because you see," and he leant forward very confidentially, "they want me to be president next year. And I want good people like you and Pramod to be behind me. And Amar, you can even be an office bearer—this fella Nitin is wanting to be secretary, but you can be—you can be treasurer—yes—treasurer. Between us we can make this society the best in LSE. Everyone will be talking of India Society. Mrs Vijay Lakshmi Pandit, our respected High Commissioner, will invite us to India House. We will be in the newspapers. And we will have big function—very big function—in big hall and invite some big musicians from India—it will be grand show. So don't miss out on this opportunity, Amar. I am like your big brother, *bhai*—listen to my advice and join with me to make India Society huge success."

Amar took a deep breath. "I have to say, Dipak *da*, that I don't quite see the need for all Indians to have to get together and form a society. After all we are in a foreign country and we need to get to know and understand them too."

"Yes, yes, I agree. I believe in getting to know them, particularly the *gaarls*." He grinned. Then became serious again. "But you see Amar, foreign peoples are in problems in England. They need to stick together. Not the problems of *fooding*. I'm not talking about *ros bif* or boiled cabbage. Although they explain why the *Engleesh* always look so unhappy and constipated. No, no, that is not important. Nor about the clothing which is so rough and smelly and which adds to the *Engleesh* unhappiness. Their tweed takes off the *skeen*. Their wool gives *bleesters*—yes, yes, not exaggerating—big *bleesters*. Taking on and off becomes so much problem that they sleep in them. And that is why they smell. You understand? But that is not the problem." He took a pull of his cigarette. "The problem is more *diffeecalt*. The problem is they look down on all foreign buggers. All foreigners are *dart* to them—the *feelth* of the streets. And we coloured buggers are not just *dart*—but *dart* mixed with *sheet*, you understand, *sheet*. So what do we coloured buggers do to protect ourselves? The only thing we can do. Stick together, *bas*, that is all. Stick together and fight together. *Shalla deir dholai ditay hobe, thoe amra ekshonge debow* (If we have to give it back to them, we will do it together). We gain strength by being together. You understand, *na*?"

"Yes, Dipak *da*, I understand. But I think you're exaggerating. I don't think either of us have had the experience of being badly treated by the locals—certainly not at college."

"Yes, yes, at college it is fine and *grandy*. But outside it is not. Take my *ward* for it. Anyway, what I really want to say is that you should consider becoming treasurer of the Society."

"Let me think about it, Dipak *da*."

"Very good, very good. And you must also join, Pramod—maybe we can make you joint secretary. I must go now, my *garl* friend will be waiting," he said with a wink and got up.

Amar sighed with relief. Pramod sipped his tea and looked accusingly at Amar, "You actually said you would think about this madman's offer? How could you do that?"

Amar smiled sheepishly, "What could I do? He was coming on so strong—how could I say an outright 'no'? I just wanted to let him down gently. I will say 'no' to him a couple of days later to show him that I have given the matter a lot of thought."

Pramod was not placated. "That is downright dishonest, Amar. If you know you don't want it—you should say an unequivocal 'no' straightaway. What if he was coming on strong? Nitin was coming on strong at lunch, and I did not see you backing down then? Just because this fellow was a Bengali, and he was an older person, you kowtowed to him."

The truth hurt. Pramod had this tiresome habit of honesty. Amar's first reaction was to hit back. He controlled himself.

"OK—OK," he said impatiently. "You're right, much as I hate to say it. Yes, I find it so much harder to be blunt with older people—even with asses like Dipak." Then with a grin, he continued, "So tomorrow I'll get hold of him and say that I will not be able to accept his kind offer, but my friend Pramod would be more than happy to be joint secretary. How about that?"

Lament

The term crossed the halfway mark more quickly than Amar had anticipated. The launching of a satellite by the USSR ahead of the Americans, who had been perennially boasting about their scientific prowess, made headlines. The newspapers went to town on this story. Some of them even speculated about the implications of this for the future. The *Manchester Guardian*, with startling prescience, said:

> The achievement is immense. It demands a psychological adjustment on our part towards Soviet society, Soviet military capabilities and – perhaps most of all – to the relationship of the world with what is beyond ...We must be prepared to be told what the other side of the Moon looks like [Lunik 3 produced the photos only two years later], or how thick the cloud on Venus may be [revealed by the Soviet Venera and US Mariner series starting in the '60's] ... The Russians can now build ballistic missiles capable of hitting any chosen target anywhere in the world.

As had now become a routine practice, Amar and Pramod met for lunch. Amar eagerly attacked his fried plaice and chips. It was piping hot and it took him a couple of minutes to recover from the scalding his tongue received. "So the Soviets have beaten America in the space race—great news, isn't it?"

Pramod, chomping away on his cottage pie, took some time to reply. "You really think it's good news? If the Soviets have acquired missile capability, how long would it be before the Americans do so? And once the Americans catch up, Russia would have to develop a more fearsome piece of artillery to stay ahead. Where will this end?"

"Sure, this arms race is frightening. But I draw satisfaction from seeing the Americans humbled. According to them, they're the world leaders, and we all have to recognise their technological superiority. Now, let them put the sputnik in their pipe and smoke it!"

"You really dislike the Americans, don't you?" Pramod asked.

"That would be oversimplifying it. The Americans as a people I don't know. The Americans as they emerge from the statements of their politicians and their press—I do know. And do not like. They emerge as an arrogant, immature, xenophobic, illiberal collection of people who can cause irreparable harm to the kind of world that we would like to have."

"But how can you condemn a whole country because some of their politicians are illiberal?"

"Come on, I said right at the beginning that I don't know the American people, and I am not condemning them. I have never been to America. The opinions I form are from hearing what the American leaders are saying, seeing what they are doing, and reading what the newspapers are printing. Reading about McCarthyism and its horrors, reading about the devastation the Americans wrought in Japan with their nuclear bombs—a Japan which by all accounts was ready to surrender well before the bombs were dropped. It is formed from the passivity of the Americans, the superpower, sitting on the sidelines and doing nothing when the Russian juggernaut rolled in to crush the Hungarians. It is formed by the unspeakable evil of segregation being practiced in this wonderfully democratic country. So—what conclusion am I supposed to draw?"

"Logical. But is it only logic that fuels your dislike of the Americans?"

Amar chewed silently for some time. "Don't know. I've been asking myself the same question for some time. Why do I react like this against any white nation, be it America, be it Britain. Where is this coming from?"

Pramod shrugged and continued with his meal. "I don't know either. But the fact is that you're beginning to sound quite racial."

"Oh, is that a fact? Are you forgetting that we suffered humiliation at the hands of the British—as a nation and as individuals." Amar retorted aggressively.

"So?" asked Pramod provocatively.

"Oh come on! You want me to forget the history books we were made to read in school which made me ashamed to be an Indian?" Amar asked angrily. "I would come out of the classroom with my head hanging down, mortified at being what I was, wishing some magical figure would leap out of history and prove that what they were saying was wrong. All my local heroes were being turned into cartoon figures. Tipu Sultan, for example, probably the staunchest opponent the British faced on the battlefield—he savaged them in the First and Second Mysore Wars and dented their reputation as an invincible power—a highly educated man, a linguist, a poet, an innovator. Reputed to have developed the world's first war rockets. A Muslim who also built churches and temples. This amazing man was written off as a stupid bumbler on the battlefield, a bigot, an inhuman creature who tortured captives and slaughtered the civilians—in short, an evil and despicable human being. Do you know, he actually gave funds to rebuild a Hindu temple destroyed by—you won't believe it—by the Marathas? The Mysore army under him became an institute of learning for the Indian princes. This individual who in terms of his learning, wisdom and innovativeness would make people like Robert Clive look like a pygmy—this person was dismissed in a paragraph in our history books. And he is not the only one … they stole our self-respect, Pramod, they destroyed our self-image—leaving us grovelling for a little attention from the white man. How can I not react to what they have done? You must have gone through the same ordeal of debasement at school?"

Pramod had become more thoughtful and less combative. He answered after a while. "Maybe not to the same extent. I was not in missionary schools as you were. Mine was an Indian school, with

Indian teachers. Our teachers tried to instil in us a pride at being Indian. So they added their own bits to what we read—they tried to redress the balance to some degree. However, until the British left, the messages in the outside world were the same as those you came across. Indian goods were shoddy. The Indian style of dressing was clumsy and ridiculous. I remember how people would laugh at our Sanskrit master because he came dressed in a dhoti with a tilak on his forehead and a *choti* (ponytail). And these were Indian children who laughed. I remember how we would listen to the BBC on a scratchy radio in order to learn the proper English accent. I thought things would change after Independence. But they didn't."

"Yes," Amar replied swept away in the tide of suppressed emotions which had been unleashed. "We're the lost generation. Neither in the West nor in the East, stuck in no man's land. Creatures without anchors in either world. Our parents and theirs had anchors in their own culture, their own civilisation and their own values. They had to start making changes when the British took over our country, but they had moorings to keep themselves steady." He paused, to collect himself.

"We? We don't know what moorings we want—where we want to be," Amar continued. "Do we believe in the caste system? No. Do we believe in the class hierarchy of the British? No. Do we believe in the puritanical values practiced in India? No. Do we approve of the permissiveness we see in England? No. Do we approve of the parent-dominated family that we have in India? No. Do we applaud the disdain with which elders are treated in England? No. Do we support the fatalism shown in India? No. Do we endorse the Western belief that man fashions his own destiny? No—I can go on and on giving examples of how we are trapped in the middle."

Pramod sighed, a little irritably, patience exhausted. "OK, OK. We've been left adrift by the huge transition that our country is making—sure. My question is how can we hold the British responsible for all of it?"

"They are the ones who tried to destroy our self-respect. Because they thought it would give them power to rule, power to plunder. That is what I hold them responsible for. This deliberate effort to demolish the confidence of a nation to satisfy their own greed."

"At the end of the day, where does all this take us?" Pramod asked a little exasperatedly.

"Maybe we need to ask ourselves some questions. What factors are really driving our feelings? The underlying pain of being regarded as personally inferior? Or the classification of our country as an inferior nation? Or both?" Pramod remained silent and Amar continued.

"Did the idea of nationhood set off this divisiveness? Suppose there were no nations—that the world was one undivided country. Could this kind of hurt still occur? Sadly, it would. A divide would still manifest itself, but this time between classes, between languages, between religions, between colours."

"So you're saying human nature seeks separateness?"

"It undoubtedly seeks affiliation. Within family, within neighbourhood, within institution. But here's the thing. Being part of a group also carries within it the idea of exclusion. So affiliation, implicitly, also means exclusion. If I belong, then there must be others who unbelong. And this means divisiveness. I must feel separate to feel that I belong. This is the paradox."

"To separate myself from others I have to choose some criteria of separation—colour, language, social customs, even accents. Then I must arrogate to my customs, my colour, my language, my religion, a certain stamp of superiority. Mine is better and therefore I am better. Is this an elemental human need? Is this driving my feeling of wanting to be superior to the whites?"

Pramod probably hadn't given thought to these ideas and felt caught on the wrong foot. "Interesting thoughts. Maybe we should think more about them"

Amar who had felt excited by these ideas felt deflated. He shook his head and said sadly, "I don't see much enthusiasm on your side. So let's forget it."

Rejection

As winter advanced, Amar found that one of the most difficult tasks of the day was getting out of bed. The central heating invariably worked less efficiently in the morning. Today, however, the morning did not seem to depress him.

As he stepped out into the icy cold air, after breakfast, he was glad that he was well clad. A freezing wind rustled through the hedges. The sky was dull and grey. The bare trees looked shrunken and cold and seemed to huddle into themselves. But all this did not affect Amar. He was going to meet Angela for a cup of coffee in the afternoon. He stepped out briskly. There had been overnight frost, and slivers of ice still lay trapped between the paving stones. He took delight in crunching them underfoot. Life felt good.

❖

As he got to the notice board outside the library after depositing his coat in the basement, he found, to his pleasant surprise, Angela standing by it. She looked a bit troubled. "Hello, Am," she said in a subdued voice, "I thought I might bump into you here. I'm afraid I won't be able to make it this afternoon—something urgent to attend to. Sorry."

Amar tried to hide his disappointment. "That's all right, Angela. I understand. Some other time, then." And he turned and walked to the library, unwilling to carry on a polite conversation.

The day moved on very slowly after that. Everything he did seemed to require a special effort, as if he was underwater, fighting a current. He wouldn't let his mind dwell on his disappointment, but it kept coming back. He kept telling himself that it was no big deal. There would be plenty of other opportunities to spend time with her.

The lectures took his mind off the subject for a while. But, later, as he sat in the library with an open book in front of him, he found himself unable to concentrate. Finally, he decided that he would go and have a cup of tea.

He chose the small cafe in the corridor to the refectory. He couldn't face the noise and the crowd in the main cafeteria. This was a smaller room and was not usually crowded. He opened the door, looked around for a table—and saw her. Angela was sitting with a man, in deep conversation. Amar's reaction was to get away from there as quickly as he could. He turned around and blundered out.

In the corridor, he paused for a moment to collect himself. His mind was in turmoil, and he walked to the main cafeteria to escape. He got himself a cup of tea and a chocolate-coated biscuit and found a table by the wall. The place was crowded and there was a babble of voices and the clatter of crockery. Life carried on—no cataclysmic event had taken place. He took a big swallow of the sweet hot tea and chided himself for overreacting to a simple incident. The truth had to be faced—that she preferred to spend that time with another man. Why should this be such a major event? She hardly knew him. She obviously knew others better. Q.E.D. Life needed to go on.

He had not, however, taken into account the human ego—ever hungry for recognition, ever susceptible to hurt. He sat alone, nursing his hurt for a long while.

Finally, he reached a decision. From now on he would have nothing to do with Angela.

A Different Christmas

There was no snow over London this Christmas. No magical purple sky, no enchanting white flakes drifting down to blanket the city.

The bright lights were strung out along Oxford Street, the shop windows glowed in colours, and snowy white Christmas cakes adorned with mistletoe appeared on shop counters. The walk of Londoners grew even more frenetic as they rushed to buy delayed Christmas presents. There was suppressed excitement on the faces of people and the papers were full of Christmas bargains.

For Amar, the euphoria of the last Christmas was not repeated. He tried hard to recapture the mood, but failed. As he walked down the cold street in the darkness of the evening, he felt depressed. The warmly lit windows of the houses, through which he could catch a glimpse of gaily decorated Christmas trees, only heightened his feeling of exclusion. He was not a part of the celebrations which were going on all around him. He felt invisible as people rushed past with brightly wrapped presents under their arms, or gathered at street corners to sing carols with gusto as the winter wind swept past their freezing ears. He was not included in any of it.

Christmas could be the loneliest time of the year in London.

❖

The Lent term began and with it the round of lectures, classes and library. The fencing class also restarted, and with it came the certainty of meeting Angela. Although he had spent the remaining part of the last term ignoring her, he now found himself looking forward to seeing her. He resolved, however, to keep conversation with her to a minimum.

He was sitting on the bench flexing his foil to get a proper bend on it when she came in with Jane. Angela, looking a little pale, seemed undecided about greeting him. Amar decided to break the ice and said, "Hello, Angela."

He thought he saw a fleeting look of relief on her face as she said, "Hello, Am. Did you have a good vacation?"

Amar grimaced. "Middling. Christmas is not the most exciting time in London for a foreigner. And you? Did you have a good vac?"

"Oh yes. It was wonderful to be home!"

Amar caught himself before he got too involved in this conversation. "See you in a few minutes. There's something I've got to attend to." He thought he caught Jane looking at him as he left the room and slowly shaking her head.

The French team would be coming over this summer, and Amar and the team members had begun a regime of hard practise. They had learnt that the coach of the French team was none other than someone whose book on fencing was actually their bible. He had been an Olympic coach for the French national team and was regarded as one of the leading theorists of this art. Amar's heart had sunk when he got the news. It made him determined to work that much harder.

Amar's regret was that he was not getting opponents of a standard high enough to motivate him to raise his own level. He was winning most of his matches.

❖

A few days later, Jane was whizzing by in her normal fashion along the corridor when she saw Amar. Amar thought he could almost hear the screech of brakes and smell the burning rubber as she came to a sudden halt. But he removed the smile from his face when he saw her grim expression. "Amar, do you have a minute to spare?" It was a command more than a question.

"Sure," Amar smiled.

She moved to a deserted part of the corridor and waited for Amar to join her. "Amar, I hope you don't mind my asking you—but what is wrong between Angela and you? You ignore her at every opportunity, you leave the group if she joins it—the poor girl is at her wits end trying to work out what's gone wrong."

Amar felt gratified to hear this. But he was determined not to show his feelings. "Sorry Jane, I don't mean to be rude, but if Angela is so concerned wouldn't it be more appropriate for her to ask me directly rather than send you?"

Jane's eyes flashed with anger but she bit back her retort. She took a deep breath and said, "She didn't send me. Anyway, I suppose you're right … thanks." She turned around and marched off.

❖

It wasn't till the next week that Amar bumped into Angela on his way out of a lecture. She looked troubled but smiled wanly at him. "Hello, Am." Then looking a bit flustered she said, "Are you free for a few minutes?"

"Yes, and if you are up to it, let's go and have a cup of coffee."

She looked relieved as she said, "That would be nice."

Amar got the coffees and sat down opposite her, feeling tense. She appeared to be equally edgy as she looked down while stirring her coffee. The air was tight with tension. "Am," she started and then cleared her throat, "Am, I've got something to ask you. If you think it's not appropriate you can tell me to shut up. God, I'm so nervous," she said smiling weakly.

She quickly had a sip of her coffee. "Am, I've noticed that for some time you've been deliberately avoiding me. I've been wracking my brain as to why this is so—but I've come up with nothing which explains it. Yet there must be some reason—and I would be glad if you could share it with me." She looked up at him appealingly.

"Well," he paused, not knowing what to say. He cleared his throat. "Well …" Then paused again. Then confessed, "I'm as nervous as you."

He wasn't certain how he should phrase what he said next. Taking a deep breath he began. "Angela, you may or may not remember, but last term we were supposed to meet for a cup of coffee in the afternoon and you cancelled it at the last moment because something urgent had come up. I was disappointed, but understood your compulsion. I decided to have a cup of coffee by myself in the small cafe, and that is where I saw you sitting with another man. I didn't want to embarrass you and dashed out immediately. But it upset me. And I decided that there was a message in this somewhere. That my company was unwelcome to you. So I decided to stay away." He took another deep breath. "This bare recital makes the whole situation sound utterly commonplace and petty—and I feel embarrassed by it. All I wanted to say was that for me it was not commonplace or insignificant. It felt like a rejection. So there you have it. Maybe I'm just a vulnerable man." Amar looked down at his cup, his hands clasped and twisting under the table. He was feeling uncomfortable with having laid himself bare.

Her pale, anxious face went through a transformation. He waited anxiously. Then to his surprise, her face lit up with a big smile. "I can't believe it! That's all it was? And here I was wondering if I had done something terrible. You don't know how relieved I feel! Oh Am, my meeting with another man is so easy to explain. I had to meet a relative of mine who was unexpectedly in town and there was an urgent family matter to discuss. He was in London only for that day and I couldn't say no to his request for a meeting. I am sorry," she said gently and stretched out and touched his hand. "I truly am. I should have explained to you—but you know how we are in this country, we're so reluctant to share anything personal with anybody. I wish I had—all this could have been avoided. I had no wish to hurt you, Am, believe me. And it was no rebuff—I'd myself been looking forward to the afternoon and felt disappointed that it did not materialise."

A huge load lifted from Amar's mind, but he tried not to show it. Some of his relief spilt over.

"Thank you for telling me all this. Being cold to you was costing me enormously."

"So can we forget the past now?" Angela asked.

"With the greatest of pleasure," Amar smiled back.

❖

"So you finally followed my advice," said Pramod as he speared a piece of fish.

"Your advice? I don't recall any advice," Amar replied indignantly. "All I recall, from our conversation at the pub, is your saying with a belch," and Amar deepened his voice, "This beer is good."

Pramod was undaunted and went on chewing. "You have to admit the beer was excellent. You also have to be able to read the underlying meaning in conversation. Everything doesn't have to be spelt out in so many words."

"So there was an underlying meaning to your 'This beer is good'? Or was there an underlying meaning to your belch?"

Pramod was not to be distracted. "You'll remember that I asked you to make up your mind about how serious you were about Angela. And that is what you have done. So—you did follow my advice. And incidentally, to set the record straight, I did not belch."

"I was reading the underlying message. When you said 'This beer is good', the underlying message was—a belch, even if it was not articulated."

"I can see that your meeting Angela yesterday has improved your mood—though not your sense of humour," Pramod said a little huffily.

"All right—all right. If it makes you happy, it was due to your advice that I said what I did to Angela—though it does stretch the truth. But I'm still not clear where this insightful advice has taken me."

"Your problem is that you're not thinking the matter through."

"You think these matters lend themselves to rational thought? You attach disproportionate weight to the logical process, Pramod.

That's your problem. The truth is, that our conscious logical processes are nowhere near being able to match our subconscious or unconscious ones. There's where wisdom probably resides." This was said on an impulse, and he wondered where it came from, since he was a firm believer in rational thought.

Pramod snorted. "You can't be serious! Hunches? Gut feel? So if I have indigestion and am feeling irritable with the world, and in my cantankerous mood reach a decision—you're saying that decision is to be valued more than a reasoned, well-thought-out conclusion? I can't believe what I'm hearing!"

Having committed himself to a position, however impulse driven it was, Amar warmed to the theme. "What I'm saying is not even remotely what you're making it out to be. I'm saying that the process our conscious mind follows does not always guarantee us the right answer. The reason is that, it either does not pick up all the information—or it does not always interpret that information correctly. Maybe our not-so-conscious mind, call it subconscious or unconscious, I really don't care—maybe this part of our mind can pick up more information—the subtle cues—the unspelt themes—which our conscious mind does not. And having picked them up, it processes them better. Can't you see that this may be a possibility?"

Pramod looked disgusted. "You will soon be saying that the spirits are speaking to you."

"And you're talking like the religious zealots who burnt people at the stake because of their divergent views. Allow some new ideas to filter through, for God's sake. You don't have to accept all I say—but at least think about them before dismissing everything just because it breaks out of the tramline thinking you're used to."

Before long they realised that this discussion was not leading them anywhere and broke up, each believing that he was the holder of the truth.

Country Weekend

As the summer term opened, Amar kept remembering that the end of term would see the end of his second year. He would be stepping into his last year next term. It had all gone so fast. There was so much to do yet—so much to see—so much to experience. It all seemed unfairly short. He didn't feel mentally ready to go back to India and settle down to a mundane job.

As he morosely stood in front of the notice board, Rod appeared at his shoulder. "Amar, my friend! Just the person I was looking for. There's a buddy of mine organising a farm party a fortnight from now—fancy a weekend on a farm? Plenty to drink, lots of country lasses! There's some of us driving down—would you like to join us? It'll be fun, I promise you!"

It sounded wonderful and Amar was sorely tempted. But thoughts of the cost it would entail, held him back from saying an eager yes. "It sounds good, Rod. Can I get back to you in a day or two?"

"Sure. And remember, it's not going to be expensive. We'll split the cost of the petrol and chip in a few bob towards the drink. The rest will be taken care of by the person who owns the farm. He's loaded—so it's no sweat as far as I'm concerned. Hope you'll say yes, my friend. The moment I heard about the party, I thought about you. So don't let me down!"

Reassured, Amar gave his assent the next day to a visibly delighted Rod. "You won't regret saying yes, Am. It's a pretty bit of country, too."

❖

The weekend for the farm visit arrived. On an unseasonably chilly Saturday morning they met outside the LSE and clambered into the battered but serviceable Austin which belonged to Rod's friend, Dick. En route to the farm they would pick up another friend, Basil, who lived some distance from London.

Leaving the grimy London houses, Amar's spirits lightened as they hit the country. A fitful sun peeked out from the grey clouds, releasing the colours of the meadows. Amar had a theory that the English countryside looked its best in bright sunlight because of the depth of the colours—the eye-blinding emerald of the grass, the intense colours of the flowers, the heavy greens of the bushes and trees. These looked shadowed under a grey sky, but exploded under the sun.

It was the opposite in India. The colours were more muted, whether it was the bleached fields or the dusty trees or the growing crops—except of course for the paddy which detonated in a dazzling green. These muted colours developed a delicate beauty under the blue-grey monsoon skies. Their colours were no longer sucked out by the harshness of a relentless sun, but glowed softly in the mellow light.

Amar sank back in his seat to enjoy the countryside celebrating late spring, while Rod and Dick animatedly discussed a new pub Rod had discovered.

They stopped to pick up Basil at a village, a somewhat plump individual who looked older than Rod. He didn't have Rod's bonhomie or Dick's unaffected charm, and Amar took an instant dislike to him. His likes and dislikes had got stronger in the last year. He believed he had been a much more easy-going person in Delhi.

Amar realised that Basil was one of those who liked to take charge. He was disappointed to see Rod deferring to him.

They arrived at the farm around tea-time and found a couple of cars parked in the yard. Amar recognised a few LSE faces. He was glad to be able to stretch his legs. This part of the farm was no more than an open patch of land with a squat whitewashed building which contained several large rooms. One of them served as a dining area and had a number of tables and a few chairs. A door connected to a large kitchen. Some mugs of coppery tea appeared and Amar gratefully grabbed one of them and went out. Beyond the open space of land and a surrounding hedge, flat cultivated fields rolled out to the horizon. There was not much greenery except for a few isolated clumps of trees. There were, however, trees along the road they had come and some attractive cottages with flower-filled gardens.

Rod appeared sipping from his mug of tea. "Could've done with a spot of rum, don't you think, old sport?" and he nudged Amar and broke into laughter. Amar couldn't find a suitable response and grinned weakly. "Hey, let's finish our tea and take a walk up the road—give ourselves a chance to stretch our legs," Rod added.

They walked out onto the narrow country lane which wound its way between gardens and cottages. A car passed by and Rod waved to them, "Aha, the troops are arriving!" They walked on towards the actual village. Around a corner, they found two horses with riders approaching them, and they got off the road to allow them to pass. The riders turned out to be two young women, one of whom looked very attractive despite her face being partially hidden by her riding helmet.

"Well now, Rod, this countryside does seem to have something to offer!" Amar said with enthusiasm. "Pity, we can't invite them to our party. Maybe you should, Rod—but you'll need to shout 'Tally ho!' or some such native war cry."

Rod guffawed. "I'll be chased by a country squire with his shotgun, if I did. But fear not, there will be talent aplenty at the party, even if they do bear the London stamp."

By the time they got back more people had arrived and the place was fair humming with activity. Basil buttonholed them, "Hey, where've you lot been? Give us a hand with setting up the bar. This is George, our host."

George was a pallid, tall, gangling young man in a tweed jacket and grey flannels who muttered a shy greeting and stuck his limp hand out. Amar shook his hand and said, "Good to meet you, George—thanks for having us."

George looked embarrassed and muttered something which sounded like, "Thanks for coming—gives us country folk a chance to kick up our heels."

The bar was set up inside the main room and comprised a long table with a white tablecloth covering it. Cartons of newspaper-wrapped glasses were unpacked and placed on the table. Bottles of beer and cider were neatly stacked on one side. "Any wine for the ladies?" Amar asked Rod.

"Those who want wine will bring their own bottles. Most will drink beer or cider, which we have in plenty."

On a side table paper plates and napkins had been placed. "The food is going to be simple—sausages, ham, some roast beef, salad from the local gardens, and farm bread. We'll also roast some potatoes on the bonfire," Rod explained.

"Perfect," Amar said rubbing his hands. "When do the festivities start?"

"They've started," Rod grinned, pointing outside where a group of people were lighting a bonfire. Some of the men had glasses of beer in their hands—the girls seemed to be doing most of the work. "Let's join them," Rod added, "But hang on, we need to be properly equipped." And he filled two glasses with beer, handing one to George and one to Amar. Getting himself one, he said, "Right, let's go into battle."

Amar recognised a few of the faces as being from the LSE. The fire had got going by now and sitting around it was comfortable in spite of the evening chill having descended. For Amar, never a great party person—not having attended many, anyway—sitting flanked by two strangers was not a very comfortable experience. On one side was a bespectacled, plump young woman whom he had seen in the corridors of the LSE, and on the other, a young man whom he could not recollect seeing before. He decided to start talking to the young woman whose name turned out to be Cynthia. She was a Sociology student, in her first year.

Gradually, with the beer reducing his awkwardness, Amar found conversation with her quite interesting. Her intelligence and interest in India helped. Until she asked the question Amar had come to dread.

"I hope you won't mind my asking this question, Amar, but what does the average Indian feel about Britain? I mean, we didn't exactly cover ourselves with glory during our occupation of India."

He paused and then said, "Cynthia, I understand your interest and respect it, but the subject is a sensitive one—one which arouses a lot of passions, especially in Indians. Can we give it a miss? I'd rather talk about the recent Teddy Boy phenomenon instead. I'm really intrigued."

She looked a little puzzled at this shift of subject, but recovered herself when she found Amar looking so interested.

"Well, it's odd that you ask, because I was reading an article on it just the other day. Did you know that the cult originated in Elephant and Castle, an area which was devastated in two nights of severe bombing during the war? The Teddy Boys emerged from this shattered and distressed area to become, arguably, Britain's first youth cult. Mind you, this area of London has had a long history of violence. In fact, there is one theory that the expression 'hooliganism' originated from the name of an Irish bouncer and a thief, called Hoolihan, who lived in this area in the late 19th century."

"Fascinating," a genuinely interested Amar said. "What is the reason for the way they dress?"

"Yes, the Teddy Boy style of dressing does mark them apart. And there's an irony about it. Post War, Saville Row had gone back to the Edwardian style for those ex-servicemen who wanted to be dandies. Strangely enough, this fashion was adopted by the teenagers around Elephant and Castle, who then came to be called Teds or Teddy Boys. Their uniform was a long drape jacket with high-waisted, narrow drainpipe trousers and chunky shoes. They also wore white shirts with narrow ties and sometimes had velvet-trim collars on their jackets. And do you know, these clothes were tailor-made, at great expense—an expense they could not really afford. They're really like any other teenager, except that they're now associated with violence after the recent Notting Hill race riots."

"Well, I would certainly get on to the other footpath if I saw them coming!" Amar said.

The boy on the other side of Cynthia, Dudley, had been listening to the conversation. He took a swallow of beer and said in a public school accent, "Actually, was the Notting Hill attack really racial to start with? The first person to be attacked by the gang was a white woman, you know."

Amar couldn't believe what he was hearing. Cynthia's reply saved him from getting involved. "Where have you been, Dudley?" she exclaimed. "Yes, a Swedish woman was attacked by a gang of whites. But surely you remember why? She was attacked because the previous day she was having an argument with her West Indian husband and the gang started shouting racial insults at him. She turned on them in defence of her husband. The gang found her the next night and attacked her. After she had been escorted to safety by the police, a 300-strong gang of whites attacked the West Indian residents of that area. And you say this was not racial? Christ, haven't you been reading the papers?"

Amar almost told Cynthia to save her breath, because Dudley probably sang "God Save the Queen" every night before retiring.

"Don't get so het up, Cynthia" a somewhat discomfited Dudley replied. "I was only making an observation. In any case, can you really blame the locals for being upset at being taken over by a different culture?" Amar almost felt sorry for the man. He was digging himself deeper into a hole every time he spoke.

"Yes, I can blame them—and I will," Cynthia almost shouted. "And I blame you too for being as racial as the hooligans were. I never thought a friend of mine could be so bigoted." She was almost in tears. Amar stretched out a comforting hand and touched her arm gently.

A welcome break was provided by a friend of Dudley's sitting down next to him. Dudley looked relieved, and performed the introductions. The new arrival, Christopher, seemed of the same ilk as Dudley. Amar looked around for an excuse to leave.

Dudley decided to steer away from the explosive topic they had been discussing. "Amar, you've avoided answering Cynthia's earlier question. Why, I wonder?"

"Because, the reply may be emotional and too strong for people to be comfortable with," Amar said coldly. He realised, too late, that this might seem like a challenge.

Dudley turned to his friend, "Cynthia had asked Amar to tell us what an Indian really feels about Britain. Amar seems uncomfortable with the question." Amar knew that he was being baited, but did not follow his initial impulse to get up and leave.

Christopher decided to put his tuppence in. "What an interesting question. I really would enjoy hearing an answer."

Amar smiled realising that it was too late to back out at this stage. But it was worth a try.

"Sorry, Christopher. With all due respect, providing you enjoyment is not top priority for me at this moment."

"Oh, let's leave the poor chap be, Christopher" Dudley said patronisingly. "He's obviously not comfortable with it."

Cynthia had been listening to all this rather bemusedly, though she recognised what the two were up to. She now turned to Amar and said, "Forget my question, Amar. I think a reply would be rather wasted on this kind of an audience."

Too late, Amar thought. He couldn't back out now. "No, I think these people need an answer."

Here we go again, Amar thought. But this time I must keep my cool, and keep it brief. "It's a question I've been asked many times and I always find it difficult to answer. As you said, Cynthia, there's a great many things that Britain did as rulers. Remembering some of them usually sends an Indian's blood coursing." Amar paused to collect his thoughts. He looked at the amused and condescending expression on the faces of

Christopher and Dudley and decided to change his mind and give these two thugs the full treatment.

"Partition was the culminating evil. You probably don't know that more than a million innocents died in the bloodshed that followed, more than 15 million were uprooted from their homes and had to flee to seek sanctuary in places which were totally alien to them. The current UK population is around 50 million? So in your terms, 30% of the population had to give up their homes. Can you even begin to imagine the scale of disruption? The Muslims had to flee to the newly created Pakistan—the Hindus and Sikhs from the newly created Pakistan. They fled anyway they could, leaving every personal possession behind. But even this flight did not necessarily bring them safety. The trains carrying Muslims had to pass through Indian territory before reaching Pakistan. Those carrying Hindus and Sikhs had to traverse parts of Pakistan before reaching the Indian border. A lot of these trains became vehicles of death. When they reached their destinations there was not a soul alive—the bogies were awash with blood from the innocents who had been slaughtered."

He continued, still a little unwillingly. They've forced me into this, he reasoned, so let them be exposed to the horrors. "This was probably one of Britain's biggest crimes—Partition—and the subsequent brutalisation of people. I was a child then and we were living in a city which fortunately did not see the worst excesses of the Partition. But I heard stories from friends and relations who had experienced the horrors first-hand. People sank to the lowest abyss in themselves—a dark and terrible depth which exists in all of us, but which civilisation has tried to keep a lid on. From time to time this lid gets wrenched off by some cataclysmic event, and then hell breaks loose. This is what the Partition did—this is the brutalisation I was talking about. Let me give you an example. Five years after this event, an older cousin, who had come to stay with us, got talking about the riots which hit Calcutta after Partition. He told of the horrors he had seen. And then—he calmly proceeded to describe how he had himself slaughtered babies with a knife. He was quite matter-of-fact in his description of events. Not a word of regret—not a hint of sorrow. Think, Cynthia, this was a very ordinary man living a very ordinary life, not a rabid killer. But his conscience had been cauterised by events. His understanding of the line between good and evil had been erased. How many thousands—no millions of such zombies had been created by this holocaust. And they are living today. Can you think what effect this has had on our present society—and will have in the future when children in the laps of these zombies will be told, not fairy tales, but these tales of blood? Can you imagine the hatred that has been created and the anger which will be passed on from generation to generation?" Amar paused.

Dudley jumped in. "Surely Partition was not just a British decision, the Indian leaders also agreed to it?"

"Sure. They were party to it. But you have to realise that history is a causation of past events. 'Divide and rule' may seem a cliché today, but that's precisely what the British did. Throughout the centuries, the Hindus and Muslims had lived in amity. Even the Moghuls respected this. Did you know that one of the most famous Moghul emperors, Akbar, took a Hindu as his wife? That the Hindus and Muslims combined to fight our first war of independence, which your historians have called the Great Mutiny? After this, the British intensified their efforts to break up this unity. Then, in 1909, came the Morley Minto Reforms which created separate electorates for different religious groups. The final blow had been struck to open up the fissure between Muslims and Hindus."

"All very interesting, but how does the Morley Minto Reforms absolve the role of Indian leaders in it?" Dudley asked.

"It doesn't, but it explains their action. The fissures that were started by the Reforms were systematically widened by the British. Jinnah, the main Muslim leader, who was initially an ardent nationalist, fell prey to the temptation and changed his stance by asking for a separate Muslim entity. When in 1947 the other Indian leaders were given the choice of having a free but split country at once, or a unified country at an unspecified future date, they succumbed to the former. They had waited long enough for freedom and wanted it immediately. And that decision unleashed the violence. Of course, the Indian leaders shared the culpability."

"So why the anger against the British then?" Dudley enquired.

"Because they initiated the split. Because they were in charge of the country when this happened. Because they sowed the seed of separation. And having achieved their objective, then set about the partition of the country with an unseemly, almost obscene, haste. Mountbatten was the architect. His vanity is well known—he had to add another feather to his cap. Radcliffe, a legal expert, who had scant knowledge about India, was given the task of carving the country up. Radcliffe arrived in India in early July and was then told by Mountbatten that the boundary delineation was to be completed by 15th August! Can you believe that? A country the size and complexity of India to be carved up in just a month? As a result, it was not possible to get together the survey and other information necessary for a well-thought-out decision. So, what resulted? A nightmare. The boundary ran through the country arbitrarily. Families woke up one morning to find that their kitchen was in Pakistan while their living room was in India! There was no transparency—no consultation. How could there be, there was no time. As I said earlier, 15 million people were uprooted. This was probably the largest forced migration the world has known. The horrors of Partition I will not go into any more."

Cynthia had been listening intently with interest. Dudley, with impatience. He jumped into the pause. "All very sad and unfortunate—no doubt. However, are you not falling into the trap that many colonised nations do, of focussing only on the negatives of colonial rule? Surely the British brought something positive to the table? Like law and order, like an education system, like public health?"

Amar hid his irritation, caused partly by having to mentally concede that there was some truth in this. But, by now, the adrenaline had started coursing in his veins, and he was not going to admit this fact. “Certainly they did. They brought a lot of goodies to the table. You had the judicial system and the concept of equality before the law. Although, it should be added that the judicial system was not unknown in India. India was governed by laws based on the *Arthashastra*, dating to 400 BC, and the *Manusmriti* to AD 100. So you can see the legal system goes back a long way, a system far older than the British legal system. There was also a decentralised structure called the panchayat system which settled disputes at the village level.” Amar paused. He noticed, uncomfortably, that by now a number of people had gathered around them, and felt isolated. But continued.

“Then, the British introduced their education system to help increase literacy. This was undoubtedly a benefit they brought. Guess what was achieved in terms of literacy levels in the many, many decades of British rule? Dudley?”

A not very happy Dudley shrugged and said, “Dunno.”

“Anybody like to guess?” Amar looked around. His initial nervousness at seeing other people gathering to listen, now dissipating. The adrenaline was really surging.

Somebody jocularly asked “Any prizes?” but was shut down by a glare from Cynthia.

“30 to 40%?” somebody else hazarded.

“No, no—much more than that I’m sure,” it was Basil now, “The British did some pretty good work, even if I as a Brit say so.”

“The literacy rate was 11% when the British left in 1947” Amar said quietly. “The result of 100 years of effort.”

Dudley looked angry, his cheeks reddened. “You’re choosing things which you can knock down. Why don’t you talk about roads, railways, health, agriculture, standard of living?”

There were grins all around and somebody said, “Come on, Amar, fair’s fair.”

Amar, after the initial discomfort of having more than one opponent to deal with, was now enjoying himself. He had the advantage of having been through similar arguments many times in the past, and so had the facts at his fingertips.

He smiled and said, "It's beginning to feel like a boxing ring—I'm waiting for the yells baying for blood! No, Dudley, you're right. I am prejudiced. So let's take the areas you mentioned. There is no doubt that the British built a huge rail system—probably one of the largest in the world. This is certainly one of their lasting legacies. On roads however, the picture is a little different. Well-laid-out roads date back to 4,000 BC and were found in the ancient cities of Harappa and Mohenjo-Daro. There was an entire network of roads criss-crossing the country. In the 16th century, a road running across the Gangetic Plain was built. This was extended by the Moghuls and added to by the British. It came to be called the Grand Trunk Road. So you see, an extensive road system existed before the British took over. Of course, they added to it and modernised it."

Dudley looked more relaxed now. "I'm glad you're giving some credit to the Brits. It was getting rather one-sided."

"Anything to keep you happy, Dudley! Let's move to health, then, since you'd mentioned it. Let's see if this makes you happy too. Everyone accepts that the British brought the benefits of modern medicine to India. However, the benefits did not percolate very far. Life expectancy in India was barely 25 in 1921, compared to 55 in London. This is a figure from a report of the International Labour Office. What is worse is that this declined subsequently—it fell to 23 in 1931. The wonders of modern medicine do not appear to have reached the Indians."

Another voice rose in support of Dudley. It came from a tall bespectacled man. "Our Indian friend would have us believe that British rule in India was a sordid story of exploitation and nothing more. Surely that is an exaggeration? Britain helped India enter the modern age, prepared the infrastructure and then left to allow the country to develop on its own. Certainly there may have been unfortunate events, but I wouldn't expect a mature person, such as our friend, to dwell only on those. Can I suggest, sir, you take a broader view and look at the general improvement in standard of living, well-being and other benefits that were brought in by the British?"

Amar's gorge rose, but before he could say anything, another voice joined in. A slightly older man sitting across from Amar, said, "Hang on—hang on. Listening to you, my friend, one would imagine that the British went to India only to fulfil a noble and Christian mission of helping a sad, backward country. Nothing could be further from the truth. They went to make money and pillage the country. If they built up the infrastructure it was because they needed it for their trade and for their military. And India was far from being a poor and backward country. As Amar—have I got the name right—as Amar has been repeatedly pointing out, India was a developed country long before Britain was. It did not need Western help. And please don't expect somebody from a country which has been pillaged and ravished to be detached about Britain's role."

"Let me just add to that," Amar said, enjoying the support. "Before the East India Company came, India was one of the flourishing economies of the world. Read Tavernier, who travelled in India in the 17th century, spoke about the prosperity he found even in the smallest villages. Read the French traveller Bernier's account of the riches he saw in Bengal in the 17th century. He described it as being wealthier than Egypt and talked with awe of its exports of cotton and silk and rice and sugar. In the 100 years that the British were there, Indian trade shrank to a cipher. Prior to the British arrival, 25% of world trade originated from India. When the British left it had shrunk to 1%."

Dudley was about to say something, but Amar held up his hand, "Sorry Dudley, just a minute more. I just want to finish by reminding you of the contribution that the money collected from India, made to Britain's development in the 18th and 19th century. Without this transfer of wealth, Britain's modernisation would not have been possible. Lord Curzon, the Viceroy of India, said sometime in the 1890s that Britain could afford to lose other dominions but losing India would mean that the sun of the Empire had set. And finally, let me just remind you of the kind of avarice that was on display. Lord William Bentinck announced plans to break up the best Moghul monuments in order to ship the marble to England where it would be sold to the aristocracy. The process began and a large number of monuments were vandalised. The Taj Mahal was on the list, believe it or not, but was saved at the last minute because it was found that the first auction was not successful!"

He looked at Dudley's bespectacled ally, "Oh, I forgot sir, you wanted me to talk of the improvement brought about in standard of living and well-being by the British. Let me, then, tell you the story of the Bengal Famine—something which your history books don't talk about. In 1942, when the Japanese overran the British in Singapore and then moved on to take over Burma, the British feared that they would enter India through Bengal, which is in the east of India. They decided to stockpile food supplies for the military, since Burma had been a major supplier of rice, and also to deny the Japanese access to food if they entered. So a scorched earth policy was followed. Fishermen's boats were confiscated to prevent the Japs access, but no rations were provided to the fishermen for the fish they were now deprived of. Huge quantities of rice continued to be exported to the Middle East to feed the Allied army. Rice became short and the prices rose. Millions of people found themselves unable to buy. People began to starve. The government reacted callously and refused to stop export of rice from Bengal. Finally, the government woke up and asked London for ships carrying food grains to be diverted to Bengal. This did not receive a sympathetic reply, as war requirements came first. So people lay on the streets begging for food, dying. Any guesses as to how many died?"

There was an uncomfortable silence. "Between three to five million," Amar said. "And everyone agrees this famine could have been avoided by timely action. So now, sir, do you still want me to talk about the improvement in standard of living?"

Finally, Dudley said, "Terrible, if it's true. Yet none of us seems to know about it. How come?"

"I can understand you wanting to deny it. Because it falls into the same category as the Holocaust. Yet, there seems little mention of it in your history books. Maybe brown bodies are less visible than the white ones."

He got up. "I think this brown body needs a drink."

Cynthia got up too. "I'll join you."

❖

As they left, Amar heard voices engaged in discussion. He was too mentally exhausted to bother about what they were talking about. As they refilled their glasses at the bar, Amar realised that Cynthia had hardly said a word. However, she had shown her solidarity with him by leaving the group when he did. He said tiredly, "Thanks, Cynthia."

"For what?"

"For your support."

"Nonsense. I did nothing except listen."

"That was support enough. You know, I got rather carried away in trying to score debating points. But this was a kind of catharsis for me. I also have to admit that I was not playing entirely fair. There are things we can thank the British for, but I was not going to admit it to the likes of Dudley and his friend. Sorry if I'm running down people who may be your friends. This will help you see the deep anger that exists in a lot of us, and perhaps help you realise the complexity of the question you had asked."

Amar took a gulp from his refilled glass as they strolled away from the bar. By now the rock music from the main room had got louder and more insistent. Cynthia was, unconsciously, shaking her head in time with the music.

"But enough," he continued. "I can see you're enjoying the music, Cynthia. Unfortunately, I am no good at this kind of dancing—so go and find a partner. The night is still young and we'll catch up with each other later."

She asked a little unsurely, "Are you sure you don't mind?"

"Yes, Cynthia, I'm sure. Go for it!"

"See you later then," Cynthia said, then turned and ran off.

❖

The night stretched on with unlimited beer, but limited excitement. No lissom country lass made eyes at him. No lecherous LSE lass dragged him to the bushes. He sat by the fire and allowed his thoughts to drift. He had been in the country for over one and a half years, yet had not been able to find himself a girlfriend. He had been to student dances at the university, had even taken out one of the girls he met there to the theatre, but had realised by the interval that it was a mistake. She did not really attract him. The same thing had happened when he had taken one of the Fencing Club girls out. She seemed to have little in common with him intellectually. Equally importantly, she also had a boyfriend. He didn't stop to ask himself why she had come out if she had a steady.

He almost convinced himself that he lacked some essential quality which women found attractive.

It had got cold and he was reminded of winter in Delhi. It would be very chilly with a light mist forming a hazy curtain around the street lamp. There would be the acrid smell of the leaves that had been burnt during the day. He would be taking the dog out for a walk on the leaf-strewn footpath, heavily clad to ward off the cold, the starlit sky just visible through the overhead branches. It was a quiet road with the bungalows protected by walls and hedges. The only sound would be the leaves crackling under his shoes and the sniffing of the dog.

His reverie was interrupted by a fresh influx of people seeking the warmth of the fire. He was forced into desultory conversation when he would have been happier left to his own thoughts.

The party drifted on and then slowly died out like the fire. He was relieved to get under a blanket and sleep.

French Team's Visit

Arrangements began for the French team's visit which was now only a month away. A rugby team and a fencing team would arrive on a Thursday and would be looked after by the Athletic Union. The fencing match was on the Friday afternoon, in the gymnasium. Later that evening there would be a get-together of the teams at the male hall of residence. Since the female participation at this do was a little in doubt, invitations had been issued to a nearby nursing college.

The Fencing Club members, Angela included, were quite excited about the event and promised to be present in strength to cheer the team. As the day approached, Amar found himself getting more and more nervous. Rod, in an effort to soothe nerves, suggested the team meeting after practise for a drink. Amar opted out. He was anxious to avoid any alcohol for the remaining days before the match. He had to be fit and relaxed, he kept telling himself. Relaxation was essential for success in a match situation, his coach had dinned into his head. Amar found this dictum a very difficult one to follow. He was relaxed enough when he took his stance, but once the judge gave the starting signal by saying "play", he found himself tensing up. He decided that over the remaining days of preparation he would spend time practising relaxation.

The week before the match he took home his white canvas fencing jacket and trousers for a thorough scrub. They came out of the wash looking gleaming white. He then used white Blanco to cover the sweat stains on his shoes.

The day arrived. Amar had a good breakfast, picked up his gear and told his mother that he would be late in returning that night because of the party he had to attend.

He was glad he had a lecture in the morning. It took his mind off the match. He had briefly met the French team when they came to see the gymnasium the previous day. He had shaken hands with their coach, who gave a brief smile when Amar mentioned that his book was their constant source of reference.

The match would begin at four in the afternoon, and Amar decided to have a light sandwich lunch. Pramod saw this and asked, "You're not eating lunch today?"

"No, have to keep my stomach light for the match this afternoon."

"Oh, yes. Sorry I'd forgotten. I'll be there to cheer you."

"Do come. We need all the support that we can muster."

"Of course I'll be there. Seriously, I will be there to proudly cheer the first Indian to represent LSE at fencing. You are the first Indian, aren't you?"

"Don't know. Probably."

After lunch Amar decided to spend some time at the library before meeting the team at the gym at three. The quiet of the library would have a calming influence. The conversation with Pramod had also raised Amar's morale.

❖

Amar sat, sweaty and dejected, in the changing room bench. An unexpectedly large number of students had crowded the gym. Sadly, the match had gone along expected lines. The French team had won comprehensively. Amar who had been his coach's main hope had not been able to fulfil the expectation. He had won the sole match for LSE in the foil section, and had received a large ovation. He had, in fact, won against their best fencer. But, that was no consolation. He knew he had thrown away both the other bouts. One by his overconfidence, and the other by succumbing to his opponent's gamesmanship. This individual had, after losing a point to Amar, said something in French which was obviously insulting. Amar had not recognised the ploy for what it was, and lost his temper. After that he had attacked relentlessly, forsaking his normal quiet skilful style which counted on creating openings before attacking. His blustering left him open to a counter and the score became 3 points to 2 against him. He had lost the bout.

As he had recovered his breath and his composure in the gym, Angela had come up to him. "Are you alright, Am?"

"No, Angela, I'm not. I'm furious with myself. I should have won all three of my bouts, instead I end up winning only one. At least the final scoreline would have read 6-3 instead of the disastrous 8-1 against us. I knew that I was the better fencer in both cases, the scores were 2-2 in each bout and I could have won the final point but for my stupidity—my bloody adolescent stupidity," he said throwing his glove and foil onto the bench.

"Don't be too hard on yourself, Am. You were the only one to win a bout, and that also against an outstanding team."

"But I had their measure, Angela, I had them lined up!" he exclaimed still fuming. "Sorry, I'm not very good company just now. Let me get myself a shower. Thanks, anyway, for what you said. See you at the party."

While the others showered and changed Amar decided to grab a snack. He wasn't keen on company just at this moment and decided to go up to the cafeteria on his own. "See you down by the clock at seven, Rod."

He got himself two cheese rolls and a cup of tea and found himself a table by the wall. He wasn't greatly looking forward to the party. The defeat still weighed on him. In the épée section, a weapon which Amar did not like and had opted out of, Roger had won the solitary bout. So the final score line read 8-1 and 8-1 in favour of the French team. It was a double blow to his ego—firstly his own 1-3 loss and then his team's trouncing. The only thing which drew him to the party was the prospect of Angela's company.

Post Match Party

The party was being held in a large room at one end of which a bar had been set up. At the other end, space had been left for dancing. A keg of beer was perched on the table accompanied by bottles of spirit and wine. “The Athletic Union is doing us proud, aren’t they?” Rod observed. “Come on, folks, let’s get our drinks and find ourselves a corner to sit in.” A number of people had already arrived and it took them some time to get their drinks. Amar got himself a mug of beer and noticed that Angela had a glass of white wine in her hand. The Fencing Club group moved to the chairs by one of the corners and sat around in a circle. Rod raised his glass and said, “Here’s to our two winners, Am and Rog—and to more victories.” They all drank.

Amar had managed to get himself a chair by Angela. “Feeling better, Am?” Angela asked.

Amar grinned, “Bee-ing with you, mademoiselle, it *ees* like all troubles have *vaneesh*!”

Angela stifled a laugh, frowned and said, “Stop it! Instead of being disastrously French you can find something for me to munch upon before this wine goes to my head.”

“Ah, but such a be-ootiful ‘ead, tres magnifique …” Amar started but was stopped by a sharp jab from Angela. “Ow—you should have been a boxer.”

Amar wandered off and found a table with rolls, sandwiches and crisps. He waited till the severe looking lady behind the table turned away to talk to someone, grabbed a plate of sandwiches and beat a hasty retreat. As he offered it to Angela, the others descended on the plate with glee and it was empty in no time. “Well, one of you greedy sods can go and return the plate and get another plate of rolls," he said disgustedly. He retrieved his beer mug from beneath the chair and was glad to see that Angela had managed to get a sandwich. As he took a long pull of beer, she nudged him, "Here, Am, I've saved one for you too." No sandwich ever tasted better.

The French teams arrived and the room began to fill up as the nurses arrived, too. Soon there was no place to move. Rod came to the rescue, "Hey, I know this place well—there is an anteroom we can move to. Let's go before that fills up too. Ed, why don't you refresh the glasses of the ladies while we move there." Amar accompanied Ed to the bar with Angela's glass and his own empty mug. Music had started but could hardly be heard above the babble of voices. There was a big crowd in front of the bar. Amar caught hold of Ed's arm, "Wait a minute, they seem to have opened another bar in that corner. Let's go there before the stampede starts." They managed to beat the crowd and get their drinks. As they returned to their group he noticed that his place next to Angela had been taken by a first-year student called Ned who seemed to be in earnest conversation with her. He handed her the drink and made his way to a vacant place next to Jane. "Hell-o-o-w, Am, come and keep me company. You did a marvellous job today against the French team. Congratulations."

Amar was tempted to just grunt in reply. She sounded so glib. He sat down and muttered, "It could have been better," and took a long draught from his beer mug. Maybe he was being unfair to her as he had been before. He really should make an effort, particularly now that he found himself sitting next to her. Just ignore her accent and concentrate on her as a person he told himself.

"Let me guess what you're drinking, Jane," he said brightly. "A gin and T?"

"That's clever of you, Am," she beamed at him. "I can tell you most of the people sitting here would not be able to distinguish between a gin and tonic and Schweppes soda."

"Don't be unfair, Jane," Amar said in mild reproof. "We're all students and for us the esoteric world of upper-class drinking is out of bounds. We're happy with our pint and an occasional glass of plonk. How would we know about gin and tonic?"

"Well then—how did you know?"

"From an overdose of Wodehouse—or maybe Maugham—or was it Kipling? I really don't know. But I remember that genteel ladies are supposed to drink gin and tonic when they're with the natives." Amar regretted it as soon as the words came out of his mouth. "Oh God, I've done it again! Sorry—Jane, for the 'natives' bit. Put it down to my tiredness, or the beer I'm guzzling, or my stupidity. That remark was uncalled for."

"Don't apologise. I understand. Do I seem aggressively upper class?"

Amar tried to hide his surprise. He had underestimated her. And she had put her finger right on the spot. However, he was reluctant to admit to it.

"Maybe or maybe not," he said moodily. Then decided that if she was challenging him with her openness, he would not back off. "Actually, you're probably right, however hard it's for me to make this admission. I despise racism—and I regard stereotyping as being part of it. Yet, I've been guilty of it. I put you in the box labelled 'upper-class behaviour, therefore brain dead' and added on the other label 'upper class, therefore racist'. And finally, I decided that white, upper class equals patronising xenophobe. And yet you're not any of these—in fact, a xenophobe is what *I'm* beginning to emerge as." He paused, "Tell me, Jane, how did you stumble onto the class angle?"

"Simply because I've been there before. This is not the first time it's happened to me." She said a little sadly. "But what am I to do, Am? I grew up in that kind of an environment. I can't be held responsible for the accident of my birth into a certain milieu, can I? Now I'm trying to learn to live with this reverse class prejudice."

She suddenly seemed vulnerable. "Let's forget what I said, Jane. Can we start on a fresh page?" Amar asked.

She smiled, "Yes, gladly. And to mark the beginning of a new friendship, I'll exercise my right as a woman and ask for another drink. May I?"

Amar got up. "My pleasure."

❖

The music had now been turned up and competed for attention with the babble of voices. Rock and roll, a new kind of music, had entered the scene around the early '50s and by 1956, Bill Haley, one of its idols, had five records in the Top Twenty. The film *Rock Around the Clock* was being shown in 300 cinema houses. So it was no surprise that rock 'n' roll music was blaring. On the dance floor, couples were gyrating and thumping their feet on the floor with great energy. Amar managed to get to the bar, get his drinks, and escape without being trampled upon.

"Thanks, Am. So what's happening in the other room?" Jane asked as he handed her the drink and sat down.

"A minor battle. Bill Haley has been unleashed and the young men and women are in full cry. It is a miracle I escaped unscathed."

"And why don't you like rock 'n' roll, my very proper friend?"

"Because it goes against the very essence of dancing. Dancing was devised to allow a sex-starved teenager to hold a girl close, with society's sanction. To enjoy a few moments of closeness and to enjoy the feel of a girl's body against his, without being put in jail. And what have we here? A manic kind of exercise done by frantic couples at more than arm's length from one another. They don't even look at each other—they're so involved in the gyrations of their own body. They don't really need to have a partner," he ended disgustedly.

"You're behind the times, Am. Wake up and look around you in the parks and streets. What you see will tell you that there are not many sex-starved youngsters in view. So the premise has changed. You don't need dancing to provide you an excuse to hold a girl close any more."

"Oh—you don't?" Amar asked innocently. But she saw the mischief in his eyes and said, "And before you leap on me, I'm going to go and rock 'n' roll. Sure you don't want to go on the floor?"

"No thanks, Jane." Amar said, appearing disconsolate, "I'll try and find somebody else to hold close."

She giggled and went off to find a partner.

❖

An hour and a beer or two later, Amar finally got a chance to go and sit next to Angela in the cosily lit anteroom, which was empty at the moment.

"Ah, what a relief to be able to take the weight off my feet. Not been dancing, Angela?"

"Nope. Didn't feel like." She seemed a bit strained and distant.

Amar looked at her and then looked helplessly into space, "Here I come, after ages of wandering and wondering when I may be able to find a place next to her … after being buffeted by the restless sea of humanity in the next room … with my hopes high of a warm, welcoming smile from her … of a little compassion, a spark of humanity—and what do I get? Miss Monosyllable. 'Nope. Didn't feel like it'—wait … that was more than one syllable. So there may be hope! I misread the signs! So reassure me, kind lady—there is really some hope?"

Her lips fought against the beginning of a smile. Finally, she gave in to a smile and said with a sigh, "How much beer have you drunk, Am?"

"Bucketfuls, oceanfuls—they've had to send out for beer wagons for replenishment." He paused. "Has the malady passed, milady? Did I notice a smile?"

She slapped him on his hands "You're incorrigible. Of course I'm smiling. I'm smiling at your pretending to be drunk—not a very good pretence, I have to say."

"Ah, always a sting in the tail. Yes, ma'am, I was pretending. And it wasn't a good act because I'm only half-drunk. Wait until you see me fully loaded." Then he sighed, "This kind of pretend-talk can be tiring. No, Angela, I'm not even half-drunk, regrettably. But I was concerned to see you looking a little morose, and thought that I would try and change your mood. Maybe a glass of wine would help complete the process? Your glass is empty."

She hesitated. "All right, just one more. Although I don't see why I should be worried, since I've been holding on to this glass for what seems hours."

"We shall set that right immediately. But—but—only on one condition." He looked grave, and Angela's expression became serious.

"What?" she asked a little hesitantly.

"That you will protect this chair next to you with your life. And not allow the assorted Teds and Freds to come and usurp my position."

Angela laughed, "Oh, you mean, Ned? Don't worry, he's quite harmless."

Amar rolled his eyes and hissed, "Them's the most dangerous, milady!"

"Oh, Am, you are a clown," she laughed and held his hand briefly. "Now away with you and get me my goblet of wine," she said sternly.

Amar came back with her white wine and a replenished beer mug. "Cheers," Amar said.

"A la votre" she replied, raising her glass.

"Beg your pardon?" A mystified Amar asked.

"That's what the French say. My mother's French."

"Oh! Yes—er—what do I say?" said Amar raising his glass.

"You respond by saying 'A la Votre' too."

"Er—*A la Votre*. I didn't know you were half-French."

"There's a lot you don't know about me, Am."

"Well, how do I find out, if every time I sit next to you somebody comes and takes the chair when I vacate it for a second?" Amar asked in an aggrieved voice.

Angela smiled, but said nothing. The silence grew. Finally Amar broke it, and said in a quiet voice, "There's a lot I would like to find out about you, Angela. But my problem is that I'm a private person and don't find it easy either to open myself up to someone or intrude into someone else's space even though I would like to. I'm crippled by my inhibitions." He looked down into his beer mug and seemed engrossed in the sight of the bubbles rising to the surface.

"I thought that was just a British aberration. You never gave me the impression of being shy or reserved. You mask yourself well."

"Yes, I follow the guiding mantra of modern civilisation—don't show what you feel, don't tell others how you feel, strip your public self of all emotions until you appear an emotional eunuch. That is what is acceptable. And that is what we are becoming slowly—emotional eunuchs."

"You're being a little unfair, Am. We do declare ourselves to those we are very close to. How do love affairs progress otherwise? One does lay one's emotions bare to somebody one loves."

"Oh yes ... love." He gazed moodily at his beer mug. "But even here, Angela, do we really lay ourselves bare or do we build a persona which we believe the other would approve of? How much do we really know of the person we believe we love? We know only what he or she has exposed—and this exposure is usually guided by canny common sense. You think I'm being cynical, don't you? Maybe you're right."

He paused. Angela remained silent. Amar felt uncomfortable. This was not the way he had wanted the conversation to pan out.

He shook his head. "Forget what I said. I don't know why I should be talking such abstractions to an attractive woman at a party."

Angela recrossed her lovely legs and said archly, "And what should you be saying to a woman at a party?"

"Not to any woman—but to a very special woman. I should be saying, that she has beautiful legs, lovely laughing eyes and a bewitching face. And that she is quite irresistible. Except that, stupid bumbling oafs like me, don't know how to proceed from there."

Angela blushed, but asked in a low voice, "And what would a non-bumbler have done?"

"He would have known the magic language, he would have known the harmony which enchants, he would have cast a sorcerer's spell ..."

"Maybe all that is not necessary," she said softly.

Just then Amar saw, out of the corner of his eye, the whole group coming back from the dance floor. He cursed fiercely under his breath. Angela frowned, "What's the matter?" she asked.

"The matter, my lovely Angela, is that the rabble are returning. Just my damned luck," he said angrily. She did not look pleased either.

"What are you two plotting so seriously?" Jane, red-faced from her efforts on the dance floor, asked as she settled down on a chair.

"A number of things, actually. But top of the list was how to get Jane a date with our eye-patch lecturer," Amar replied. This endearing young lecturer in Economics, who sported an eye patch, was a great hit with the women."

Among the "ooo's" and "aah's" from the other women in the group, Jane replied, "Jane doesn't need any help with dates, thank *yeow*. What she does need is a drink. And, since Am has been so solicitous about my welfare, maybe he'll get me one. Will you, Am, please?"

Amar grunted and got up. "What one has to do to maintain peace in the Fencing Club. Come to think of it, this is actually part of the president's job remit—fetching drinks for obstreperous women members. Oy Rod, what about doing your duty for Queen and Country?"

Rod was contentedly leaning back with a full glass of wine in his hands. "Jane is too charming to be the Queen. But I'll do the next round, I promise!"

"The East India Company again," Amar grumbled. "The natives do all the work while the bosses cavort with the ladies. Ah well, duty calls ..." and Amar shambled off in a tired walk.

He was gone for a long period. So when he returned, he had to face a barrage of innuendos, "Hey, Am, did you find that delectable thing with her shoulder straps slipping off—lucky, sod," "Not only did he find her he also found a room with a bed." "But it takes only seven minutes, Am, you were gone for fifteen." "With all the beer in him, it would take longer."

Amar smiled beatifically. "Quiet, children, quiet. Do you want to hear a tale?"

"We don't want to hear a tail, we wanna see one."

"Then go to the US of A, my friend. No, mine is a tale of Europe. But if you lot are not interested, I shall find myself a more receptive audience," Amar said loftily.

"Tell me a story—tell me a story …" somebody started singing.

"All right, in view of the overwhelming response," Amar ignoring the catcalls, said, "Let me tell you why it took me so long."

"And don't spare the detail, mate."

"Shush. I have a much more interesting story to tell than you think. Can I have some quiet, ladies and gentlemen? Thank you. Well, it started off with one woman's unfair demands on me."

"What happened finally, Am—was she satisfied?"

"We'll know in a little while, after she's tasted her drink. Well, to meet her demands I had to trudge through dangerous territory to get to the next room. There were bodies all over. I finally managed to enter the next room, only to be met with semi-darkness. A strange kind of languorous music was playing. And there were more bodies. These were not recumbent, but upright, or as upright as you can be when you are clutching another. I noticed one such unupright couple because they were directly in my path to the bar. The man I recognised as being one of our friends from across the channel. The woman, was probably from the nursing college. But that was of little consequence. As I tried to make my way past them I noticed—any guesses?" Amar paused and took a swig of beer.

"Get on with it, Am." "The suspense is killing us."

"I saw our friend from across the channel unbuttoning the woman's blouse. He succeeded and then proceeded to the bra. I was hypnotised. The mesmerising music continued. And then I noticed one of our burly LSE Rugby knights approaching the couple, anger writ large on his face. The expression said, 'Lay off the fair English rose, you dirty swine from across the channel.' He walked up to them, and I thought this is the end of my quest—the police will be here in a minute—poor Jane will be drinkless. And then … ?" He paused and took another sip of beer.

Before there was a riot, he continued. "And then—I heard the impact of flesh on flesh—a blow." He deliberately paused. "The Rugby knight staggered back. The woman dusted her hands after the blow and proceeded to help her partner take her bra off. The Rugby knight retreated into the night."

There was a stunned silence, and then laughter and cheers. "More, more tell us more." "What colour was her bra?" "Did you get her name and address?"

"Silence, you men. We have ladies present," Am said sternly.

❖

The evening unfolded like a roll of luminescent ribbon, sometimes rapidly, sometimes in slow motion, sometimes brightly, at other times darkly. But soon it became apparent that the end of the roll was near. The girls started looking at their watches, and muttering about the last train. The men weighed the possibility of one last drink against the near certainty that they would be puking on the pavement if they drank any more. Amar, semi-inebriated, was feeling depressed that the evening was ending. He wished that they could continue somewhere else. Reality, however, reared its cold head. If he missed his last train, he would have to take a taxi home. Since he did not have the money for that, the only option would be to walk home—a traverse of many miles across London. This sobering thought got him up from his chair.

He muttered a good night to Angela, got his coat and wandered out to the Russell Street Tube station. He felt the numbness of an evening's drinking. Everything seemed to move slower than normal. Sounds seemed to come from a distance. His steps became more measured, to allay any suspicion of inebriation.

Slumping onto the seat in the train was a relief, and Amar suddenly realised how tired he was. He willed himself to stay awake, since sleep was creeping in very stealthily. He changed trains at Green Park and subsided onto his seat. He woke just before Willesden Green. The walk home from the Tube station seemed a Herculean task. But he made it.

Club President

The term drew to its close with the approach of July. The Fencing Club activities tapered off with the year-end examinations getting closer. There was one last class on a Friday evening, and Amar was quite surprised to see a full house. Rod was beaming at the attendance. "Hey, Rod, how come we have so many attending at the end of term?" Amar asked.

Rod stared at him. "Have you forgotten? You're going to be appointed the new president, dear boy."

When everyone had assembled, Rod handed over to Amar with a fulsome speech. As the applause subsided Amar said a few words of thanks.

Next, the secretary was announced. There was muted clapping. Greg, a cold-looking individual, who appeared older than the others, did not inspire much affection. Amar himself did not care for him, but could not deny his efficient and methodical approach.

After showering and changing, they all strolled down to the Three Tuns for the customary farewell drink.

A toast was drunk to the departing *el Presidente*, led by the ginger-haired Gary, who was usually the life of any party.

Following that, Gary asked, "Hey, Rod, what's the provenance of this glass of water before me?" Rod was well known for his love of the arcane traditions of wine drinking and would take great pleasure in unloading, onto an unsuspecting listener, the unasked for provenance of any drink he was having. Many had suffered, and Gary was now paying back.

However, Rod was equal to the occasion. "That may be a little difficult, Gary, since, as you know, all London water is recycled.

But there is a chance you might be drinking your own pee." Gary, to his credit, joined in the laughter.

Greg decided to join the fun, partly, Amar suspected, because he felt that Gary was hogging the limelight. "Am, are we going to have an Indian orientation to our activities? What about an Indian dinner party where we all contribute?" This was weak, but Greg was not known for his wit.

An unjustifiably irritated Amar, pondered for a moment. "Sure, Greg, sure. We have a particular dish we can cook with your contribution. It's called *gurda kapura* and is a rich and tasty curry made with balls—yes, literally balls."

There was silence for a minute and then sniggers, which exploded into laughter and drowned Greg's reply.

Later, Angela who was sitting next to Amar whispered to him, "You were rather cruel to Greg, Am. He was only trying to follow Gary and be funny." And I know he's interested in you, and that's one of the reasons I reacted, Amar said to himself.

"I know, Angela, I know. He's someone I'll have to work side by side with for a whole year, so I need to keep him on my side. I reacted because I don't like patronising national references. What the hell did he mean by an 'Indian orientation'? Why bring in nationhood into a light-hearted conversation?" Amar whispered back fiercely.

"I still think you overreacted, Am," she whispered back. And I think you probably enjoy his attention, Amar thought angrily.

"OK—I probably did. Maybe I should make amends by telling him that his vital organs are safe, since its only sheep's testicles we use in this dish."

Angela was not amused. She turned away to start a conversation with her neighbour.

Later, when everybody had left and only Rod, Jane and Angela remained around the table, Amar decided to make amends.

"Look folks, I have an apology to make. I think I was a little over the top with my remark to Greg. Angela has rightly ticked me off, and since I did not feel up to making an apology to Greg and the others around, I thought I would at least apologise to those few whose opinions I value. So—sorry if I said something which might have been offensive."

"No need for any apology, old sport. If Greg can't take a joke, he shouldn't crack any himself," Rod said.

Jane looked a bit bemused, "Am, you're confusing me. If you were offensive to Greg, then the apology should be directed to him, not to us." It's directed at Angela, woman, not you, Amar said to himself. "Having said that, let me also add that I think he deserved the reply he got from you. There was absolutely no call for him to have talked about an Indian orientation being introduced, now that you were president. For Christ's sake—would he have talked about a North Country orientation if somebody from the north was made president? No. I think he was being a bit patronising. So, don't lose any sleep over it. He's a bit reptilian anyway—can't say I like him."

Angela reacted, "Jane ... ! You can't pillory someone because of his looks!" Amar hoped that this was just her sense of fair play.

"Sorry—I got carried away," Jane said, not very apologetically.

It seemed to appease Angela. "Jane's right though, Am, don't lose any sleep over it. I brought it up with you only because what you said seemed a little out of character with you."

"It probably was" Amar said gloomily.

Helga

Summer had arrived and the city rejoiced in an explosion of flowers of brilliant hues. The spring crocuses had given way to daffodils, tulips, jonquils and bluebells. Daisies carpeted the green swards in the parks. The sky was a lazy deep blue. Amar marvelled at the miracle of the English summer and the change it brought to this grey city. A season of joy.

On this summer weekend, Amar had dragged a folding chair into the garden, by the apple tree, and sat soaking in the sun with an unread newspaper on his lap.

Sometime earlier, Amar had received a letter from Sudipto. It was a tentative one. Obviously, Sudipto was not sure how it would be received.

> I am writing this in spite of your not having replied to my earlier letters. I hope by now some of your anger has dissipated. It would be sad if our friendship foundered on a silly incident, though I agree it is difficult to forgive or forget such an unfeeling act on my part. But what can I do now but to ask for your forgiveness? If I could live my life again I would make sure that this incident never happened.
>
> The purpose of this letter is to apologise once again as I have done in my earlier ones. And to tell you that Helga—you remember her?—will be coming to London for a holiday in July. She doesn't know anyone there. Do you think you could spend a little time with her? I will fully understand if you can't. But please let me know, so I can give her your address.

Amar had been taken aback. During Amar's second year in college in Delhi, Sudipto had acquired a German penfriend called Helga. Photographs had been exchanged. Amar was allowed to see them and also hear the story which went with them. The pictures showed Helga posing, wearing very short shorts which exposed her attractive legs. However, the story was sad. During a cycling holiday in Germany she had got friendly with a man in the group. He had, apparently, forced himself on her and raped her. She got pregnant and refused to have an abortion. Her well-off father disowned her, and she had to manage on her own. She had the child and found a job to sustain herself and the child. That is when Sudipto and she had become penfriends. Sudipto, ever the romantic, wrote to her saying he was ready to marry her. She had said neither "yay nor nay" but their correspondence had got more intimate after that. Sudipto had told her he would come to Germany to marry her after he finished his Master's course in Delhi. And that is where it rested.

That is why the letter took Amar by surprise. Why would Sudipto thrust his wife-to-be on him? Possibly, this was Sudipto's way of trying to renew their friendship—by saying I trust you enough to ask you to take care of her. Whatever the reason, Amar found it difficult to refuse. So somewhat grudgingly, he had written back that he would be happy to meet her and show her a little bit of London. In his own mind he was clear, he would do no more than the minimum that politeness demanded. He did not owe Sudipto anything.

A few weeks later he had received a letter from her. It was a brief one, thanking him and asking for his phone number so that she could contact him on her arrival in London. She also gave her arrival date.

The term had ended. Amar had forgotten her arrival date, until one evening his mother told him that someone called Helga had called during the day. Amar had called her back next morning, a little nervous but determined to be as matter-of-fact as possible. An English voice answered and he asked for Helga. She came on, "Hello, is that A-mar?"

"Yes, Helga. Sorry, I wasn't in—got back from college a little late."

"Oh, that is all right. It is kind of you to take the trouble." Her German accent was very obvious.

"No, no, it's no trouble at all. Sudipto and I were very close at college in Delhi, and I am only too happy to be able to help. So when can we meet? Say, tomorrow at around five in the evening? I would have finished at the library by then. I tell you what would be best. Can you take the Underground to reach Holborn Tube station at five? I'll be waiting for you at the exit—on the main road."

"Yes, that will be very fine. I will travel by the Underground—you call it the Tube, no? Now you will spell the name of the station, please? My English, not so good."

So he spelt it out and assured her that her English was fine. "So till tomorrow, then, Helga".

"I look forward to that, and thank you for calling."

"Oh, I forgot—how do I recognise you?"

"Is it not silly of me? I forgot too. I will wear a yellow summer dress and carry a brown bag. And I? How do I know you?"

"Now let me think. I will wear a white shirt and a sports jacket."

"Moment, please. Sorry—I do not understand *spots* jacket."

"No, don't worry. I will wear a long college scarf around my neck. The colours of the scarf are purple, yellow and black. In any case, I have seen your picture and should be able to recognise you."

"Thank you—till tomorrow, then."

❖

The next day was pleasant, with a gentle cool breeze blowing as he strolled down Kingsway. He realised that the scarf as a distinguishing mark had not been such a brilliant idea. This area was full of students with LSE scarves.

As he approached the Holborn station exit, he saw a young woman wearing a lemon-coloured dress already waiting by the newspaper stand. She had her back to him and he had to go past and turn around to have a look at her. He pretended to be reading one of the posters outside the station, while he stole a glance. She was slim but not tall, about his height. She had a pleasant face, not film-star beautiful, but a face with character and lively eyes. A younger, more animated and leaner version of Mona Lisa, he thought, fancifully. He tried to compare her face with the photograph he had seen. Yes, it seemed to tally. He went up to her and said, "Excuse, me."

She turned around and smiled, "A-mar?"

He smiled back, "That's me. It's good to meet you Helga, Sudi has told me so much about you."

She grinned mischievously, "Do not believe everything you hear."

"No, only the naughty bits," Amar replied, grinning back.

"We must compare sometime," she said mischievously.

"I was wondering what you would like to do," Amar asked, "Maybe visit the National Gallery, and also see Trafalgar Square?"

"That sounds very good, but—may we have some coffee first? I am expiring—no—dying—for some good coffee."

"Sure—you don't mind walking down a little way, do you? There are some reasonable places near the Gallery."

"No, I do not mind. In fact, I like to walk. It is such a nice day."

They crossed the street and went up Kingsway. "So were you looking for the purple, yellow and black scarf?"

"Yes, and I was thinking what kind of identification has A-mar given me—because the road was full of men wearing the same scarf! I could have gone off with a dozen A-mars."

"So, you see, how I have saved you from being kidnapped by turning up on time."

"No," she furrowed her brow as if considering, "I would not have minded being kidnapped by some of them." Then seeing his expression she burst out laughing, "I was just joking! I was waiting for only the right A-mar to come—no one else would do." And she touched his arm. They walked on chatting companionably.

They found a table at an Italian cafe and Amar fetched two steaming cups of coffee. She tasted hers and sighed, "What happiness to get some good coffee. At the place I am staying, it tastes like dirty water." They sipped their coffee in a comfortable silence.

She broke the silence, "Can I say something? I do not know you at all, so you must not mind—you will not, I hope?"

Amar shook his head, wondering what bombshell was going to land on him. She continued, "You are not like what I had expected."

Putting on a brave face, he said, "Go on, I can take whatever terrible things you want to say."

She frowned and bent forward, catching his hand, "No, no, no—it is not like that. I just had a different picture from what you are. I am not criticising—the opposite. I thought you would be—how to say—studied, no, studious, serious, talking about Indian philosophy, looking down on me for not having studied in college like you. I was lot nervous about meeting you. But now I see—you are … fun, and that you also can laugh."

"Thank God," said a relieved Amar, "I thought you would make me stand in the corner for not having said 'good afternoon' to you, for not having brushed my hair and for not having had my shoes polished." They both laughed. Realising that she still had her hand on his she blushed and quickly withdrew it.

They went to the National Gallery and Amar took her to his favourite paintings. Later, they sat on the steps and chatted while the London traffic rumbled by below them. And still later they went for another cup of coffee. Before they knew it, it was time for her to get back because dinner was at a fixed time at her boarding house. They agreed to meet the next afternoon after Amar finished in the library.

Amar went home feeling relaxed and at peace with the world. He had enjoyed the evening, and felt good about doing the right thing by Sudipto's friend. After tomorrow's meeting he would find some excuse to avoid meeting her till it was time for her to go. He would have done the minimum that was necessary.

The Tate Gallery

The next day dawned cloudy and the sky was overcast as Amar walked to the Tube station in the morning. However, it did not dampen his spirits. He had to admit that he was looking forward to meeting Helga in the afternoon.

He had lunch a little earlier than normal and missed Pramod who was just queuing up as he left. He waved out and said, "Have to attend to some work—see you tomorrow."

Helga was there looking fresh in a white printed dress with a belt emphasising her slim waist. She welcomed him with a warm smile. "Hello, A-mar. I hope you will not get into trouble coming away from college like this."

Amar's expression became grim. "I didn't want to worry you. But since you've asked, I'll tell you. As punishment I will be made to run up and down the Thames Embankment balancing my text books on my head and saying over and over again in Latin 'I must not miss my classes to meet Helga.' If I drop a book, then I will have to immediately eat a plateful of boiled cabbage and resume running."

"Oh, that is very severe punishment, A-mar. English boiled cabbage won them the war—the German army was terrified of it."

They walked down Kingsway to Aldwych and then down Lancaster Place to the Embankment. The day had cleared and patches of blue sky were now visible. As they reached the Embankment he stopped. "Before I show you my punishment course, I want to show you something else."

He took a deep breath and declaimed, "There in front of you is one of the most romantic bridges in history—Waterloo Bridge. Romantic because of the beautiful paintings of the bridge done by

Claude Monet, romantic because it's wonderful to walk down it at night with the lights along the river sparkling in the dark—it helps if you are holding someone's hands. And even more romantic because of the famous film with this title, starring Vivien Leigh, I think. But I've not walked down Waterloo Bridge or seen the film, so I can't speak first hand."

"Not walk down Waterloo Bridge holding a lovely woman's hand? How could you not do it?"

Amar looked bereft. "Well, every girl I started walking down the bridge with, let go of my hand after a few yards, and grabbed someone else's hand. So what could I do?"

"Grab another girl's hand! Oh, A-mar, these are things you should have learnt in kindergarten," Helga said in exasperation.

"You mean like this?" He asked, clutching her hand, and surprising himself.

"Taking advantage of a poor German girl visiting London? Shame on you," she said severely, yet not letting go of his hand.

They walked slowly down the Embankment watching the boats drifting down the river. A cool breeze blew, and the cloud and blue sky battled for space in the heavens. On earth, Amar walked awkwardly holding Helga's hand, wondering what had made him clutch it in the first place. This was not right. This was not correct. She was Sudipto's girl—how could he forget that. He now racked his brains for an exit route. The tension must have been transmitted to his hand, for Helga gently withdrew hers in the pretext of looking for something in her bag. Amar almost sighed with relief.

She found what she was looking for and offered him a peppermint. Amar who disliked peppermints, accepted one, such was his state of mind.

They walked on silently with the brown river flowing by like a strip of oil, while a battle raged in Amar's mind. What had he been thinking he was doing when he grabbed Helga's hand?

The struggle must have shown on Amar's face. Helga stopped suddenly and pointed to the river and said, "Look, look, was that a fish jumping?"

"The river is too polluted to have fish," Amar replied in a dead voice.

"And the world is coming to an end," Helga said in a deep voice trying to copy Amar's sepulchral tone.

Amar could not hold back a smile. "And why is the world coming to an end?"

"Because A-mar thinks this is the end of the world," she continued in her imitation voice.

"All right, all right," Amar smiled. "You're too observant for comfort. So now, what would you have wanted me to say in reply to your imaginary fish sighting?"

"So many things. Let your mind free and say—that was not a fish but a mermaid raising her head to greet the sun. Or, an angel raising her face to look at the beautiful sky. Or, a goblin pointing to the pot of gold at the end of the rainbow."

"But there is no rainbow."

"A-mar, A-mar … what I am to do with you?" she cried. Then in a calmer voice, she said, "Obviously, there is something dark and not nice on your mind. Throw it out, and begin again to appreciate this lovely day. See the white clouds chasing each other—see the blue sky smiling at the way the clouds play—see the lazy bird wheeling in the sky—see all this A-mar—not what you have been seeing."

"Just like that—so simple? Grow up, Helga," Amar said more sharply than he intended to.

Helga said nothing, but the angry expression on her face was eloquent enough.

To placate her, and with a resigned look, Amar closed his eyes. He actually made the effort to throw out the battling voices in his mind. But they continued, if in lower register. He tried to think of something which was pleasurable. A green meadow sloping down to a lake—blossoming trees dotting the meadow—a tender breeze blowing the fragrance of the blossoms towards him—the sun sparkling on the gentle waves in the lake … He let himself enjoy this for a while. But before long, extraneous thoughts invaded, and he slowly opened his eyes again. However, the respite seemed to have done something for him.

He found Helga looking at him with a quizzical look on her face. He cupped his hands above his eyes and stared at the sky. He kept staring for a long time and Helga's expression grew more puzzled. Finally he exclaimed, "Look, look, I see it—I see it—there is a fairy flying in the sky … and … and … oh my God …"

Helga looked alarmed and asked, "What … ?"

"She's not wearing any clothes," and he quickly clapped his hands over his eyes.

Helga angrily said, "You are very funny, A-mar. Ha-ha-ha. Forget what I said." She flounced off. Amar caught up with her, and saw to his relief the beginning of a smile on her face. He walked beside her without saying anything.

Then he looked at his watch. "You have another minute to be glum—then it's my turn. Fair's fair," he said petulantly.

This time she laughed. "Do not make me laugh. I am supposed be in bad mood."

After walking for a while she asked, "You have not told me where we are going."

"In the West every action must have a goal, every step must have an end," Amar said with a resigned sigh. "A myth. A myth which we are trying to get the West to recognise. Our philosophy says—immerse yourself in the action, the results will follow. However … our philosophy also says defer to the wishes of your guest. So, where are we headed? To the bastion of democracy, the fountainhead of civil liberty—the Parliament. Ah—there it is."

"We walk all this way to see the Parliament? I am not interested in being American tourist, please—all the sights of London in thirty minutes," she said crossly.

Amar grinned. "But who said I brought you here to see the Parliament?"

"Then—what are we doing here?"

"Walking. Watching the white clouds chasing each other—seeing the blue sky smiling at the way the clouds play—watching the lazy bird wheeling in the sky." Amar was enjoying himself. But he realised that she was coming to the end of her patience. "And soon, if you are patient—are German women always so impatient?—Soon, if you are patient, then what we are really going to see will reveal itself."

Helga did not appear to be amused. "I do not enjoy being treated as a child, A-mar," she said crossly.

"Well, if you must know, we are going to the Tate Gallery which you had expressed an interest in yesterday. I just wanted it to be a surprise for you."

They walked silently for some time, their feet clip-clopping on the pavement. Then imperceptibly the distance between them seemed to diminish and she caught hold of his arm. They walked like this for some more time, and he could feel his arm brushing her breast. He was confused by her change of moods and did not know what to say. She broke the silence.

"What do I say when you have been so thoughtful and I—so not understanding?"

"Don't say anything. Just look to your right. *Voila*—the Tate Gallery!"

The Tate, while not as imposing as the National Gallery, still was an impressive structure. As they entered, Amar again noticed the high ceilings and the grand scale of the gallery. This never ceased to impress him.

He did not try to influence her in respect of the rooms to visit. She wandered as she wanted, and he followed. Then they came to the Impressionists and Amar could not help saying, "This is my favourite room." He wandered off to allow her to enjoy the paintings in her own space. He had realised, some time ago, that viewing a work of art was a very personal affair. It was an individual interaction with the artist. There was no room for anyone else.

Eventually she sat down on one of the seats at the centre of the room. He sat down beside her, but did not say anything for a while. Then she turned and smiled at him and just said, "Thank you."

"Tired?" he asked gently. "I find that more than an hour at a gallery exhausts me. And we have been here for an hour and a half or more."

She nodded. "Yes, I am tired—but nicely so."

"Then let's go and get some fresh air and revive ourselves."

They walked down the steps and Amar felt the peculiar tiredness and restlessness he always experienced after being closeted with works of art. He did not particularly want to make conversation, and she seemed quite content to walk in silence. He decided that they had earned a drink, and more importantly, that he had adequate money for a visit to a pub. He guided her steps towards a nearby one which he recalled had a couple of benches on the pavement for those who wished to brave the London weather.

A cool breeze still blew off the river and there was still some blue visible in the sky. They sank down on a bench and Helga turned to him. "A-mar, this will be expensive. Why not instead go for coffee?"

Amar smiled, "Because it is not every day that I get a visit from you. And I wanted to introduce you to English beer."

Helga looked aghast. "*English* beer?" Then said with resignation, "Well, since we have lost the war, I cannot say no. But if I need to be rescued, you will finish the beer for me please."

Amar went in and got two half-pints of London Pride. She looked at her glass apprehensively. "It looks quite dark, A-mar."

"As dark as the Thames on a moonless night—and as full of mystery. Cheers, Helga!"

"Cheers, A-mar," she said and took a tentative sip.

Amar waited a little tensely for her reaction. She grimaced and shook her head, and his heart sank. "It tastes like the Thames." Then she grinned mischievously and had another sip, "But it does not taste so bad."

A relieved Amar took his first sip.

They sat back companionably on the bench, letting the tension of the day slowly recede as the river breeze caressed them. For the first time Amar realised that he had been tightly wound up. Was it being with Helga? Or was it the Sudipto baggage that he carried? Or was it both?

Helga looked reflective, and Amar wondered if he should try and cheer her up. But he realised that he had been putting on this flippant front continuously with her, and it was quite exhausting.

After a while Helga turned to him. "A-mar—I wanted to thank you for being so sensitive at the Gallery. You kept silent and let me enjoy what I wanted. Usually, when you go with someone to a gallery you have to keep up a stream of words—'Oh, my dear, is not that arrangement divine—like God's unwashed lingerie!', 'Oh, what masterly treatment of a dead fish's intestines!'—I am so happy you spared me all that. But then, you are different."

Amar was quiet for a while. Then in a soft voice he said, "Thank you for the nice things you have been saying, Helga. I'm not used to it."

He was silent for a while. "At the same time, I feel nervous—I wonder if you can understand that? I go back to my childhood days—when I used to think fearfully, is it right for me to enjoy things—will some punishment be visited on me? When I take pleasure from the nice things you have said about me—these fears are faintly revived at some deeper level. Odd, isn't it?" Amar ended gloomily.

Amar had been surprised at his confession—spontaneous and unpremeditated as it was. It had slipped out, but it seemed a natural piece of the mosaic of their developing friendship. It felt as if it belonged.

Helga broke the silence. "Not so strange as you think, A-mar. I have felt like that too. We are still children in many ways. Do you feel a lot of guilt, A-mar?"

"Yes—sometimes at the most unexpected moments. While enjoying a piece of chocolate, for example. Or, receiving a gift. The common thread is my enjoying myself—feeling good about something I'm experiencing. And then—bang. Guilt. As if I'm partaking of something I have no right to, enjoying something which is not my due, biting into the proverbial forbidden fruit."

"How you deal with it?"

"Not too well. I push it back to some corner of my mind and shut the door. But the guilt keeps peeping out." He paused. "Maybe I'm exaggerating a little—it's not as bad as it sounds. But as a phenomenon it intrigues me." He realised that he had, unwittingly changed the tenor of the conversation. He had put back the mask he had temporarily discarded. He felt a sense of loss.

Helga, too, sensed this change. "What happened, A-mar? You were speaking from your heart—and suddenly you changed to cocktail-party conversation? 'Phenomenon intrigues me'—what does that mean? Sorry, maybe my English is not good enough. I do not understand."

Amar was embarrassed and irritated. He did not relish being caught out. He was about to reply sharply, but then stopped. She was right. She had reflected exactly what he was feeling. "You're right. I don't know what made me change gears." He paused. "No, the fact is—I don't reveal myself like this to anyone, and suddenly I felt I was exposing myself too much."

"Oh, A-mar! I like honesty. For me, listening to you was like crossing a bridge together to find out what lay on the other side. I am not interested in 'phenomenon'. I am interested in listening to what your heart says. And your heart was talking to me—but suddenly you stopped. And I did not like that."

"You believe in saying what you feel, don't you? It's not something I'm used to, but I don't dislike it."

Helga smiled. "A-mar, A-mar—how English you sound! 'I don't dislike it.' Why not simply 'I like it'?"

Amar was again taken aback. She was right.

The evening seemed to have inexplicably run down. The conversation continued, but it was on a different plane. Both seemed to realise it, and both seemed to be saddened.

Ultimately they parted, promising to meet the next day.

❖

That night, as he lay in bed, his thoughts returned to the afternoon. He guiltily recognised how much he was enjoying Helga's company. He was forgetting that this was his friend's territory he was trespassing on. The voices would not cease.

After struggling with the conflicting voices for a long time, he tiredly decided that this conflict was taking too much out of him. He resolved that he would restore his relationship with Helga to a more casual and matter-of-fact level. No more hand holding. No more baring of the soul.

He slept the sleep of the virtuous after that.

Guilt

Another sparkling summer day greeted them when they met at the Marble Arch Tube station. Helga was in a light blue dress and greeted him cheerfully, "Hello A-mar, did you have a good day at the library?"

Amar responded to the hello and added, "Yes, thanks. What about you, did you have a good dinner and sleep?"

She made a face, "The dinner was not good. The lady believes in overboiling and overcooking everything. So—I ate a little to be polite, but I was still hungry. I went back to my room and finished a whole slab of chocolate." She patted her stomach, "You can see the effect, no?"

Amar was forced, in spite of his earlier resolution, to look at her midriff which looked pretty trim, and weakly shook his head, "No, no, you look fine."

They walked across to the Speakers Corner at Hyde Park and then wandered on to the park. The wide expanse of green was impressive and Helga shaded her eye and looked, "It is very big. You people are lucky to have such a big park in the centre of the city." Amar did not say anything and they walked for a while. Seeing a bench, Helga sat down. Amar followed suit.

Helga looked pensive. "A-mar, is something wrong? You seem so occupied—is that the right word no, no—preoccupied."

Amar said, "No, no, nothing wrong. Where would you like to go after this?"

Helga looked at him and did not say anything. She turned her head and stared out over the park. Amar was feeling wretched. He so much wanted to tell her what was bothering him, but doing so would breach the decision he had made last night. He just wanted to get this afternoon finished and done with, so that he could go back to his old life.

"Helga, why don't we take a walk down Oxford Street—it's one of the sights of London."

Still staring out over the park, she said coldly, "No, I do not want to do any shopping—oh, I forgot I must say, thank you. You British have to have one thank you in every sentence, do you not? "

"I'm not British—and in any case you don't have to be so critical of the British—the war is over."

She glared at him and said angrily, "You do not have any right to talk to me about the war. You did not go through what I and a lot of Germans went through. So let's drop the war, OK?"

Everything seemed to be going wrong for Amar. He flared up. "And what would you know of what we in India faced during the war? Your war lasted six years, ours went on for over a hundred years, from the time the English landed in India to the time we finally got independence. If you want to know about hardship, come to India."

She finally said more reasonably, "Then we are both on the same side, A-mar." She paused, and looked at him, "Why are we fighting? Do you really want to?"

Amar glumly shook his head, "No … no." Then, added in a low voice, "I'm just feeling awful."

Softly she asked, "Why, A-mar—why? Yesterday you were charming, laughing. Today you are opposite. What has happened?"

Amar could not hold back any more, "I don't know how I can explain it to you."

Helga moved a little closer and said gently, "Please, A-mar, please. I will listen to whatever you have to say. And if at the end you do not want me to say anything, then I will not."

"Oh, it's too difficult. Too difficult. I don't even know where to start." He paused and then, unable to hold it in any more, went on, "Sudi had told me a long time ago, how he felt about you—and that he wanted to go to Germany to be with you. When he wrote and asked me to look after you in London, I hesitantly agreed. I had decided to just have a polite meeting with you and maybe see you once more before you left—so that I could feel I have discharged my responsibility. But it's all turned out to be very different. Being with you, I feel as if I have known you for a long time—I feel at ease with you—I can chat and laugh and tease you. I agreed to meet you again—and then again. But going back yesterday, I realised that I was betraying Sudi. You are his, and here I seem to be doing the same thing that he did to me." He stopped.

"What was that, A-mar?"

"Oh, that's a sordid story. Let's just forget it." Amar sat forward looking into the distance. It was all going awry. He felt a gentle hand on his.

"A-mar, don't stop now—tell me the rest. Please?" And Amar quietly told her about Preeti without more prompting. About his breaking off once he was in England, and how he learnt about what had happened in the taxi between Sudipto and Preeti on the way back from the airport. "And now, I am doing something similar to what he did," he said.

In an urgent voice she said, "A-mar, listen to me please. First of all, nobody owns me, neither Sudipto nor anyone else. Just because Sudipto likes me does not make me his. No human being can be owned. And neither was Preeti owned by you—however much you two liked each other. What happened between her and Sudipto in the taxi was something which had to happen. So do not blame. And why blame yourself for being friendly to me? If I do not want it I can say so. And what have the two of us done, in God's name? Nothing, but enjoy each other's company. How is that wrong?"

Amar sat with his head down and let what she had said sink in. He recognised, uncomfortably, that his unloading had not been entirely unselfish.

"I don't know, Helga, I just don't know. Things are just happening without my being able to control them."

"Then let them just happen. Let us just take things as they come."

❖

They walked down Oxford Street in a companionable silence. Something seemed to have changed in their relationship. A barrier lifted? He did not feel the need to be witty or clever in his conversation, nor did he feel uncomfortable with silence.

She seemed quite content to dodge the crowds, moving away from Amar and then coming back when a pedestrian had passed. Occasionally she would grasp his arm as they crossed a lane, and then let it go. Once he found her skipping on one leg, like a little girl, from one pavement tile to another. She stopped, looked back at him, grinned and wrinkled her nose endearingly.

After a while they found themselves in the Soho area. They wandered around and Amar pointed out Dean Street where Karl Marx had once lived. As a counterpoint, he also showed her the Raymond Revue Bar which was apparently the first legally permitted strip club in London, and told her about the Soho area being home to a number of brothels.

They walked along Shaftesbury Avenue to Piccadilly Circus and sat on the steps below the statue of Eros. Amar told her how the nude figure being used in this public monument caused controversy when it was first installed, and how, to temper this criticism, it was renamed "The Angel of Christian Charity"!

They walked and they chatted and they joked, had another coffee, wandered around some more until she reluctantly looked at her watch. It was time to go back. Slowly they walked to the Oxford Street Tube station. As they neared the Tube station, Helga's steps seemed to become even slower. She became quiet. Amar noticed it and trying to bring a smile to her face said, "Is the prospect of facing your landlady's cooking so depressing?"

She smiled weakly and said, "No, it is nothing." She stopped and seemed to be struggling with something in her mind.

"Is something worrying you, Helga?"

She nodded absently, and then seemed to make up her mind. "I was just thinking—that after what you said today about Sudipto ..." and she tailed off.

Amar's heart sank. He put on a brave face and said quietly, "You're wondering, after what I said, whether we should meet again? Is that what's bothering you?"

She did not seem to know whether to say yes or no. There was an indecision on her face which Amar had not seen before. She looked down at the pavement, then looked up at him. "I was wondering … I was wondering … whether you would go back home and feel guilty again about spending time with me."

She looked away and continued, "I was wondering if you would think it is not good for us to meet."

Amar said in a flat voice, "Is that what you want—not to meet?"

Still looking away, she said in a low voice, "Would it not be better for you?"

Amar could not contain his irritation, "Are you deciding what is good for me?" he asked harshly.

She turned around angrily, her eyes flashing. "I am not deciding anything for you! I am wanting opening of your eyes. You are so miserable to meet me. So worried about your friendship with Sudipto. I do not want to be the cause of guilt—and I do not want to ruin your wonderful friendship. I have enough problems of my own." And she turned away.

Amar had recovered himself. He slowly walked up to her and turned her around. "What do you want then?" he asked quietly.

She shook her head, closed her eyes and said gently, "I do not know, A-mar. I do not know. I do not want to cause complications in your life—and I do not want to complicate my life further, it is in enough of a mess. At the same time …" and she tailed off.

"So meeting me is complicating your life," Amar said coldly. "Then not meeting me will solve the problem, won't it?"

She looked at him, exasperated. "Oh, A-mar, why you do not want to understand? You are angry. I am also not good in mind. You cannot understand. I cannot speak with anger. So, let us not do this now. If you want to, give me phone call tomorrow."

Amar said curtly, "If I want to," and turned around and walked off, seething with anger.

The Beginning

Sleep did not refresh the mind, neither did it provide any answers. He woke drained and irritable. All he knew was that he wanted to phone Helga, and he was not going to.

The cheerful, brightly lit kitchen with its red table and chairs failed to raise his spirit. He wasn't in the mood for breakfast. He made himself a second cup of tea and buried himself in the morning papers. He tried to read the papers but found himself gazing blankly at the columns. He knew what he was waiting for, but would not admit it to himself. So when the phone rang in the hall, he pretended to continue reading the papers. His mother answered it and he waited tensely to see if it was for him. It was.

"Is that A-mar?" Helga's voice sounded strained.

"Yes."

There was a pause and Amar wondered if she had cut off sensing the coldness in his voice. But she was still on the line, because he could hear her breathing.

"Everything okay?" Amar could not keep up his distant voice. He was worried by her silence.

She sighed. "Thank you for asking. It has made difference. And you? Are you fine?" she asked anxiously.

"Yes, yes, I'm still in one piece."

"What means that, A-mar? Do not make jokes with me—I am not in mood. I do not expect you to be in many pieces. Just tell me that you are all right. Is that too difficult?"

Although his mother was in the kitchen and could not hear him, he lowered his voice. "Well, I did not sleep too well."

"I also." She paused. "A-mar," and her voice sounded strained. "A-mar, can you manage to meet me today—even for a short while?

I will not take so long, I promise. And then you can go back to do whatever you really want to."

"I would like to meet you, Helga, in spite of whatever happened yesterday. But what is this business about 'a short while'? If you are so busy, we can talk on the phone."

There was another pause. This time her voice sounded angry. "If we can talk on the phone I would not ask you to meet me. Please understand. Do not make things more difficult for me—please?"

Amar said wearily, "I don't have the energy or the desire to fight with you, Helga. I am just tired—weary." He paused. "Can we meet at, say, 3 pm?"

"Yes, yes—3 pm would be fine. Where shall we meet?"

"Outside Marble Arch Tube station?"

"Yes—I shall be waiting."

❖

While initially Amar had felt a fleeting relief—as if he had got a kind of reprieve—on the tube to Marble Arch, he began to worry. Whatever Helga wanted to tell him was obviously not pleasant, otherwise she would not have said the meeting would be short.

He climbed up the narrow steps leading out of Marble Arch Tube station, tense and edgy, wishing he had not come. The fresh air, even though tainted with petrol fumes, felt better than the stuffiness underground. He took a deep breath and tried to collect himself. Helga was not around, and he waited by the newspaper vendor near the entrance, keeping an eye on the stairs. Five minutes passed and there was no sign of her.

Getting exasperated, he turned around to look up and down the street. As he turned, he found her standing behind him with an unsmiling face. Startled, Amar said, "Where did you appear from? I have been watching the staircase for the last five minutes."

She gave a wan smile. "And I have been watching you for all five minutes. I arrived early."

"Then—then—why didn't you tell me you were here?" Amar spluttered.

"Can we go across and sit on one of the park benches before I start answering your questions? I am feeling a little tired."

She did look pale with dark circles under her eyes, her hair limp and lifeless.

She looked vulnerable and helpless. He suddenly felt protective and took her arm while they crossed the street. As they walked towards Hyde Park she looked up and said, "It is all right, I am not weak." As he tried to disentangle his hand from her arm she prevented him by bringing her arm closer to her body. "I never said I did not want your hand on my arm."

The tension broke. Amar sighed and said, "I wish LSE had a course on understanding women!"

They found a bench which was still a little damp form the earlier drizzle, but their coats protected them. There was a chill to the air, and Amar dug his hands into his coat pocket to warm them up. Helga leant back and closed her eyes. The Oxford Street traffic rumbled in the background. Rain drops still dripped from the trees. The sky was a sombre grey.

Amar looked at Helga whose eyes were still closed. He decided not to disturb her, and enjoy the view of the wide expanse of green parkland instead. But too much was going on inside. After a time, he gruffly asked, "Are you awake?"

She opened her eyes and turned her head towards him while still resting it on the bench, her hands in her white coat pocket. "Yes, A-mar, I have been awake," she said in a low voice.

"Are you feeling all right?" Amar could not prevent some concern creeping into his voice.

"I am fine now. I was not until a little while ago."

"What's wrong—do you need to go to a doctor?"

She smiled sadly. "No doctor can cure what I'm suffering from. No, no, it is no disease—do not look so worried."

Amar shook his head. “You’re talking in riddles.”

She said with a sad smile. “Sorry if I confuse you, but I am confused myself. I thought I had found answer and that is why I wanted to talk to you. But what my brain decides may not be what I want to follow. So I am confused.” She paused, and asked hesitantly, “Do you think—do you think you can stay with me for a little while today?” Then, as if collecting herself, she hurriedly said, “But if you have to go—I will understand.”

“I wasn’t thinking of going anywhere. You were the one who said on the phone that this will be a brief meeting! I’ve been concerned that you will suddenly look at your watch and say, ‘Times up’ …”

She looked up at him, and he could not read her expression. She nudged closer and put her head on his shoulder. After a while she said in a low voice, “Thank you.”

Amar was not sure what this meant, but was quite content to sit and enjoy her closeness. He closed his eyes. However, thoughts kept crowding in. Finally, he turned to her and said, “You still haven’t told me why you said this would be a short appointment.”

Without looking at him she asked, “Why do you need to know, Amar?”

“Because the thought keeps bothering me that this will end too soon.”

“A-mar, what will happen we do not know,” she said tiredly.

“You’re sounding very philosophical—but at the moment I’m feeling far from philosophical.”

“What are you feeling?”

“Never mind,” Amar said quickly, hoping that his desire did not show on his face.

“Actually, I’m feeling like a glass of beer. Can’t you see the thirst showing on my face?”

She looked at him searchingly, and then turned her face away. “I know what your face shows.” And then said briskly, “All right, we have to satisfy the male of the species—so we will go looking for beer. But you must let me pay.”

"We'll see—we will see. But we have a more difficult problem—it's still not opening time for the pubs."

"Yes, I remember. The British have this strange belief that drunkenness goes up if pubs stay open throughout day. So what do we do until then?" she asked.

At a loss, he said, "Er—maybe, walk in the park for a little while?"

She looked at him appraisingly and got up. "If that is what you want to do," she said quietly.

Amar felt uncomfortable. This was the last thing he wanted to do. "When in Britain do as the British do. When in difficulty, go for a walk—or have a cup of tea."

As they walked she held his arm, and sensed the tension in him. She herself was on edge. "Why are you so tense, A-mar?"

"Because there are so many unanswered questions tumbling around in my mind and you're refusing to answer any."

"Oh, please, can we stop going over same thing over and over again. I am tired," she cried out in exasperation.

"And I'm tired too, of all this mystery and the drama," he exclaimed in irritation. They had both stopped. She let go of his arm as he walked away.

She followed. They walked in silence, both in turmoil. After a while she could not hold out any longer. She said, "A-mar?" When there was no response she grabbed his arm and shook it. "A-mar—why do you not say something?"

After a pause he replied shortly, "What is there to say?"

"Oh, God! Must we always fight?" There was anger beneath her despair. She said something in German. "Must everything be written like company report? Can you not appreciate what I have been going through? Can you not feel what I am feeling and have been feeling? Oh God, you are so blind!" She shook her head and muttered, "And, time is so short!" Her voice broke.

Amar was shaken at the rawness of her despair. It jolted him out of his self-centred sullenness. It broke through the walls of anger and self-justification he was building up. Because he sensed its honesty.

He tentatively stretched out his arm across her shoulder. When she did not resist, he gently pulled her to his side, and with the other hand softly wiped away her tears. She suddenly crumpled into his arms and he felt her body against him, her wet face tucked into his collar. He held her gently and stroked her hair, as she sobbed against him. He let her cry until her body stopped jerking spasmodically. He held her tighter and said gently, "Helga—Helga—come on, tell me what's bothering you. You're not alone. I'm here for you."

She did not say anything, but her sobs continued, this time in a quieter rhythm. As they stopped and her body became more still, she started talking against his neck. "A-mar—oh, A-mar," was all she could say in the beginning as she clung tightly to him. Then as she composed herself, her voice became a little more audible. "I have so wanted to hear this from you. But I was afraid. Afraid about your thinking of me as bad woman. A woman with an illegitimate child. But, please understand A-mar it was not like that. Please believe. Please … I was raped—and—thrown away. I had become pregnant. Doctor said, do not have the child. Friends said the same. I said no—no—no. I cannot kill my own child. My family did not help. Nobody helped. Then, a kind friend took me to her flat. I had the child—I found a job and my friend offered to look after the baby while I was away."

She wiped her eyes with a handkerchief and then continued. "After long time my father who is rich agreed to see my face. He bought me small flat—not wanting to do more. I do well at my job and can pay for person to look after my baby. I live alone. This is first holiday after having the baby."

She was speaking in a low voice and seemed reluctant to continue. However, she did.

"Then I meet you. You are the first man I am comfortable with. You are gentle, kind—funny. I miss you when I go back to my room. Then you spoke about Sudipto and everything was spoilt. I felt frightened you will disappear from my life. I would be lonely again. I could not sleep at night. But I could not ruin your life—so

I wanted to meet you once more, even if for short while and then go back to my aloneness. I came early because I wanted to look at you and keep you in my mind. Then I became weak and asked you to stay longer. But now the minutes are going and I cannot my stop tears, because I am a lost woman. Oh, A-mar what will happen when you leave me ...'' She buried her face once again into his neck, and he felt the warm tears wetting his collar.

Amar felt the weight of grief in her as if it was his own. And he felt the sense of imminent loss which her words brought. The hours were indeed passing, and he was helpless to stop them. He felt the panic. Would he not see her again? Would he go back to his humdrum existence and lose forever this intense emotion he was feeling? Would he lose this warm body which was pressing against him for comfort? His sense of panic intensified. He had never felt like this before, and now it seemed bounded by hours—by minutes.

He held her tighter. He did not want this to end. "Helga," he said softly. "Don't you see that I care for you too? I feared I was losing you. Then when you rang this morning the sun was shining again. I need you ... I want you," he whispered.

She whispered back, "Just keep telling me you need me!" It was almost an entreaty.

She slowly raised her head and sought his eyes and saw the hunger. He lowered his head and brushed her lips with his. They were soft and light—like the petals of a flower. He kept his lips on hers in a gentle kiss. He did not know how long they stayed in this chaste kiss. He was woken by the feel of raindrops on his face. He drew apart, but saw her eyes were still closed. A few drops were trickling down her face. He leant forward and kissed them off her. She made a sound and seemed to settle into him. Then opened her eyes and met his. He bent down and kissed her again. This time his lips were harsher on hers, and he felt her lips opening, and her tongue emerging to meet his. This time the kiss was passionate—all the pent up feelings exploding in a wild probing of each other's mouth.

The rain grew in strength, but they were oblivious. After a while their lips parted and they gasped for breath as if they had not breathed all this while. Amar brushed the drops off her hair and said, "You're getting wet, darling." Startled, he realised he had never used the word before. "Darling" had been on his proscribed list. Yet, now it just flowed naturally.

She burrowed into his chest and murmured "A-mar, oh A-mar … just hold me close."

❖

The rain slicked their hair and trickled down their face. A chilly breeze made it seem colder. But they were unconcerned and stayed in a warm, life-giving embrace. Finally, Amar seemed to wake up to the reality around him, "Hey, my little crazy woman," he whispered, "If you insist on getting wet like this, you will end up with the very English ailment of a running nose and a frog in the throat! Not to mention bleary eyes and a bulldog look! So, for my sake, will you get out of the rain?"

He was glad to hear her giggle. "Since you will not kiss a bulldog—I will have to agree."

They hurried to the shelter of some trees, and Amar did his best to wipe her head dry with his handkerchief. But it was a futile exercise, since the handkerchief was soaking wet in a minute. Amar shook his head. "No, this won't do. We need a more drastic remedy. A glass of something strong to improve the blood circulation. What do you say?"

"I say yes, but not to beer—I am too wet and cold."

Amar snapped his fingers. "We'll go to one of the few wine bars we have in London. It's on the Strand. We'll have to take the tube to Charing Cross station, and then it's a short walk. Are you up to it?"

She glared at him for a minute, "Why do men think that women are weak? You have been exposed to same rain that I have. If possible for you, why not for me?" Then, her voice softened.

"Especially when you will hold my hand."

He sighed. "What men have to do to earn a drink! All right it's a deal."

She hugged him. "Even though you sound American, I will forgive you." Then she added in a low voice, "With me—you do not have to do any deals—you silly man."

❖

They found a table at the end of the long narrow room. He asked her what she wanted to drink. "Anything which will warm me up—and stop me from turning into a Churchill," she said, running her hand through her hair to dry it.

"That's very helpful. You want me to go up to the bartender and say, 'My friend wants a drink which will stop her from turning into a bulldog.'"

She kicked him under the table. Then slipped off her shoes and sent her toes sliding up inside his trouser. It felt incredibly erotic, and Amar for no reason found himself blushing. He recovered enough to clear his throat and say, "If you don't stop, you'll have a crazed man on your hands."

She was unfazed. "Good."

Amar got up and said pleadingly, "Before I go totally crazy, let me at least have a drink!"

He returned with a brandy in a snifter for her, and a glass of red wine for himself. She looked at her drink disapprovingly. "A-mar, why did you have to get me such an expensive drink? I would have been happy with just glass of simple red wine."

He smiled. "Relax, relax. This is not cognac. It's just the glass which looks expensive. What I've got you is a Spanish brandy—much, much cheaper than cognac. Now sip it and tell me if you like it. The bartender swears this is just as good."

She lifted her glass, cradling it between her hands. He said, "*Salud*. Cheers, *Prosit*, *A votre sante* … anything which says good cheer—good health."

She lowered her glass, looking pensive. Then she raised it once again and toasted, "To eternity," and drank.

He drank too, but the beginnings of a cloud appeared in his mind. How much time did they have with each other? She was here for only another five days. And then? She had looked wistful as she raised the toast, and now he understood her melancholy.

They sipped their drinks in silence. He stretched across the table and took her hand. She clutched it as if it was her lifeline. "Helga, this is not a vanishing moment in time. This is not us meeting while the clock ticks away. It will go on—it will endure—if we want it to."

She reached for both of his hands and imprisoned them in hers, then crushed her face against them and closed her eyes. Slowly, she seemed to relax. After a while she opened her eyes and smiled. Her entire face was transformed with light. No words were needed.

Sensing the easing of her tension, Amar broke the silence. "And now, if you give me back one of my hands, maybe I will be able to drink my wine."

"No," she said promptly. "These hands are mine. But, I am a considerate woman. So I will give you the wine. Now open your mouth like a good boy." She grasped both his hands in her left hand and held the wine glass to his mouth with the other hand. He took a swallow and spluttered. He was amazed at how difficult it was to drink if both the hands were incapacitated.

"Oh, A-mar—you are worse than little baby! A baby drinks better," she scolded.

"It's not my fault if I was not trained in wine drinking as a baby," Amar said in an aggrieved voice. "And anyway, how can I drink when you have imprisoned my hands?"

"You don't drink with hands. There are ways of drinking—come and sit beside me and I will teach you," she replied with a glint in her eyes.

Amar looked apprehensive. She sighed and said, "Come on, A-mar—you can sit beside me without looking as if your life is in great danger!"

Hesitatingly, Amar got up and sat next to her. She said, "Now, place your hands on my lap—go on, nothing is going to happen. Next turn your face towards me and close your eyes."

Amar did as he was told, but protested. "I am not sure I like this game."

"Just shut up, and do as told."

"How long do I have to keep my eyes closed—I might get vertigo," he complained.

He heard her pick up the wine glass. Then she said "Just open your mouth a little."

He parted his lips waiting for the cold rim of the wine glass. Instead he felt a pair of soft wet lips against his and wine warm from her mouth pouring into his. The wine swirled in his mouth, but her lips stayed on his. He hurriedly swallowed the wine and concentrated on the kiss.

After a while he opened his eyes. She sat primly looking ahead of her, as if nothing had happened, while he tried to recover his breath.

She turned to him calmly and said, "Did not I tell you there are many ways of drinking wine?"

"If there are even more ways, maybe you should teach me only behind locked doors," he said breathlessly, his eyes wide.

"Are you really shocked, A-mar?"

"I am shattered. I think I need another drink of wine to revive myself."

She rewarded him with another drink.

❖

They sat side by side and Amar could feel the warmth of her thighs against his. He could smell her cologne and her damp hair. There were a hundred thoughts which were trying to float up in his mind. But he was not going to let them impinge on his enjoyment, and he shut them out. All his senses seemed to be awakened to razor-sharp receptiveness. His lips felt swollen and hot and yearning for the cooling touch of hers. His skin seemed to magnify the heat from her body, until he feared that she had a fever. His face felt flushed with a continuous rush of blood. His nose smelt every subtle scent of her body. It was a kind of agony, and a kind of rapture.

The evening slipped away through their laced fingers. There was no way to hold it back. Before the sense of desolation could take hold, Amar said, "I won't go to the library for the next few days. So from tomorrow we can spend more time together."

Her face lit up like a child receiving a Christmas present. "I cannot believe it. Truly, you can spend all the time with me?"

"Well, no—not all of it." Her face fell. "Some of the time I'll have to spend with a woman who fights with me. But apart from that, I have no other commitment."

Her brows furrowed—then cleared. She grinned, "And if the woman promises not to fight—then?"

"Well, then I'll have another problem—because then I'll have to start believing in Santa Claus!"

Richmond

As he opened his eyes in the morning, Amar habitually registered the quality of light in the room to judge the kind of day it was. He would part the lacy white curtains and confirm the dull leaden sky. Today, there was the gloomy half-light which was the norm in London. This usually sent his mood into a downward spiral until the first reviving cup of tea. But today his mood was buoyant as he tied the belt of his dressing gown and went downstairs. Not even the absence of the papers, commandeered by his father, could dampen his spirits. Humming to himself, he put the kettle on.

His mother came in, plump and comfortable in her housecoat. "*Arrey*, Amu, you're up early today. Are you feeling all right?" She was quite serious in her concern about his health.

Amar grimaced. "Did not sleep a wink—had indigestion and gas."

His mother couldn't resist a smile. Then putting on a serious expression she became the dutiful wife. "Amu, you mustn't make fun of your father like this. You know he doesn't keep good health."

"But, Ma, I tease him to his face and he takes it very sportingly. You get more upset than he does!"

"He has suffered from ill health all his life—just see how thin he is."

"Come on, Ma, he is fitter than most people his age! He just follows the Bengali tradition of providing a health digest at the slightest opportunity. And being thin doesn't equate with being sickly—it is often a sign of good health."

"These are all ill-thought-out, new-fangled ideas—everyone knows that good health and a good weight go together. I've learnt this from my childhood, and I'm not going to change my beliefs in favour of these modern notions. Just look at you—all skin and bones. You just don't eat enough."

"I know," Amar said in a weak voice. "I'm dying. Maybe now you'll cook some *kheer* for me—as a last meal."

"Don't joke about these things," she said sharply.

"M-a-a, tell me when have you last seen me ill? Come on, tell me. See, you can't remember—and that's because this skinny son of yours has never been ill. Nor is his weight any less than normal. All he needs is some good creamy, thick *kheer* to bring back the roses to his cheeks."

"Amu, don't say you have never been ill—it's inauspicious and it's not right. Fate does not take kindly to this kind of jesting."

"All right—all right, I'll do penance—no *kheer* for a week?" Then seeing her severe expression, he said tentatively, "All right then—for two weeks?"

She sighed in exasperation, but a smile was fighting its way into her chubby face. "Oh, why has God given me crazy children like this!"

❖

Amar felt inexplicably edgy as the train rumbled on towards Paddington Tube station where they were meeting. He would have the whole day with Helga, and he was overjoyed. But a nervousness clouded the anticipation.

She was there waiting by the clock, in a dark blue dress with a lemon cardigan against the unseasonal chill, and her off-white raincoat draped around her shoulder. Her hair was drawn back in a ponytail, giving more length to her face and highlighting its planes. It suited her, and Amar watched her for a while before approaching her. In spite of yesterday's closeness, Amar felt awkward. Undecided whether to kiss her in greeting or be more casual, he said an uncomfortable, "Hello, Helga."

Helga looked a bit startled. Then said, in a very proper voice, "How do you do, A-mar. Miserable weather, is it not?"

Amar was disconcerted. This was the girl he was holding in his arms yesterday? How do you do? Had she decided that yesterday was a mistake and must be wiped off the slate? He had read that women were unpredictable. Or was this the Western norm—a little bit of snogging over a drink and back to normal routine the next day, as if nothing had happened. Or, had he missed out on some aspect of the Western dating ritual and was being punished?

Then he noticed the beginnings of a grin stealing over her face. He stepped forward and pulled her into his arms. "You little minx, you almost had me traumatised. What's all this nonsense about 'How do you do, Amar?'?"

"Well, if all you can say to me is, 'Hello Helga', in your most British voice, then what must I do? I must be equally British, no? Was my 'miserable weather' not good?" She asked proudly, arching her head back to look at him, and in the process pushing her body more firmly into his. Very conscious of the feel of her firm limbs against his, Amar tried to be casual.

"Not bad," he frowned. "But to be really British you've got to speak through your nose and say, 'Rather nippy, what?'"

She glowered at him. "You do not appreciate my good English because I do not speak through my nose? Sometime I will show you how good my English is." Then she bit her tongue in alarm, "Sorry—sorry, I forgot the no-fight treaty." Smiling sweetly and batting her eyelids she said, "You will see what a good girl I am. Can I ask, please, why we are meeting at a railway station? Are you going to kidnap me and take me away to some lonely place while I struggle wildly and faintly cry for help?"

"Patience, woman. All will be revealed. In the meantime we will take the Underground—but since it is the District Line it will be Overground."

She looked at him curiously. "A-mar, you are all right?"

Amar looked puzzled. "Why, is there something wrong with me?" And hastily looked himself over.

"*Nein—nein*. Let us go." And taking his arm she started walking, humming something to herself. Amar listened carefully and finally caught the words, "... let's go underground—to go overground ... overground to go underground ..."

"What on earth are you singing?" Amar asked.

"Not singing—practising my English," she said with an innocent face and continued humming.

Realisation dawned on Amar. He stopped and glared at her.

"Let me tell you that while the District Line is part of the Underground system, it functions as a surface transport. That is why ..."

"You have to go underground to go overground," she sang softly.

Amar couldn't help but smile. She was adorable. He wanted to take her in his arms and plant a big kiss on her lips, but refrained.

At the platform Amar had to keep holding her back from boarding the trains that drew up. "Not this one." "Not this one either." "No, not ours."

She looked around in exasperation "A-mar, I know this platform is a romantic place, but are we going to picnic here for day?"

"Who knows? Isn't it exciting, though, not to know where you are going and when you are going?"

"Yes, as exciting as going to the dentist."

Just then another train appeared round the bend, and Amar grunted in satisfaction. "That's ours."

They boarded and found two vacant seats. "And how did you know this is right one? Or did we just get on the train to stop my complaining?"

"If you had looked at the sign carefully you would have noticed that this goes to Richmond—and that is where we are bound."

"Oh, Richmond!" she nodded knowledgably. "Of course—Richmond." She paused and then asked in a flat voice, "And what is Richmond?"

Amar settled back smugly and started talking confidently, since he had done his research. "Well, to begin with, it is the largest of the royal parks."

Helga didn't seem particularly moved by this fact. "A-mar, are you also affected by the American size sickness? Everything big is wonderful. Is that only reason we are going to Richmond, because it is big?"

Amar was a little taken aback at his research not finding a receptive audience. But he was sure that the reaction would change once he presented the other facts. "Just listen, Helga, and you will know why we are going to Richmond. From there you get a magnificent, uninterrupted view of St. Paul's Cathedral. Although its royal connection goes back to the 14th century, this park became famous when Charles I moved his court from London in 1625 to escape the plague."

Helga's impatience seemed to be growing. "And are we also going there to escape some plague?"

"Helga, be patient. When you get there you will see what a magnificent park it is. Acre upon acre of rolling green meadows—magnificent forests, beautiful woods, wild deer—you don't feel you are in London at all …" his voice began tailing off as he noticed that he was not making much impact, "… and … and … you can feel lost in it, without people looking over your shoulders all the time …" he ended lamely and looked out of the window morosely.

He sensed a change in her. Her thigh seemed to press against his more firmly, and her voice became more lively. "A-mar, I love woods and trees. Can I go rolling down the grassy hills?" she asked with the eagerness of a little child.

Amar was unaccustomed to such mood changes, but enjoyed her sudden enthusiasm. "Well, I'm not sure. We'll have to check with the keeper of the royal keys," he said solemnly, having no idea what the keeper of the royal keys was. But it sounded appropriate—after all they were going to a royal park. "Rolling in a royal park is only allowed to inebriated royalty, you see."

"Oh, please tell him I will be good—I promise to follow all the traffic rules, and not bump into any highnesses."

This surreal conversation ended as a buxom young woman with Rubenesque thighs swayed sensually down the aisle and lingeringly brushed Amar's shoulders. Amar, guiltily enjoying the feel of the silky thighs brushing him, was suddenly brought to earth by a nasal voice saying loudly, "Rather hippy, what?"

He quickly turned to Helga to shush her. But she wore an implacable expression as she looked ahead. "Helga," Amar whispered fiercely, "not so loudly."

"Only practising my English," she said calmly.

"Yes, but what I had said was 'Rather nippy' not 'hippy,'" Amar whispered.

"That crude woman was trying to flirt with you. So I said hippy. What is wrong with that?" she asked combatively. "Anyway, she was very fleshy."

Amar gave up arguing.

❖

The sky had not lightened, but in its vastness and with so much greenery to set it off, it acquired an added dimension of colour, which was lacking in the city which had only grey, dusty and sooty buildings for contrast. As they stepped into the park, with grassy meadows stretching out all around, the area seemed huge, and they felt like little inconsequential ants scurrying about in a massive universe. They turned into one of the walking tracks and after a while found the undulating downs they had been looking for. Amar stopped and drew a long, deep breath. The air smelt and tasted different—it was sharp and fresh and smelt of grass rather than petrol and burnt coal. He took Helga's hand and said, "Drink it in—it's more uplifting than any champagne!"

Helga said contemptuously, "Ha—this city man teaching me the beauty of the countryside! I've drunk more country air than you, I bet."

"And how will you prove that, my country lass?"

She turned around to face him, and said with an impish grin, "Well, they say the proof of the freshness is in the tasting."

Amar tried to say something, but his voice would not emerge. His heart had begun to beat more violently, and he felt breathless. He drew her to him. He kissed her gently, and then held her close to allow his heartbeat to slow down. Her body felt warm against his, and he was conscious of the pressure of her breasts. He kissed her again. They slowly broke away and looked at each other. "This is the first time we've really been alone," he whispered.

"This is what I wanted," she whispered back. Her face looked content as she closed her eyes and sighed happily.

She opened her eyes and it widened as she said, "A-mar, A-mar, look at that beautiful butterfly flying drunkenly against the wind!"

Amar turned to look and she broke away and was off running with arms outspread. "Come on, let us follow the butterfly". She ran, zigzagging as the butterfly kept changing its mind. Or maybe it was just exulting, drunk on the champagne-air.

They topped a small rise and the grassy meadow fell away gently. "Come on, A-mar—let us roll!" She tugged him over as she sank down on the grass and started rolling down. Amar rolled too, if a little more clumsily, hampered by his coat. They reached the end of the slope—a little hollow with daisies dotting the grass. They lay on their backs getting their breath back. All they could see was a vast expanse of grey sky—and that was their world. Amar realised that the grass was damp. He got up and spread his coat on the grass for them to lie on.

He lay down next to her and looked at her lying a little dishevelled and breathless, her cheeks flushed. She turned to him and held out her arms. This time the kiss was long and deep, each one reaching into the other as if in desperation. Amar cupped her breast gently in his palm and felt the rigidity of her nipple. They were both breathing heavily, as if air was difficult to find. He breathed her in—the warm feminine smell of her, overlaid by the cologne fragrance which he had begun to associate with her. He felt the softness of her thighs, the warmth in between.

She put out her hand, unbuttoned his shirt and put her hands on his chest. Her light fingers played about on his chest in a way he found very exciting, especially when they caressed his nipples. He began to realise that there were a large number of pleasure points on a human body. He decided to experiment too. And undid her bra, with some effort and help from her.

As their fervour mounted, Amar became bolder. He put his hand under her skirt, up her smooth, warm thighs and reached the mysterious warmth in between. Afraid that he was going beyond the point he would be able to control himself, Amar stopped himself.

She did not say anything but closed her eyes and lay still.

"Sweetheart, you're precious to me, more than anyone has been," he whispered. They kissed again, long and hard and Amar felt his excitement growing. Unable to restrain himself, Amar whispered breathlessly, "I want you darling, I want you."

Helga was equally breathless and murmured, "I want you too, A-mar."

"But I have not come prepared for ..." Amar said in anguish.

She pushed him down, propped herself on her elbow over him and whispered with a hint of triumph "Don't worry—I have just started my period. You don't need a protective."

Amar could not believe this was happening. Helga did not give him any more time to think as she got up to slide her panties off, then closed his mouth with her lips. He found the space between her legs and felt his way in. At last they were one. He could feel her soft warmth engulfing him. They lay quietly for a while, savouring each other's warmth, but nature took over. They moved in rhythm until the final moments of obliteration. He felt his whole being pouring into her. For a suspended moment he seemed to lose consciousness. Then there was stillness.

He had made love to a woman for the first time. The sad encounter with Jasmine did not count. This was real.

After a while Amar opened his eyes again. Shouldn't the momentous event have changed him in some way? Shouldn't the world look altered—shouldn't he feel different?

Yet here he was, lying uncomfortably on an uneven surface and worrying about the drizzle which had started intensifying.

"What are you thinking of?" Helga asked petulantly.

"What I'm thinking, my little pumpkin, is that the drizzle is becoming heavier. We need to get to some shelter, before we get soaked."

She just grunted and cuddled up closer. Slowly, a sense of peace came over him and they lay contentedly ignoring the drizzle. Finally, as it intensified into rain, Amar got up, and said sternly, "Come on, get up you crazy woman, we're getting soaked."

❖

At the cafe, which fortunately was not overcrowded, they took off their wet coats and found a corner table. The coats added a damp odour to the prevalent stale smell of frying. The white neon lights were cold and impersonal. The windows had misted over and hid the greenery outside—but to the two of them this was a wonderful haven. The warmth helped them dry out—the smell of food suddenly awakened their hunger.

Amar loaded two plates at the counter and returned to the table.

As he attacked the ham, eggs and chips he said, "I'm ravenously hungry—I don't know why, since I had a heavy breakfast."

Helga smiled enigmatically and looked at him. "I hope you will be equally hungry for the next few days."

"Oh no, I don't think so, I'm not a huge eater ..." then stopped. He raised his eyes, and said with a shy grin, "I promise to be very hungry." He shook his head, "Stupid of me not to have caught on."

"No. How were you to know that lovemaking can make you hungry?"

❖

On his way back home that evening, Amar leant back in his seat and closed his eyes, overcome by a pleasant lassitude. They had taken the train back to central London, and wandered, hand in hand, around the streets. Stopping for a coffee when the thought took them. It had been a lazy, leisurely afternoon. His mind seemed too lethargic to think now—all he felt was a gentle, satisfied glow.

He had begun to feel wanted again, to be at the centre of a woman's thoughts. It seemed a miracle to him because he still found it difficult to believe that he could be the focus of a woman's attention.

As he came out of the station, the night sky had the usual depressing coppery tinge. However, today it seemed warm and comforting. The cones of light cast by the street lamps caught the slanting, glistening drops of rain, and Amar marvelled at how beautiful they looked. Yes, today was a different day.

He had crossed the invisible line into adulthood.

Helga's Last Day

They spent the next few days "avoiding the plague", as the Richmond trip had now come to be termed by her. On the day before her departure they decided to do something different after a morning visit to Richmond.

Their lovemaking that morning was particularly passionate, tinged as it was by the impending separation. Amar voiced what he was feeling. "I don't want to think that from tomorrow it will be an existence without you, Helga."

Helga put her finger over his lips. "Hush, my darling. Do not talk that way. You are making it sound as if this is a final parting. Remember, we are only separated by the Channel. And you have promised to come to stay with me next summer."

"But that seems so far away," Amar whispered.

"Yes, it does—for me too. But letters will bring me close to you. Promise you will write often."

"Of course I will write, sweetheart, I will write my heart out. For the moment though, I'm feeling bereft." He feverishly clutched her to him as if to obliterate the thought of the impending parting.

❖

They had decided to have one last walk in Hyde Park. The sombre grey sky reflected their mood, and in a strange way Amar was glad. A bright, sparkling sunny day would have been inappropriate, and unbearable. There was a certain melancholic beauty in the gloom, and Amar found himself responding to it, despite the bleakness in his soul.

They sat on a bench under a tree, holding hands. Amar watched the drops dripping in front of him from the leaves, and found himself fascinated by them. They were so perfectly shaped, so pure and transparent, so simple and uncomplicated. If only life could be so simple. If only his mind could acquire this stillness.

As he watched the drops fall with metronomic regularity, his thoughts drifted back to his childhood days in the pine-covered hills of misty Shillong. He remembered how he would gaze with wonder at the drops drifting down from the spiny leaves of the pine trees—as each drop fell, the pine needle would spring back and then begin to bend again as the water gathered on it. He could smell the woody smoke from some nearby cottage.

"You know, Helga, this weather takes me back to happy childhood memories. We lived for over three years at a hill station called Shillong where it used to rain for nine months in the year—we would even have a 'sunny day holiday' at school—and grey skies and damp were a part of our lives. We would go to school in our raincoats and gumboots. Rain became part of normal existence. I used to enjoy the feel of cold drops on my face and the drum of rain on the raincoat. I would walk home down a muddy side road, along a whispering stream overhung by trees, enjoying the smell of wet earth and the solitude, and looking forward to reading the book I had borrowed from the school library."

"The last bit of the walk was the hardest," he continued, "since we lived at the top of a hill and, weighed down by the school bag, my short legs in the bulky gumboots would strain to climb the slope. I would console myself by saying that this climb would build my leg muscles. I was only about eleven then, but I had dreams of becoming an athlete. Once I got home, I would kick off my gumboots in the veranda and get into some dry clothes. There was great pleasure in rinsing my feet in warm water, towelling them and then putting on dry socks. The next pleasure was to sit at the table where there would be a plate of hot buttered toast and a jar of jam, with a glass of hot milk—which I loved. Then the crowning pleasure. I would get the book from my school bag, sit on the veranda chair, and let the pages transport me to a different world. From time to time I would look up and watch the raindrops drip down from the gutters, or look down the hill to the pear trees which were shrouded in a rain mist. Those were moments of great joy for me. And today, ten years later, sitting here looking at the raindrops, I get pleasure thinking about it."

"Your memories have cheered you up—your face looks less sad, your voice livelier."

"But now come back to the present," Helga continued, reaching up and pulling down Amar's head and kissing him. It was a long, lingering kiss. "I'm going to miss you, sweetheart," she whispered.

Then she buried her face on his chest. Looking down, Amar found tears trickling down her cheek. He stroked her hair.

He tenderly wiped her tears and then said, "Hey, my little funny face, there is something I want to show you. But it can only be done at one particular place. Come on, it's not far." He gently pulled her up and, holding her hand, walked into the park. He stopped after a few minutes, looked around and said, "Yes, this is the place. Do you remember?"

Helga looked around and nodded.

"This is where we first kissed. And no place could be more appropriate for me to give you this." He pulled out a packet from his jacket pocket.

Helga seemed to be in a daze and did not respond immediately. Then her face started breaking into a smile and for Amar it was like the sun breaking through the grey clouds. She clutched the packet to her breast and said in delighted surprise, "For me? You got something for me?"

Amar, not used to giving gifts, fidgeted embarrassedly. "Of course it's for you, silly woman! Who else would I buy a present for? But it's a very small gift. Go on, open it."

She opened it very carefully. Then paused and slowly drew out a scarf made of silky material. She put it to her mouth and kissed it and then looked up at him with swimming eyes. "This beautiful scarf from the man who I most wanted to have a keepsake from.

But this is too expensive—oh A-mar, why did you spend so much on me? I would have been happy even if you had given me a single flower as a remembrance. This—this is just too magnificent. How do I thank you?"

Amar was even more embarrassed, unused as he was to receiving such a heartfelt response to something he had done. "You don't have to thank me. This is what I wanted to give you. And incidentally, it isn't silk—so it wasn't as expensive. It's amazing what effects synthetic fibres can achieve these days."

"Oh, I am not interested in what you paid, A-mar—for me this is the most valuable gift I could ever receive." She hugged him. "Just let me hold you—I want to remember this moment."

She disengaged herself from him after a while and said, "Can I now give you something I had got for you? I know it is wrong moment—I know it will seem like a gift being given only because you have given me something—but you will know it is not like that. I have been carrying it around. I have been so tense today that I forgot to give it to you earlier." She fished in her bag and drew out a packet wrapped in coloured paper and gave it to him.

Amar said, "It's so beautifully packed that I feel bad about tearing the packing. But I have no patience, so here it goes." He drew out a small journal with a leather cover. It had a small clasp which locked it. A ribbon around the clasp held a key.

"This is something for you to write your innermost thoughts in. That's why it has a key—so that only you have access to it."

Amar groped for words. "Helga … Helga, this is too extravagant—I'm not used to getting gifts—I—I, I don't know what to say. Thank you is such an inadequate expression—yet I don't know what else I can say. This diary will be my closest companion."

❖

They sat at a table by the wall at the wine bar with glasses of wine in front of them. Try as they might, they could not conjure the spirit that had engulfed them the last time. Their mood was sombre.

Amar finally could not restrain himself. "Both of us are trying so hard to be cheerful, but it just is not working. I'm not going to try any more. If I sound morose, it's because that's the way I am feeling."

She did not say anything but just clutched his hand tighter.

They finished their drink and walked slowly towards the Tube station. They had decided that there would be no lingering parting, so after a last kiss Amar watched her slipping slowly out of sight on the escalator. He turned and walked to his train.

Next day, at college he bumped into Pramod. "Ah, the *Id ka chand* (rarely visible moon)! Where have you been all these days?" Seeing the expression on Amar's face, he added with a grin, "All right, it's obvious you don't want to talk about it."

"Let's not go on about it, then," Amar responded tiredly. He was in no mood for banter.

"What about some lunch?"

Amar hesitated. "Actually, I've had a heavy and late breakfast. I was thinking of going for a coffee and sandwich rather than for a refectory meal."

"That's all right, I'm quite happy to have a light lunch too."

They got their sandwiches at the third floor cafe and found a table.

"Sorry, Pramod, if I was short. It's just that I am feeling a bit low."

Pramod shrugged. "OK, you don't have to talk if you don't want to."

"I don't really know whether I want to or not. Helga has gone back and her absence is depressing me."

"She's gone back?"

"Yes, she left today and I don't know when I'll see her again."

"Well, Germany is not too far off, Amar. Maybe you can go and visit her sometime."

"Be practical, Pramod. You know my financial situation. Where do I find the money to go to Europe?"

"Well, there are vacation jobs, you know. Half the students here do these jobs to get some extra money, so why can't you?"

Amar was startled at what seemed such an easy solution. He smiled. "You're a genius. Thanks for suggesting it."

Pramod's very practical suggestion had, suddenly, eased the tension in Amar's mind. Soon he found himself telling Pramod about the last few days with Helga, but in an abbreviated form. "So, now you know why I'm depressed. I had a few days of pleasure and happiness, and now it's all behind me. Trust me to get involved with a girl who lives hundreds of miles away and is unreachable," he said bitterly.

Pramod did not seem sympathetic. "What are you moaning about? At least you've got somebody you like and somebody who reciprocates your affection. Remember, that's more than a lot of people have," he ended wryly.

"But you haven't as yet got anybody because you want the moon with silver tassels on. She has to have an IQ which qualifies her for Mensa International, she has to be able to do ballet, Bharat Natyam and Kathakali—preferably simultaneously—she has to have the body of Brigitte Bardot and the face of Meena Kumari ..."

Pramod smiled dryly and said, "Thank you for being polite, Amar, but let's face it, I've not been successful with women because I do not have what they find attractive. Nature did not bless me with looks."

"That's a load of rubbish, Pramod, and you know it. What women look for in a man, I don't know. But you're insulting them by saying they're just looking for a male stud."

"So what is the magic ingredient, then, which draws the women to some men, like bees to a honey pot. The secret formula?"

Amar laughed. "You're certainly asking the right person, Pramod. The 'Casanova of Willesden Green'! What I know about such matters won't even fill a thimble, mate. Maybe we should ask the 'Lithi man' who smugly announces each conquest to us." Manpreet, inexplicably successful with women, would pass by in the morning after a date with a girl, nod, and out of the corner of his lip mutter with a smug smile, "*Lithi* (Taken)".

"Oh, that born-again socialist? No. I'm not in the mood for the dialectics of sexuality."

"Well, you may not have any choice—I see the man himself headed to our table."

The slim, moustached Manpreet sauntered over and said, "May I join you, gentlemen," in a hard, practised clipped accent, which, sadly, slipped frequently.

Before Pramod could intervene, Amar said, "How can we say no to the loin of Punjab? Had any good conquests lately?"

As he sat down, Manpreet turned with an uncertain half-smile to Pramod, "Amar seems to be in good form this afternoon, ha-ha."

Pramod shrugged and went back to his coffee. Amar beamed at Manpreet. "Of course, I am, Mun—of course I am. Pramod and I have been searching for the secret formula for attracting women, and sad to say we are at a total loss, having had no success in this field ourselves. Just then, who should come along but our resident expert from India. What a stroke of luck—the gods are obviously smiling on us—sorry, the Politburo is obviously smiling on us. They sent you."

Manpreet, not very comfortable with the trend of the conversation, managed to force a smile. "*Kya yaar*, how come God has started to creep into your conversation? Are we seeing a conversion? Is there a sexy, religious woman responsible for this?" He paused, and his smile disappeared. "Incidentally, I think you know that I don't like being called Mun."

"Oh, my apologies. I thought they all called you Mun in college in Delhi. Anyway, Manpreet it will be from now on. So, now tell us about this magic potion you Casanovas have—or is it a mysterious chant—or the intoxication of an unwashed body—that gets the women running breathlessly to you."

Manpreet wasn't sure how to react, but in the end his vanity won over. Smiling modestly, he said "Who knows, *yaar*, why women behave as they do?"

"Come on, *Badshao*, don't be so modest. Let's face it, the women don't come running to me or Pramod. So what's your secret?"

Manpreet sat back in his chair, and looked at both of them smugly. "Shall I tell you a simple truth? Women love to be dominated. Show them who is master from the word go. Don't pussyfoot around worrying about their sensibilities. If you want something from them, just take it. You'll be surprised how willingly they'll give it."

Pramod woke up. "The caveman gambit? Throw a woman over your shoulder and race off to ravish her in your cave—to hell with what she wants? I thought you scientific socialists were against such gross feudal excesses?"

"No, you're missing the point I was trying to make. The point was—women enjoy being dominated by their men. This satisfies some latent need in them. So, by being controlling with them, you're actually satisfying their own need."

"And who has decided that women want to be dominated by men? You?" Pramod asked angrily. "You know, your thinking is not very different from the kulaks."

The uncomfortable Manpreet managed a smile. "Calling me names does not answer my arguments."

Pramod asked, "What arguments? I don't recall hearing any from you. All we heard were ex-cathedra pronouncements about the nature of women."

"Well, that is what you wanted—in fact, that's what Amar specifically asked me for."

"Did I now?" asked Amar, who was the only one seeming to enjoy himself. "I thought I asked you to tell us about the secret of your fatal charm—the secret of your hypnotic allure. You haven't touched on that at all."

"I think you'll have to ask the women that. I have an appointment to keep, so I must be off. But we'll continue this discussion some other time. See you folks later." Manpreet got up and left.

"Insufferable twerp," Pramod said disgustedly. "Why did you welcome him to our table, Amar?"

"To have a bit of fun! Come on, Pramod, don't be so uptight. We need some comic relief from time to time. Also, we needed an answer to our conundrum. Now we've got some kind of an answer."

"That the secret of seduction lies in hitting a woman on the head and dragging her to your bed?"

"No, the answer is—if morons like him are so successful with women, then we have some hope. The message is that we have been prisoners of our own inhibitions and lack of confidence. What this insufferable prig has got, is a sublime belief in himself. That is what we seem to lack."

Pramod was still seething. "So, what are you suggesting—we start speaking with a clipped Punjabi accent like him? Look at our profile on every reflective surface—you've seen him crane his neck every time he passes a glass-fronted notice board? Walk as if we've got a rod stuck up our backside?"

Amar grinned. "No. What I'm suggesting is we forget about discovering the Casanova code. And start believing more in ourselves. That's what we need—more self-belief, more pride in ourselves."

Pramod snorted with disgust. "Yes, thumping our chests like prehistoric apes. Let's just forget the whole subject." But he couldn't. "What I cannot get my mind around is that this professed socialist, is a total male chauvinist. How do these totally opposed standpoints coexist in the same mind? Is schizophrenia a part of the make-up of an educated Indian male?"

"You're forgetting that we are children of two ill-matched halves. The British pull us one way—the Indian ethos, the other. The English we meet every day have a much lesser problem, because there is a continuity in their mores and traditions. For example, the suffragist movement began in the early 20th century, women got their right to vote in 1928, and what we are seeing today is a continuation of that trend. Women are demanding their other rights—including the right to be as sexually free as men. In our country, the right to vote for women came suddenly with Independence. From being tied down to producing children and doing the cooking and cleaning, women suddenly found themselves being given the same right as the men—the right to choose their government. This was a huge step jump—a massive leap—and not a part of a continuum. The women were as shell-shocked as the men. But while some of them rejoiced, the men retreated into sullen mutiny." He paused and then continued.

"Manpreet is just one example of this simmering discontent. For him, the women have to be put back into their place. On the other hand, he has been exposed to the Western tradition—the socialist ideology. But his journey stopped right there. Free the exploited serfs, unchain the oppressed workers. But don't get carried away. The place of women is in the home. It's their natural role. Who's going to bear children? And once they are born who is going to look after them? Men have to earn their livelihood after all and feed the family."

"You almost sound as if you agree with this line of thinking."

Amar laughed. "I know you're pissed off with our friend Manpreet, but don't take it out on me! I was trying to find an explanation for his schizophrenia, as you called it."

Overture

Amar began to feel Helga's absence more acutely as her departure receded. Initially, he had guiltily admitted to a feeling of relief at being able to go back to his normal routine, away from the high-voltage few days he had spent with Helga—days which had made great demands on his emotions. He had felt emotionally exhausted and sought comfort in the day-to-day routine which he was used to, a more placid existence. But soon he began to miss her voice, her smile, her banter and most of all—her body.

He also began to notice a worrying change in the way he responded to women. Earlier, an attractive woman had usually been an object of somewhat abstract sexual longing. Now he found that he looked at the woman with the same desire, but with fantasies which were more graphic. This more vivid awareness disturbed him—it made him feel guilty and unfaithful to Helga.

He was finding that an emotional involvement with a woman did not automatically lead to a signing on to the one man–one woman charter. He had thought that this would be a programmed thing—you find a woman who is dear to you, and bang—the door would close on any further interest in other women. But this wasn't happening.

❖

Amar remembered that he had missed his usual weekly visit to Kanika's for dinner. He did not feel greatly inclined to see her, but decided to call and apologise anyway. A promise to come to dinner the next day was the price he had to pay.

"Sorry, Kay *di,* I should have rung earlier and told you I couldn't make it last week. You're not too angry are you?" Amar said as she opened the door.

"Only a little," she smiled, "But having you here makes up." She hugged him, and Amar was very conscious of the feel of her soft breasts against him. "More than me, it's your little friend you have to placate."

Buri was sulking behind a chair. Amar knelt down and hugged her. "Hey, what kind of growly face is this? Doesn't Amar Mama deserve a smile?"

"You didn't come last week," she muttered in a low voice, looking at the floor.

"What could I do – I saw a snake on the road and it reared up at me and would not allow me to move forward or backward. I don't know how long I stood there … "

Buri's interest had been aroused and she followed the story interestedly, until she saw the twinkle in Amar's eye. "There are no snakes on London streets!" she said indignantly.

Amar started laughing, "At least the growly look has gone from your face! I made up the story to get you in a better mood. But you know Buri, I actually have seen a snake on a London road. And this was in our neighbour's hedge."

Buri's curiosity was aroused. "What happened, Amar Mama?" she asked, wide-eyed.

"My neighbour called Scotland Yard."

Kanika burst out laughing. "You and your fibs."

Amar held up his hand. "No, its God's truth."

After the mandatory story, Buri was put to bed and Kanika and Amar sat down to dinner. Amar ate with relish, since Kanika was a good cook, and complimented her.

"Thank you. So, Amar, what have you been really up to? All this talk of urgent work I take with a pinch of salt!" Kanika said with a sly smirk.

"Why, what do you think I could have been up to?" Amar asked innocently.

Kanika rolled her eyes. "So much—you could have been up to so much! London is full of young women wanting a good time—and with a good-looking young man like you available, they would be stupid not to try something."

"Would you, Kay *di*, have tried something if you had been unattached in London?"

Kanika looked pensive, and her eyes seemed to focus on a distant beyond. Then slowly she came back to the present and a blush suffused her cheeks. "Yes … why not? I have never been a conventional person. I do not believe in blindly following custom. So—yes. I would have been quite willing to enjoy myself."

"Kay *di*, do you really mean it? There are not many Indian women who would say this."

Kanika bristled. "What do you mean by—'do you really mean that?'? Don't you understand that women have desires too? What's wrong with their satisfying these desires? And are Indian women biologically different from Western women?"

"No, Kay *di*, I don't believe that. But wouldn't a person have a sense of guilt going against convention?"

"What conventions? Have these been written down in stone anywhere?" she said agitatedly. "Have they been etched in the sky by a divine hand? These have all been made by ordinary human beings like you and me, Amar. They mean as much as my fixing a rule for Buri that she must wash her hands before she starts a meal. OK, so on some days she doesn't. That does not bring the sky crashing down. Deviating from some of society's rules doesn't mean the end of the world either. These are all man-made rules."

"Yet some of society's rules have some value. Without them our social order could collapse. There have to be rules to protect human life, for example. Or rules to protect individual property and individual freedom."

"Sure. That is why they have been enshrined in our constitution. These rights stand the test of time. But there are other conventions that don't, because they vary from age to age, from society to society. They are contextual and do not have universal relevance.

And sometimes they are downright laughable. Take, for example, the convention that there must be no kissing shown in our Indian films. Does this make any kind of sense? You just have to go to Khajuraho to see how irrelevant this is. This is what I mean by saying that some conventions have no relevance. Why should I feel guilty if I breach them?"

"That's wonderful—not to be bothered by guilt."

Kanika looked thoughtful. "I'm not sure that I'm completely free of it, Amar. All I can say is that I've probably got thick skin, like a callous growing over my soul, so I've probably got desensitised to it."

Amar grinned, "Ha! Got you. Callouses only grow from regular friction—so have you been sinning so often that callouses have grown?"

Kanika laughed. It was a head-thrown-back, throaty, abandoned laugh. "*Ai, dushtumi korchish* (You're being mischievous now)! But I like it! Of course I've been naughty—and I continue to want to be."

Amar leant back and then rather recklessly said, "So what's the next convention you're considering breaking?"

Her face slowly broke into a smile, and he thought there was a faint blush which appeared. "Nothing too drastic, but it requires some help from you."

Amar's heart beat faster. He felt a growing sense of nervousness, but tried not to show it. He seemed to have wandered into something which was over his head.

Kanika was enjoying herself. The smile stayed on her face. "Don't look so anxious, Amar. All I wanted to do was learn to dance. Will you teach me?"

Amar felt a mixture of relief and disappointment. He had been expecting more than this innocuous request.

"Of course, Kay *di*, I would love to. However, let me warn you, I'm no great dancer."

Kanika looked pleased. "One condition, Amar, no one—but no one, must know about this. I would really be embarrassed if anyone did. Learning dancing at my age ..."

"Why should anyone know? This is just between you and me." Amar felt a twinge of guilt as he said this. It sounded so much more intimate than just a dance class. Then, being more practical, he said, "But what about Buri?" He had a faint hope that this might be a clincher against the dance class.

"No. We'll only do it after she falls asleep. She won't wake up, as long as the music is not too loud. Why don't we try it out now?"

Amar was taken aback. "Now?" Then he collected himself. "Sure, why don't we try a few steps? Do you have any music?"

Kanika nodded. "I do. It may not be very good, but it should be okay." She got up and got out a record from a cupboard and placed it on her turntable.

Feeling as embarrassed as when he had first learnt some steps from his sister's friend, Amar got up and cleared a little space by removing a few chairs. He felt his heart beating faster than normal.

"Shall I start it?" asked Kanika, and for the first time, sounded a bit nervous.

This hesitancy on her part gave Amar some confidence, and he said, "Yes, but don't make it too loud."

She started the record player and walked hesitantly to where Amar was standing. "My God!" she exclaimed in a tremulous voice, "I'm as nervous as a school girl. Remember, Amar, I'm a complete novice."

Amar took her in his arms and murmured, "So am I."

Amar recognised the beat, and was relieved. He knew the basic steps. She had a sense of rhythm, or maybe was more experienced than she made herself out to be. After a few initial stumbles, they were able to glide to the music reasonably well. It was a slow rhythm and soon Amar found that they were dancing closer than he had planned to. He felt the warmth from her cheeks and her body which was touching his. After a while Amar's initial nervousness gave way to a sense of enjoyment. He exorcised the ghost in his mind, which said you're dancing too close, by deciding that this kind of music required close dancing. He pushed back the thoughts of Helga by saying that this was only a dance and did not compromise what he felt about her.

The music ended and they drew apart. He noticed that her cheeks were a little flushed. "You're pretty good, Kay *di*," Amar said, "certainly better than the normal beginner."

Kanika shook her head in denial.

The next number began—another slow one. This time Kanika came in to his arms without any hesitation, and Amar found himself dancing cheek to cheek with her. He could feel her breasts against him, and her soft stomach pushing against his midriff. While enjoying the sensation Amar realised, nervously, that both were now in a dangerous zone. Helga's face floated into his mind, and he decided that he must end the evening before it was too late. The music ended. They were still in each other's arms, and his body was very aware of her thighs and breasts against him. His heart was beating painfully fast.

"I've got to go now, Kay *di*, or I'll miss my last train" Amar said a little hoarsely.

She did not seem to register. Her eyes had a faraway look. Slowly she brought her focus back to him and seemed to hesitate. There was a look in her eyes which he could not read. Then a curtain seemed to come down, and she turned around and went to turn the player off. Amar felt relieved to be able to go to the corner to collect his bag and coat.

Kanika came back to see him to the door. Her face now seemed dead and empty. "See you next week, Amar," she said in a flat voice and shut the door.

PART THREE

Imagined Slight

Michaelmas term began in October and stalls were put up for the freshers in the corridor outside the library. The atmosphere was a bit like an open-air market with each stall holder shouting out his offer. Amar shared the first shift with Angela and Jane, clad in his grey trousers which had got shiny at the knees and the seat from overuse, and his tweed jacket which had now acquired patches at the elbows. He felt quite comfortable being scruffily dressed. Two years ago, he would have been embarrassed.

By the time their shift ended at lunch, Amar's voice was hoarse. Greg and Beverly and Rod relieved them, and Amar asked the girls whether they would like to keep him company at lunch. Jane pleaded another engagement, and Amar saw Angela hesitating. Raising his hand he quickly said, "I promise not to steal any of your sausages." "Though, the pudding is another matter, because I come from a part of India where anything sweet is regarded as nickable."

Angela laughed, "Of course I'll come. I was just thinking about the unfinished project which I should have completed during the holidays. We'll make it a quick meal."

"Oh, the sadness of a civilisation which imposes time limits on pleasure," Amar sighed. It was an unexpected gift—the first time by themselves after the Passfield party.

Angela laughed again and allowed herself to be led by him to the ground-floor lift. They ended up by going to the cafeteria because Angela preferred a sandwich to a hot meal.

They were both hungry after the morning's exertions and chewed on their cheese rolls in silence, surrounded by the comforting buzz of conversation. Amar broke the silence. "It's this business of selling yourself that I find tiring. I suspect you feel the same way."

Angela wasn't going to speak with her mouth full and Amar had to wait until she had finished the mouthful. "Yes, like you, I feel uncomfortable about selling anything, myself most of all."

"Yet, today, can you imagine a politician being successful without this ability? Or a businessman? Or a company executive? Or, indeed, a novelist? It's scary. We've grown up with the belief that doing something well was its own reward and acknowledgement would come automatically. But now doing something well is not enough. You gotta advertise."

"And maybe you should be doing a little of it, Am. You should be in line for your full colours in fencing, going by your performance last year. But your achievements have to get known."

Amar shook his head and replied with an embarrassed grin, "Talk about myself? Cannot do."

"Come on … you did better than anyone else. Your scores against various teams have been very good. So stop being modest."

"Angela … I have not even seriously thought about the colours so far. It would be wonderful if I do qualify, but I leave the Colours Committee to do their job. I just cannot imagine advertising myself."

"I don't expect you to do that, Am. But what the Fencing Club can do is to undertake some groundwork. For example, prepare a small report of each of their matches for the *Beaver*. Other clubs do that regularly, and I don't see why we can't grab a little space in the college paper."

"Yes, that makes sense. The club could do with a little more exposure. Good idea, Angela. I'll have a word with Greg about it. Thanks. Thanks a lot for thinking about me—my colours, I mean," he ended embarrassedly.

A brief silence followed, each conscious about this passage into personal territory.

"You know, I woke up the other morning feeling depressed because it had suddenly registered that this was my last year at the LSE. There's so much I will miss when I leave. The lectures, the library, the Fencing Club, the theatres, the art galleries, the walks in the country … but most of all my friends. Special people … like you."

As he said this, a wave of embarrassment swept over him. Saying something like this out of the blue? God! At the age of twenty-one couldn't he have been more urbane? He looked down at the table, unable to meet her eyes.

He felt a light touch on his hand and looked up. She looked serious, but her eyes were dancing with a repressed smile. "Oh, Am, your face is so transparent at times! Did you think that you had offended me by what you said? Don't you know that a woman cherishes being regarded as special? That was one of the sweetest things you could have said to me. As for this being your last year, just remember, a year is a long time."

Amar felt a huge relief. Hiding it, he mumbled, "Thanks, Angela."

He wanted the conversation to stay at the warm personal level, but was at a loss on how to continue.

"You look preoccupied, Am. Probably time for me to get back to my project."

"No, no, don't go yet," he said almost in panic. "Just stay on a bit longer and help me get out of the blue mood I seem to be getting into."

He felt guilty at playing on her sympathy. It seemed to work, though, because he saw her face soften. "Of course, I'll stay. But will you tell me why you're getting into this blue mood?"

Amar didn't know what to say. Then it all bubbled over and he found himself saying something he had not planned to. "Because, I'm not able to say what I really want to." He stopped himself, but was unable to prevent the next sentence. "Will you come to a play with me this Saturday?"

Angela looked startled. Then a smile broke through. "Oh, you *are* a crazy man, Am! You change subjects so fast! Here we were into serious stuff—and you suddenly ask me out!"

"The element of surprise. I thought I would use surprise to get you to say yes."

She looked at him with a gentle smile, but said nothing.

"So what's the answer going to be? Don't keep me in such terrible suspense—I'll have to jump out of the window if you don't hurry up, it's an old Indian custom."

Her smile widened. Then patiently, she said, "Oh Am, how can you forget! We're booked for this Saturday."

Amar looked bewildered. "Come again?"

"Hasn't Jane told you? She's planning a little get-together at her flat this Saturday?"

"She is? That's the first I've heard of it."

It was Angela's turn to look confused. "But she's supposed to have told you! She made out the list with me and you were on it. She said she'd speak to you."

"Well, she hasn't," said Amar somewhat peevishly.

"I'm sure she will," Angela responded, though a little nervously. "I'm certain she will." This time with more confidence.

This didn't improve Amar's mood which had dived into gloom. "Whatever," he replied morosely.

There was an uncomfortable silence. Angela murmured, "But there are other Saturdays."

Amar did not respond to her overture. "Yes, I suppose there are." He didn't feel in the mood to be civil. He had asked and the request had been rejected, oh, ever so delicately. Within himself he was desolate. It was as if suddenly the colour had leached out of the room, the music had suddenly stopped.

There was little left to talk about.

Amar affected a nonchalance he did not feel. "Back to the library now for me, I'm afraid. Thanks for sharing your lunch break. See you later." He got up and left.

He walked away simmering. He knew he had been rude. But the fact was, she had turned down his invitation. Anger brought with it a curious sense of exhilaration, a satisfying vindication of self.

Downstairs, he stopped at the pigeonhole to check his mail. He found a note for him addressed in unfamiliar writing. It turned out to be from Jane, inviting him to the Saturday get-together at her place.

Jane's Party

A healing night's sleep seemed to put things into perspective. What else could Angela have said, given that she was already committed? At least in her turning him down she had been inclusive—she had said, "You're forgetting we're booked for this Saturday." He really should be apologising to her.

The sun was making one of its fleeting appearances and patches of bright blue sky peeped out from behind racing white clouds, as he walked to the Willesden Green Tube station. This would normally have uplifted Amar's spirits. The need for sun in this grey foggy land was like a physical want, a bodily craving. Whenever he saw the sun, Amar wanted to rush out and exult in its warmth on his skin. Today, however, he was blind to it. As he walked along he kept kicking at pebbles on the pavement. There was a riot of conflicting thoughts jostling in his mind. Every time he thought of Angela, the thought of Helga sneaked in. Why was he allowing this adolescent crush on Angela to interfere with the much deeper relation he had with Helga?

He turned his attention to the present. How should he respond to Angela if he bumped into her? Apologise? Pretend that the previous day had not happened?

He could not make up his mind and vented his frustration on another pebble.

The tube ride did not help solve the problem, nor the walk up Kingsway to college. It was resolved by an unplanned response, as such matters often are, when he saw her in the corridor. He said a curt, "Hello," and marched on.

❖

Sitting in the library, he felt repentant. Head in hand, he brooded. But it was too late to undo the damage. He now wondered if he should go to Jane's party.

As Saturday approached, however, his mood changed to one of truculence. He was well able to manage without Angela. He was tired of this wretched man-woman game.

As he climbed up the steps to Jane's third-floor flat on Saturday, however, his mood was no longer one of truculence. He did not enjoy meeting people in groups, he was not good at social chatter, and he found parties taxing. So what was he doing here? As he rang the bell, his hands felt cold, his stomach queasy and his mind unsettled.

The no-nonsense, down-to-earth voice of Jane and her wide smile helped reduce his tension. "Ah, the wise man from the East arrives! Good to see you, Am," she said as she hugged him. "And a bottle of wine to boot! Why hadn't I invited you before?"

"Because your cellar was full, you scheming woman!" Amar smiled back. Banter seemed to come so easily with Jane. With Angela, he would have been tongue-tied.

"You beast!" Then she lowered her voice and whispered with a mischievous smile, "Just for that, I won't let you sit next to Angela!" Then taking his hand, she said, "Come and meet the other guests, most of whom you know, of course." Amar was taken aback by her reference to Angela. Was his interest so transparent?

Jane led him into a large high-ceilinged living room, very comfortably furnished. The size of the room was unusual for student digs, as was the South Kensington location. But it was hardly surprising, given her wealthy background. There were a number of people scattered around the room, some sitting on the oriental rugs which covered the wooden floor. Jane raised her voice and said, "Most of you know Amar, but for those of you who don't, meet our friend from mysterious India. He also happens to be captain of our fencing team."

Amar felt embarrassed but managed a grin. "Hello. And shortly I'll do the Indian rope trick, but first, I need some sustenance." There was scattered laughter.

"Well, let me take you to the source of sustenance," said Jane and led him by the hand to the table in the corner which had bottles and glasses.

Amar had noticed that most of the people were from the Fencing Club, one among them being Greg who had found himself a place next to Angela, much to Amar's irritation. Amar poured himself a glass of beer and made his way to an attractive girl sitting in a corner. Drawing up a chair, he asked, "Hello, may I?" She had an upswept hairstyle which emphasised her high cheekbones. And a low-cut dress which showed generous cleavage. A very sexy lady, Amar decided somewhat nervously.

She smiled and said, "Of course. I'm delighted to meet somebody from the mysterious orient."

He spread his hands in dismay. "Sadly, I've left my bag of tricks behind, and I won't be able to conjure up a handsome prince or the Taj Mahal."

She grinned impishly, "And you believe I'm in need of a handsome prince?"

"Which woman isn't? Men are no different—they're in search of the fairy-tale princess."

"But suppose I've already found my handsome prince?"

"Ah, my dear lady, then your need is even greater."

"Please explain."

"I will, but first, your name. I can't go through the evening calling you 'my dear lady'. I'm Amar."

"And I'm Priscilla. So, explain please, Amar."

Feeling sorry he had started this, Amar could not find a way out and decided to soldier ahead. "Tell me, Priscilla, if you ask all the women that you know if their relationship with their man—whether husband or boyfriend—has turned out as they expected, what do you think they would say—yes or no?"

"Well... probably 'no', but they would add a lot of qualifications."

"Such as?"

"M-m-m-m—maybe, that there are pluses and minuses. That you can never know a man properly until you've been with him for some time. So there are some good things that emerge from his personality and some which are not so attractive. In any case, when you go into a relationship you're a bit in cloud cuckoo land. The harps are playing, the sun is shining, the birds are singing and life promises an endless vista of bliss. So there will have to be disappointments, because life ain't like that."

"Brilliant. What you're saying in essence is that the answer would be 'no.'"

She didn't seem to like that, but reluctantly said, "Yes, I suppose so, if you insist on a 'yes' 'no' answer, which actually over-simplifies life."

"Right. Life is too complex, human beings too complicated. But we do build up expectations, don't we?" He continued with enthusiasm. "You know what Kahlil Gibran says? 'Every man loves two women; the one in the creation of his imagination and the other is not yet born.' The same applies to a woman. A woman, or a man, builds up this beautiful picture of the partner she wants. It's made up of a lot of elements—some as banal as the way he looks, the way he talks, the way he reacts, etc., etc. The list goes on and on to make, finally, a composite model of an ideal man. Right?"

"Well, I suppose so."

"No, Priscilla, there's no supposition here. Either women do or they don't—maybe they're not even conscious of it. So do they?"

"Okay—yes, they probably do, though not deliberately or consciously. And when they do, the picture they build up is rather hazy around the edges."

"Agreed. But the picture is built of a myriad of expectations, all fused together to form this superman. Now, do you really think any one man can live up to all these myriad expectations? Is it humanly possible? As Gibran said, we have a fictional image of a partner who is not present in this life. The one who is, we clothe with imaginary qualities which are impossible to live up to."

Priscilla looked uncomfortable, as if she was struggling between agreeing on the one hand to what seemed common sense, and on the other hand not giving in to this dehumanising logic which took away the magic from romance. Finally, she gave voice to her unease. "All right, what you say may be true. It isn't possible for a man to live up to all the expectations, yet I'm uncomfortable because you are taking away all the music from life. It would be a cold dead world if we tried to live just by logic."

"I couldn't agree with you more. But remember, the discussion began with the question of why a woman who has found her man may be in need of another prince charming. And the reason—no man can live up to the mass of expectations the woman loads him with—nor for that matter a woman who struggles under the load of expectations the man places on her—so he slips, not just once, but many times. And each time he recedes further from the ideal. Can you then see why his attractiveness also recedes for the woman?"

Priscilla thought and then nodded uneasily. "Maybe you're right. But then how do you explain all the happy marriages you see around you?"

"Happy marriages? Where? Priscilla, from the figures I remember reading, in the USA at least one in four marriages break up, or was it one in three? I don't know the figures for the UK, but I doubt they will be very different. So, if one in four marriages actually break up, there probably will be double the number which struggle through, unwilling to face the social stigma of divorce, but unhappy in their relationship all the same. So only one in four marriages may be reasonably stable—and that is a very optimistic estimate. Would you say that paints a picture of marriages being happy?"

"So what are you saying then," she said sounding peeved, "Don't get married, avoid relationships—maybe enter a convent?"

Amar shook his head. "No. No. No. Please. We weren't born to stumble through life in darkness, wondering when we could get relief from this existence. We were born to be proud and free—to enjoy the light and sing our song. All I'm suggesting is—let us be realistic and see life for what it is. Nothing in life will work out exactly as we expect it to. So, let's just not build huge expectations. Let a woman enjoy her prince charming for what he is, let the man enjoy his princess for what she is. Let's enjoy what we have. So of course we have to enjoy life. Let's savour the moment, just as I am now, talking to a very attractive woman."

As often happens at a party, there is a sudden lull in conversation when everybody falls silent, and there is only one voice. Here it was Amar's. He realised this and looked up uncomfortably, wondering how much had been heard. Just then Greg's loud voice broke the silence. "Don't believe a word of what you hear, Pris, it's the Indian spell that our Amar is trying to cast on you!" And he grinned and looked around for appreciation.

There was silence.

Then Priscilla slowly turned to face him. "I'm having a wonderful conversation with Amar, thank you. Why don't you go back to yours? And my name is Priscilla," she ended coldly turning back.

Greg seemed taken aback. He grinned weakly and said, "Ouch!" then turned to his neighbour to find a way out of his embarrassment.

Amar was embarrassed too. Partly because of Priscilla's aggression, and partly because he had not had anyone publicly standing up for him before. He did not know how to react.

He took a sip of his beer and then looked up at Priscilla. "Um—weren't you a little severe on him, Priscilla?" he asked.

She seemed quite unperturbed and Amar marvelled at the unflappability of women. If he had been in her place, he would still be fuming with anger. She on the other hand, smiled and said calmly, "I don't like nosy parkers nor do I like unsolicited advice."

He looked worried and said, "Phew … then, I've been skating on very thin ice!"

She smiled serenely, "No, it was solicited advice, so you are safe." The tension seemed to dissipate.

She was lost in thought for a while. Then she asked him, "Do you really believe in all that you've said?"

"What, that I'm enjoying talking to an attractive woman? Of course I believe in it—loving every minute of it!"

She smiled, "Not that, you ass. Everything else you said."

Amar did not reply immediately. He thought for a while and then said quietly, "You've got me. The ideas make sense to me. But … but … I have to say, they make me uncomfortable. I'm still a novitiate."

Priscilla heaved a sigh of relief and grinned, "Thank God! You belong to this earth, after all. I was getting worried about being in conversation with an ethereal being!"

Amar looked alarmed and suddenly extended his hand, "Quick, feel my hand—it's there, isn't it? It hasn't dematerialised, has it?"

Priscilla laughed and held his hand and then released it with a little slap, "You're quite a practised man about town, aren't you? And you look so innocent!"

Amar joined in her laughter. "I wish I were a man about town, Priscilla. But believe me, I'm as green as they come."

"You're sure you don't have a long list of girlfriends in your phone book?"

"Now, that is flattery! Sadly, my dear Priscilla, my phone book is as blank as a baby's conscience."

"I don't believe it."

"Well, actually, there is someone I'm very fond of, but she lives in faraway Germany."

"Ah—h—h, now we're getting somewhere."

Just then Jane came by, "I see you're monopolising my friend from Oxford, Am. I hope you've convinced her that she should get away from that backward rural university and come to where it's all happening. Your glass is empty, do get yourself another drink. Pris, come and meet some other friends."

With that she bustled away and Priscilla, rising with a resigned smile on her face, shrugged and followed. Amar smiled too. Jane, as always, dominating and wanting to be in charge. At the moment he was feeling happy. He knew that he had made an impression on Priscilla, and also realised that he had not thought about Angela, although she had been only a few feet away sitting with the odious Greg. Maybe he was not as obsessed with Angela as he had feared.

He sighed and decided to forget these complications and made his way to the bar.

❖

It was much later in the evening. A number of people had said their farewells and gone. The core remained. Amar had been chatting with a couple of people near the drinks table and then gone to the loo. On his return he decided to join the main group, most of whom were now lounging on the carpet. He found Angela sitting on the carpet with her back propped against a sofa. With his head on her lap, lay Greg.

Amar stood still for a moment and then chose a low stool to sit on, swept by an unreasoning anger. His mind told him that he himself had ignored Angela the whole evening, apart from a perfunctory few words, and lavished attention on Priscilla. He could, now, hardly complain. Also, Greg had been humiliated and needed to get his own back. So, what was happening should not surprise him. But his emotions held sway, not reason. They raged at Angela.

The party was at that stage where, thanks to the liberating effect of alcohol, conversation often turns to matters which were usually regarded as *passé* among senior students.

God was being discussed, a tired subject in Amar's view. But as is often the case with such topics, very passionate responses were being aired. Amar sipped his drink and nursed his anger, which had now turned to Greg.

Jane decided to draw him into the conversation. "What do you think, Amar?" This after a passionate harangue from Greg about the need to have a belief in God.

"About what?" Amar responded listlessly.

"About God, Amar," she replied a little impatiently.

"Oh, that poor harassed man?"

Greg bristled. "You're talking about a presence that brings succour to millions."

Amar woke up. He asked Greg, "If you've caught a cold walking unprotected in the rain, would you take medication?"

"Of course," an irritated Greg replied.

"If you've eaten and drunk to excess at a party, would you come home and have a digestive?"

This time Greg frowned as he said "I suppose so … but what has all this to do with religion?"

"Patience. Some of the people you know, smoke. When they get a sore throat and start coughing do they seek some medication to relieve the discomfort?"

"Of course they do. I can't see the relevance of all this …"

"Well, it's simple really. I believe that people treat God like an anti-misfortune tablet. They will be immoderate or intemperate in their actions and then rush to the church or temple to ask God to get them out of the mess that their actions have got them into. They swallow the biggest pill of all—the God pill, in the hope that absolution will follow."

There was a disapproving silence. Amar was, however, past caring. Then Priscilla spoke. "There are people who lead disciplined lives and still go to church. How will you fit them into your categorisation?"

"Oh, they are the cleverer ones who believe in preventive medicine—they take the advance God pill by entering into this contract—I'll go to church every Sunday, please make sure nothing untoward happens to me."

A displeased Jane said, "Thank you. My family and I go to church every Sunday."

Amar shrugged. "Sorry, Jane, but you asked me my view."

Greg now intervened. "OK. Forget about the normal churchgoer. There are people who devote their life to religion without asking for anything in return. What about them?"

"You're not going to like this, but you asked the question. The people you mention are those who truly play it safe. They are the life termers who enter into a long-term contract with God by promising to suppress all their God-given desires for their entire life, in return for a promise of eternal salvation. If they are not asking for something in this life, they're registering their demand for the next world. Or, they're asking for something for someone else, in a great act of self-sacrifice. But it is asking just the same, it is a contract just as the others are. They swallow the God pill daily—morning, noon and night. So you see what it all boils down to? A kind of pact with God—you look after me and I'll do obsequies to you. You remove my pain and I'll sing hosannas to you. You smooth my path and I'll sweep your temple floor with my hair."

Greg shook his head. "Sorry, but this is utter nonsense."

Amar's smile had disappeared and he leant forward earnestly. "Do you believe that God is all-powerful and all-loving?"

"Of course—that's why he is God," Greg replied condescendingly.

"But here's the rub. Do you know the old Greek paradox? It questions this hypothesis. It says that God cannot be all-powerful as well as all-loving. God is either all-powerful or all-loving. Not both. An all-loving, all-powerful God would extend his love to everybody and would protect everybody. But then how do you explain an infant being crushed under the wheels of a car?"

"Is it because God is not all-powerful?" he continued. "Or is it because, while being all-powerful, he is not all-loving? There has really been no satisfactory answer, in the Western world, to this paradox. And until there is, the kind of pact that people make with God seems even sadder. For what's the point of entrusting your life to someone who has no power to protect you, or if he has the power, no inclination to save you?"

Angela joined in, seeming somewhat shocked. She asked, "So are you saying that there is nobody who worships God without an ultimate motive?"

"No, there are people of wisdom in this world. There are individuals who are unselfish, there are some who have transcended petty concerns. However, these rare individuals have not reached their understanding by necessarily believing in an external God.

They have found their God within themselves—they have found a profound source of wisdom in themselves and in their relationship with the world around them."

Jane said, "I'm not sure I'm comfortable with the idea of a godless world. It makes me feel panicky and anchorless."

Amar nodded sympathetically. "I understand. Sorry, Jane, these are just my beliefs. You don't have to accept any of them."

❖

Most of the people had left, including Greg.

Jane got up. "I think it's time for another round of drinks. Okay, people, get yourselves to the bar—or if the men feel especially gallant, they can help the ladies."

Amar got up and ambled towards Angela, checking to see if his step was steady enough. "Can I get you a drink, Angela?"

"No thanks, I've drunk enough for the evening."

"I've wanted to talk to you, but there was never any space for an interloper," Amar said.

Angela's smile as she replied was not entirely warm. "Those who want something usually make the effort."

"You're right, I suppose," Amar said tiredly. "I'm going to get myself a last drink."

Angela looked concerned as she said, "Am, do you think you … ?" and then stopped.

He was touched by her concern, but equally sure that he was all right. "Don't worry, Angela, I'm not drunk."

He thought he saw her shrug, but by then he was moving to the bar area.

❖

Amar was now feeling a euphoria, a conviction that he was on the edge of great truths. If he could only take that final eventful step. He sat slumped against a chair, not far from Angela.

By now, there was a pause in the half-hearted conversation.

Amar, in whom an accumulated sense of frustration had been welling up, finally gave voice to it. "You know, the trouble with us," he mused, "the trouble with us … is we have chosen to live stunted lives, anaemic existences … one of your great poets recognised this when he lamented that life was measured out with coffee spoons … that's what we're doing, living life parsimoniously."

He continued after a pause, but this time he seemed to be muttering to himself. "We've lost those magnificent gestures, the gigantic dipping into the chalice of life, the extravagant flourish, the true generosity of spirit. Why have they disappeared? If I was a writer, I would pour my soul out in my writings and sweep away the reader with the cadence of my words. If I was a painter, I would take a huge canvas and paint it wildly in the most brilliant of colours and challenge the sun and the moon and the sky. If I was a musician, I would send my music soaring to the heavens and have the universe aquiver. Yet, what I do, what I sadly do, is live life in a tiny, cramped corner of my own creation. It is so small that I cannot spread my wings. It is so confined that I cannot fly …"

Nobody spoke for a while. The late-night bus rumbled by. Finally Priscilla broke the silence. "You obviously like T.S. Eliot."

"You recognised the quote," he smiled at her, bleary-eyed.

Jane broke in, "I can sense your longing for expression, Am. But why don't you do something about it? Paint, write or play music?"

"You're right, Jane … you're right. Nail on the head. Why do I just lament? Why not do something about it? That's where I've failed. I do not listen to the wild bird's song. I listen, instead, to the caged bird's chant."

❖

He suddenly seemed to wake up. He looked at his watch in alarm. "God, I'd totally lost count of time. I think I may have missed my last train home."

This roused the others too and they all stirred. “Where do you have to get to, Am?” Jane asked.

“Well, I need to get to a Bakerloo line station.”

One of the men, called Peter, said, “Hang on, I’ll be driving past Marble Arch—maybe I can drop you there. It should be possible to get on to the Bakerloo line from there.”

“Thanks, Peter. That would be fine. If nothing else I can get a bus from there.”

Jane broke in. “Am, if the worst comes to the worst you can spend the night on the divan here. So, if you don’t feel like chancing the bus, you’re welcome to stay.”

Amar was touched. “Thanks, Jane. Thanks a lot. But I’ll be okay, honest.”

The farewells were said. Amar followed Peter to his car.

❖

When they reached Marble Arch, Amar said a hurried “Thank you” and sprinted for the bus stand. But it was too late, the last bus had left. He now faced the daunting task of walking home, a distance of over four miles, through some not very salubrious areas. Since he did not have money for a taxi, there really was no option.

He took a deep breath and looked down Edgware Road. It was a chilly October night. The coloured lights of the neon signs above the closed shops glinted on the wet pavements in their magenta, red and blue. Beyond, the valley of darkness stretched. He reassured himself that he felt fit and strong, tightened his coat around himself and started on his walk. He realised that it would be past two in the morning before he reached home and rang his mother from the next phone booth he passed. He told her he was going to be dropped home by a friend, but could be a bit late because he wasn’t sure when his friend would leave. His mother had sounded worried, but he had reassured her.

As he walked, some of the nervousness he had felt earlier left him. There were still some people about. A few walking their dog, some shift workers making for the late-night cafe for a cup of tea and a sandwich.

His thoughts returned to the party. He had obviously made an impression on Priscilla. But not on Angela. His mind played back the party, dwelling at length on the pleasanter parts, but inevitably going back to the more brash statements he had succumbed to.

❖

A cold wind and the change in surroundings brought his mind back to the present realities. He had comfortably traversed the Maida Vale area and was now in Kilburn, one of the less salubrious parts of London. A number of the street lamps were not working, the buildings were dark, the shadowed shopfronts looked bleak and unfriendly, the walls with bare bricks showing through were covered with graffiti. Amar felt a growing nervousness. There was hardly anyone to be seen on the street except for what looked like a group of Teddy Boys on his side of the pavement, a couple of hundred yards ahead. He slowed his steps and quietly crossed to the other side, hugging the shadows. They had not noticed him, and he was relieved, though he quickened his steps.

A little further on he saw a bulky figure approaching him. There was not enough light to see him clearly. Amar kept walking with muscles involuntarily tensing up. As he got closer, he saw the figure was wearing a battered hat, a grubby coat and carrying something in his hand. Amar's heart beat faster. The man's face was unshaven, he was muttering to himself. He raised a bottle to his lips and shambled on in the darkness looking for a doorway to shelter in from the cold night wind, leaving behind the sour smell of unwashed body, stale beer and loneliness. Amar's tightened muscles relaxed.

He came to Willesden Lane, which he was tempted to turn into since the name carried with it the comfort of the known. But he knew this was the longer route. He had to find Mapesbury Road where he should turn left. He continued along Kilburn

High Road, which then became Shoot Up Hill Road. By now he was bone-tired, and wondering if he had missed his turning. He continued doggedly and finally was rewarded with a sign which said Mapesbury Road. From here it was a short distance to Exeter Road which led to Teignmouth Road, his final destination.

As he neared the house, he worried about waking his parents up. It was close to 2.30 am. He unlocked the door, and tip-toed up the stairs praying that the floorboards would not creak.

Dicing with Desire

Friday came and it was time for Amar's weekly dinner visit to Kanika. He was not looking forward to it. He had begun feeling that there were too many swirls and eddies in his relationship with her. He was not sure of what she wanted, but recognised the sexual attraction he felt. He had to remind himself that she was a married woman, and worse, a friend of the family.

Buri greeted him as warmly as ever. "You should actually come more frequently than once a week. I get no chance to be with you, because as soon as you finish your story, Ma puts me to sleep."

"So now, what story shall we have today, a man-eating tiger one?"

"Yes, yes!" Buri said excitedly, "a man-eater!"

"In the hills of Kumaon ..."

By the time the story ended, Buri's eyes were as big as saucers. "So it was the wrong tiger shot in the beginning because they thought it was the man-eater?"

"Sadly, yes. But as you saw, the man-eater was killed in the end."

"That was a good story, Amar Mama." Then looking around to see if her mother was listening, she whispered, "Do you think you can slip in another short story? Ma doesn't know this one is finished."

But, she had underestimated the hearing abilities of her mother who had been fussing around the stove. "I heard that, Buri. No, you've had your share, now time for bed."

Buri went off grumbling. "Sit, sit," said Kanika sinking down into a sofa. "God! I'm tired. Thank God that tomorrow is a Saturday! So tell me all about the fun you've been having. Let me live vicariously."

Amar sat down in the sofa next to hers. He was close enough to catch a whiff of her sweaty but musky odour, and found it disturbing. He wondered again why he had let himself get into this situation.

"Do you enjoy yourself only when you're young? You're making the post-youth phase sound very daunting."

"No, no. I didn't mean that at all. I'm not your age any more, but I like to enjoy myself—and do."

"Kay *di* … so are you going to admit to indiscretions now?" Amar asked.

"What indiscretions, Amar? If you're young, it's called an adventure. If you're older, it's called an indiscretion? What's the difference? Is it just because I'm married? You know my views on marriage—certified sex, as somebody has called it. You're allowed to produce babies without society's disapproval." She paused and looked thoughtful. "No, I wish I had indiscretions to tell you about. Sadly, I don't."

Amar did not believe her. He felt she had been on the brink of telling him something and then stepped back at the last minute. He recalled that on one of his evenings here, the doorbell had rung while he was telling Buri a story. Kanika had opened the door. He heard a male voice which sounded familiar. Through the partly open door he caught a glimpse of the man. It was Dipak, the middle-aged Lothario from the LSE. He heard a muffled argument and then Kanika said, "No, not now, I'm busy." She had shut the door. Amar remembered being surprised that she knew him, but had not raised the topic.

They chatted desultorily for some time. She seemed preoccupied. He was uncomfortable at the thought of what might follow dinner.

"Let me get dinner on the table before you start complaining that I'm starving you."

Amar ate, but not with his usual gusto.

After they had done the washing up, she broached the subject he had been dreading. "So, are we going to have the second dance lesson today?"

Amar's heart fell. This business of erotic Russian roulette was proving too taxing for him. Yet, he could think of no way of backing away. So, with an enthusiasm he was far from feeling, he said, "But of course—as long as Buri is fast asleep." Like a little girl, and with an air of complicity, she tip-toed across to the curtain and peeped in, and then nodded her head.

Initially, as the music started, both were stiff and self-conscious. But then the soft music worked its magic, and soon Amar found himself dancing close to her. She danced with her eyes closed, lost in her own private world. But her warm body was very much alive. He found himself guiltily enjoying it.

But, before long, he realised that they were skating dangerously near the edge. This game of sexual brinkmanship could easily get out of control. He recognised that his body wanted it to. Yet he knew he had to stop.

"I need to get back, Kay *di*, there is an assignment I have to sit down and complete tonight, because I'm meeting my tutor tomorrow."

"Tomorrow? But tomorrow is a Saturday. Who is this crazy tutor who works on a Saturday?"

"They don't usually work on Saturdays, but he has to go out of town next week for a lecture. So he is trying to finish pending work over the weekend." Lies following lies.

Kanika was not convinced, and seemed displeased. Her face hardened. "Well, it's up to you. I had thought that this being the beginning of a weekend we could have spent more time together. Anyway, please yourself."

As he walked out of the door, Amar decided that he could not continue with this charade any more. It was taking too much of a toll on him.

The next week he rang up and made an excuse for not being able to visit. She sounded cold and distant.

Kanika's Allegation

With winter round the corner, a watery sun had made an appearance. It had encouraged Amar to drag the folding canvas chair out to the garden. The apple tree had shed some time ago and the damp blackening leaves carpeted the grass. There was a chill in the air, but it was bracing. Autumn brought with it its own melancholic charm, of memories which had lost their sharp edges and returned more rounded and gentle. There was the feeling of an end, but also the promise of a new beginning.

It was while he was in this gentle reverie that his sister called out to him that there was a phone call. It was Kanika. She sounded aloof, but went through the required polite chatter. Finally, she said that there was something important she wanted to discuss with him and could he please come next week. Amar agreed to go on the following Tuesday.

He went back to the garden, but the enchantment had faded from the morning. He wondered whether her summons had been prompted by the same need to terminate things. Yes, that was why she had asked him to come.

Had she begun feeling that he had been coming on to her? This thought caused Amar deep embarrassment—the thought that he could have been seen as making overtures to a married woman, and that too, a friend of the family. He cringed at the thought.

❖

Tuesday evening saw Amar ringing the bell at the flat. He had the hollow feeling in his stomach which came before the beginning of a difficult examination paper.

Kanika let him in. She seemed unaffected and chatted casually about the weather. But he sensed a slight unease. Her bantering was absent.

Buri ran and clung to his legs. Amar felt a sense of relief at this gesture of normality.

Kanika said, "Buri, only a short story today from Amar Mama. You've got school tomorrow." Buri grimaced but said nothing. She had obviously been spoken to earlier by Kanika.

Amar seemed to see the evening unfold without being a part of it. He told Buri her story, watched her being put to bed, helped Kanika lay the table and heat up the dinner, engaged in idle chatter over dinner and helped with the clearing up. Inside, he could feel a knot becoming tighter and tighter. So when they finally sat down after dinner he was almost relieved that a resolution was at hand.

Kanika seemed a little pale, but her voice was steady. "Why are you so tense, Amar? You haven't been your normal self. Is anything wrong?"

"No, nothing. Just the usual pressures at college."

"Everything okay at home?"

Amar was now getting edgier. He wanted the whole thing to be over quickly, so that he could go back to his normal life. "Yes, why shouldn't they be?" he asked a little tersely.

"You don't have to be so touchy, Amar. I only have the welfare of you and your family at heart."

She paused for a while, then with a sigh began again.

"Actually, it's your family that I wanted to talk to you about." Here it comes, thought Amar. A lecture on how a family should not be let down by the errant behaviour of their college-going son. He steeled himself. "It's something I feel very embarrassed to talk about with you, Amar. You know how fond I am of you—I didn't want to hurt you in anyway. But I think there is something you should know." Amar waited for the axe to fall. How young men should behave with married women, etc., etc. He did not say anything, wanting to get it done with swiftly.

"You know, there is this friend of yours called Kamal, who visits you all quite often?"

Kamal was somebody Amar knew from his Delhi days. His family had been friendly with Amar's, but Amar and he were not close. He had come to London for some diploma course and taken a room in Kilburn. Because of the old connections he would often drop in and stay for a meal. Usually, Amar would never be at home when he came, but Kamal seemed quite happy chatting with his mother or Chotku.

"Yes, he does drop in occasionally. What about him?"

"Did you know he is a homosexual?"

This came as a shock to Amar. "Where did you get this information from, Kay *di*? It's probably so much gossip."

"Sadly, it's not gossip. Somebody's son had an unpleasant experience with him. That is why I felt I should warn you."

Amar laughed, relieved that it wasn't what he had been afraid of. "Don't worry, I'm quite capable of looking after myself. I don't think he poses a threat to me."

Kanika sighed exasperatedly. "It's not you I'm worried about, Amar. It's your brother. They always pick on the innocent boys. Already people are talking about it."

"Talking about what?" Amar asked sharply.

"I knew you would get angry. But I thought you must know, however unpopular it might make me."

"Know what, Kay *di*—what?" Amar asked, not hiding his irritation anymore.

Kanika hesitated, as if she was unsure whether to proceed. Then she said, "People are talking about your brother and Kamal."

Amar felt the anger rise in him, as much as for what she had said as for the fleeting glimpse of cruelty he had seen in her eyes. "And you listen to all this gossip? Believe in it? I'm really surprised at you. You should throw this kind of filth out of the window when you hear it. You should be defending my brother rather than encouraging this kind of character defamation. Don't you women have anything better to do than wallow in muck?"

Kanika appeared to be startled by Amar's vehemence. "No, no, don't misunderstand me. I'm not implying anything about Chotku. But, there are these rumours afloat, and I thought you should know."

"Why?" Amar was still fuming and unwilling to let her off the hook.

She seemed taken aback. "Because … because … it's not nice to hear these things said about families you are friendly with …"

"So squash these rumours when you hear them. Why transmit them?"

"For heaven's sake, Amar, don't start blaming me for something your brother might have done. I was only trying to do you a favour by warning you. If you don't want to hear it, forget I said anything!"

"What do you mean by 'what your brother might have done'? Let's get this straight. He—did—not—do—anything. DID NOT. Is that clear? He has enough girlfriends hanging around him to leave me with no doubt about his sexual orientation. And you can tell your friends that, when the vultures next sit around to feed off carrion."

He got up angrily, collected his coat and briefcase and made his way to the door. As he opened it, he got a glimpse of Buri's frightened face peering from behind the curtain. The angry voices must have disturbed her. Amar tried to muster a smile and a cheery wave as he closed the door.

❖

His anger abated a little as he walked to the Tube station in the bleak, steel cold night. He knew why he had overreacted. He had seen something in her eyes. A smug satisfaction at having drawn blood. It was almost as if she was seeking some kind of revenge, a reprisal for his having stopped his visits.

He now had to decide what to do. If Kamal was in fact gay, Chotku needed to be spared his attention. Now that he thought of it, there was something effeminate in his mannerisms. And why should someone in his twenties feel the need to spend so much time with a young boy just entering his teens?

He would have to tell his parents about this, because the rumour would ultimately reach them, but hated the idea of having to do it. He reluctantly got out of the train at Willesden Green.

A renewed wave of anger towards Kanika swept over him. She was no longer the sultry siren of his fantasies, but a tired, middle-aged woman with dark circles under her eyes, and darker motives in her soul.

He wanted time. He walked home as slowly as possible. The ten-minute walk ended, and he was at the front door with his heart beating wildly. Pori answered the door and her smiling face heightened his discomfort.

His mother was in the kitchen putting the dinner things away and humming to herself. He made his way upstairs and heard his father in his bedroom. He decided that he must take the plunge now, before his resolve failed.

His father was looking for his pyjamas in the cupboard. He turned around when Amar entered and then went back to his search.

"Baba, there's something urgent I have to talk to you about."

His father frowned, "Can't it wait till tomorrow? I'm tired and want to get to sleep."

Amar steeled himself. "No, it can't. There is something that I've heard, which Ma and you must know about."

Irritated, his father turned. "Make it short, I am exhausted."

"I'll call Ma."

When she came up, puffing with the effort of climbing the stairs, Amar made them sit down. He then repeated the conversation with Kanika.

His father burst out spluttering, "I'll—I'll—I'll—sue them. I'll take them to court for spreading such malicious falsehoods. I'll—I'll—make them pay for making these dastardly allegations against my family …"

His mother was even more agitated. She had turned red with anger. "What does Kanika mean by spreading such nasty rumours? Hasn't she got any loyalty towards us? Maligning my innocent son like this! I thought she came from a good family. I don't want to have anything more to do with her."

It took him some time to calm them down.

"I always thought this fellow, Kamal, was a bit odd. Always wanting to spend time with Chotku, and coming here at times that Amu is not here. After all, he is supposed to be Amu's friend, not Chotku's," his mother said. "There is another thing—some things have been disappearing from the house. There is a valuable old pen I can't find, your rucksack vanished … I think he's involved. And then—what about Chotku's new tennis racquet's strings being slashed? It was lying in his room, and the only outside person who goes to the room, apart from the maid, is Kamal."

"Just get a night's sleep, both of you. I'll have a chat with Chotku, and find out if he has anything to say."

His mother looked worried. "You're usually so hard on Chotku."

Amar closed his eyes, took a deep breath and then said as quietly as he could, "Just trust me to handle him, okay? Stop getting so worked up. Nothing earth-shaking has happened. We all know that Chotku is not involved in anything unpleasant. So just get a night's rest now."

❖

He got a chance to talk to Chotku the next evening when he was in his room studying. "Chotku, sorry, I shouldn't be disturbing you while you're studying, but there was something urgent I needed to talk to you about. Won't take long."

Chotku looked up apprehensively. Amar grinned and reassured him. "No, no, this is not one of Chorda's lectures. Relax. Actually, I wanted some information from you about Kamal. We're still trying to understand who damaged your tennis racquet. Now Kamal spends a lot of time in your room, doesn't he?"

"He's a strange fellow. Even when I'm not here, he comes into my room. I don't know why."

"That's what we're trying to understand, Chotku. He also likes to spend time talking to you, doesn't he?"

"Not only that, he tries to grab hold of my hand whenever he can. I've pushed him away quite a few times. I've a feeling that he's queer. I don't like him."

Amar was taken aback at Chotku's uninhibited reference to homosexuality. Obviously the school milieu was different from the one Amar had grown up in.

"I'm glad you're sharing this with me, Chotku. Has he behaved oddly in any other way?"

Chotku grinned in a way which belied his tender years. "You mean has he tried to get fresh with me? Not likely. He knows he would get a thrashing from me if he tried." Chotku had an athletic build and would probably have been quite capable of it.

"Good for you. He is a strange character, and maybe he is queer. That may be no fault of his, but as long as he doesn't pester others, it's really his business."

"Chorda, how can you take such a tolerant attitude with this kind of behaviour? It's not normal. He should be given a sound public beating to make sure he mends his ways."

"You can't judge people so harshly, Chotku," Amar said gently. "Nobody is quite sure how people become homosexual, there are a lot of theories doing the rounds. But most seem to agree that it's not just an acquired habit, like say, smoking. Maybe it's an orientation that they can't do anything about. Would you beat someone up just because they have, say—blonde hair?"

Chotku was dismissive. "How can you say this is the same thing? Queers are abnormal people. People with blonde hair are just born that way."

"That's just what I'm saying. It may be that the homosexuals are just born that way, and it's no fault of theirs. Anyway, as far as Kamal is concerned, I think there are additional complications. So it's best that we keep a distance from him."

“How are we going to do that if he just barges in as he has been doing?”

“We’ll work something out. Don’t worry,” Amar said.

He told his parents about his chat with Chotku. His mother was appalled that Kamal had tried to hold Chotku’s hand. His father growled, “People like this should be put in jail,” and kept pacing up and down the bedroom to work off his anger.

❖

Amar arranged to meet a surprised Kamal, at a coffee house on Kingsway the next afternoon after his lectures were over.

He reached early and took a window table, wishing he didn’t have to go through this ordeal. While he felt a distaste, he could not summon up a strong sense of anger. Could a homosexual help responding to his deepest urges any more than a heterosexual could?

Kamal hadn’t turned up by the appointed time. In a moment of weakness, Amar considered waiting no longer. But then, through the window, he saw his slightly mincing walk. He had a round plump face, narrow sloping shoulders, and broad hips. He looked a little worried.

After the usual pleasantries had been exchanged, Amar said, “There’s a serious matter I have to discuss with you, Kamal.”

Kamal seemed to pale a little but said nothing. He stirred his coffee.

“There’s a rumour going round the Bengali circles about a nasty relationship between Chotku and you.”

Kamal did not look at him, nor did he respond immediately. Finally he said “What? You—you can’t possibly believe in such horrible rumours.”

“Well, whether I believe it or not is immaterial. My family has heard about it, and God knows how many of our acquaintances. So my brother has been branded a homosexual through no fault of his.”

Kamal did not say anything. He seemed to be looking at the side wall.

Amar ploughed on. "Look, Kamal, I don't have anything against homosexuals, but a lot of people do. For my parents, this has been a very heavy blow. I don't want an opportunity for more fodder to be created to feed this rumour. So I'll have to ask you to stop visiting us." It was finally out. Amar felt an intense discomfort. He was sitting in judgement for an unproven crime on, maybe, an unoffending individual. But a visceral dislike for Kamal took over and justified his action.

There was a long silence during which Kamal looked out of the window. He finally said, "So you're ending a long friendship on the basis of unsubstantiated rumours."

"Well, friendship carries with it certain responsibilities."

"And in what way have I fallen short, pray?" Kamal asked, seeming to regain his confidence.

His tone irked Amar. "Do you really want to know? Then let me tell you. Chotku had been given a brand new tennis racquet. He used to leave it in his room. Then suddenly one day it was found slashed. Nobody would go to his room but you. I had a very nice rucksack in my room. That disappeared. Do you want me to go on?"

Kamal pushed his chair back angrily. "I'm not going to listen to any more of this nonsense. Why don't you ask your dear brother why he used to sidle up to me whenever I was in his room?"

Amar controlled himself. "You'd better go, before I lose my temper."

Ordeal

Ten days later, Amar's mother had a heart attack.

Amar knew nothing about it until he returned from college. Pori had come back from school to find her mother looking unwell. She complained of chest pains a little later and asked Pori to ring the doctor. Fortunately, the doctor was available and came to the house without delay. He called for an ambulance and rushed her to the local hospital. Amar's father arrived at the hospital as fast as he could. Her condition had stabilised by then.

Amar sat in a daze as he listened to Pori bringing him up to date. He wanted to rush to see her, but it was past visiting hours. His mind seemed unable to grasp what had happened. He slumped at the kitchen table with his head in his hands. His mind felt like an inferno, with fear and guilt burning fiercely in it. Why had he told his parents about the Kamal rumour? He could have discreetly dealt with it on his own. And now his mother was on the verge of death.

Pori got him a cup of tea which lay cooling in front of him. At her repeated prompting he finally took a sip. He had to control his panic, he realised, before it spread to the rest of the family.

His father returned from the hospital that evening looking exhausted. "She's all right—all right," he muttered, taking off his coat. The doctors had assured him that the worst was over, but she had to be kept under observation for some time. He sat in the drawing room gazing unseeingly at the wall. It was the gloomiest of all the rooms because of the drab olive walls and heavy brown drapes. Amar put on all the lights to make it a little more cheerful. His father seemed to have aged suddenly. The skin on his face hung loosely from the bones. His neck seemed thinner as it stood out from his loose collar. His eyes looked stricken.

"How did this happen to her—how did this happen …" he kept muttering and shaking his head. Amar realised that Pori was standing in the room. "Pori, why don't you make Baba a cup of tea?"

Amar tried to comfort him with reassurances he himself did not believe. "Baba, Ma's attack is now a thing of the past. It's over. She's on the recovery path now. We have to look ahead—we have to think of how to make Ma's recovery more comfortable."

This seemed to bring his father out of his reverie. "Yes, yes, we have to make her more comfortable. She is in a general ward," he said with some disgust. "She has no privacy, just a curtain to separate her from the next patient. And the stupid nurse has the gall to call her 'dearie.'" His indignation would have been comical in other circumstances. "I'm going to move her into a private nursing home tomorrow. I want her to have the best treatment possible."

Then he began brooding again. After a while he said, almost to himself and Amar had to strain to hear, "My fault … my fault … too strict with her … not been able to give her the kind of life she was used to in her father's house. I should have seen this coming. I should have made it easier for her to talk to me … let her indulge herself a little. But where could I find the money to indulge her? I had my sisters to be taken care of on my limited salary. What could I do?" he whispered in desperation. He coughed and cleared his throat. Then took out his handkerchief ostensibly to wipe his glasses, but surreptitiously he quickly wiped his eyes.

"No," he continued in a more stable voice, as if noticing Amar's presence for the first time. "I wish God had punished me instead of her. The poor woman is suffering in a dingy general ward …" and here his voice broke. But he recovered quickly. "She'll be out of there by tomorrow. I promise you, she'll be out of there by tomorrow."

Pori came in with the tea. He did not seem to notice and sat gazing into the darkness through the French window.

"Baba, have your tea. Pori and I will organise dinner." He escaped into the kitchen unable to watch his strong father break down.

❖

His mother's recovery was steady in spite of her childlike defiance of the doctor's instructions.

On her first day back home from the hospital Amar heard muted voices from her room. His mother was talking to Kishan Singh.

"... and buy haddock or cod, no other fish, you understand. We'll need some meat too. Don't buy New Zealand lamb—you remember the last time we cooked it how smelly it was. Get some English lamb. Have you got any vegetables in the house? No?" She sighed.

Aghast, Amar rushed in. "Ma, what's going on? You'd promised to stay away from household matters. Don't you realise how seriously ill you've been? The recovery process will take time, the doctor's told you that. And you have to take complete rest, the doctor's told you that too. Why don't you understand?"

"I'm not exerting myself. All I'm doing is getting things in order once again. I had a look at the fridge and it's full of small dishes of stale food. There was no meat or fish in the deep freezer. There were no vegetables apart from some shrivelled specimens at the bottom of the fridge. The kitchen looks a mess—the maid hasn't been cleaning the window panes. All I'm doing is getting things organised."

Amar tried to look serious in spite of the laughter bubbling up inside. "Ma, you went to the kitchen before coming up? Weren't you supposed to come straight up to the bedroom?"

She looked like a little girl caught with her hands in the cookie jar. She tried to bluster her way out. "In my own house I can't go to my kitchen? I went for a few minutes, anyway. You and your father don't know anything about running a household. Just leave me alone now, while I finish giving Kishan his list."

Amar sighed and said, "All right, five minutes is all you get. And no more getting involved with the household."

❖

However difficult she was being, having her back lightened the atmosphere in the house. The children, though perfectly capable of looking after themselves, found a kind of pleasure in pestering her with trivialities.

Chotku would complain, "Ma, I can only find one of my white socks, the other one is missing."

She would summon Pori and say, "Pori, why don't you help your little brother find his other sock—he will be in trouble in school otherwise."

Pori would put on a disgusted expression and say, "My little brother is old enough to find his own socks. Why doesn't he look in all the drawers?" And sure enough it would be found in one of the drawers.

Or Pori would go to her and say, "Ma, can you do a bun for me?" And their mother would take the comb and start brushing Pori's hair, exclaiming "My God! When did you last wash your hair Pori? It's filthy—see that you shampoo it today when you get back."

Amar, after his initial concern about this kind of pestering, soon realised that this was a way for the children to reach out to the comforting presence of a mother. More importantly, it brought his mother back into the mainstream in not-too-strenuous a fashion, by feeling wanted. The doctor had told them that the most important part of the healing process was the gradual reintroduction to normal routine. So he joined the game.

"Ma, there's a button missing from my shirt and I don't have any other clean shirt to wear!" complained Amar, although in other circumstances he would have quickly stitched the button on himself.

"O-o-f … I don't know how you people coped when I was away," she exclaimed in exasperation. "Get me the needle box and my glasses. You so-called modern children are as helpless as your father."

Amar hid his grin as he handed her his shirt and the needle box. She looked at the collar with a grimace. "Is this how you wash your clothes? Just look at that ring of grime around the collar!"

"Ma, you don't understand. That ring of grime is the badge of an undergraduate. You'll be considered an imposter if you had clean collars. Our student's union has a collar inspection every week," he said with a straight face.

"Yes, yes, and elephants fly and the Queen does the rock and roll. Give me the shirt tomorrow so that I can ask the maid to do a proper scrubbing."

As they sat at dinner on the third day, Amar heard the stairs creak. He thought it was Kishan Singh and went back to his chapattis and *keema* curry, a particular favourite of his. Looking up, he saw Pori staring through the door. He turned to find the round podgy figure of his mother shuffling in with a defiant and determined face.

"Ma, have you lost your senses?" Amar burst out. "You aren't supposed to be downstairs for another four days! Do you know how much the heart is taxed when you climb up and down? The doctor's going to be livid."

His father was apoplectic, and as was his wont when excited, started stammering. "You—you—just don't listen. How many times have I told you that—that—you have to rest? And—and—what do you do? Just the opposite. Just the opposite. And the result—the result—you will suffer, and we all will suffer. Just selfishness—selfishness."

Her face still rebellious, she came and sat down on her customary chair facing the television. There was an uncomfortable silence for a little while. Then she broke it.

"Why are all of you making such a big thing out of my coming down? I was all by myself for a week in the nursing home. I've been all by myself for the last three days at home. I just wanted to have the company of my family for a little while. Is that such a crime? As far as the doctor is concerned, you all can tell him that we are made of sterner stuff than the ever-ailing British. The amount of newspaper space devoted to health. The TV ads on medicines. Gilbert Harding proudly claiming on TV that he has indigestion. Of course, they'll have indigestion with the kind of food they eat—boiled cabbages, boiled turnips, boiled cauliflower, boiled Brussels sprouts. If these don't give you gas, what else will? So if the doctor asks just tell him I'm doing fine—which is the truth. And that I don't have indigestion," she ended firmly.

Amar had to make an effort to stop himself from laughing at the non sequitur. Pori and Chotku looked a bit bewildered, as did their father.

"Besides, there's the *Harry Secombe Show* on TV tonight and I did not want to miss it," she added defiantly.

She took the opportunity to convey her message to the doctor directly on his next visit. Amar overheard her telling him, "It's all in the food that we Indians have grown up with, doctor, that's the secret of our health. We don't cook in this artificial stuff like the mixed oils that the West do. We use good pure ghee—a type of butter made from pure cow's milk. Or we use pure mustard oil. And as part of the seasoning we use turmeric which has medicinal properties. Then we eat a lot of lentils which are very strength giving. Our vegetables are chosen to provide iron and vitamins ..."

Amar crept away. His mother was still fighting the nationalist battle. The doctor emerged a while later, looking a little shaken.

Jane's Interference

Amar was by the pigeonholes, in the corridor, checking to see if he had any mail when he felt a tap on his shoulder. It was Jane. It was some weeks since the party, and apart from bumping into her in the corridor once, he had not spoken to her. Jane was not her ebullient self but managed a smile as she asked, "Fancy a cup of coffee, Am?"

They got their coffees and found an isolated corner table in the buzzing cafeteria.

"That was a very enjoyable party, Jane, though I may have got a bit high. I hope I didn't prove an embarrassment."

Jane looked at him and grinned. "Not in the least. You were your usual charming self."

"So you haven't invited me for coffee to chastise me?" Amar asked with a smile.

"No, darling. What I do want to know from you, though, is what the hell you told Priscilla? She doesn't seem to be herself since that evening!"

Amar was perplexed. "What do you mean, not herself?"

"Well, for one she seems to be considering breaking off from her current boyfriend."

"That's sad, a relationship breaking down—but surely not that unusual?"

"Maybe not. But what is strange is that it may have something to do with the other evening. That's why I was keen to know what you two discussed."

Amar looked surprised. "Are you saying that the break was related to our conversation that evening? Come on ... isn't that a little far-fetched? A stable romantic relationship breaking off because of a conversation a woman has at a party with a stranger?"

"Don't get uptight, Am. Of course it sounds ridiculous. But if you know Priscilla, it won't sound absurd. She's one of those people who acts very impulsively. So what did you tell her that evening?"

"Hang on. What makes you think that our conversation had anything to do with it?"

"Because she keeps referring to it. About how it helped to open her eyes. About how she woke up to some of the illusions around her life. It's pretty scary to hear all this."

"This sounds crazier and crazier! Our conversation was little more than party babble when it started off. I had no idea she would take it all so seriously," Amar said in a self-justificatory tone.

"You said 'started off'—how did it end then? Can you tell me what you said?"

Somewhat slowly and reluctantly, Amar told Jane about the whole conversation. Jane listened patiently and at the end sighed and said, "That's quite strong stuff, Am!"

"But surely not life-changing?"

"Well, she seems to have taken it all seriously, and decided that her relationship was not worth continuing with."

"You're forgetting, Jane, that what you take out of a conversation is often what you want to get out of it. Hasn't it struck you that she may already have been dissatisfied, and that what she heard from me gave her an 'out'?"

"Maybe. Maybe," Jane said ruminatively. "Tell me honestly, Am, do you truly believe in all this? Or was it a bit of intellectual gymnastic to impress a woman?"

Amar stared into space for a while. Then, slowly, said, "If I am honest I have to say, yes, the idea of creating an impression was there. But it is also a fact that I did believe in what I was saying. I find that this line of thinking explains a lot I see around me, as well as some of what's been happening to me. However, not for a moment did I want to create a crisis in Priscilla's life."

Jane toyed with her coffee spoon. "Now that you've been so frank with me, Am, I'll tell you in confidence—and mind you, this must not go any further—that you may be right. What you said may have just given her an 'out', because she's been having problems with her boyfriend. So don't lose too much sleep over it."

Priscilla

A couple of days later he was sitting at his desk in his room, working on a tutorial, when Pori shouted from the ground floor, "Call for you."

A little irritated, Amar walked down the stairs to the little hall which housed the phone, as well as served as a coat room, wondering who could be calling. He said hello and was answered by a female voice he did not recognise.

"Amar, you may not remember me—this is Priscilla. You remember we met at Jane's party?"

Amar was nonplussed. Why was she calling him? To berate him for having ruined her life? He collected himself and said with as much enthusiasm as he could muster, "Of course, I remember you, Priscilla, how could I forget my inquisitor? None of my other inquisitors have been so attractive!"

"Flatterer! But we poor creatures are very susceptible. So you've earned a bonus point."

"Wonderful," replied Amar. At least the first hurdle had been crossed. She wasn't going to yell at him. "Are you in London, Priscilla, or are you in your village, surrounded by the smell of cattle manure and swarms of midges?"

"I'm in a place where there is clean air and the song of birds," she answered loftily. "Unlike the fog-filled wasteland called London. Unfortunately, I'll have to be visiting the wasteland this Saturday morning and wondered if we could get together for a cup of coffee?"

"That would be wonderful. Shall we meet, say, at Leicester Square Tube station—the Charing Cross exit—and find a nice coffee place? What time would suit you?"

"That sounds super. Say eleven?"

"Perfect. I'm looking forward to seeing you again. Thank you for taking the trouble to contact me."

She laughed. "You don't have to be so formal, darling! I just wanted to meet you. Ciao."

"Bye," he said, not yet accustomed to the new Italian import of "Ciao".

But he began to feel an apprehension as he climbed the stairs back to his room.

❖

Pramod was amused. "So why are you getting your knicks in a twist anyway? You should be thrilled to be meeting her again."

They were having lunch at the refectory the next day. Slashing fiercely at the meat in his steak and kidney pie, an irate Amar said, "What's so bloody funny? Here's a girl whose life has apparently been disrupted by what I said, and you think that I shouldn't be concerned by the fact that she wants to talk to me?"

"Well, at least she didn't shout at you over the phone," Pramod said equably. "Maybe she just wants to know you better."

"Yes, of course. I'm Cary Grant and Errol Flynn rolled into one. No woman can resist me," Amar said angrily. "Can't you get it through your thick head that there can be other reasons why she wants to see me?"

"Oh, you mean she might have set this up so that her boyfriend can beat you up?" Pramod asked interestedly.

Amar looked disgustedly at him and didn't bother to reply.

❖

On the grey Saturday morning, Amar walked with reluctant steps out of Leicester Square Underground station. He could see the crowded street—the weather didn't seem to stop the locals from going about their day-to-day chores. And Christmas was drawing close.

Priscilla was standing by the news stand in a beige duffel coat and black trousers. She still looked sexy, thought Amar, in spite of the bulky duffel coat. She had high cheekbones, a sharp but delicate nose and hazel eyes. Even in her bulky attire, she looked quite breathtaking.

He wasn't sure whether the few hours together at the party entitled him to peck her on her cheek, so he said a loud, "Hello, Priscilla," instead. "How nice to see you again!"

She smiled, "Good to see you too, Amar, in spite of the truly awful day London has produced."

Safe ground. The weather. "And did your village produce anything better?" he asked.

"There was at least more oxygen to breathe in Oxford."

"Ah, but give it a little time. I'm sure there's research going on to prove that London smog actually promotes good health."

"Do you think the research will frown on a cup of coffee? I could do with one."

"I don't think coffee has been put on the restricted list as yet. So let's hurry and get a cup."

They walked out onto Charing Cross and after a few minutes of searching found a quiet, cosy-looking coffee place.

Sitting over steaming cups of coffee, Amar asked, "So what brings you to old London town?"

She had taken off her duffle coat and revealed a tight-fitting black sweater. Her reddish gold hair struck a nice contrast with the black. Amar noted this with approval, while at the same time also registering the way the tight sweater outlined her breasts, and showed the deep cleavage. He had to make a deliberate effort to avoid looking at them but gave up the battle when he found that an impossible task. She must have registered this, because with a mischievous glance she settled herself so as to make her breasts more visible. She enjoyed his discomfiture for a while and then grinned and said, "Looking at a girl hasn't been proscribed by parliament as yet, Amar."

Taken aback by this frankness Amar was at a loss for a response. He spluttered trying to find a suitable rejoinder. He failed. Finally he said, "But a law should be brought in to ban décolletage. Do you realise what a disastrous effect it has on the equanimity of us God-fearing men?"

She said innocently. "Oh, women are off your list then?"

Amar looked at her and said with the beginning of a smile, "Devious women, maybe."

She looked affronted. "Devious—me?"

"Devious, charming, attractive—a combination designed by the devil! How can a poor man from the back woods deal with this lethal blend?"

"By being himself," she replied.

Amar felt himself colour. He didn't like what she had said. "So you think I try too hard," he responded in a level voice.

She looked concerned. "Oh dear. Have I offended you? I'm sorry. It wasn't meant as a criticism at all, Amar. I just wanted you to know that I like the basic you, the person you are within."

Amar wasn't completely mollified. "And how did you get to know the person I really am?"

"Through my instinct. Through the sensors that all of us have, but pay scant attention to. Through gut feel—if you like to call it that."

Amar felt a little more placated. "And what a lovely gut to be processed by," he said smiling.

She smiled too, but slapped his hand and said sternly, "Wicked." Then let her hand linger on his for longer than necessary.

"You still haven't told me what brought you to London," he said, deciding to move on to safer ground.

"Not shopping for winter bargains, I can assure you."

"What—no visit to the mecca of shoppers?" Amar asked, knowing that a well-known upmarket departmental store in London was located in Knightsbridge, where she had said she was staying.

"No, I'm not one of the worshippers. Though the friends, whose flat I'm babysitting, buy everything from there—even their sausages."

"Good luck to them. But I wouldn't want to be run over by the bargain-hungry tourist hordes, either. So we agree on something."

"So we're a bit of a snob, are we?" she said teasingly.

"Snob? No, I don't think so. Snobbery implies a cultivated sense of superiority based on social rank or wealth. I don't buy into that. But I do try to distinguish between what I give value to and what I don't. So, following the herd is not an idea which is attractive to me." He realised how pompous he was sounding, but it was too late.

"Implying that the masses give value to the wrong things? Isn't that being snobbish?"

"To the extent that it implies a separateness from those who unthinkingly follow a popular trend—yes. But I wouldn't call that snobbishness."

"Yet, you would support—say—democracy, which has millions as its protagonists. Isn't this an idea supported by the masses? Aren't you then following the herd?"

"No. I'm not applauding democracy because the movement of the majority pushes me to it. I believe in democracy because I have given thought to the concept and it seems a sensible political model."

"Neat footwork, Amar," she said ironically. "But I still think you're a snob. Which isn't always a bad thing."

The friendly sparring continued, until they were both looking at empty cups. Priscilla said, "I could do with more coffee, but not this sort."

Amar nodded. "I couldn't agree more. Let's try some other place."

Priscilla looked doubtful. "I'm not sure there would be much of an improvement." Then her face brightened. "I know. There's some fresh coffee beans at the flat—I can make you a really good cup. How about that?"

Amar was taken aback by the invitation, but tried to maintain a calm exterior. "What a wonderful idea! Yes, let me put your coffee-making skills to the test!"

They strolled down Shaftesbury Avenue to the Piccadilly Circus Tube station. The morning had got darker, with an icy drizzle developing. However, the coloured neon lights from shops and cafes reduced the gloom. Amar took all this in absently. His mind was still grappling with the thought of being in an empty flat with this gorgeous woman. It was a prospect he would have longed for in his fantasies. But when reality presented it, he was gripped by a crippling nervousness. Red lights were flashing danger.

As he sat by her in the tube compartment he was very aware of the warmth of her thighs against his. She chatted away blithely, seemingly relaxed. "Have you been to the new musical at Drury Lane, *My Fair Lady*?"

"The comic book version of *Pygmalion*?" He was sounding even more priggish, he realised.

"Don't be so uncharitable! It's a fine production. And immensely popular. Do you know that for the first time in history, touts were operating in the West End and one-pound tickets were selling for five?"

"Well, the producers have another dubious first to their credit then."

"Oh, Amar, lighten up. Do."

He patted her hand and smiled. "I will—as soon as I have your divine coffee trickling down my throat."

"Don't raise your hopes too much. I'm not sure I can operate the grinder."

"Never fear. Amar will grind them between his rice-strengthened teeth."

"And I drink the coffee straight from the grinder—is that what you're planning you wicked man?" she said roguishly.

"Now that you suggest it, it sounds a charming idea! Saves the washing up," he said as they got up to alight. She uttered a muffled "Mmmph" in disgust and pushed him out of the door onto the platform at Knightsbridge station.

They climbed the steps up to the road. It was a short walk to the sedate but imposing three-storeyed building they entered through a side door. The small, lushly carpeted lobby led to an old-fashioned grilled lift which creaked its way to the second floor. A large, ivory-painted front door led them into the flat.

The living room was furnished with understated elegance in warm beige and brown with maroon and gold cushions providing the counterpoints. The lamps which she switched on, cast a warm glow on the off-white pile carpet. Several Persian rugs were scattered about the floor. A large French window overlooked the road. On the walls were several paintings. Some of them were Impressionists, and Amar assumed they were prints. If they were originals, they would be worth a fortune, and Amar couldn't even bear to think that they were, since he felt uncomfortable in the presence of so much wealth.

"*Voila*—home," said Priscilla spreading her arms wide. "At least for the next couple of days!"

"And very nice too," Amar said as enthusiastically as he could, very aware of her breasts thrusting through the sweater.

She sensed his lack of fervour. She came up to him, looked up at him and said, "You—no like?"

"Oh, I like, I like … it's just that I'm a little uncomfortable with opulence. But everything around is in such good taste, that I can't help but like."

"Opulence? That's LSE talking, I take it. Just forget about your socialism for a while and let's enjoy the surroundings we are in."

"Which I'm doing. And will do more, when my poor parched throat gets its caffeine fix."

"Right. This way then. You can help me fix the grinder—and I mean the real one."

They came out into a corridor. The kitchen was on the left, all neat closets, drawers and chrome. It looked so tidy, that it seemed never to have been used.

"Now, here's the grinder. Let me get the beans. Marguerite, my friend, keeps them in the fridge—believes they stay fresher."

She opened the giant refrigerator and rummaged around. "Now w-h-e-r-e are the damned beans? Here we are—all set." She was about to close the refrigerator door when something caught her eye. Her face lit up. "Oh, look Amar, look! There's a chilled bottle of white wine!" She took out a bottle full of a pale golden liquid and checked the label. "And it's French!"

She put the bottle on the counter. "Now, here's the situation, as the Yanks would say. We have a choice between coffee and wine. Which one will it be? You have to take a call—more American."

Amar was at a loss. The golden liquid looked very appealing, but it was an expensive French wine. Yet, Priscilla looked so enthusiastic. He mumbled, "The wine looks nice—but it's an expensive one, and maybe we shouldn't open it when the host and hostess are not present."

Priscilla's eyes widened. "You mean, would it be within the rules of propriety—would it be ethical, etc., etc. Well, the only rule between me and Mags is 'do unto her what she would do unto you'. And I know that, if she was in my flat, she would not think for a half a second before she opened a bottle of my wine. So argument settled. And if you're still worried about the cost aspect, rest assured." She came close, her breasts brushing against him, and whispered, "They're loaded, darling, loaded. They would think nothing of giving this bottle away to their maid, because their cellar contains hundreds of bottles. So—no further argument. Wine wins hands down. Now where the devil is the opener. Found it. Now you open the bottle and I'll get the glasses."

She came back a few minutes later to find Amar still struggling with the opening of the bottle. He'd got the corkscrew in, but couldn't get the cork out. "This—damn—cork—just refuses to—come—out," he muttered through his teeth while pulling at the cork. Priscilla watched him with a smile for a minute, and then said, "All right, darling, just relax. Pass me the bottle, like a good boy." When Amar looked rebellious she said, "No reflection on you—a wine bottle has beaten the strongest of men. What you need is a woman," she smiled sweetly as she took the bottle. With a deft twist of the wrist she had the cork out. "All you need is leverage, darling." Seeing Amar's woebegone face, she came close and hugged him.

"Relax. The world has not ended. It's only a bottle that would not open." She looked up into his still distressed face, hugged him closer and said, "This is what I like so much about you—you're so childlike and unspoilt."

Amar felt the warmth of her body and her firm thighs against him. She was looking up at him. He wasn't even conscious of lowering his head. Suddenly he found his lips on hers. They felt soft and tremulous like a butterfly. She closed her eyes and responded by tightening her arms and opening her lips so that their tongues were touching. The kiss lasted a long while. Finally, she gently took her lips away, and whispered, "Let's make ourselves comfortable in the living room. Bring the bottle, darling, I'll take the glasses."

This 'darling' somehow seemed to have a different resonance from the earlier ones. Amar followed her. She placed the glasses on a peg table, sat down on the floor with her back supported by a sofa and patted the space next to her. Amar sat down. She poured the wine and passed him a glass. "*Salud*," she said, "to cloudless skies in London." They drank sitting side by side, thighs touching. Her flesh seemed to burn through the fabric. They kissed, this time deeply. His hand slid to her breast and his fingers found her erect nipple. They tumbled onto the carpet and his hand caressed her taut stomach, her flank and moved to her thigh. They were both breathing hard, their lips locked.

The phone rang. She ignored it for a while, then broke away cursing. "I'll take the bloody thing off the hook." She said a fierce "Hello", then softened her voice. "Where are you now?" She listened and then said in a flat voice, "Right," and put the phone down. She stood by the phone dismally, then turned around and faced Amar, almost in tears. "They've changed their bloody plans and are coming back.'

"Who?" Amar asked, though he guessed the answer.

"Mags and David. They're already in London and will be arriving any time now." She collapsed beside him saying, "Shit, shit, shit … I hate this …", then threw a cushion at the nearby chair just missing a lamp. "I'm so, so sorry, Amar. They were supposed to be away the whole bloody weekend …" She sat with her head cradled in her hand.

Amar tried to hide his frustration and gently rubbed her back. "Not your fault, Priscilla. It's just—just—the wrong place and the wrong time. I'm feeling just as miserable as you … oh, what the hell. Time for me to go."

"No, don't go—I don't want you to go," she cried, holding on to his hand.

"But I have to, Priscilla," he said softly. "It'll be worse for the two of us to have to sit miles apart having to make polite conversation."

He helped her to her feet and they clung together in a long embrace. "Will you ring me in Oxford?" she asked as they broke apart.

"Of course," he promised her.

❖

Out in the open Amar welcomed the cold air which soothed the flush which was still on his face. He felt strangely relieved to be out of the miasma of lust and desire he had found himself engulfed by. He needed the fresh air and decided to walk for a while before entering the stuffiness of a Tube station. Taking one of the lanes off Knightsbridge he soon found himself in Kensington Palace Garden. He crossed the horse riding tracks and entered the park proper.

There was a sadness in the air. The bare trees were mourning the passing of summer. The sky was sombre. The birds hushed. And there was the ever-present smell of burning leaves.

He found himself a bench and sat down. A few drops fell from the overhanging branches, but Amar didn't care. He gave himself up to enjoying the sight of the drops falling like live transparent pearls onto his coat and then rolling off. He breathed in the damp air deeply to help clear the jumble in his mind.

Where had his self-control been? And where did this leave Helga, to whom he had professed undying love? He was paralysed by guilt.

❖

"Of course, I wanted it. Wouldn't you? But the untimely phone call was a much-needed wake-up call for my conscience."

Pramod and Amar were sitting in the Nell, a pub just a short walk from Aldwych, for the fortnightly drink they treated themselves to.

Pramod looked aghast. "Conscience? After being exposed to two years of post-war permissiveness and radical thought in England, you still have one? Look, conscience is no more than a bundle of outdated dogmas printed onto our brains by our upbringing. Are you telling me you still cling to them?"

"I don't know whether I cling to them or not. But I do know that all my ingrained values have not been destroyed. And from time to time they make themselves heard."

Pramod sat back and looked at him with pity. "You certainly need a wake-up call, but of a different kind."

"Have you thought about a small thing called loyalty? I've made a commitment to Helga—don't I need to uphold that?"

"Uphold what? Having sex for the first time in your life, you felt the need to paint it in virtuous colours. 'It was not just bodily gratification—it was something above and beyond that, something sacred and pure!' Now, you can't extricate yourself from the pious bullshit! If honesty is what you're looking for, look at yourself more carefully. How honest were you in your professions of love for Helga? Go on, be ruthlessly honest. Look at yourself again, Amar. "

Amar looked uncomfortable. "I don't know. It's a meaningless question to ask, anyway."

"Why?"

"Because words carry with them their own truth. What is behind those words doesn't matter. The words cement the truth."

"A beautiful bit of sophistry. You might even have convinced me, if I didn't know that you're just evading the original question. Why don't you admit the truth?"

"Because I myself don't know whether I was honest or not," he burst out in exasperation. Then he said in a quieter voice, "Oh, the hell with it … I've been asking myself this same question for a long time. And, yes, I've been suspecting that I said what I did to satisfy my conscience—to make me feel that making love to her was not just a purely carnal act, but was supported by the underpinning of emotion. Somehow in my mind, sex accompanied by emotion is acceptable. Without, it isn't."

"So where does it leave you now?"

"I don't know. Maybe the emotion of love is just so much window dressing, so much self-delusion. I have to accept that, in the heat of desire, things are said which may not always be the final truth."

"Ergo, there is no such thing as genuine love then?"

"Who knows? Do you? My problem is I'm not sure I would recognise it even if I bumped into it. Because there are so many imposters on the scene."

"In which case, how do you deal with Helga?"

"I'm not sure," he said in exasperation. "Can't you see—that is my problem. She still is a person I'm very fond of. Someone I would like to spend time with. But more and more I begin to realise that there are also others who I would also like to be with, who I would also like to be close to. So where do I go from here?"

Pramod who had been getting somewhat restless, finally heaved a sigh and said, "Lord knows … I know where I'm going—and that's to get another half-pint of beer. What about you?"

Amar nodded. "Thanks, the same for me."

Jane's Repeated Meddling

Priscilla called him at home, but he had not returned from college. He did not return the call. She called him again on Sunday. This time he was out at the ULU playing table tennis with friends.

A week later he was buttonholed by Jane in the corridor. "Amar Das—don't pretend you haven't seen me. You're going to buy me a coffee this minute." She grabbed his arm and marched him off.

Amar settled himself opposite her once he had got the coffees. "Your highness seems in a bit of a lather?"

The beginning of a smile tugged at the corners of her lips. "Don't try to change the subject," she said, trying to look severe.

Amar gazed at her, open-mouthed. "But, your worship, I don't even know what the subject is!"

"Stop clowning. What are you doing to my friend?"

"Hey, we seem to have been over this before. I'm getting a sense of déjà vu. Weren't we sitting at the same table not so long ago when you accused me of ruining your friend's life?"

Jane was not to be diverted. "I'm serious. What went on between Priscilla and you a few days ago?"

Amar still didn't want to enter into a serious discussion on the subject. He sighed. "Why, has she ditched another boyfriend?"

"On the contrary, you seemed to have ditched her."

"Look, Jane," Amar said, beginning to get exasperated, "You probably have Priscilla's best interests at heart, but she's an adult now—and quite capable of managing her life. Yes, she and I met, but what went on between us is between two adults. Don't you think we're entitled to some privacy?"

"Of course you are. I'm sorry if I've given the impression that I want to pry." She looked contrite, which was unusual for her.

She went on in a quiet voice, "I'm asking you these questions only because Priscilla seems distressed at your not having returned her calls. As it is, she's been going through difficult times. I just wanted to help her."

"Jane," he said patiently, "Listen to me. She's a lovely woman and any man would consider himself lucky to have her company. I would have rushed to Oxford the moment she rang, if it wasn't for other circumstances." He wondered how much he should divulge to her.

Jane raised her eyebrows. "What does that mean?"

He decided to be honest. "Well—I'm involved with a girl who lives in Germany. She and I are very close."

Jane looked angry, "Then why on earth … ?"

"Did I spend that morning with Priscilla?" Amar sighed and said, "I think you'd better ask her. She's the one who rang me."

Jane did not reply, but kept stirring her undrunk coffee. Then she shook her head and said, "Oh, Am, what a mess this is. She gives up her boyfriend because she finds you attractive, spends a blissful morning with you, is bereft when you don't respond to her calls—and finally … finally, she will find out that you were never there for her in the first place."

Amar started feeling the beginnings of guilt, and then suddenly woke up. He said coldly, "We're playing the old 'find a scapegoat' game again, are we? Let me spoil it for you. She knew about my girlfriend in Germany—I told her at your party. So I'm afraid you'll have to find another scapegoat. I'm getting tired of this game."

"And who elected you as judge and jury in the first place?" Amar continued with intensity. "You're probably well-intentioned, Jane, but you could be doing irreparable damage to Priscilla's relationships with this kind of interference." Amar got up angrily.

Jane looked pale and suddenly ten years older. She reached out and caught Amar's hand, "No, don't rush off like this, Am, please … please?" Amar stood for a moment, undecided, and slowly sat down. She freed his hand.

She stared down at the table. Then she opened her bag and took out a packet of cigarettes. Amar had never seen her smoke, but he was not in any mood to comment on it. "Do you mind if I smoke?" She asked. Amar shrugged.

She lit her cigarette and inhaled deeply. "This is a recent habit," she muttered. To Amar's eye she had the mannerisms of a long-time smoker. She seemed to draw strength from her cigarette and said in a stronger voice, "I don't really know where to start. First of all—I need to apologise. I had no intention of interfering in your personal life, but I seem to have done it willy-nilly. Priscilla is my dearest friend. We've known each other since we were children. She's always been a wild thing, and I've always kept a protective eye on her. I know she doesn't like it. She'll be furious if she knows I've been talking to you." Jane looked anxious and kept clasping and unclasping her hands. Then, with a great effort, she blurted out "You're not going to tell her, are you?"

"I was going to talk to her sometime. I have to. I can't leave things hanging uncertainly. I need to explain things to her."

She looked stricken, "You mean, you're going to tell her all about today's conversation?"

Amar looked puzzled. "If you're such a good friend of hers, would you not like her to be given some explanation? Surely she deserves that?"

"Yes, she does. She does. But can you not leave me to give her the explanation?"

"No," he said sharply.

Jane was now looking distressed. "Please, Am, don't talk to her please—please … if you do, she'll blame me again for ruining her life."

"Again?"

Jane sat with her head in her hands. After a while she said in a barely audible voice, "She believes my meddling has made her lose friends." In a voice close to tears she added "You don't realise how much she means to me."

"I'm sorry, but I can't promise that I won't talk to Priscilla. All I can promise is to try not to hurt her." With that he got up and left, his mind still reeling from the entire conversation.

Labyrinth

"Priscilla?" he was in a call box.

There was no response for some time, and he wondered if she had disconnected. "Priscilla?" he said again. This time she responded.

"Yes," she responded in a dead voice.

"This is Amar."

"I know."

"Priscilla, I need to talk to you."

"What about?"

"Well … well … about us," said a discomfited Amar.

"There's nothing to talk about."

"If that's the way you feel about it, fine."

"What other way should I feel after what Jane has told me?"

"Jane? But … right, now what's that bloody woman said?"

"You don't have to raise your voice. And she's a friend of mine."

"If only you knew," Amar muttered. Then more loudly, "Right—fine. I think there's little point in trying to talk to you."

She hesitated, and then said, still in a flat voice, "Well, if you're so anxious to talk, I'll be in London this weekend."

"Can we meet then?"

"I suppose we could."

They fixed to meet on Saturday morning.

❖

They sat on a park bench in Hyde Park not far from the Knightsbridge flat. It was grey and cold, a dank mist hung in the air. Amar was glad he had his coat on, though the raw cold penetrated through the protective wear. He had not suggested a coffee, neither had she. They sat side by side, though a formal distance away from each other.

"I just wanted to say sorry," Amar mumbled, when she waited for him to begin.

"Sorry for what? For having been nice to me? I don't feel at all sorry about that morning, except for the fact that we were so rudely interrupted." She was staring straight in front of her. Her profile looked beautiful. With her high cheekbones she looked like a Slavic princess, Amar thought absently. In spite of the cold, her coat was unbuttoned and the top of her proud breasts were revealed. He tried to switch his mind from these distractions.

Amar was confused because he had expected that his apology would set loose a tirade of reproaches, and had been bracing himself.

"But … but … uh … aren't you upset that I err … that I …"

"Kissed me?" She laughed without mirth. "This is not the first time I've been kissed, Amar."

This hurt Amar as it was meant to. He had thought that their kiss was special and memorable, but here she was relegating it to the collector's cupboard.

"Well, in that case I have nothing to apologise for," he said more firmly, "particularly to such a seasoned campaigner."

She looked at him coldly. "I think you do."

He was equally cold. "And what would that be for?"

"You didn't have the decency to return my calls, and then you go running to Jane to discuss what is, essentially, a private matter …"

"Hold on a minute. Jane told you that *I* went to her?"

She nodded. "Yes, she said that you felt you had to unburden yourself and buttonholed her. And that she did not want to hear about it, but you insisted."

Amar was speechless. After a while he said, "Say again—I buttonholed her?"

Some of his incredulity must have been conveyed to her, because for the first time she turned and looked at him. "You seem surprised?"

"Surprised? I'm struck dumb!" he burst out. He shook his head, "I didn't expect this from her."

She looked puzzled. "What do you mean?"

"I mean that I had not expected her to be such a bloody liar," he said heatedly. Then he recovered himself. "Sorry, as you reminded me the last time on the phone—she's a friend of yours. So let's end the conversation here."

"No. I'm not ending any conversation until I know the truth," she said firmly.

"You may not like the truth."

"I'll chance that. Now, will you please tell me what actually happened between the two of you?"

Amar hesitated. There seemed little purpose to be served in souring their relationship. "No, Priscilla, I don't think it would be a good idea. Let's just forget it."

This time it was Priscilla who seemed agitated. "For God's sake, don't treat me like a little child! You don't think I know Jane? I've known her since childhood, Amar, and nothing that she does surprises me anymore. I just want confirmation of what I have long suspected." Her voice softened and she put her hand on his arm, "So will you tell me. Please?"

Amar told. At the end, however, he began to feel somewhat debased at the disclosure. Some of this must have shown on his face, for suddenly Priscilla moved closer and put her cold hand on his.

"What's the matter?" she asked.

"Nothing much. I don't like carrying tales," he said rather shortly.

Her hand tightened on his. "You stupid man. You don't know the good turn you've done me. This is not the first time she has lied, nor will it be the last. But I needed to know the extent she would go to."

However, this did not make him feel any better. Coming to meet her had been a mistake. His irritation seemed to convey itself to her. She moved even closer, and he could now feel the warmth of her body. "You're still cross, aren't you?" she asked gently.

"Yes, I am." He had nothing to lose, and he wanted to be out of this situation as soon as he could. "I don't really know why I'm here. Anyway, at least one set of lies has been nailed. So it did serve some purpose, I suppose. Anyway, I can't see any further purpose being served by being here, so … have a good weekend." He got up.

"No, no, Amar—don't—please don't go. Please …" she said in alarm. She stretched out and grabbed his hand.

Amar's surprise must have shown on his face. She pulled on his hand and dragged him to sit next to her.

She sat close to him and held on to his hand. He wasn't sure what was happening. This same woman had been cold and unpleasant minutes before. Now, her body warmth and her proximity seemed to convey a different message. Her coat had parted further and he could now see her breasts straining against her deep blue pullover. Unused to what he considered women's whims, he tried to extricate himself from this confusing situation. "Priscilla, the purpose of this meeting has been served. You now know what transpired between Jane and me. There is nothing more that either one of us can add. So it seems pointless for both of us sitting out here, freezing our asses off. Let's just call it quits, shall we?"

"You sound so cold and matter-of-fact. I can't believe this is the Amar I've known," she said sadly.

"That's really rich, coming from someone who would have put an ice maiden to shame just a few minutes ago."

"You don't understand, do you," she said softly. There was warmth and something else in her voice, which Amar could not identify. She still clutched his hand, and moved even closer to him.

"Yes, I just don't understand what the hell is going on," Amar began in perplexity. But before he could continue she closed his lips with a kiss.

Amar was bewildered. He sat inert while her lips stayed against his. He noticed absently that his lips were thawing with the warmth of hers. Then his body took over, seemingly, without his volition. He responded to her kiss. They sat locked in an awkward embrace in the cold misty parkland. He finally whispered to her, "What are we doing, Priscilla?" And she whispered back, "What we should have done long ago."

She got up.

"Where are you going?" he asked, even more mystified. Then a wave of anger swept over him. She was playing games. There was a crude name for this type of a woman and he was tempted to use it. Just then she spoke.

"Not where I'm going, but where we're going," she said calmly, dragging him up. "We—are going to the flat."

"To the flat? Absolutely not. I don't want to meet your friends," Amar responded in a surly voice.

She pulled him harder by his hand. "You won't. They're out to a late lunch with friends."

"And then they'll decide to come back early," Amar replied "And we'll have the same sordid replay."

"No, we won't. Trust me." She replied with confidence and entwined her arm into his. By now, most of his anger had evaporated, but he was not totally mollified.

"And how would you ensure that?" Amar asked sceptically. He was very aware of her soft body pressed against his, as they walked. Aware also of the need to stop. But he could not summon the resolve. The urgency of desire overcame the staid voice of conscience.

"Oh, hush." She scolded him. "Just trust me. Everything's been taken care of." They entered the building and she dragged him into the lift.

As they got out of the lift and approached the flat, Amar asked disbelievingly, "Taken care of? How? You didn't even know that we would be coming back."

She looked back at him with an enigmatic smile and unlocked the door. Amar stepped gingerly in and looked around for signs of a jovial Mags who would thump him on the back and say—"Hello there, don't mind us, just carry on, jolly good."

But, there appeared to be no one.

He stood in the passage and said, "Come on, Priscilla. I can't take this mystery any more. Just tell me what's going on."

"Oh, what a persistent young man." She took him by the hand and started walking down the corridor. She stopped in front of a door and said, "Well, if you must know," and stopped and looked down at the floor. Then she continued in a lower voice, "I was hoping that you'd come back with me to the flat. Mags told me that they were going out to lunch and promised to make it a long lunch. She also told me that she would ring before returning."

Amar stared at her. "So all this was planned?"

"Not planned—it was what I was hoping for," she said in a small voice.

"And what about all the coldness in the park where you even refused to look at me? Was that all rehearsed and play-acted?"

"No. I was furious at you having cold-shouldered me. The anger was genuine, as was the warmth which replaced it. Don't ask me how the transformation took place. Oh, must we discuss this? Can't you understand a girl's wanting, can't you see that wanting to be with you led to my so-called planning?" She turned away angrily.

He gingerly reached out and touched her shoulder. "And why are you touching me as if I were made of glass? Can't you take hold of me properly?" she said furiously as she turned back. Then seeing Amar smiling she started laughing within her anger and was in his arms, "Oh you are such a fool—you—you …" And she crushed her lips against his with great force. Her anger seemed to slowly subside and her body softened against his. Her lips now caressed rather than bruised, and her tongue sought his. Amar wasn't aware how long they stood their kissing, but was very aware of his body responding.

She gently disengaged herself and opened the door they were in front of. It was obviously the guestroom. They went in, she closed the door and turned to him and they were kissing again. They soon tumbled onto the bed. Amar's hand caressed her body while hers slipped through his shirt. They undressed each other with an urgency which neither could hold back. When she had nothing but her black panties on, Amar suddenly stopped. Priscilla raised her head, "What's the matter?" she asked in a concerned whisper. Amar looked embarrassed and whispered back, "I didn't come prepared ..." She giggled. "Well then, you'll have to support an illegitimate child when it comes." Amar wasn't amused. "It's not funny, Priscilla," he whispered fiercely. She rolled over on top of him still giggling. "Well then, you'll have to pay for an abortion." Seeing his expression she kissed him. "Relax, my darling. There's something we girls use which is as safe as a condom. It's called the Dutch cap. Just give me a minute—and take the y-fronts off while I put it on." She got up and disappeared into the bathroom. When she returned she was totally naked. Amar caught his breath. She clambered onto the bed and to his body. He turned her onto her back and entered her. She was moist and ready, as was he.

Later, as they lay breathless, she curled herself into him and rested with her head on his chest, her leg across him. Amar closed his eyes. It had been good. But it had been too hurried, as if each wanted to get the most of the other before it was too late. Yet, he was happy that she had cried out at the end.

She lay in his arms and played with his chest hair, running her finger through them gently. "You won't get angry if I say something?" she asked in a soft voice. He murmured "No," and lay back enjoying her gentle touch.

"I wanted to sleep with you from the first evening we met."

Amar was shocked. Women didn't say such things. And he did not want to feel like an object in a shop window which a woman takes a fancy to and must possess. Yet, he couldn't resist the feeling of satisfaction which also crept in.

They lay together in silence for a while. Then she said, "You're cross, aren't you?"

He shook his head.

"I know you are. But you shouldn't be."

Amar didn't tell her what was really going through his mind, but managed a forced smile. She got up, kissed him and left the room, returning a little later with a chilled bottle of white wine.

As he lay back against the headboard with a glass of wine in his hand and her naked body stretched out beside him, he stared into space and said quietly, "I feel utterly decadent. Totally corrupted. A slave to hedonism."

"God bless the Greeks for hedonism," she murmured sleepily.

There was no more conversation and Amar was left to his thoughts. He felt a drowsiness creeping over him and, without wanting to, dozed off.

He tumbled into wakefulness a while later, wondering desperately what was worrying him. And then he realised—the time. What time was it? They might be back any minute, he thought in panic as he sat up.

"What's the time? When are they due back?" he asked urgently.

Half awake, she sighed. "Is that what's worrying you, you foolish man? Actually, I should have told you. I called them when I went to get the wine. They're going to an art exhibition from there, so we have plenty of time. At least a couple of hours more. Come and lie by me," she said falling back onto the bed. With her hand wandering over the sensitive parts of his body, it wasn't long before he was ready. This time she straddled him.

He enjoyed the lovemaking but realised that he felt a strange detachment. He seemed to be watching the entire act from outside. It was as if his body was being used, albeit pleasurably.

Once it was over, she snuggled up to him. They lay together in silence. There was a lot going through his mind and she probably sensed the tension in his body. "There's something bothering you, darling."

He smiled wanly and said, "Oh, nothing ..."

She rolled away from him and reached for her glass. "Post-coital depression, obviously."

"You seem to have a lot of experience in these matters," Amar replied tersely.

"What's that supposed to mean?" she asked sitting up.

"Nothing more than what you implied earlier in the park."

"Oh, you were expecting a virgin, were you? Sorry, darling, you'll have to go back to India for that," she replied coldly as she sat up.

"No, I wasn't expecting a virgin. At the same time I wasn't expecting to be another notch in a huntress' belt."

"So, that's it. That's what it's all about. I don't believe this. Any other man would have taken what I said as a compliment."

"You must go around in strange company. To a normal man it would mean that he has been marked down as a target, which will lose its value as soon as it's been conquered."

"Right. So I'm the seductress. And you, the poor victim. I'm immoral and jump from bed to bed to capture victims. You, of course, believe in the one man-one woman principle. No wandering. Good for you. So, how come you tumble into bed with a dissolute woman when there is a woman waiting for you in Germany?"

All pretences at politeness were now off.

"I've been wondering about that myself," Amar replied. "I let myself be drawn into something I could have avoided. My weakness. My mistake."

"Oh, you poor dear. Swept away by lust through the machinations of a scheming woman." Her voice still cold.

"Right on both counts," he answered angrily. She seemed to flinch.

She looked down at her glass. "Is the idea of a woman being attracted to a man so foreign to you?" She asked in a less hostile voice.

"No, it isn't," he replied quietly.

"And a woman acting on her desire—is that such a criminal act?" she looked up at him almost in entreaty.

Amar saw a sad woman sitting naked in front of him, legs folded to one side, a neglected wine glass cupped in both hands, hair covering one eye, waiting a little tremulously for his answer. She was no longer the calculating siren he had been thinking of her as. Just another human moved by desires, just as he was.

"No. And I'm sorry if I implied that." He stretched out his hand and touched her arm. It was cold. He moved over to her and put his arm around her shoulder. "I'm sorry," he repeated. Her body seemed to thaw slowly. She dumped the wine glass on the bedside table and settled herself in his arms, her head resting on his chest. "I'm not an evil woman, Amar. Will you believe that?" she whispered imploringly. "Please?"

"I'm impulsive," she continued in her low voice. "But I'm not wicked. And I really am attracted to you. Oh, I'm so lonely, Amar, so—so lonely …" her voice broke and Amar felt her warm tears on his chest. "I wake up in the morning in despair that there is another day I'll have to go through. The black desolation that engulfs me is terrifying. With nobody to turn to. Nobody who can fill this yawning gap within me. The acquaintances and men I have known were no more than temporary analgesics whose effect wore off as the light dimmed in the sky. I wanted something to feed the hunger of my soul. And then someone who seemed to be different came along … can you blame me for wanting to be with you?"

This seemed to come from the heart. He could relate to her loneliness and the panic it could engender. He wanted to reach out to her, but felt helpless. All he could do to comfort her was gently caress her shoulder. He knew how inadequate it was.

She snuggled into him. "Hold me tight, please Amar, please," she implored with tears flowing again. He wrapped his arms around her and she lay quietly against him.

The ringing of the phone gave him the excuse to get out of bed, go to the bathroom, and dress. They would be back in half an hour. She put on a bathrobe. They stood facing each other awkwardly, not knowing what to say.

She asked, biting her lips, "I'm not likely to see you again, am I?"

He shook his head. "It's best that we don't meet."

"Will you promise not to think badly of me?" she asked, restraining her tears.

"I'm hardly in a position to judge you since I've been involved in all that has happened."

"Equivocation," she sniffed. But she clung to him. Her voice broke as she said, "I'll miss you so …" The teardrops finally fell.

He felt like a heartless monster as he kissed her lightly and walked out of the door. This would be the last time he saw her. Yet all he was feeling was a sense of relief. No sadness. No sorrow. His soul, he feared, was beginning the slow process of atrophy which seemed to mark modern society.

Unwanted Truths

It was a Sunday morning and Amar sat in the garden in the weak sun, browsing through the *Observer*. The apple tree projected a long shadow with the low winter sun behind it. The flowers on the bed had gone and all that remained were brown stalks and brown earth. A blackbird hopped around on the browning grass looking for worms.

Although it was quiet and restful, Amar's mind was not at peace. The episode with Priscilla kept stoking the fires of guilt. What was he doing to Helga? What was he doing to himself? In the battle between his bodily desires and his conscience, it was the former that had won. What did that do to his beliefs, his soul? Was he succumbing to the western religion of mindless gratification?

It got colder and he went in. The restlessness pursued him. The house seemed oppressive and he decided to escape to the ULU after lunch.

Getting himself a coffee at the ULU cafeteria, Amar wandered into the lounge and sat down on one of the Rexine sofas with an old and well-thumbed copy of *New Statesman*. He still had a couple of hours to kill before his next destination. His mind was really not on the magazine, and he was relieved when he found a noisy group coming in. Two of them were from the LSE. They dragged him along to the TV room to watch a replay of a football game.

As the darkness gathered outside, he said his goodbyes, fetched his coat from the cloak room and walked out into the lonely street. The street lights had come on, although it was still early evening. A cold wind swirled the leaves from the park onto the pavement. He made his way slowly to the pub on Marchmont Street, not being sure whether he would find the person he sought, although this was where he normally came every evening. He lived nearby and this was his local.

The pub had started getting crowded, but was not packed. Amar looked around but could not find the face he was looking for. He hesitated, wondering whether he should stay or go home and then decided to walk across to the bar.

The pub grew more crowded as he, perched on a stool at the bar, nursed his half-pint of bitter. After a while his patience deserted him and he made up his mind that it was a fruitless wait. As he raised his glass he made out the familiar grey-haired figure limping in. He stood up and waved and Ben finally caught his eye and smiled. "Hello, Amar," he said as he limped over. "Good to see you, Ben. Here, I've saved a stool for you."

"Thank you kindly, my friend."

"Let me get you a drink—what will it be?" Amar asked.

"A half of bitter please, Amar."

Ben was very sensitive to the financial condition of students and normally would refuse a drink when offered by Amar. But, Amar had made a fuss and said that he could not be the recipient all the time, and needed to reciprocate.

Settling himself on the stool, Ben said, "Haven't seen you for some time, Amar. Tell me all your news."

Amar had met Ben at this pub in his first year, when he had come in by himself on a dreary evening. He had waited at the bar for an unconscionably long time and had seen others, latecomers, being served. Finally he had asked the bartender why it was taking so long to serve him when others who had come later were being served. A man standing next to him said in a low voice, "You'd get better service if you spoke English." Amar was so taken aback that he took a while to digest what had been said. He turned furiously to him and said angrily, "And what the hell is that supposed to mean?" "Oh, just that you foreigners need to go to classes to improve your English," said the other man calmly. "Listen, mister, I could give you lessons in English for a year and you'd still not catch up with me ..." Before Amar could continue, a slight, grey-haired man pushed his way in and put a restraining arm on Amar, "Just give me a minute, young man."

Then turning to the other man he asked coldly, "And what are your educational qualifications, sir?" The other man frowned and said, "I don't see what business it is of yours." The elderly man said calmly, "Nor was it any business of yours to comment on this young man's English, which, incidentally, is far superior to yours in diction. Be that as it may, since you seemed so knowledgeable about English, would you mind telling me what your educational qualifications are? Did you finish your A-levels for instance?" The other man responded angrily. "It's none of your business, but I did my A-levels and then went on to do my accountancy—for your information." The elderly man raised his eyebrows and nodded his head as if impressed. "Oh, that's impressive," he said. Then gently, "And which college may that have been from?" The other man hesitated but seeing the approving look on the other man's face, mentioned a name. The elderly man's voice changed and became stronger. "A polytechnic. You passed out from a polytechnic. Now do you happen to know where this young man is studying? Maybe his scarf will tell you … no? Of course not—how would you know! Let me tell you, sir, this young man studies at the London School of Economics, one of the leading institutions of learning, not just in England—but in the world. Does that register? One of the best in the world. An institution you would not have had a chance in hell of getting in on merit. And you have the temerity to suggest to this young man that he does not know English?" The other man, now looking uncomfortable, sneered and said, "Oh, go to hell," and went back to his beer. The elderly man smiled. "I probably will, when my time comes. But I don't think there would be place there for the likes of you. Even hell has its standards." The other man picked up his glass and wandered off.

They had got chatting at the bar and it emerged that Ben had served in the army in India during the war. He had got injured in action and now walked with a limp. He had fond memories of India, and remembered Poona and Calcutta well. He and Amar had hit it off and it became a long evening. Amar found in him a good and sympathetic listener which, he would come to realise, was an endangered species.

Over the last year an improbable friendship had developed between the two—an elderly, slight Englishman who looked older than his years with his craggy-lined face, grey hair and intelligent but gentle blue eyes, and an introspective Indian student not far out of his teens. Amar would come to the pub whenever he had some time and, more importantly, some money. It wasn't very often, but often enough to build a friendship. In Ben, Amar found a compassionate elder person who, while being very well read, did not pretend to know all the truths. He was prepared to discuss and listen to opposite views. Ben did not talk too much about himself. Amar knew that he had been married and was now a widower. Also that he had a daughter who was at Cambridge. Apart from that he knew little.

Amar kept his friendship with Ben to himself. Not even Pramod knew. Amar wasn't sure why he did not share this with his closest friend, but was determined to keep this relationship in a separate compartment.

"My news," Amar said slowly and paused. "Well, my love life is in a mess. Apart from that, everything is hunky-dory." Amar replied with a wry smile.

Ben listened patiently, while Amar recounted all that had happened, and then asked with a gentle smile, "And you feel the end of the world is nigh?"

Amar was taken aback. "Ben, I've made a commitment to one girl, and soon after, gone and slept with another! Shouldn't this bother me?"

"Why?"

"Why? Why? …" Amar spluttered. "Because—because I've betrayed a trust! I've cheated! I've been unfair …"

Ben remained silent.

"Oh, come on, Ben. Don't tell me you can't see all this. I've been stupid and … and … intemperate."

Ben took a sip of his beer. "You still haven't answered my question—why're you so agitated?"

Amar furrowed his brow in anger. "You haven't been listening, Ben. It's simple. I've a set of values, and I've gone against them."

"Ah, now you've answered my question. Values. I think you've earned a refill."

When the beer arrived Amar absently noted that they were pint mugs, not halves. Normally Amar would have commented on this. But he was too worked up with Ben's seeming insensitivity.

Ben took a deep pull from his glass and sat back looking satisfied. Amar waited impatiently for some time, then said in exasperation, "So that's all there is to it? Just a petty clash of values? Could you expand your cryptic comment a little?"

Ben did not seem in a hurry. Finally he said, "Isn't it self-explanatory?"

"The meaning maybe," Amar responded heatedly, "but not the implication that all is solved once you attach a label to a situation."

"Isn't that this generation's need—to attach labels to problems and then decide that the problem is over?" he replied seriously. Then his craggy face broke into a smile. "Sorry—inappropriate joke. Though it is a fact that in the States, giving names to issues is quite a pastime. But seriously, don't you now see where the problem lies? It's not just about letting down one girl in favour of another. You've been brought up in a certain tradition, and your actions have flouted those."

Amar said sarcastically, "A wonderful statement of the obvious. How does it help?"

Ben remained calm. "It doesn't. Nothing will, until you realise a certain basic truth."

"And what may that be?" an irritated Amar asked.

"Nothing very difficult to understand intellectually. Much more difficult to follow emotionally."

"I'm still waiting for enlightenment."

"You're waiting for absolution," he replied in a harder voice. "And I can't give it to you—I'm not a priest."

"I'm looking for counsel from a friend, no more," Amar replied tersely.

"Look—there are no quick fixes to matters of the soul," Ben's voice had softened. "Nor for the conflict of values. The only thing I can say is that it is a myth that values are absolute."

Amar did not reply.

Ben continued. "You're not your normal sharp self today. If you had been, you would have asked the obvious question. If values are flexible, how does morality exist? Well, it exists only because people feel a sense of comfort with order, and a sense of security with society."

"So, according to you, there is no *right* course of action?" Amar asked in a deprecatory tone.

"For me, and others more enlightened than me, the right course of action is one you can live with the consequences of. That is all that morality should be, in essence. Now let's come down to your individual case, since you are so keen on a judgement and a solution. Can you live with the consequences? If you can—fine. If not, you've acted unwisely. What can be the consequence for you? Losing your German girlfriend. If you can live with that—where's the problem? So decide for yourself. Just don't expect the world to find a solution which will absolve you."

Amar was too taken aback to respond. Then the anger started building up like a mounting fever. He put his full glass down on the table, got up, picked up his coat and said as coldly as possible, "Thank you for your kindness," and marched off.

Ben sadly shook his head and went back to his drink. Truth was as painful to deliver as to receive.

Christmas Job

With the Christmas vacation approaching, job notices started appearing on the notice board. Amar had been determined to get a job this winter. However, by the time he applied, the only ones left were the post office ones. The more prized jobs were on the delivery team, where there were tips to be earned and maybe an occasional piece of cake or a drink. He had been too late for these. He finally got a job as a sorter at the Mount Pleasant Post Office, the largest sorting centre in London. It meant being on the early morning shift, but the novelty of working and earning was enough to push that in the background. Two weeks should earn him enough to make the trip to Helga.

The vacations began and he looked forward with excitement to his first working day. He woke up at 4 am, dressed warmly with a full-sleeved sweater under his jacket, swallowed a hurried cup of tea and walked down, through the freezing but quiet darkness, to the Tube station to take the train to Piccadilly Circus from where he would have to take the Piccadilly Line to Turnpike Lane.

Turnpike Lane station turned out to be a gloomy building with poor lighting and dirty floors. Amar hurried out to breathe in the fresh air, which in spite of being tainted with traces of coal smoke, seemed preferable to the stench of urine and phenyl. He had to walk a little way to the bus stop for the bus which would take him to Rosebery Avenue, from where the post office was a short stroll. A scything cold wind penetrated his winter wear and froze his extremities. He was glad to reach his destination.

The post office building, though large, was depressing. Not surprising since it was built on the site of a 19th century prison. He was signed in and issued an apron and told he could get himself a snack at the canteen before the shift began at 6 am. He chose a cheese roll and a large cup of tea in the bleak, neon-lit canteen with dirty yellow walls, and found a Formica-topped table and a battered metal chair. His initial enthusiasm started evaporating in the dreary surroundings.

He was taken in to his place of work by a phlegmatic man and introduced to the person who would be his boss. He found himself in a huge hall with the ceiling disappearing into gloom. There were long tables in pairs, facing each other, separated by a partition which contained pigeonholes. The senior sorters sat at these tables facing the pigeonholes which were labelled by destinations. Some distance away were long chutes coming down from the first floor. Bundles of mail came down these chutes at regular intervals and Amar's job was to carry these heavy bundles to his sorting table where the senior sorters took over. That was all he had to do. For eight hours. It required no exercise of mind, just the exercise of muscles, like mules carrying loads. Initially the physical challenge was exciting. How to carry a heavy bundle to the table in the quickest and most efficient way. There was also the exhilaration of simple physical exercise, which the young enjoy as a test of strength.

By the time the breakfast break came, the novelty had worn off. Amar went to the toilet to wash off the dust and grime from his hands, which the regular workers regarded with some amusement. "Don't waste your energy, son," an elderly man said with a smile, "It'll take just five minutes to get all the grime back again."

The exercise had given him an appetite and at the service counter he piled his plate with fried eggs, bacon, baked beans and toast. A large cup of copper-coloured tea in a thick china cup completed the tray. He tucked in with gusto and felt some of the gloom lifting once the food was inside him.

Back at work, he schooled himself to let his mind wander over pleasant thoughts. A gurgling stream in Shillong and the smell of pine trees. A meadow in Kashmir with snow-clad blue peaks in the distance ...

It was not an easy exercise, but it seemed to have helped because the morning tea break seemed to arrive sooner than expected. Amar blessed the British for their tea tradition, and sat down in the canteen with his cup with great relief, resting his tired legs.

When his shift ended in the afternoon, he felt truly exhausted. It was already dark by the time he walked out of the post office, because of the shortened winter day. He just wanted to stretch out and rest his weary muscles, but there was a bus and tube journey to negotiate. He was walking like a robot by the time he climbed the steps at the Tube station at Willesden Green. The ten-minute walk home seemed to take an eternity.

He hung up his coat and scarf, and wearily climbed the stairs. Collapsing on the bed was such a luxury. His mother came in to ask whether he wanted something to eat. He was a little short and said that all he wanted was to be left alone.

After opting for an early dinner which he had all by himself, he realised that he had not read the papers. He got hold of the *Manchester Guardian* and took it up to his room. Before long he found himself drowsing with the paper in his hand. Manual work, he realised, was a harsh taskmaster in more ways than one. Not just for the physical energy which it drained from the body, but the mental energy it seemed to have sucked out of him. His mind just refused to function. The words on the newspaper were just words—they did not seem to mean anything.

Over the next fortnight he began to realise the plight of workers faced with monotonous repetitive work. It deadened the mental faculties, blunted the mind, shut it off from thinking beyond the basics. It emasculated the intellect, the exercise of which was one of the vital human needs, and engendered an alarming restlessness. Amar began to glimpse the kind of frustration which led to the growth of labour agitations.

The days dragged drearily by. More than once, Amar wished he had never started this job. At home, he was too exhausted to speak to anyone. At work, there was hardly an opportunity, except during the breaks. He felt like an automaton and was in a state of depression throughout the day, watching the clock and urging it on. On the last day he collected his wages and staggered out. There was not the euphoria that he was expecting. Just a mind-numbing exhaustion, and an overwhelming desire to sleep.

❖

They were at a pub close to Holborn station, celebrating the end of Amar's servitude. Amar feeling flush with his new earnings, had offered to treat Pramod. Christmas was over, but the new year had not yet been rung in.

Pramod looked more relaxed than usual, and Amar asked him about his newfound equanimity.

"Just maturity, son, maturity," Pramod said, grinning.

"Bollocks."

"Not quite. It's not quite the nether region, a little higher."

"God! Don't say it's another one of your crushes!"

Pramod looked offended. "I don't have crushes like a teenage school girl. And I'm amazed that you find it necessary to resort to this kind of adolescent colloquialism. What's happened to your English?"

"Never mind. Who is the latest target then?"

"I wish you wouldn't refer to her as a target. She is a highly intelligent girl studying at Cambridge."

"And?"

"And what?" Pramod said in an irritated voice.

"A little more about her?"

"Well, her parents are Indian born, but they moved to this country a long time ago. She was born here and grew up here. And I met her through Sushma. Is the inquisition over?"

"Oh, come on. You're dying to talk about her. So—have you been out with her as yet?"

"No, we're meeting this weekend."

"And her name?"

"Anisha Kapadia. Her father is an engineer working for a large company and her mother works in an office in London. And that's about all I know."

"All this is wonderful news, Pramod." Amar was delighted. "Drink up, we need to celebrate!"

❖

Amar had felt rich when he received his final salary at the post office. Apart from the money itself, what excited him was the prospect of buying gifts for his family. This would be the first time he had the wherewithal to indulge this long-held ambition. He bought his mother a cologne; his father a scarf; Pori a long playing record of her favourite singer, who currently happened to be Pat Boone; and Chotku a book on cricket. He had felt somewhat embarrassed in handing over the gifts. While Pori received it gleefully and gave him a big kiss, Chotku was less effusive though he didn't forget a dutiful hug. His mother told Amar he shouldn't have spent so much on her, while a tear rolled down her cheek as she held her gift to her breast. His father gruffly asked, "What's this—what's this?" When Amar explained that this was bought from his first earning, he seemed taken aback and did not know what to say. "No—no—don't waste money on these things for me—I don't need it. No—no—buy books for yourself, they are the best investment."

Amar said that he had enough for himself and as this was his first earning, he had to buy gifts for the family. Still looking dazed, his father looked short-sightedly at the package and asked, "*Etta kee—ẹtta kee* … (What is it)?"

His mother now spoke sharply to her husband "*Khullay dakho na* (Why don't you open it and see)? Your son has brought you a gift—you can be a bit more gracious about receiving it."

He fumbled while opening the package and took out the rust-coloured woollen scarf. He stood looking at it, and then looked away blinking. He turned, hurriedly embraced Amar and walked out of the room. Amar thought he saw him wiping his eyes as he went out.

Dusseldorf

Amar slung his rucksack onto the overhead rack and slumped onto the seat in the second-class compartment of the Dover train. He had left home without breakfast, fearing he would be late, and was beginning to feel hungry. The snacks counter on the platform looked enticing.

He came back with his purchases—a sausage roll, a Danish, an apple and a bottle of water. He ate with relish and wondered whether this hunger was some kind of reflex brought on by a train compartment. During his childhood in India, one of the joys of travelling by train was the mini-feast which began the moment the train steamed out. His mother would always travel with a couple of baskets of food or sometimes even a small tin trunk. One of the baskets would be unpacked almost as soon as the train left the suburbs of the city, and *parathas* and spicy *chops* (meat and potato croquettes) would emerge, together with *achaars* (hot pickle). This would be a pre-lunch snack. Lunch, when it came, would be a *thali* provided by the railways. It would be a large metal plate with bowls containing different courses. There would be a *dal*, a vegetable preparation, a chicken curry floating in oily orange gravy laden with spices, a curd preparation called *raita* and crispy *papads* to provide a crunch to the meal. In the middle of the plate would be a mound of rice and *chapattis*. And finally, in the corner would be a bowl of dessert, maybe a *halwa*.

They would all tuck in with gusto. For Amar, however, the pièce de résistance would come after the meal was over and the trays had been tucked under the seats to await the bearers at the next station. His mother would bring out a tin box which contained a homemade dessert. It would quite often be a *narru*, a small ball made of coconut, milk and jaggery, all cooked together over a slow fire until they became a thick glutinous mass which could then be shaped into balls. These balls when cooled became a delicious kind of stick jaw which took a lot of chewing to dissolve. They were one of Amar's favourites.

Thinking of all this awoke a craving for something sweet, and Amar dashed out to buy a slab of chocolate. Chewing on it, he thought how inadequate it felt against the memories of the *narru*.

"Not enjoying the chocolate? Don't blame you. Our confectionery is awful. Here, try some Swiss chocolate. You'll bless the difference." An attractive middle-aged woman, who had entered the compartment when Amar was out on the platform, was holding out a slab of chocolate. Amar broke off a piece and thanked her.

"Amazing! How did you know I wasn't enjoying the chocolate?" Amar asked mystified.

She smiled. "In my profession, expressions are the currency of the trade. We have to study them and reproduce them when the scene requires it. Your expression was very clear."

"No, no—it wasn't that I wasn't enjoying the chocolate," he said, thinking that politeness demanded it. "But I was remembering a kind of confectionery that is common in our country. And the taste that you have grown up with can never be supplanted by a newly acquired one."

She looked at him searchingly, and then smiled again. "You don't have to apologise. Our English chocolates are terrible compared to the European ones. And I know about childhood tastes and memories. They cannot be equalled. Where are you from, anyway?"

"India," he said.

They chatted comfortably after that, as the train moved out. It emerged that she was an actress. Amar now realised why she had looked familiar. He had seen her on TV.

❖

The ferry set off from Dover to the cries of seagulls and arrived at Calais to the call of more seagulls. Nature had imposed a unity which human beings tried so hard to pull apart.

On the train to Dusseldorf, a sense of fatigue started creeping in. Helga was still several hours away and he found himself restless, almost counting the minutes. A refreshment trolley came by, and he realised that part of the fatigue was due to hunger. He bought some cheese rolls and sausage rolls, together with a large pastry. And a large container of coffee which actually smelt of coffee! The joys of travelling in France!

With the food inside him he managed a nap, and was woken up as they crossed the border and passports were required. As they set off again, he realised dusk was approaching. It would be night by the time he reached. To stretch his cramped legs and to quell his edginess, he decided to take a walk down the corridor. Walking from one bogey to another he came across the refreshment car. There was a counter selling snacks and drinks and his eyes fell on bottles of German beer. He decided to treat himself to one and carried it back to the compartment. Used to the heavier English beer, he found the golden lager somewhat different. But it seemed to take some of the edge off his tension.

The last half hour was the most difficult. Had she got his last letter providing the train details? If she was not there at the station would he be able to find his way to the flat with no knowledge of the language? Would he be imposing on her by staying a week, given her tight finances? He realised that there were satisfactory answers to all of these, and he knew them. But the mind throws up unnecessary questions when there is a deeper one squirming in the depths. That question finally surfaced. Were her feelings as intense as they had been when they parted? He had to admit that, if he was brutally honest, his had been diluted somewhat. A lot of time had elapsed, could her romantic focus not have shifted'?

Finally, the train slowed down, and Dusseldorf appeared on the board on the platform. Amar, who until now had been raring to arrive and jump off the train, suddenly found himself holding back from disembarking. After all the others had filed out, he hesitantly picked up his rucksack and slowly got off the train.

The platform was full of hurrying passengers wanting to get to the buses, taxis or cars. Some had been met by family, and after the first hug, were engaged in the banalities that surface when people meet after a break. Soon the platform emptied and Amar stood looking around. He could see no sign of her. He wondered if there was any place as desolate as an empty platform.

Slowly he hefted his rucksack and started walking towards the exit. He felt low. Why had he come, he wondered, if this was the kind of enthusiasm that she showed. Maybe he should make this a short visit. His feet seemed to be reluctant to move and he was reduced to a shuffle. His worst fears had been realised. She had not come.

Announcements in German kept reverberating through the system. Should he try to find a youth hostel to spend the night in and go back to London the next day without seeing her? The idea seemed to have merit, though it did not arouse any enthusiasm in him.

The noises of a busy station swept by him. The shuffle of feet, the sound of people running to catch up with some train. He heard the sound of running feet near him. A passenger who had left something behind on the train. Suddenly, a shadow appeared in his peripheral vision and he felt arms go around him. Startled, he looked around to find a tearful face next to his.

"Oh, A-mar, I was afraid I had missed you! I went to a mistaken platform—and then realised what I had done. I have been running …" and then she couldn't speak anymore and buried her face in his chest. He held her close and smelt her familiar cologne. It seemed to release something within him. He held her tighter and inhaled her closeness.

After a while she slowly disengaged herself and looked at him. "You've got a stain on your shirt," she admonished, picking at the fabric with her fingers. "I'll wash it out when we get home."

"I've got a strain in my heart, you little devil!" he grinned, "I thought you weren't coming!"

She stopped and looked at him angrily. "Not coming? What kind of person do you think I am? Somebody who forgets her heart so easily? You are—stupid … very stupid." She drew away from him and walked ahead.

He followed, feeling foolish. When she turned around there were tears in her eyes. "Did you really imagine that I could just put you behind me? Oh, A-mar you are so foolish." She came and clutched on to him. "I have not been sleeping at nights waiting for you. I have not been able to concentrate at my work because I was impatient for you. And—you—you think I forget you? How could you do this … ?"

"Because, I need you so much, my little cabbage—not seeing you made me feel terrible and alone. I'm sorry if I upset you."

"And you have not even kissed me," she sniffed.

So they kissed long and deep, under a street light. When they parted, she opened her bag and took out her handkerchief to wipe away her tears. Then she scrabbled around in her bag again and took out something. "I brought an apple for you because I knew you would be hungry."

Amar's eyes suddenly filled at her thoughtfulness. He blinked his tears away and took the apple from her. "Thank you," he mumbled.

They held hands and walked slowly to the bus stop.

❖

The flat was a small one on the third floor overlooking a crossing. The door was opened by a sturdy but shapely young woman who was introduced as Hilde. She was the live-in help who looked after Helga's baby. Amar's heart sank. In this tiny flat, where would he and Helga get any privacy? They entered into a small living room area which, apart from a dining table and chairs, also had a baby bed with railings. The bedroom was on the left and Helga led him through. It was tiny, and had a single bed. Amar dropped his rucksack into a corner and looked around. There was a big window overlooking the street and a built-in wardrobe in one corner, adjoining a dressing table and stool. His eyes came back to the bed and Helga smiled. "Don't worry, we will both fit in, if you hold me close enough." Amar felt a little embarrassed. "I know what you are thinking A-mar, you are uncomfortable because of Hilde. Don't worry, she sleeps on the floor next to the bed. She doesn't snore so we won't be disturbed." Then seeing the expression on Amar's face she burst out laughing. "She sleeps in the living room, silly! And there's a door between here and the living room. Now it all depends on how noisy we are," she giggled mischievously.

Amar, unused to this casual attitude towards sex, looked stern. "Don't joke about this, Helga."

She folded her hands together and looked serious. "I will say the Lord's prayer before we make love, and another prayer after we finish. That will satisfy you?"

Amar couldn't restrain a smile at the vision of a naked Helga kneeling and saying her prayers. "As long as you tell your Lord to keep out of this room, I will be happy."

"Maybe I'll tell him to attend to Hilde."

Madelena, the baby was fast asleep. They had dinner out of a large bowl of beef stew with crusty bread to go with it. Hilde did not speak English, so conversation was limited. Amar was keen to finish dinner as soon as possible.

The bathroom was off the living room and Amar brushed his teeth, changed into his pyjamas and self-consciously went into the bedroom after saying goodnight to Hilde. He still had not got used to the idea of openly sharing the bedroom with Helga. She kept him waiting for some time before she appeared in a housecoat. Amar's throat had gone dry with expectation and his hands turned cold. Helga seemed quite collected as she closed the door, switched on a bedside lamp and switched off the main light. He stood up and she came into his arms. Her body felt soft and warm as he crushed her to him. Her mouth found his and her tongue darted between his lips. It was a long kiss and Amar was breathing heavily after it. He unbuttoned her housecoat and found her wearing a short flimsy nightdress through which he could feel her warm silky skin.

"Let's get to bed," she whispered. "But let's wait a little before we start anything. She'll be asleep in a few minutes."

The lights in the living room, visible through a chink under the door, went off. Helga carried on a conversation while lying in his arms, as if they were sitting at a table. Amar's hand was busy caressing her breasts. "Was the journey comfortable, my darling?" she asked.

Amar mumbled a reply.

"Did you get enough to eat on the train?"

Amar was now nibbling at her nipples and found it difficult to answer.

"I know that you got enough to drink, I smelt it on your breath."

Amar did not bother to reply, busy as he was sliding his hand down her stomach. "Not yet, darling—not yet," she whispered.

"And what about your travelling companions—did you meet a sexy seductress?" She carried on the one-sided conversation.

This time Amar nodded his head vigorously and said yes, before continuing with his exploration.

"What?" asked Helga alarmed. "What did you say? Be serious now, A-mar, I want an answer," and she took his hand away from her thighs. "Who did you meet?"

"Only an actress. Good-looking." His hand went back to where it had been and decided to probe further.

"You serious?" she asked suspiciously. "Or are you joking?"

"She was only a TV actress," and he went back to her nipples.

"Oh A-mar, don't joke with me." Then as his hands started caressing her she muttered, "Oh—oh—darling." Their conversation stopped.

The lovemaking was hurried and desperate. Once it ended they lay in each other's arms breathing raggedly.

"Oh God, how much I needed that!" Amar gasped.

She gently kissed him and said, "This is what I have been dreaming about since London."

❖

Their sweat dried and they got their breath back with Amar lying with his head on her breast. He loved the smell of her—animal, warm, musky. He did not want to talk. It was enough for him to lie there and take it all in.

Helga stroked his back slowly and was lost in her own thoughts. After a while she asked casually, "And who was this actress?"

Amar groaned. "Darling, let it go! She was just somebody I met on the train and got talking to because she offered me a chocolate. It wasn't important."

Helga stiffened. "She offered you chocolate! You realise that was symbolic."

"Helga! Don't get Freudian on me at this time of the night. We've just had a wonderful experience."

She didn't reply but kept rubbing his back.

Sometime later as Amar was drifting into sleep she asked, "How old was she?"

Amar lifted his head from her breast and said, "Who?"

"The siren who offered you her chocolate."

Amar sighed. "She was middle-aged—may even have been forty. And to put the matter to rest, let me tell you that we chatted for some time and that was it. I'm not going to meet her again. So, can you now relax, sweetheart?"

She looked at him with a forlorn expression. "Oh, A-mar, I'm so jealous of anyone who can get your attention. I want to be all you think of. I don't want anyone to take the space in your mind or thought or emotion that I occupy. I want you all for myself." She buried her face on his chest. Her muffled voice said, "Oh, A-mar—I do love you so much." He felt her damp face on his chest and held her closer, feeling a special tenderness.

She caressed his stomach and then slid her hand down to his groin. Her hands caressed him and soon he found himself ready again. This time she straddled him. Their lovemaking was prolonged and languorous. At the end as she lay recovering her breath, she said, "Now you see—you don't have to do all the work."

As Amar finished the messy job of taking the condom off, she took it from him as she had done the time before and wrapped it in her handkerchief. Amar asked why she was doing this and she said that she would go to the bathroom and get rid of them. She got up, put on her housecoat and slid out of the room, opening the door only partly.

After she came back she got into bed and into his arms. They chatted desultorily and Amar dozed off, overcome by a gentle tiredness. He woke sometime in the night and saw Helga's sleeping face next to him. She had a small smile on her face as if she was dreaming of something pleasant. He watched her with a sense of contentment for quite a while. Then in gratitude, he gently kissed her on her lips. She shifted and muttered something in German. Then with her eyes still closed she put her arms around him. His body responded to the pressure of her thighs against his. But he did not want to wake her. He tried to ease out of her grasp, but when he moved she tightened her grip. Still with her eyes closed she wrapped her legs around him and started rocking slowly. Amar's hands slid between her thighs and he found her moist and ready to receive him. They made love with great gentleness. At the end as she gasped, she opened her eyes and said, "Oh, A-mar, oh darling, it was so wonderful!"

Trying to get his breath back, Amar muttered, "I thought you were asleep."

She replied sleepily, "So … you were raping me while I was asleep? No, sweetheart, I was awake from moment I felt your kiss."

"Then why did you keep your eyes closed all the time?"

"Because it was such a lovely experience with my eyes closed. I felt I was being pampered and pleasured without having to do anything myself."

They fell asleep in each other's arms.

The Longest Bar

Amar woke up disoriented looking around confusedly at an unfamiliar room. The walls were at a different angle, the light not the same. As the sleep cleared, memory came back. Helga was not in the bed, but her body aroma remained. He savoured it and then realised that the source was not far off. He called out to her. She came looking preoccupied, but he made her sit down on the bed. "Where have you been?" he asked petulantly as he buried his face in her lap.

"Getting breakfast ready, you great baby," she smiled as she stroked his hair.

"I've been missing you," he replied, his voice muffled as he nuzzled into her lap further.

"You're worse than Madelena," she scolded gently, still stroking his hair. "Now get up and brush your teeth."

"Why can't you just get into …" he wasn't allowed to complete his sentence before she slapped him gently and said a firm, "No."

"Now up you get," she said dragging him up. "To the bathroom," she commanded.

❖

At breakfast Amar found himself with a ravenous appetite. The heavy bread tasted good with just butter, although there was also cheese to go with it. The apples were crunchy and sweet. And the coffee was fragrant and rich.

Little Madelena sat on her high chair and smeared her face with butter as she tried to eat the slice of bread in front of her. She carried on an animated conversation with Amar who could not understand a word. Nor, he guessed, could Helga. He walked his fingers towards her slice of bread and she looked on intrigued until his fingers neared the bread. Then in alarm she picked up the piece and held it to her and frowned at him. When his fingers retreated she looked relieved and put the piece down in front of her. Then she raised her chubby hand and waved it from side to side to indicate that Amar should not do it again. Amar pretended to cry and Helga explained to her that he was hungry. Wouldn't she share some of her bread with him? She thought for a little while and then lifted the by-now-grubby piece and offered it to Amar. He kissed her little hand and thanked her, then put the piece of bread to her mouth. She looked at him and then bit into it and smiled. After that it became a game. He would walk his fingers up, she would snatch up the piece of bread and try to hide it, he would pretend to cry, she would offer it to him, and he would then feed her while she gurgled with delight.

'She likes you," Helga said contentedly. "And you are good with her."

"Not as good with Hilde, though," Amar said as she went to the kitchen for more coffee. Hilde had been polite, but seemed to treat him with some suspicion.

"You do not have to be so good with her," Helga said with severity, kicking him under the table. "Her boyfriend would not like it—and—neither I. So behave."

"All I wanted to do was to say what a lovely figure she had," Amar said, deftly moving his chair back from her kick.

Just then Hilde came back with the coffee pot and Helga said something to her. Hilde blushed and muttered something.

"I told her that you thought she had a nice figure," she grinned mischievously. "And she said to thank you."

Then she said something to Hilde and both laughed. Hilde replied and for the first time looked at Amar with a smile.

"I said what will Dirk think of this? And she said that this is a secret between you and her and Dirk will not know. See—you're now a hit with her also. I don't like it one bit."

Amar gestured to Hilde to say that now he would be beaten up by Helga. Hilde grinned and put her hand on his arm and said something.

"She says she will protect you from me." Helga said and then added something in German to Hilde. Hilde blushed again and with a smile still on her face, managed to frown.

"I told her that she should take my place in the bedroom tonight, and I would look after Madelena. She is shocked and embarrassed," Helga said with a grin.

Amar was shocked himself. "Hey, stop this. It's not funny."

❖

Helga had taken the day off. She asked Amar whether he would like to go out. He looked at her as if to say what a stupid question—when there were other things they could do. She smiled enigmatically.

He showered and found himself at a loose end because there was no newspaper to read. He played with Madelena for a while and then stared out of the window watching life go on in the street below, while Helga busied herself with household chores. This wasn't turning out quite the way he had imagined.

He watched idly while Hilde bustled around. He realised after a time that she was preparing to go out, and suddenly the morning took on a new life. She appeared to be taking Madelena with her and he realised that this was the reason behind Helga's enigmatic smile. As Hilde wheeled the small pram out and smiled meaningfully at Helga and closed the door, Amar grabbed Helga from behind and hugged her "You're a magician! How did you organise all this? How did you know that this is what I wanted?"

"Because this is what I wanted, stupid!" she said as she came into his arms. They made love on the carpet in the living room.

❖

Later, after Hilde's return, Helga and Amar walked down to the neighbourhood store to stock up on groceries. The street did not look very different from a London one, except for the signs being in German and the traffic moving on the right. The buildings, though, did not look as sooty and the streets as dirty. The tramcars were a novelty too.

She took his hand. He felt self-conscious and tried to withdraw, but she held on and quelled him with a stern stare. At the store he followed Helga down the aisle holding the basket while she tossed things into it from the shelves. Is this what married life was like? he wondered. It was not too bad a feeling doing things together. At the cash counter he would not let her pay, in spite of her protests, though it depleted his stock of Deutsch marks significantly.

They slowly strolled back. Amar asked whether the city had been severely damaged during the War, because he saw few signs. Helga smiled. "Do you know, almost half the city was reduced to rubble by incessant bombing during the War? In 1939, there were 5,40,000 civilians in the city. At the end of the War there were just 3,70,000. Oh yes, the city has really suffered."

"But then, why don't I see more signs of it—it's only about eleven years since the War ended?"

"The reason is interesting. This area came under British occupation, and in 1946 the British decided that this city should become the capital of the newly formed county called Nordrhein-Westfalen. As a result, the city's reconstruction proceeded at an unbelievable pace. Nobody could have dreamt of it in 1945. So, you see, we are indebted to the British in a way." She smiled wryly.

It was cool with an overcast sky, but there was a pleasant breeze. Amar suggested that they should go for a longer walk. "We will," she said, "but in the evening. Right now we need to get back and prepare lunch. You're going to help me."

Back at the flat, she busied herself with preparing pork ribs in mustard, a local speciality. Amar did odd jobs like fetching the herbs and spices, pots and pans. While he did that, he would surreptitiously give her a kiss or caress her bottom. She finally banished him from the kitchen.

The lunch was delicious and Amar had to admit to her that she was a better cook than he was. He did the washing up and then as he was drying his hand looked at her meaningfully. She fractionally shook her head looking in the direction of Hilde and then with the suggestion of a smile whispered, "Tonight".

❖

After a light supper that evening Helga took Amar to Altstadt, the city centre. "This is referred to as the longest bar in Germany because of the number of drinking places on this road," Helga said. "Here you must drink Altbier which is one of our traditional beers. It is better than the light lagers which are so popular, and which have so little character."

This was the old part of town. Tall houses with their typical conical hats lined the river. There were sculptures on the road, but Amar had never been enthused by carvings. His interest now was in tasting the Altbier.

They found a place at one of the bars, an old-fashioned place with plain wooden tables and chairs. Helga engaged in a conversation with the blue-clad waiter. "He says we should order the Fuchsen—that is supposed to be the best, but don't believe what he says. Maybe they have a special deal with the brewery."

"Let's order it anyway," Amar said with mounting anticipation.

The beer came in stubby glasses carried on a metal tray. The waiter just plonked down a glass in front of any customer whose glass was empty and kept track by putting a tick mark on the beer mat. The beer was an inviting copper colour with a creamy looking head.

"Prost," said Amar and lifted his glass. "*Hagalakayi,*" said Helga with a grin and Amar collapsed with laughter.

"You remember?" he asked delightedly.

"Of course. It is an Indian prayer," she replied with a straight face.

"You know, this is not as bitter as the English ales. In fact, unlike the British ales this is full-bodied and malty."

Helga grimaced. "You are suffering from English disease of trying to be technical about everyday things. Just enjoy the taste and let the Britishers write their doctorates on malty or whatever it is."

Amar was not amused at being labelled a closet Brit. He just sat back and drank. Conversation languished. Until Helga took a deep breath and said, "Actually, the Altbier is a very complex beer. It has a great similarity to the British pale ales, but it is made with warm top fermentation followed by lagering at a low temperature. This may sound a contradiction, but it is not. Altbier has had to cope with a lot of competition from bottom-fermented beers and there is fear that it may lose market share to them."

Amar sat up. He had no idea what she was talking about, but was impressed. "Er … right. Yes, yes, quite right. I had no idea you were so knowledgeable. Er … where did you pick up all this knowledge?"

Helga just shrugged. "Altbiers, as you would know, have a hoppy finish. There are a lot of copies of Altbier, but the newer versions can never match the complexity of the original …" And she continued for a few more minutes. Amar began to feel quite overwhelmed in the face of so much knowledge. Until he noticed her glancing down every now and again. He glared at her and covered the back of the menu card with his hand. She continued "… it's the top fermenting process which gives the Altbier its fruity flavour. There is a hint of smokiness due to the malting process followed, and your nails need cutting, though I do love your fingers …"

"You're a little crook," Amar said sternly. "You've been reading the menu all the time. And here I was being greatly impressed by your knowledge."

"What does it matter, A-mar, whether I read it out or recite from memory? If I recited it, you would have been impressed. But because I'm reading it out, you are not. Why? It is same information. Why worship memory?"

"You're not just a little crook, but a highly intelligent little crook."

Helga blinked her eyelids and maintained an innocent expression. "My memory now tells me that Schlussel is even better than the Fuchsen that we have had. So can we please have a Schlussel?"

❖

The lovemaking that night was especially tender. Maybe it was the beer that had slowed them down. Maybe it was the knowledge of each other's bodies which took away the tension and edginess. Maybe it was the languor induced by a lazy day. But they took their time and savoured each other. Amar drank in the experience through all his senses.

They lay in the soft aftermath of lovemaking. Amar closed his eyes as he got his breath back. He felt the softness and warmth of Helga's body next to him, and turned his head to nuzzle into Helga's breasts. Outside, the night was quiet, except for the desultory car which passed by in the road below. The neon sign on the other side of the road reflected on the room wall in faded red and blue. He felt a great sense of peace as Helga gently ran her fingers through his hair.

"Are you top-fermented or bottom-fermented?" Amar asked drowsily.

"If you still do not know you have obviously not drunk enough," she murmured equally sleepily.

He rectified it a little later.

The Parting

Outside the window, the night drifted by as if this was just another night. The late-night bus ground by in the street below, the cars crept along, a few pedestrians crouched under umbrellas walked home on the glistening pavements. The world just went on—another day ending. But this was not. It was their last night together. For how long, Amar did not know.

He would be going back to India in a few months' time, once his exams were over. What would happen to their relationship? Was she willing to make this a permanent relationship—for that matter, was he? They had never talked about it nor had he seriously thought about it.

Would he like to be with her for the rest of his life? He could honestly not say yes. The past week had taken some of the gloss off the relationship. They had had arguments about trifles. He had learnt enough about human nature to know that these reflected a deeper discontentment. Yet he had sworn love to her, something he had not done with any other woman. Had he been honest then? Was he being honest now? These were the questions churning inside him.

The rain pattered against the window pane. On any other evening this sound would have filled him with joy, because this was a sound he loved. Today it depressed him.

Helga had saved up a bottle of white wine for their last evening. Amar watched the liquid in his wine glass glinting golden against the light from the table lamp. The glass was frosted and a drop of condensation ran down the side. "A tear of sadness or a pearl of joy?" Amar mused.

Helga's reply was sharp. "A-mar, stop finding sadness in everything around you. I do not understand you ..."

"I don't understand myself, Helga." Amar looked out of the window pensively. "But we Bengalis tend to be a collection of depressives. We get a perverse pleasure from sadness. Maybe we are somewhat like the Russians. How they love to dwell on the darkness of their winters, the melancholy in relationships. Except that they have a redeeming feature we don't have—they shed their tears while knocking back vodkas!" Amar hoped this would introduce a bit of lightness to the conversation.

Helga was unmoved. "But this is not healthy, A-mar. Feeling sadness when there is a reason is all right, but we must also feel joy when there is reason for it."

"You're right, my wise princess. Oh by the way, did you notice the pimple developing on your nose?"

Helga got up in alarm to look into the mirror. "Where is it? Where …" she kept frantically looking.

Amar couldn't control his laughter. He got up and held her from behind "There is nothing, my little idiot—your flawless skin remains flawless. But do you see how easy it is to lose your sense of joy—even over trivial issues?"

She turned around and started pummelling his chest. "You horrible man. That was mean—mean …" and she kept pummelling him. "I do not want to talk to you," she pouted.

He held her closer and whispered, "Who's interested in talking?"

Fencing colours

After returning from Germany, Amar had not had time to think about the problem which had been taxing him in Dusseldorf, but the issue was always at the edge of his mind. He had hoped that his visit would help cement his feelings for Helga, but realised with disquiet that it hadn't.

Was Helga also experiencing this sense of deflation? Her first few letters had not revealed any such feelings. But the frequency of her letters had reduced. And was there just—ever so faint, but a discernible preoccupation with something else? Or was he being fanciful?

He decided that enough was enough. He had to return to the business of preparing for his examination which was due at the end of this term. Time was short. Terribly short.

❖

A couple of weeks later, he was taking a walk in the corridor after a concentrated session in the library when Greg sought him out. He held out his hand. Bewildered, Amar took it.

"Congratulations, Amar. The Athletic Union have decided to award you full colours for fencing. And that means something, because full colours are not easy to come by. Most good performers have to be satisfied with half colours. Well done!"

Amar looked befuddled. He had really not thought about this since his conversation with Angela, which seemed years ago. Fencing colours! His mind seemed unable to grasp it, and he found it difficult to respond. "Thanks—Greg. Thanks a lot. This … this is a—a—wonderful surprise. Quite honestly, I had forgotten that this was the time that colours were handed out! Thanks for bringing me this good news. I—I really don't know what to say!"

"Well, let me tell you, this was no fluke. You thoroughly deserved it."

Amar was even more surprised by this fulsome praise, coming from someone he had had words with. He had misjudged him. Misjudged the sense of fairness that the English possessed. "Thanks again, Greg—thanks for fighting my corner. I know the AU doesn't release these things easily, and a lot of persuasion and argument is involved. You did all that on my behalf—my grateful thanks."

He wandered away in a bit of a daze, still not fully absorbing the news. At lunch, as he was getting up from his table at the refectory he heard Angela's voice. "Am—Am, I just heard the news," she said as she ran towards him. "Congratulations!" she said holding both his hands. "All of us are so happy for you. Well done! And it's full colours too!" She gave a final squeeze and released his hands. He couldn't help thinking, why not give me a hug instead, you stupid girl.

"Thanks, Angela. I still haven't absorbed it all. I can't still believe it!"

"Well, to help you absorb the news properly, we're getting together in the Three Tuns at six this evening—make sure you're there!" she said, shaking her finger at him.

Pramod, who had been listening to the conversation in some bewilderment, asked him as Angela left, "What was all that about?"

"Oh, I forgot to mention this earlier. Apparently I've been awarded fencing colours."

Pramod didn't seem particularly enthused. "Good. Congratulations."

Amar bristled. "Show some more enthusiasm, you *unpad dehati* (illiterate villager)! It's not every day that an Indian gets full colours for fencing in a white world!"

"All right, all right—it's a praiseworthy performance. You've done well."

Amar burst out laughing, "You sound like a constipated Brit having to praise an Indian curry at a diplomatic dinner."

"What would you have me do? Dance the bhangra and shout *Balle Balle*?" Pramod replied testily.

Amar laughed even louder. "Our good Sharmaji doing the bhangra! That would be a sight for the Brits to see! Why didn't Gandhiji think of this as a secret weapon in our fight for independence? What havoc it would have caused—what terror it would have unleashed ..."

Pramod was not amused. He particularly disliked being reminded of his surname. He got up, and collecting his tray, said coldly, "When you've got over your schoolboy seizure, we can perhaps continue the conversation we were having."

Amar clapped. "Better and better. You know Pramod—you sound more and more like the upper-class Brit every day. They'll be offering you club membership at the Raffles if you can maintain this progress!" But this was said to a retreating back.

Amar wondered if he had been unnecessarily aggressive towards his friend. Had Pramod's dismissal of the colours achievement upset him? Or was it the unresolved Dusseldorf problem which was making him needlessly edgy? Amar felt an unfamiliar sadness, as if another era was coming to an end. He feared that the Dusseldorf one, maybe, was.

❖

The Three Tuns was less crowded than usual, probably because of the impending annual exams. Amar made his way a little self-consciously to the table with some Fencing Club members crowded around it. There was a muted cheer as he arrived. Amar was embarrassed. "You lot should be in the library, not swilling beer!" he said in the severe tones of one of the not-well-liked lecturers.

This was greeted by good-natured jeers. "Can we have refills all round, Guv?" "Where's the magnum of champagne you'd promised us?" "Drink up lads, there's a table booked at his club by Am" ...

Amar held up his hand. "Steady on, troops. As all of you must know, the magnum of champagne went to the AU Colours

Committee earlier as a sweetener. And none of you lot would be allowed entry into my club, anyway."

There was a chorus of boos, and Amar sat down. He found himself next to Angela, whether by accident or design, he did not know. She put a warm hand on his arm and asked, "What will you have, Am? Remember you aren't allowed to buy a round today—it's all on us."

There was a chorus of disapproval. "You let the cat out of the bag! We wanted him to sweat a bit as he saw the tab mounting. You're a spoilsport, Ange!"

Angela smiled and said firmly, "Quiet everyone! Let the man have a drink in his hand before all of you descend on him like a wolf pack! And now that he has—let's congratulate and toast him. To you Am, and the great achievement of yours! Well done!"

There were cheers all around and everyone drank. Amar took a long draught of his beer and relaxed. He turned to Angela, "Hey—after all that, don't I at least get a kiss?"

Angela blushed, but planted a kiss on his cheek amidst laughter. Amar looked around the table "What, no other takers? Not you, Ed. You're the wrong sex ..."

Conversation resumed, and Amar sat back. For some reason he was feeling quite exhausted. Angela seemed to realise this. "What's the matter, Am? You don't seem to be enjoying your moment of triumph," she asked quietly.

He replied in a low voice, because he did not want the others to hear, "I'm not sure why. Partly because, between you and me, I'm not sure I deserved the colours. And I'm not being modest. I know, I know ... I have a good score of wins against the teams we fenced with. But I really don't think that they were of a particularly high standard. I would have felt better if I had been pitted against really high-quality fencers. And partly it's due to a feeling of disillusionment which seems to assail me every time I have some success. The glamour and the colour seem to disappear the moment I reach the goal. Sorry, I shouldn't be getting into all this on an occasion like this. But you asked—and I felt you were one person I could share my feelings with. Forget it—let's return to the festivities."

Angela touched him lightly on his arm. "This is the first time you've opened yourself to me, and I'm happy that you have."

"Hey, you can't monopolise all the pretty girls just because you're a colours man!" Rod yelled across the table. "Share her with us!"

Amar grinned mischievously and turned to Angela, "Are you willing to be shared?"

Angela blushed a deep pink.

"Isn't that a rather anti-woman thing to say?" Jane asked out of the blue. So she's back to her dysfunctional ways, Amar thought, creating discord out of nothing. Was it her need to be at the centre of things? He could see, though, where her remark came from. She'd been carrying around Simone de Beauvoir's *The Second Sex* for some time, and possibly felt it appropriate to flaunt her newfound intellectual property.

Aloud, he said, "Is sharing friendship anti-woman?"

"No, but regarding a woman as an object which can be distributed amongst men, is," she replied.

"I'm afraid you're twisting meanings to win a debating point, Jane." Amar went on, "What Rod said was that I was monopolising Angela, and that others should also be given a chance to enjoy her company. This could equally have been said about a man. And if you're reflecting Simone de Beauvoir's thinking, let me add that you've got it wrong. Her position was that there was a tendency for men being treated as a norm to which women should aspire. That women were being regarded as belonging to a different category. Here, if the remark made could equally apply to a man or woman, where is the discrimination?"

Before Jane could reply, Angela intervened somewhat angrily. "Hold on, people, hold on will you? I'm the one who is supposed to have been the subject of discrimination, and yet I have not been asked for my opinion! Jane don't you see that *you* are treating me like an object by by-passing me? If anyone is treating me like a second sex, *you* are. Don't you think I'm capable of standing up for myself if I felt slighted? I know I should feel grateful at your rushing to my defence—but quite honestly, I don't. I just feel irritated at the implication that I can't fight my own corner and need someone to defend me. This is the stereotypical attitude to women that you're displaying, I'm sorry to say. And you as a woman shouldn't be doing it. In any case what's all the fuss about? *I* don't see anything wrong with what either Rod or Am said, so why all the kerfuffle?"

Jane looked quite taken aback by this outburst, as did most of the group. Amar had not seen this side of Angela before either, and was equally surprised. Maybe it was the built-up resentment at constantly being "managed" by Jane which had burst its banks. Whatever it was, Amar felt delighted, though he did begin to feel a little sorry for Jane who was, metaphorically, almost gasping for breath.

"I'm sorry, Angela, if that is the way you see it. At no time was it my intention to belittle you or treat you like an object. I'm sorry."

Rod saved the situation by clapping his hands and raising his voice. "OK folks, time for another round, I think. I can't put my head around all that's being said because Simone de Beauvoir is beyond my intellectual capabilities. Maybe another pint would help me see the light. Jane, I think you need a refill, and deserve one for introducing a bit of crackle into the evening. Give me your glass, darling, and what about the other ladies? Could you give me a hand with the glasses, Am?"

Angela gave her glass to Amar, and said in a low voice, "Gin and It, please."

Amar collected the other glasses and accompanied Rod to the bar. "Rod, well done. You saved the situation."

Rod grinned through his newly revived straggling beard. "Yeah, well, I was just being honest. I don't have a clue about Simone de Beauvoir or existentialism. For me existentialism is—I pee therefore I am."

Amar laughed. "You are a madman, you are, Rod! Maybe we should start a pee-existentialism school of thought with you as the founder! But seriously now, tell me—do you fancy Jungle Jane? I think she fancies you. And now suddenly her outburst falls into place. She was jealous at your asking for Angela's company."

Rod looked a bit sheepish. "W-e-e-l-l," he drawled, "I do like Jane. We seem to get on well together. We've been out together a bit."

"Ah—hah! There you are. Now it all fits!" Amar exclaimed.

Back at the table, peace seemed to have been restored and Ed was recounting some story of his experiences as a postman during Christmas. "It was a cold evening and I was finishing my round delivering mail at Swiss Cottage. I rang the bell—and bingo, all my fantasies seemed to have been realised. Would you believe it, the door was opened by this gorgeous woman, with a glass of wine in her hand, who smiled welcomingly. I handed her the mail and she said, "Oh, thank you so much. Won't you come in out of the cold and have a drink?"

Ed paused and drank from his glass. He seemed disinclined to continue, so somebody asked "And … ?"

"Well, I went in—end of story. What I wanted to show is that doing a Christmas job can have its bonuses."

Andy, who knew Ed better than the others, chipped in, "Not quite the end, Ed, was it?"

Ed wasn't to be drawn further. He turned to Amar and asked, "So, Am, tell us how it feels to be a colours holder."

Andy was not going to relent. Stifling a smile he said, "Come on, Ed—if you don't tell 'em what happened, I'm going to …"

By now Ed had begun to turn red. "Nothing much really. She gave me a glass of wine and that was it."

"Except that," Andy was laughing so much that he had to pause. "Except that he'd got too close to her and her dog decided to intervene, and last seen, he was haring out of the door with the dog in chase and he almost had to have stitches on his rump!"

"Don't exaggerate, Andy, you weren't even there," a red-faced Ed remonstrated.

Buxom Beverly made comforting noises amidst the laughter and said, "Don't worry, Ed darling, don't pay any notice to these rude people. You've still got a nice rump!"

Somebody said, "Did you notice any scars, Bev?"

Equal to it, Beverly replied, "No, darling, the lights were out."

❖

Jane was among the first to leave and looked at Angela as she got up, since they usually left together. Angela shook her head and said, "You go ahead, Jane, I'll stay for a while longer."

The party started to break up and people began collecting their scarves and coats. Rod, Angela and Amar were the only ones that remained. Rod got up and said, "Come on, one for the road."

"Not for me, thanks," said Angela.

Rod grimaced, "Hey, folks, don't let me down. I want to end the party with a bang. It's not every day that a friend of mine gets elected to the House! You're not going to say no too are you, Am?"

Amar laughed, "All right, you old reprobate, I'll have one last drink—but just a half please. I'll have to see Angela to the Tube station before I head for the House, and I need to have a clear head to go through the Cabinet papers!"

Rod wandered off a little unsteadily to fetch the drinks. Angela looked a little worried. "You think he'll be all right?"

"Oh yes, I know his capacity for drink—nothing to worry about."

"That was sweet of you to offer to see me to the Tube station."

Amar had been surprised himself when the offer just rolled off his tongue without premeditation. "It's a pleasure I've often promised myself, but never been able to achieve. And time rolls on remorselessly."

She gently reached out and touched his hand.

Rod came shambling back. "Here you are, old man. And here's to a friend I will miss—cheers." Suddenly, the thought of his end-of-term departure became more real to Amar. The genuine sense of loss which came through from this tall gangling Englishman who would normally hesitate to show his emotions, greatly moved Amar. His eyes threatened to fill up, and he had to use a lot of self-control to prevent it.

He raised his glass and said, "Thanks, my whiskered friend. Hey—I've not gone yet—the obituaries needn't come out so soon." He immediately felt ashamed at the lack of graciousness in this reply and decided that the world-weary poseur was not what he wanted to be just now. He sighed and said, "Sorry, Rod, that did not come out right. That is not what I'm feeling just now. I'm feeling an intense sadness that I'll have to leave my dear friends behind soon. And what you said almost brought tears to my eyes. So in the best British tradition I was trying to not show it—and a clumsy ungracious sentence came out. I will miss you lot a great deal—and I'll particularly miss you two." He had to resort to another sip to control the emotions which were teetering on the brink. "What kind of people are we becoming? Is it only alcohol that allows us to make our emotions public?"

The evening folded up soon after. They climbed down the stairs and emerged into the chilly night. Rod said his goodbyes, "I'm going the other way—congratulations again Am, and take care. Bye, Angela." Amar blessed Rod's delicacy in leaving the two of them together.

Instead of turning right towards Holborn Tube station, Amar took Angela's arm and turned left. "Do you mind a small walk, Angela? I just want to clear my head, so much seems to have been compressed into one evening."

"I could do with a walk too," she said, gripping his arm more closely.

They came out onto Aldwych, turned right towards Lancaster Place, and walked in silence for some time. "Shall we go to the river?" Amar asked. She nodded.

At the Embankment they turned right and walked slowly along the river. The air was cool and the river a liquid bronze under the street lamps. They leant against the Embankment and looked at the oily river which seemed still except for an occasional brown swirl. Amar could feel the warmth of Angela's body next to him. "You won't believe, Angela, how often I've dreamt about this—being with you, away from the crowd. And of the wonderfully witty aphorisms that would emerge from my mouth which would have you laughing, and of the terribly clever things I would say which would have you regarding me with new respect. And now when it actually happens, I'm more or less speechless, with my heart thumping inside me in panic."

Angela moved a little closer and took hold of his hand. "Your hands are icy."

"Just shows how scared I am."

"But of what, Am? Do I frighten you so much?"

"No, not you. It's the feelings which you evoke in me. It's like a storm inside me struggling to emerge. And it's an almost impossible effort to keep it under control. It frightens me."

"Why should a genuine emotion frighten you, Am?" she asked softly.

"Because—because—of the fear of rejection."

"And why should there be rejection?" she asked even more softly—so softly that Amar wasn't sure he had heard her.

He turned to her and tilted her face towards him. Her eyes met his and he seemed to be drawn into them. He gently lowered his face and found her lips. They were soft and light but they responded. They stayed together kissing tenderly in an envelope of silence while the world sped by around them.

As they came apart, Amar looked at her and she kept her eyes on his. They seemed to reciprocate his yearning and he gently took her into his arms. This time their lips met and parted and her tongue played on his. He became conscious of the warmth of her body pressed against him and his kiss became more demanding. How long they stood there in their own little world, lips clasped, bodies pressed, eyes closed, he did not know. He seemed to be in a dream. When he came out of it, he gently led her to a nearby bench and they sat down.

She put her head on his shoulders and whispered, "Oh … Am …"

"Do you know how long I've wanted to do this?"

She shook her head.

"Almost from the time I first met you."

She smiled and burrowed her head into his collar, "Liar."

"Honest—I did."

"Then what took you so long? I thought you didn't hesitate to take what you liked … Priscilla for example …"

Amar laughed quietly. "Oh, Priscilla. Yes … Priscilla. In her case I think it was a question of *her* taking what she wanted. I was just there to be added to her list."

Angela sat up, "Oh Am—don't be unfair. She really wasn't that much of a man-eater. She obviously liked you." Then she added archly, "And in any case, I thought it was you making the play at the party where you first met her!"

Amar grinned, "And you know why? Because you were flirting with that incorrigible Greg."

This time Angela laughed. "You can't be serious! He just put his head on my lap and there was nothing I could do to get it off without being rude in the middle of the party. I was planning to get up to find a polite way out of it, but then I saw you making hay with dear Priscilla. And I thought—well, if he's going hammer and tongs to charm her, I'll teach him a lesson. So I let him lie."

"I don't believe it—you were actually jealous?"

Angela giggled. "What do you think?"

"I just find it so hard to believe …"

"For all your intelligence, you're an incredibly obtuse man—you know that?"

"Ah, such soft words of endearment … ! And why was I obtuse?"

She did not say anything for a while. Then said quietly, "It should have been obvious that I was attracted to you."

"That sounds like the sweetest music to me. I wish I could hear it again and again. I just can't believe that the Angela of my dreams was actually interested in me." He was quiet for a moment. Then almost to himself he muttered, "So much time lost …"

Angela did not reply but put her head back on his shoulder. He caressed her hair. "In my dreams, you would creep into my mind silently, and dispel the darkness I was enveloped in. Suddenly there would be a smell of fresh jasmine, the doors would open to a wild playful wind and I would hear the song of the *koel*. I would look around for you—but you were there and not there. I could feel your presence—you were there in the cool wind which caressed me—you were there in the sweet smell of jasmine which intoxicated me—you were there in the mysterious light which washed over me. But—but—you were not there for me to touch or see. I reached out to the wind, I swam in the light, I drank deep of the fragrance, but you were there and not there. You were in me and out of me. I could sense you, but not see you. Yet that left such a feeling of peace and contentment. I would wake refreshed and bathed in your warmth."

Angela had closed her eyes. There was an expression of serenity on her face. As Amar stopped, she slowly opened her eyes. She turned her face slowly and looked up at him. "That was beautiful, darling." Then she reached up for him and dragged his head down. The kiss was full and warm. Amar felt lost. The kiss seemed to go on for ever, she would not release him.

They eventually parted, but she kept a firm grip on his coat lapel as she nestled into his shoulder. Amar realised that he had not experienced this kind of happiness before. Dusseldorf and its memories receded to the background. This moment in time was everything. This realisation of dreams so long held.

He bent down and kissed her again. She responded. They were in a zone that was timeless. They heard no traffic noise, they felt no drizzle, they sensed no pedestrians.

Eventually, she, leaning against his chest, murmured, "Tell me why you became interested in me." Amar noticed that she did not say "attracted to me" but a lower level "interested in me". She fought so hard to keep her emotions hidden.

He sighed. "If I could, I would become the toast of the century—it's oracle—its prophet! I would be able to break open this mystery known as love—be able to establish a logic in a realm where no logic exists! Does anyone know what weaves this web of desire and love over a human being? I don't know, my sweetheart, what drew me to you. Was it the gamine aura surrounding you? Was it the quality of inapproachability you showed while at the same time inviting me with the mischief in your eyes? The duality you displayed? I don't know. All I do know is that I would wait in the corridors to get a glimpse of you. I would ache in the cafeteria to have you next to me. I would chafe at the Fencing Club at having to share you with so many."

Angela lay against him in a bliss-laden silence, eyes closed. When he stopped she snuggled up even closer and murmured, "Mmmm, I love listening to you. Go on—and on—don't stop."

"No, fair's fair. You tell me now how you became interested in me."

"No-o-o, I'm too embarrassed ..." and she burrowed her face into his coat.

Amar said nothing and let the silence grow. She began playing with a button on his coat like a little child. Amar felt an almost uncontrollable urge to crush her to him but resisted it. Then he heard her low voice beginning.

"Actually, I didn't like you at first," she said. "I found you rather cold and unapproachable."

"Me?" an incredulous Amar asked.

"Yes, my sweet, you." Now her voice was stronger. "You seemed to live in your own private world into which you welcomed no one. You seemed too self-contained. Yet, despite myself, I felt attracted. You had so much grace in your movements, particularly while fencing—the others looked clumsy by contrast. Then when I started getting to know you, I realised that you were not the arrogant person I thought you were. I also found you caring. You gave so much extra attention to the people who were not progressing in the fencing class. You were sensitive too—I noticed that you would steer the conversation away when somebody seemed to be at the receiving end and was uncomfortable. All this added up, and after a while I found that I would look forward to the fencing classes because I would see you there. But sadly, you would hardly notice me."

"Not true—no—no—not true," Amar protested. "I was just afraid of making a fool of myself by starting a conversation with you and then having you turn your back to me. There are so many times I wanted to ask you out, but I did not have the courage."

Angela raised her head and said a scornful, "Ha!" Then continued, "I didn't see a lack of courage with regard to Priscilla."

"But that's not the same thing," Amar complained. "I had nothing to lose with her, don't you see? If she turned her back to me it wouldn't have meant anything more than a slight dent in my self-esteem. With you it was all so different. If you went out of my life, everything would have turned dark. I would have been desolate. You must see that?" Amar ended almost pleadingly.

Angela looked up at him with a fond smile. "I was only pulling your leg, my gullible Am. I loved hearing what you said about your feelings for me being different. But we have so much to make up for," she ended with a sigh, "and so little time in our hands."

"So—we'll cram everything into our limited time—we'll make time expand. We'll make a minute into an hour, an hour into a day. We'll let nothing else intrude …"

Angela smiled sadly, "Except for the exams …"

"Spoilsport!" Then taking her head between his hands, kissed her deeply. "Your punishment," he declared when he had finished. She sat limply leaning on him and murmured, "That was nice."

The callous night ground by on wheezing bus wheels, with nary a pause to give the two lovers more time.

Suddenly, Angela sat up with a start. "What time is it, darling?"

Amar, with a sinking heart had to tell her.

Her face mirrored the despair he was feeling. "Oh God!" she murmured, "I'll have to go soon if I'm not to miss my last bus." In a childlike voice she added, "I don't want to, I just want to stay on here with you … oh, Am, what will happen to us—you will be leaving in a few months …" she seemed close to tears.

"Hush, my little darling. We will take one step at a time. As the first one—will you promise to go out with me this Saturday?"

Tearfully she said, "Yes, yes—a hundred times yes …"

He gently kissed away her tears. Then he found her mouth and they clung to each other as if their very life was ending.

They walked with unwilling steps to the bus stand. As her bus appeared and she climbed on, she looked around with a stricken face to him. He blew her a kiss trying to look composed. But within, a creeping fear was stealing in. Would this idyll last? Would his dream of togetherness be realised?

The thought of Helga inevitably crept in. He didn't feel any paralysing guilt. His feelings towards Helga had been on a downward slope. A break would have come sooner or later. Was he trying to justify what happened this evening? He didn't think so. Something had been building up inside him much before today.

Hunched inside his raincoat against the heavy drizzle, he slowly walked to the Tube station. The aura of Angela still enveloped him. He could still smell her personal scent, a lavender made fleshier and more intoxicating by her own body aroma. He could still feel her light fluttery lips on his own, he could still sense her lithe body straining against him. Yet there was this feeling of foreboding which he could not get rid of.

Jolt

The letter came two days later. It was the usual blue and red slash-bordered airmail envelope from Dusseldorf. Amar had returned from a tiring day at the library and found the letter lying on the table in the hallway. He took off his coat and hung it up with his scarf and went upstairs to leave his briefcase.

After a relaxed dinner, he decided to read the letter from Helga. He slit the envelope and took out the two flimsy sheets of blue airmail paper. He read, and sat down. He couldn't believe it—and read again. But the message did not change.

She had missed her period, and was now certain that she was pregnant. She did not believe in abortion and was determined to have this baby.

Amar found it difficult to breathe. He sat paralysed. He could not absorb the news. He could not take it. His mind was reeling.

It could not have happened—it was not true. Not true. They had taken all the precautions. It must be a mistaken diagnosis. Surely the period would come. But the denial could not last in the face of her clear assertion that the pregnancy had been confirmed. This explained her silence over the last couple of weeks—a silence Amar had started believing as signifying a fading of ardour.

He sat in a daze.

Anger followed. How could he be sure this was his child? She was no sexual innocent. There were men she had known.

Then the horror which was at the edge of his consciousness, flooded him. Angela. He could not think further. He was immobilised. He sat vacantly staring out of the window at the darkness, his mind in a terrifying disorder. His world collapsing.

The anger came bubbling back. How could he have made her pregnant when he had used the safest protection? Unless—unless—she had cheated. Yes—maybe that was it. This explained the nonsense of bundling the used condoms into her handkerchief with the excuse of disposing of them in the bathroom. From that to impregnating herself was a small step. Yes, that must be it. In which case he had no responsibility. This was all the result of her scheming.

The anger continued to seethe. Helga continued to be the scapegoat, the source and cause of the problem. The same thoughts went through his head over and over again, in an unceasing cycle, until his mind felt exhausted and ready to burst.

He changed mechanically, and lay down to sleep. Sleep eluded him. When it ultimately came, it was a troubled one.

He woke early to a grey dawn, feeling a sense of disquiet which he could not immediately explain. Then he remembered. The passage of the night seemed to have created some distance from the problem, allowing him some time to think. Even if his suspicions were true, that she had engineered the whole thing, he was forgetting that it was *his* baby she wanted to have. She did not want to abort. This should mean something to him. The decision could not have been easy, given the past history where she had to face public scorn as an unwed mother. The idea of bringing a child into the world again, without the sanction of marriage, must be haunting her. She had gone through the experience once, had lived through the sly glances of the upright God's anointed around her, the innuendos, the knowing looks of the virtuous world. She had stood up to it all, alone. Now she would be faced with the same disparagement and scorn again.

He imagined her sitting by herself in her tiny lonely room facing this crisis, desperately seeking a way out. She had shown courage in reaching the decision she had. How could he now leave her isolated. She needed his support.

He sat down at the desk and with an immense effort began to write to Helga. He tried to be honest. The news about the baby was a shock to begin with, but that was because it was so unexpected.

The immediate thought was of an abortion, but then came the realisation that it was his baby—and more important, that she wanted to have it. He appreciated her decision against an abortion, and applauded her courage. There were a lot of issues to think about—a lot of things he had to get his mind around. However, she was not to worry. Things would be sorted out. It was essential that she look after herself and the new life that was growing inside her. As he wrote this, he felt a fraud, as thoughts about Angela kept intruding. There was a deep sense of despair within, but he kept writing out of a cold sense of duty.

❖

He struggled through the morning in the library. His mind kept wandering away from the book lying in front of him in its pool of light. In the hushed silence of the cavernous room, his thoughts kept coming back to Angela, the precious woman he was about to lose. The one he had yearned for, the one who had, ever since he had met her, been part of his internal life. With whom, suddenly, wonderful new vistas had begun opening up, exciting dreams had begun unfolding. They now lay shattered. The fairy tale had ended. He would have to face her and tell her that the beautiful idyll, which had enriched their lives for a few days, was over. He felt a physical pain inside him. Found it difficult to breathe. He was suffocating.

He roughly closed his book and stumbled out of the library. Stood in the corridor to recover.

After a while the disturbance subsided and he took a deep breath. He realised he was standing next to the pigeonholes and decided to restore normality by checking his mail. There was a small note for him. It said "The Embankment has acquired a new meaning for me—life a new depth. Thank you for both. I can't wait for Saturday!" It was signed "A".

❖

In the cafeteria, Amar sat slumped over his untouched coffee staring unseeingly at the wall. Pramod, who had also decided to take a break, found him there. He sat down at the table with his coffee and asked, "Having discovered Angela's feelings for you doesn't seemed to have cheered you up. What's wrong?"

Amar hesitated and then said, "Something serious has come up."

Pramod looked concerned. "What?" Then sensing Amar's hesitation, he asked, "Something you can't talk about?"

"Well—it is a bit difficult to talk about …"

Pramod shrugged and said, "Up to you."

"At the same time, you're the only person I can talk to about it." He told him about Helga's letter.

Pramod took time to absorb the news. He looked shaken. "This is terrible, Amar, awful for you …"

This sympathy brought tears to Amar's eyes. He hurriedly brought out his handkerchief and wiped his eyes while blowing his nose. Pramod looked down at his cup while stirring it.

After an uncomfortable silence, Pramod said hesitantly, "Let me test my knee-jerk reaction. What about an abortion?"

Amar smiled wanly. "I had the same knee-jerk reaction. But it's clear that she wants to have the baby. And on reflection, I respect her decision."

Strangely, Pramod looked relieved. "I'm glad. She obviously wants to have your child. A lot of women would have grabbed at the abortion option. At least she seems to respect what is between you and her."

"Yes. And I've decided that I'll take her and her existing child back to India. We can get married there, so she'll be able to have a child with society's sanction."

Pramod looked even more shaken. "Marriage? You're already thinking of marriage? But—but—you don't even have a job … how will you support two people?"

Wearily, Amar shook his head. "I don't know, Pramod, I don't know. These are some of the questions that are plaguing me. I've no answers yet. But, I don't see any alternative to marriage. The poor girl has been through enough with her first child. I don't want that experience to be repeated for her. I'll just have to find a job of some kind."

"What will your family say?"

"To my marrying a pregnant foreigner? What do you think?" Amar managed a mirthless grin. "I just hope my mother's heart can take it."

"Then shouldn't you think again?"

"What choice do I have, Pramod? What do I do?" he asked despairingly. "Leave her in this mess and scarper? That is not a choice. Twist her arm to have an abortion? That is not a choice either—I cannot be party to the murder of my own child."

"When will you tell your parents?"

"Haven't decided. Before that I'll have to tell Angela. I don't know how I'll do it. It's going to be unbearably painful. But I'll have to tell her. The shortest love story to be written. An hour or two together, and the idyll ends," Amar said bitterly.

Pramod remained silent.

❖

Leaving the library in the evening he walked down to the nearest post office. He wanted to phone Helga to reassure her. As he heard her phone ringing, his nervousness overcame him and he almost replaced the receiver. Just then her voice answered. She did not appear to be overjoyed at hearing his voice. Or was it just his imagination?

He said that he was happy at her decision to keep the baby. He repeated to her more or less what he had written this morning. Her voice seemed to warm as the conversation progressed. Finally, to lighten matters, he said that he hoped she was practising her Hindustani and getting some cotton dresses stitched. There was a pause, which lengthened. Then finally she said that she had not given any thought to these matters as yet. He again felt the warmth disappear from her voice.

Darkness

Amar looked with dread out of his bedroom window and wished this Saturday had not come. The dreariness outside matched the darkness inside his mind. There seemed a lump of lead suspended within him. He had hardly slept.

He had decided that he would spend the day in the library and meet Angela in the evening.

❖

Just before six, Amar dragged his unwilling feet up the stairs at Green Park Tube station. Angela had not yet arrived and he waited outside in the corner by the newspaper vendor. His heart was beating wildly and his hands felt clammy. He took a few deep breaths to compose himself. He felt a light touch on his elbow and turned around to see her radiant face smiling up at him. Without thinking, he gathered her in his arms and held her close. Her arms went around him and they stood in close embrace for a while without saying a word. She turned her face up and he kissed her. This is going all wrong, he thought in alarm. But his body and heart went their own way, and the kiss was a long one. She drew back and looked at his face. "You were holding on to me like a drowning soul! Is something wrong, Am?"

He shook his head and managed a smile. "Let's find a bench in the park."

Angela took his hand as they walked into the park, but continued to look troubled. They found a bench on one of the long tree-lined avenues. As soon as they were seated Angela turned around and searched his face. "You don't look right, Am—what *is* the matter?"

Amar looked away. After a while he said, "No, physically I'm fine—so don't worry." Then added in a quieter voice, "It's just that emotionally I'm in a mess."

Angela's brown eyes clouded. She took his hand and said evenly, "Tell me. Even though I have the feeling it's not something I want to hear."

Amar lifted her hand and rubbed it across his cheek. He kissed it and held on to it with both hands. He found himself unable to speak. Finally, he found his voice, though it cracked with stress. "It's not something I want to speak about either. But things have happened—unexpectedly. You know, there was a girl I was seeing in Germany? Well, there is a situation now which makes it necessary for me to be with her. Please don't ask me to explain. It's difficult enough for me to say what I have said. But it means in effect that I won't be able to …" and here he found his voice seizing up again. Tears gathered, uncalled, and he found his cheeks wet. He wished he were dead. Then he gathered himself, took a deep breath and rushed through his words, "… it means I will not be able to see you again." He closed his eyes. He couldn't bear to look at her anguish.

Finally, he opened his eyes to see Angela's stricken face. It had paled and the eyes were staring at him as if willing him to say that all this was not true. Her hand in his, went limp and cold. Then she took it away. She slowly turned and looked unseeingly into the distance. In a dead voice she asked, "So—it's—all—over?"

Amar remained silent. He couldn't bring himself to repeat her words.

The silence grew and grew until Amar thought it would drive him mad. He mentally pleaded with Angela, say something … anything … shout, scream, utter obscenities … call me names … hit me … but please, please break this silence …

Finally, she said in a strangled voice, "There's no chance of things changing?" It was a question and a statement.

Amar managed to reply. "I can't see … I seem to be hemmed in—I've nowhere to turn."

She kept looking blankly at the trees in front. Then slowly, she got up and walked away. She walked without looking back. Her blue coat swayed with her graceful gait. The sky had darkened, the lights in the park had not come on, because this was summer when the evenings lasted long. She was a solitary figure slowly disappearing into the gloom. Amar could only helplessly watch with a heart-twisting emptiness within him.

He sat alone on the bench, unable to summon the energy to walk. Life had ceased for him. It had begun to drizzle. He didn't notice it.

The rain got heavier. He struggled up and stumbled to the entrance of the park. The couples hurrying for shelter were invisible to him. His main aim was to get to the Tube station and get into the train. It was as if he had drunk too much and could only focus on one thing at a time.

As a result he missed the graceful figure in a blue coat seated on a bench in a side avenue, shaking with sobs.

❖

The next morning he woke up with a fever. He lay miserably in bed the whole day. The thought of the impending exams dragged him to college the next day.

Awakening

The next few days passed in a haze. His body went through the daily business of living. But it was as if he did not inhabit that body. He was not a part of it. He avoided people and spent the whole day at the library. Pramod sensed his need for solitude and did not press.

He blanked out his thoughts of Germany, and was grateful that there were no letters to read. He tried to concentrate on his exam preparation, but with limited success.

Eventually, nature played its healing role and he woke one morning feeling more alive to the world. He noticed that he had not been shaving properly and remedied that. His hair felt sticky and dirty, so he shampooed himself. He emerged from his shower feeling a sense of freshness and an urgent hunger. He wolfed down a large breakfast much to his mother's delight. He stepped out onto the pavement with his briefcase and walked briskly to the Tube station. He noticed the crack on the cement pavement at the road crossing, the tree which was dying on the other side of the road, the hedgerow shining clean after the recent rain. His body felt alive, but inside, a part of him felt dead and inert. He was carrying the remains of dead emotion like a non-functioning organ—a lump which refused to dissolve and disappear.

In the library, he was able to concentrate on his books for the first time in days.

At lunch in the refectory Pramod noticed the change. "Welcome to the land of the living," he smiled.

Amar managed a weak smile. "I'm not sure whether I am in the land of the living or of the walking dead."

"I know you're suffering. I know you're upset. But don't get carried away. There are countless people who go through this break with their loved ones. It happens every day now, and has happened every day in the past. Yet these people recover, they begin to lead normal lives—and they are able to find love again. I know it feels as if life has ended—but it hasn't. There is so much to experience, so much to encounter in the years ahead, Amar. Look around you at the people eating lunch. I would bet that at least 50% of them have been through your kind of experience. Yet here they are—leading a normal existence. They're laughing, chatting, planning their weekend, enjoying themselves. So, the experience you've been through doesn't end your existence. It merely pauses it."

Amar was irritated by his friend's well-meant efforts. He resented his situation being trivialised. "Don't. Don't. Don't. I know you mean well. But you're trying to generalise, because all of us find comfort in wide, universal statements. You're forgetting that each person's experience is unique—it's his own. Each situation is filtered by his unique experiential framework."

"Alright. Agreed that your experience is unique," Pramod said patiently. "But grief is not unique. It is universal. And all I was saying is that grief is something that people recover from and that there are examples of this all around us. Acceptable?"

Amar shrugged. "I don't know. I don't even want to know. Yes, people recover from pain—like they recover from serious illnesses. But small pox leaves scars, tuberculosis leaves scars, as do most serious diseases. I feel scarred—and these scars are deadening a part of me. That was what I was trying to tell you."

Pramod recognised the self-pity, but decided not to comment on it. "Look—I don't dare say that I know what you feel—but let me at least say that I can see that you're suffering. So why don't we postpone a chat on this for the evening when we are more relaxed—say over a glass of beer? Come on—say yes. It's a long time since we've had a drink together, and with some work that I did over the summer holidays I can afford to buy you a drink."

Amar remained silent for a while, and then with some reluctance, nodded.

❖

That evening they collected their coats and briefcases and walked down to The George on the Strand. The first sip of beer brought back memories of the evening at the Tree Tuns with Angela and with it, a revival of the pain.

Pramod noticed his mood and decided to risk confronting it. "What exactly is bothering you, Amar? It's not just the loss of Angela, is it?"

Amar did not reply immediately. Then in a quiet voice he said, "I know you think I've been melodramatic about what's been happening. Maybe I have overreacted, I don't know. But the fact is, my whole world has turned upside down. I've lost the one woman I've really cared for—cared for in a way that I've not done for any other woman. I also face the prospect of spending the rest of my life with someone who has been forced on me by circumstances, not by choice. I have no job and no wherewithal to support her and her child. So … life is proving somewhat difficult for me just now."

After a pause, Pramod asked, "Amar, I understand what you're saying. But don't you think you're being a little unfair to Helga? When she came on the scene she seemed like an answer to your prayers. If you were so enamoured by Angela, why did you throw yourself wholeheartedly into the relationship with Helga? And now you're decrying this relationship which seemed to have given so much to you?"

Amar did not reply, but sat looking at his glass. The pub noises swirled around them. "Hey Fred, mine's an Adnam Extra …" "And then this bird sways up and says …" "Cor, that right footer was somethin', wannit …" "Nah, you ain't seen nothin' if you ain't seen Stan Matthews …" "Take my word for it—it'll be Nottingham Forest in the finals …"

Amar heard none of this. He sat looking at bubbles in the glass as they slowly fizzed to the top and burst. Eventually he shook his head and looked up at Pramod. "You're right. I've been going on as if I've been the victim of a terrible injustice." He sighed tiredly. "The reality is that in all that has happened I did what I did of my own volition. Nobody forced me. Nobody coerced me. I could have walked out at any stage, if I had so wanted."

He paused, seeming unwilling to continue. "The truth is that it's very easy to fall into a victim mentality—where everybody else is to blame but you."

Pramod looked startled at this sudden turnaround and said nothing.

Amar brooded for a while and then continued in a reluctant voice, as if the words had to be torn out of him. "If I'm honest, I'm not really helpless, even in the present situation. I have choices. I have the choice of not marrying Helga. I have the choice of asking her to abort. I have the choice of just walking out and leave her to sort herself out. And by deciding not to do any of these, I'm making a choice." He stopped. Then added, "And now, having made my choice, I need to start thinking of practical steps to tackle the situation."

Pramod looked surprised. Amar noticed it. "I know I seem to have suddenly turned around in my thinking," he said.

He thought back to some of the things Pramod had said. They deserved an answer.

"Why did Helga happen? If I'm honest, I have to admit that it was because she was there. I dived impetuously into the experience because I was so desperate for companionship. From there, it was not a difficult step to convince myself of a deeper emotion, especially when sexual deprivation helped the process. This is not to take away anything from Helga, she is a remarkable woman, and I do feel affection for her." He paused and continued.

"With Angela, it was different, though probably not very different—who knows? When I first saw her, she did not bowl me over. She was a pretty girl, but not film-star pretty. Yet she appealed to something inside me. There was something … God knows. It's futile to try and analyse the anatomy of attraction. I've realised that it's a mystery and will always remain one.

"Angela took root in my mind, and as her image grew, she seemed to become more and more unattainable. She was always friendly, but I could not sense if there was anything more. When I was around her I was walking on eggshells, afraid that one misstep might break the bond. Now you can probably see why I was so afraid to express my feelings to her. Then some days ago it all changed. That was a moment in paradise for me. I have never felt such joy. Yet paradise turned out to be a fickle host. Within a few days it had expelled me."

Amar was fighting back the emotions that were choking him and did not continue. A sad silence grew. Around them there was laughter, loud voices. But the small round table they were at seemed buffered against these sounds. Silence is uncomfortable, and finally Pramod broke it.

"Have you fully made up your mind about being with Helga?"

Amar slowly nodded. "Yes."

Pramod decided to be ruthless. "Why?" he asked.

Amar looked startled. "Because, in all conscience I cannot do anything else. I got Helga into this situation—now I have to help her out of it. As simple as that."

"Let me be even more provocative. Are you sure it is your child?"

Amar did not react with the outrage Pramod had been expecting. Instead he looked troubled. He hesitated and then said, "It would be stupid for me to say that the thought has not crossed my mind. It's possible that she may have had a fling with someone else—but somehow I don't think that it happened." He leant his head on his hands and said wearily, "Ultimately—ultimately, it's a matter of trust, isn't it? And I have to trust her."

Pramod shrugged and said, "Well, I suppose you're right. Anyway, it's your decision," and went back to his beer.

At the mention of "decision", a sudden panic hit Amar. He was taking a terrifyingly momentous step, transforming his entire life, closing all other avenues, constricting himself to a limited existence, building his own little prison. This was a life-changing decision he was making and he was doing this on his own without the benefit of mature advice. Yet, there was nobody to turn to.

Pramod's realism rescued him. After another sip of beer he said, "Now, let's start looking at the practical issues. Your exams will be over in July, results will take a little time, and it's only then that you can start looking for a job. You can't land a job straightaway, so allow a few months. This will take you to the early part of next year. Now, when is the baby due?"

Amar had not even thought of this and had to do a quick calculation. "I suppose around January—February."

"Well then, Helga will have to be able to take care of herself at least till then, because I can't see you getting a job before that. I don't know what their national health system is like, but presumably she will be taken care of?"

"I really don't know. She's working—so maybe there is some support she will get from there. I'll really have to find out."

"OK, let's now think about the job options you have in India. The Indian Administrative Service is obviously out—you'll have an exam to do, there'll be a long wait, and there is no guarantee. So it'll have to be a company job, or a bank. What about teaching?"

"No, there's not enough money in teaching. I'm not really enthused about a bank job either, but I suppose I'll have to apply anyway since I can't afford to cut down my options."

"Your father should have a lot of contacts. That should be useful."

Amar's face darkened. "Contacts? Contacts? Credit me with some self-respect! You think I could live with a job earned through the old boy network? You don't believe I can get a job on my own merits … ?"

"Sorry, sorry—my apologies. It wasn't meant to be any reflection on your abilities. It's just that company jobs and influence tend to go together."

“Well, that’s not the kind of company job I’m going to look for.”

So the discussion continued. Amar felt a sense of comfort talking about tangible, practical matters. By the time they went into their second pint, his spirits had improved.

❖

When he returned home, he found a letter from Helga. It was briefer than the normal ones. At the end of the letter she mentioned that she did not think that moving to India would be such a good idea. Perhaps Amar could think of trying for a job in Germany. With his LSE qualification she was sure he would be able to land one. And German was not all that difficult a language to learn.

Disbelief

"I can't believe this. She now wants me to look for a job in Germany! Me, with not a word of German. I just don't understand," said Amar agitatedly to Pramod the next morning over coffee in the cafeteria.

Pramod took off his glasses and polished them, seeking time to absorb this shock. "Well, you'll have to tell her in no uncertain terms that the idea is nonsensical. The only jobs you could aspire to are a labourer or a house-painter or waiter. Is this what she has in mind for you after an LSE degree? She needs to have her head examined."

"What I can't understand is why she's doing this. I've offered her marriage, a home in India, security and comfort. And the comforts she will get in India are far more than she could dream of in Germany. So, what's stopping her from coming to India?"

Pramod shook his head. "Sorry, Amar, I'm no expert on the female psyche. All I can say is that there is probably something she hasn't told you."

Amar did not reply, his mind too occupied with confusing thoughts chasing each other. Pramod had a sip of his coffee and continued, "Amar, with this emotional turmoil you're going through, are you going to be in a fit state of mind to take the finals? They're almost on us now."

"Don't I know it! Until yesterday, I couldn't read a paragraph without my mind wandering off in all directions. I had just begun to be able to concentrate again, but now this bombshell has knocked me off my equilibrium once more. I can hardly sleep at night for worry about my lack of preparations, yet there seems little I can do. I'm trying to get myself together somehow and buckle down to serious study, but it's an uphill battle."

"Well, then, I think you just forget about Helga for the moment and concentrate on the exam preparations. You've told her all that she needs to know about your supporting her and so on—now just let her be. She can cope. You'll have to now push everything out of your mind and focus every scrap of your energy on the preparation. There's so little time left."

Amar's face showed irritation. Then controlling himself, he said patiently. "Yes, Pramod, I'm aware of the seriousness of the situation—you don't have to spell it out. I just hope to God that I *can* focus my mind."

❖

He followed the discipline for three days. Then, in the evening after he had finished with the library, he found his steps leading him to the post office phone booth near Holborn station.

Helga's voice sounded strained. After answering his enquiries about her health, she paused as if she wanted to say something but was finding it difficult. "What's the matter, Helga, are you all right? You're not sounding the same."

She paused again. Then said in a low voice, "Sudipto is coming to Dusseldorf."

Amar did not grasp the import of it immediately. "Good, good," he said breezily. "Is he coming for a holiday?"

"He is coming to stay."

"He's coming to stay? He's coming to stay—with you?" Amar exclaimed.

"Yes."

"What do you mean—'yes'?" Amar was shouting now. "He is going to stay with you—in your flat?"

There was silence from the other side.

"Helga—Helga—can you hear me"

A faint voice said, "Yes".

"What is the meaning of all this, Helga? Have you taken leave of your senses? How can you even think of him staying with you?"

"He says he wants to stay and work in Dusseldorf."

"So let him. But he can damn well find somewhere else to stay, can't he?"

Again the infuriating silence.

"What the hell's going on, Helga?" Amar lowered his voice when he realised he was shouting again. He said fiercely, "Have you forgotten you're carrying my baby? Have you forgotten that I've asked you to marry me and come to India with me?"

"I want to stay on in Dusseldorf."

Her voice was low but firm.

"So you told me. And you expect me to find a job there. What kind of a job do you think I'll get when I know no German—maybe as a street cleaner, or a labourer? Is that what you want?" he asked fiercely.

No answer.

"Well, let me tell you something," said Amar beside himself with anger, "That is not going to happen. I'm going to go back to India to find myself a job. I would like you to come there. If you don't intend to—then fine. But that will be the end of our relationship. Do you understand that? And remember—everything will also end if Sudipto moves in with you. I'm just sick, sick—sick—of all the drama you're creating. I'll ring tomorrow to ask your decision—and I want you to think long and carefully before that."

He banged the phone down and stormed away from the post office. His mind was a maelstrom of emotions. There was disbelief. Had he heard right or did he mishear? No, there was no doubt because she had repeated it a number of times. Anger took over. What was she playing at? She was pregnant with his child and she asks somebody she has only known through letters, to come and stay with her? The bitch was playing a game, using both Sudipto and him as pawns. Her need was to find a husband who would live in Dusseldorf. Was she even pregnant—or was it part of her complex manoeuvring? Anything was possible.

Then the lash of rejection hit him. The love she had professed for him had been false. She had just been playing on his weakness. His gullibility.

Pain and fury took possession. He wanted to shout out in agony, despair and rage. He wanted to tear at her with his nails until blood poured, to crush her with his bare hands until life left her, set flames raging and hear her cries of pain ...

Cool drops of rain on his fevered face calmed him down. He closed his eyes and let the coolness envelop him.

It did not strike him that she was doing to him precisely what he had been planning to do to her.

Termination

Curiously, he slept better that night than he had for some time, and woke to a rare sunny morning. Something seemed to have relieved the unbearable tension in his mind. Maybe it was his acceptance deep down that it was all over, although at the conscious level he still hoped that the door was still slightly ajar. It was this that stopped him from calling Helga. He was afraid to hear what she would say.

Possibly because of the closure that his deeper mind had accepted, he found himself able to concentrate, once more, in the library. He worked steadily through the day and avoided Pramod at lunch. The next day it was the same.

On the day after, his restlessness began to reappear and he decided that he would steel himself and call her. He had walked past the Holborn Tube station before taking this decision, and continued on to a post office on Old Gloucester Street. Her voice sounded remote. He found it difficult to bring out the words he had rehearsed in his mind. When he was able to, they came out gruffly. "Well … have you thought about what I said that day?"

She did not reply.

"For God's sake, have you lost your voice? Or are you leaving me to draw my own conclusions?"

Her voice now came firmly across. "Sudipto is here."

Amar controlled himself. "I see. I hope you know what this means?"

There was silence at the other end.

"Let me tell you then, clearly, that it's all over between us. You hear me? It's all over." He was now shouting. "The sick web of deceit and lies you wove round me—is now lying torn and crushed. You had me convinced, did you know that? You had me believing you were in love with me, did you know that? Of course you did—that was your intention, wasn't it? That was your carefully conceived plan—build up an insurance policy in case Sudipto lets you down? Well, you succeeded brilliantly. Congratulations on being such a wonderful actress! You had me actually believing your lies …"

In a low and angry voice she said, "I never lied to you."

"Oh no. Of course not. All the protestations of love were true, weren't they? Yet all of a sudden you decide to shack up with another man. So what happened to your love, sweetheart? The genuine, 24-carat love just melted away? Maybe you should have gone to a better store to buy your love—they gave you shoddy stuff—they cheated you, didn't they? Poor thing! And when you found out, you naturally had to throw it away. Who keeps shoddy imitations …"

"Stop it—stop it, A-mar," she interrupted angrily.

"Why? Is the truth so hurtful? You think pain is something only you have the right to hand out? Have you any idea of the agony I've been going through? It's about time you learnt about pain too. But what am I talking about?" Amar laughed bitterly. "*You* feel pain over this charade? Lord God Almighty! You were the one who planned it—where's the question of pain! No—no—you should be celebrating with champagne tonight. Drink a glass for me and raise a toast to 'the absent gullible fool.'"

"I'm putting the phone down," she said in a strangled voice.

"Why, is your new friend listening? Well, tell him from me that he is welcome to the gold-plated bitch I had made the mistake of loving."

He emerged from the stuffy booth smelling of stale cigarettes, urine and damp, and breathed in the fresher, cooler air. He was emerging into a different world, one without the woman who had occupied so much of his life. That foul, contaminated world he was now leaving behind. He should rejoice at having escaped. He should now savour his freedom. But did the London air feel any fresher? It carried the usual smell of petrol exhaust and coal smoke. The sky had clouded over and reflected the fevered, coppery hue of London being lit up for the evening. It didn't really feel a different world—just the tired, soiled, malodorous world it had always been, like the stained mattresses one found lying by some roadsides. He felt an immense weariness. His legs felt weighted down. His mind benumbed.

He dragged his feet to Bloomsbury Square and slumped onto a bench. He did not feel like returning home just yet. Pramod was the only person he could talk to, and he would probably be on his way home now. There was no one else. It was an empty city. Empty.

A midnight wave of darkness engulfed him. He was an insignificant speck in this huge city. Alone. He felt a frightening, yawning emptiness within himself. As if he was falling—falling into a bottomless blackness, his heart beating so rapidly that it could not cope.

On the street, men clumped by after a day's work, women rat-tatted by on their heels, a group of students sauntered past laughing, couples walked hand-in-hand, the red buses lumbered along—life surged on, but he was alone. He was invisible. He saw the scene as if on a screen in a starkly empty, dark cinema house. He was alone in the darkness. Did he exist? Not to the moving figures on the screen. He existed only to himself—he was non-existent to the others. Existence which was not an existence. Unbearable pain and aloneness. He had to escape. His head throbbed. He found it difficult to breathe.

Many ways out. People taking them every day. The river. The oncoming train. The wheels of the bus. His mind went blank. He didn't know where he was. He got up. He heard the squeal of brakes suddenly applied.

He could almost feel his body being torn under the heavy wheels, his skull being crushed. The blessed relief. The termination of pain. The wailing of a siren sounded, becoming louder and louder. Was he lying crushed under the bus? When would the pain hit him? Was he losing his mind?

Then, he saw an ambulance speeding by. The spell was broken.

He was emerging from a nightmare. He could hardly breathe because of panic. He needed to force some fresh air into his lungs. He walked down to Southampton Row and kept walking towards Russell Square, breathing in deeply. He walked in a panic-driven hurry. At least the cold air was reviving. He walked round the square and then slowing down, headed for the Russell Square Tube station.

Around the corner, he saw the lit windows of the Friend at Hand pub. It looked a welcome haven. He had been there once before, drawn by the story that Oscar Wilde had used it as a drinking place.

Today, it was a sanctuary that provided life. His heart was still beating wildly. He didn't want a drink, but ordered a half-pint of bitter which he carried to the corner of the bar. He collapsed onto a stool and felt grateful for the crowd around him. There were noisy college students, sporting their scarves, having a drink before returning to their lonely bedsitters. There were office goers in their grey suits downing a pint and pulling on a cigarette before taking the train. There were pipe smoking regulars at their customary tables reading the evening papers in their local. It was a picture of normality, and a comfort for the emptiness he felt within. He just sat and allowed it to warm him. After the first sip, he left his drink untouched. Slowly, he seemed to draw strength from the babble and the noise, though the pain remained like a jagged piece of lead which had torn up his insides.

After a long while he felt strong enough to go home.

Examinations

He lay in a tortured half-sleep throughout the night. In the morning he opened his eyes wearily to a bleak dawn. He felt too tired to get up. He could not summon up the energy to go to college and lay in bed, bothered by the unwanted fussing of his mother. Finally, he closed the door to his room.

He lay listlessly in bed the whole of the day. He slept deeply that night.

He woke the next morning feeling a sense of calm which he could not understand.

❖

"I'm glad you called her a bitch to her face. She really has been a calculating, conniving bitch," Pramod exclaimed angrily as they sat at lunch at the refectory the next day.

Amar was touched by his friend's loyalty. He knew that what he was about to say would provoke a strong reaction. "You know, Pramod, I was angry that day—angrier than I've ever been. I told you about the crazy thoughts that went through my mind when everything seemed so dark and hopeless. But the turmoil seems to have lessened."

"And … ?"

Amar shrugged.

"So you're willing to forgive her?" Pramod asked unbelievingly.

"Forgive her? Not likely, not for a long time, maybe never. But try to understand her action? Yes, that I may be able to do."

"And you don't feel any anger, any rage?"

"Be your age, Pramod—of course I feel rage!" Amar replied exasperatedly. "I feel a terrible sense of rejection—a burning urge to hit back … but the anger and angst were proving very corrosive. It was burning me up. Leaving that furnace behind has given me a sense of peace. Don't ask me how the change happened, I don't know. Maybe there can be some life-affecting experiences which change your perspective."

Pramod did not seem particularly convinced but decided to change direction. "Well, if you insist on being a modern-day saint, I can't stop you. You've been let down badly—and used. If you're okay with that, fine. Let's look at the practical side now. With all this turmoil in your life, do you still think you can do the examinations? Do you feel your state of mind, and lack of preparation, is going to allow you to go through with it? I'm just wondering whether you should drop a year—it could be the difference between a good and average result."

Amar looked startled. "Drop a year? Are you serious? How do you think I'm going to support myself for a year in London? My father would have retired and certainly will not be able to support me. I'm not going to be able to work part time and pay my way through college as they seem to be able to do in the States. There just are no opportunities for that kind of thing here. And finally, I will need to find myself a job in India soon after my father retires since he will need financial help. Remember, my younger sister and brother still have to go through college. No, there is just no way I can stay on for another year."

Pramod shrugged. "I suppose you're right. I was just thinking of a way to reduce the pressure on you."

"Thanks. But I see no alternative to going ahead with the examination—and hoping for the best."

❖

Over the remaining few weeks, Amar spent all his time at the library. He would arrive at nine in the morning and leave at eight in the evening. He became obsessed by the need to prepare. In his sleep, he had nightmares, where he would find himself in the examination room but unable to write. Or unable to remember the answers. Or having answered only the first question when the invigilator announced time was up. Each time he would wake up in a cold sweat.

He tried to banish thoughts of Germany, though not very successfully. In weaker moments he would be tempted to ring, but then wiser counsel prevailed. Angela also occupied his mind. She had not spoken to him since that fateful day, although he caught glimpses of her at college. He wanted to talk to her, but what could he say? That he was sorry? What a feeble and inadequate gesture that would be. Or could he perhaps explain what had happened? That would be worse. It would seem as if he was trying to crawl back into favour. There was nothing really he could say which would not make matters worse.

❖

Finally, the examinations began. By now Amar just wanted everything to be over. He was tired and stretched. He was on edge and tended to snap at everybody at home. The family kept away from him. Yet he needed them more than ever before. He seemed to be living in such a different world of books and tension that he craved for the familiarity of day-to-day life—his brother and sister squabbling with each other; his mother giving instructions to Kishan Singh or pottering about in the kitchen or complaining to his father about the rising prices of vegetables. He needed the commonplace, to feel rooted and avoid the feeling of floating around in an unreal world—of desks, pens, question papers, the inexorable clock ticking away his future, the heart-stopping moment when the mind goes suddenly blank, the impersonal invigilator parading up and down, the stress of scribbling fast to beat the clock, the agony of not having the time to revise what was written, the panic of missing out some important point … and overall, the pressure—the temple-crushing pressure—to perform.

At last, the examinations were over and as he came out of the examination hall, Amar felt a depleting weariness which made him wonder whether he would be able to walk to the Tube station. He managed to get home, collapsed on his bed and went to sleep. A long, dreamless sleep.

Accidental Encounter

There were still a few days left of the summer term and he decided to keep going to college, partly because he did not know what else to do and partly because he wanted to savour as much as possible of the college, which he had grown to love, before he said his final farewell to it.

The errant sun had made an appearance and it was a beautiful summer day when he decided to take a walk by the Embankment before going to the LSE. There were few cities which looked as wonderful as London did on a bright summer day. The parks were aflame with flowers—tulips, daffodils, roses, pansies, iris. So were the grass verges. Even the river, swirling by in its brown turbidity, shone with flashes of sun and seemed to be smiling with the recollection of its ageless memories. It was a day when even tired spirits soared.

A lot of the students were taking advantage of the sunny day to walk by the river. He thought he saw a slender figure in a summer dress he recognised, but realised as she turned around that he had made a mistake. This was happening to him with increasing frequency. He kept seeing Angela lookalikes.

He walked slowly back to college.

Pramod had also finished his examinations and they met up for lunch at the refectory. The cold white neon lighting seemed an affront to the bright sunshine visible through the window, but there was a palpable end-of-term excitement which lightened the mood.

"So, is it going to be the LSE or some other university? Have you decided?" Amar asked. Pramod wanted to do postgraduate work since he felt that it would help him get the teaching job which he aimed for. If his results were good, and they were likely to be with the effort he had put in, he might get some financial assistance.

"I think it will be the LSE. Let's see what the results are."

"Don't worry, your results will be good, and you'll do your PhD. My only problem will be imagining you as Dr Sharma! I wonder what nickname your students will give you. Let's see … hmmm … yes … hic-dick-doc would do, quite euphonious, don't you think? Hic for your fondness for beer—dick for …"

"You don't have to get down to street-level vulgarity to be funny," Pramod intervened irritated.

"Hey, it's all innocent stuff. Hickory dickory dock—the mouse ran up the clock … it's an innocent nursery rhyme, for God's sake. It reflects your child-like goodness—your innocent nature. All good, wholesome stuff!"

"Yeah—yeah—healthy, innocuous stuff. I think your Fencing Club associates have managed to infect you with their gutter-type humour," Pramod said huffily.

"All right, we'll make it 'Doc Sham' or 'Sham Doc'. 'Sharma' is too long a word to pronounce. So—'Sham Doc', how's that?"

Pramod didn't think this deserved an answer, and concentrated on his cottage pie.

Amar recognised the tall, shambling figure of Rod approaching. "Hello, old man—good to see you," Rod said.

"Good to see you too, Rod. Come and join us—you know Pramod, don't you?"

"I think we've met—no, I'll not stay, thanks, as I'm in a hurry. Just wanted to book you for this Friday evening. Some of us are getting together in the Three Tuns, before term closes. Hope you'll be able to make it?"

"Sure, Rod. Will be delighted."

"Good—good. It's a sort of farewell party for you, though there won't be any speeches!"

"Thanks, Rod. I'll be there with my ten-page screed."

Rod laughed his braying laugh. "See you then."

Pramod raised his eyebrows. "Farewell party? I'm impressed."

Amar looked embarrassed. "Oh, they'd do it for anyone who's leaving, I'm sure." Secretly he was pleased and touched.

❖

He bumped into Angela in the corridor the next day. There was hardly anyone else around and there was no way they could avoid each other. He looked at her and decided to venture an awkward "Hello, Angela". She looked around like a trapped animal, then quietened and said, "Hello". An awkward silence developed and Amar did not know how to break it. She looked pale and drawn, and her eyes avoided him and looked at the notice board over his shoulder.

Finally, Amar said in a strained voice, "Do you think we could talk once before I leave?"

She didn't answer straightaway. Then asked, "What for?"

"For no reason I can give you, for it's beyond reason. I promise not to take up too much of your time."

"I don't know …"

"Please?"

She hesitated, then said, "I'll let you know," and was gone in a swirl of a summer dress.

As he walked away he kicked himself. Why did he go out of his way to be humiliated? What was he going to say to her anyway?

It would be best if she refused to see him, which was very likely. Yet, perversely, he still hoped she would agree.

Farewell Party

At home, packing had begun. The family would leave a week before Amar did. He had persuaded his parents that he would join them in India later, since he wanted to spend a few days in Europe on the way back. He was surprised at their easy agreement, but put it down to the cheerful mood brought on by the offer of a post-retirement job that his father had received. The plan was that Amar would spend a few days in Pramod's place, sleeping on his couch, and then leave for Europe.

He had received a surprise phone call from Sudipto. His voice seemed warm, if a bit wary. "*Kaamon achheesh* (How're you keeping)?" he asked. Amar had been taken aback, but recovered sufficiently to say coldly, "As well as can be expected." Sudipto went on, "I know things have been messed up, but nobody is to blame." Amar lost his cool briefly and said, "I'm glad you think so, because I don't." "You know we need to talk to clear the air," Sudipto replied. Amar had paused and then said, "Look, this is not the best time to discuss these things. I'll call you from a phone booth later."

As he walked to the Tube station Amar wondered why he had agreed to continue this discussion. A slow burning anger had set in and this time Sudipto was the target.

Why reopen old wounds? And his feelings for Helga were dead, weren't they? Weren't they? He had to admit that her cologne fragrance still drifted across his memory, as did fragments of their time together.

He walked into a call booth and called Sudipto. Helga answered and he said, "This is Amar."

She replied after a pause. "I know. I can recognise." Her voice still had the ability to unsettle him.

But he wasn't going to give anything away. "I'm glad to know that," he replied coldly. "Is Sudipto there?"

She seemed about to say something, then changed her mind. "I will put him on."

He came on the line. "Thanks for calling back."

"What is it you wanted to discuss?" Amar asked.

Sudipto sighed. "You don't sound like you are in the mood for any discussion."

"I'm not sure that it will achieve anything."

"Well, at least let me clear Helga—whatever has happened, she is not to blame."

"Sudipto—what I think about Helga is my business. Let's just leave it at that. I know you're trying to help, but it's not working."

"I wish you could be fair with respect to Helga. However, since you don't want to discuss it, we'll leave it at that. But I would like to see you again for old times' sake. Could you not pass through Dusseldorf on the way back? Our friendship dates back a long time, Amar, and I wouldn't like it to founder on a misunderstanding. I have too many happy memories of our college days."

There seemed to be genuine feeling in his voice, and Amar softened. Then collecting himself again he said, "I haven't firmed up my plans. Let's see."

He hung up after a few desultory sentences.

❖

Friday came, and Amar decided to go to college in the afternoon.

As he walked up the Kingsway to the LSE on another bright day he wondered if Angela would be there at the get-together. He doubted it. As soon as he got in, he went to his pigeonhole hoping for a message from her. There was nothing.

He met Pramod and said, "Let's take a walk down to the National Gallery. It's too nice a day to waste."

"Okay, let me just return this book to the library."

They came out onto Aldwych and walked along to the Strand. The tall grey stone buildings, streaked a darker grey from the pollution, shut out some of the sky but the sun still penetrated and lit up the coloured shop awnings along the way. The red double-deckers splashed their colour. A few wisps of fleecy white cloud wandered in the blue sky.

"I really have grown to love this city. I'm going to miss it," Amar sighed.

Pramod, not given much to sentiment, grumbled, "Could do with a bit of a clean-up, though."

"Yeah, yeah—but that's part of its charm isn't it? Who wants an antiseptic showpiece like Geneva?"

"You're an impractical romantic. Do you know that the Thames is so polluted that there are hardly any fish left in it?"

"Now *that* is serious. River fish have to be saved. No self-respecting Bengali can eat sea fish."

"Here we go again. The divisive 'we Bengalis'. When will you be able to think of yourself as an Indian?"

"The day you north Indians get to appreciate river fish."

The arguments continued until they reached the National Gallery.

However they did not end there. Pramod liked Picasso. Amar didn't. Amar admired Turner, particularly the *Rain, Steam and Speed* which hung at the National. Pramod thought Turner was overvalued. Pramod enjoyed Monet's *Water Lilies* series, while Amar, though an ardent admirer of Monet, thought this series was overrated. The only painter they seemed to agree upon was Van Gogh. Amar said that this probably reflected the incipient madness in both of them.

Exhausted by an hour of viewing and arguing, they found a cafe outside where they sat down to rest their weary legs. "So, what's the latest on the Germany front?" Pramod asked idly while stirring his coffee.

Amar told him about his conversation with Sudipto. Pramod almost choked on his coffee. "You were pleasant to this fellow who has done so much damage to you? Worse, you're planning to go to Dusseldorf? Are you out of your mind?"

"I don't think the blame game is going to help, Pramod."

"The halo is still there, I see," Pramod said disgustedly. "I don't think anything I say is going to change things, so let's get away from the subject."

"Yes, let's," Amar said amiably. "Tell me about Anisha—how are things going?"

"Well, as you know, her parents were initially opposed to our friendship. But they seem more reconciled to me now, although her father and I argue all the time about politics. He seems to be a true-blue conservative, complete with pipe, cravat and glass of sherry."

"Another Indian settled here who feels this need to be a true-blue Brit. Are you going to go the same way?"

"Let me tell you what happened when they invited me to lunch. They'd also invited some English friends across, and I was sent a message by the father through Anisha. I was instructed not to ask for beer—it was too working class. Sherry was what I should opt for."

Amar was intrigued. "So what did you do?"

"I declined the invitation. I asked her to tell him that Debrett's was not available in the LSE library and I still wasn't sure which fingerbowl I should drink from."

"Good for you. But how has this affected your relations with Anisha?"

"She can't stand her father, in fact, regards him as a comic character. She was in splits when she gave me the message about sherry. In any case I don't think she delivered my message to her father verbatim. She would have been banned from seeing me, if she had."

❖

He got to the Three Tuns a little after six to find a number of the Fencing Club members already there. They had taken over one corner by joining tables. Along with the drinks on the tables was a bowl containing coins and notes. They were obviously the contributions for the evening and Amar dropped a ten shilling note into the bowl. "Hey, this party's for you, Am. You can't be contributing to it!" Rod protested.

"Worry not, Rod. I'll make up for it by drinking more than my contribution! Cheers …" and Amar took a long draught of beer from the glass which had been handed to him.

"Drink up, lads, before this wily Indian drinks up all the money we've looted from his country," said Gary with whom Amar had a special bond because of his fun-loving nature.

"Nah, this is not his tipple—he prefers the Virgin Marys," said Greg.

"Mary was no virgin, it was Elizabeth—the Virgin Queen," retorted Amar. His chemistry with Greg still had not improved.

"Bit mature for you, old boy, don't you think?" said Rod who liked to periodically lapse into the public school idiom.

Beverly, in an effort to move away from what was becoming a men's locker room conversation, asked Amar, "So what are your post-LSE plans, Am?"

"Find a job in India, Bev, to keep body and soul together."

"No chance of you getting one here?" Beverly asked.

"Sadly, no. There are enough locals crowding the job market. I would have loved to have stayed on."

"Oi—that's a change, isn't it? You used to be very critical of this country, if I remember correctly," intervened Greg.

"I still am. As I am of my own country. That doesn't stop me from loving it." Before the argument grew more heated, two more people joined the group. Amar noted to his surprise and dismay that one was Jane. And the other, Amar couldn't believe his eyes—the other was Priscilla.

"Hello, everybody," Jane said cheerily. Turning to Rod she said, "I've brought Priscilla along because she's staying with me. You don't mind, do you?" her smile was wide enough to mesmerise Rod.

"Not at all—not at all," Rod said getting up. "We're delighted to have Priscilla here. Now let's find a place for her to sit." And it just so happened, that a place was found next to Amar.

"To all of you who don't know her, this is Priscilla, a dear friend of mine. You do remember Priscilla, don't you, Am?" Jane asked. You bitch, thought Amar. But outwardly he nodded. "Good to see you, Priscilla. What will you drink?" he asked, ignoring Jane.

As Amar got up to fetch the drink, Rod followed. "I say, I'm sorry, old boy. I didn't know Jane was bringing this girl along. I know you're not happy meeting her." Obviously his brief dalliance with Priscilla was public knowledge due to, he suspected, jabberer Jane.

Amar smiled to put poor Rod at ease. "Not to worry, Rod. I can deal with it. What's important for me is that you went to the trouble of organising this little get-together. Thanks so much."

Ever-modest Rod said, "No, no, it wasn't just me. Others wanted it too." They went back with the drinks.

"How's Oxford treating you, Priscilla?" Amar asked, handing her the drink.

She was wearing well-cut beige slacks which clung to her shapely hips and thighs and a white flimsy top through which her bra was clearly visible, and looked quite fetching.

"I was expecting a more exciting *bon mot* from the fascinating man from the Orient," she said coquettishly.

Amar's initial reaction was one of exasperation. Could she never stop flirting?

"All right—how are you treating Oxford?"

She made a moue. "Better, but still not your style."

"Sorry, you Oxford nobs may be consumed by style, but we LSE plebs don't have time for that luxury," Amar said coldly.

"Now I've upset you. And here I was hoping that you'd be happy to see me."

Amar looked at her. In a low voice, he asked, "What made you come today?"

Her composure seemed to falter. "You seem a lot harder than you were."

"You haven't answered my question."

She did not reply immediately. Her expression changed and she looked away. When she turned back her voice had lost its party banter tone and was quiet. "If you really want to know, I myself am not sure. It was Jane's idea and initially I was a bit reluctant. Then I was persuaded, and I have to confess I didn't need much persuasion. Is there anything terribly wrong with wanting to see someone again?" she asked a little sadly.

"I thought it would be Jane. You still haven't figured her out yet, have you? She loves feasting on the entrails. Never mind." Her candidness had softened Amar. "I'm sorry if I've been abrupt. And if it's of any relevance, it's nice to see you." He smiled.

Her face and posture relaxed and for a moment he feared that she would reach out her hand. But she controlled herself, and went back to her bantering tone. "Do you often use that party line?"

"Only when I'm confronted with a see-through blouse," said Amar getting into the game and grinning at her.

She blushed. "You're wicked," she said, obviously enjoying herself. "What would you say if it was a see-through bra?" she whispered.

"I'd say what your House of Commons speaker says—the *eyes* have it, but the rest don't."

"And what would you do about that?"

Amar was now tiring of the game and said, "Have another drink. Excuse me while I get one." He got up, leaving a rather miffed Priscilla behind.

When he returned with his beer he found, to his relief, that Gary had taken his chair. "You can't be monopolising the sexy women all the time, Das" he grinned.

"Wait till I complain to my tribal tough. He'll do yer," said Amar.

He found a place between Beverly and a petite blonde called Dawn who was in her first year and regarded Amar with a bit of awe. He thought back to his first year and recalled how he had sat in this same room with the senior fencers. How much time had elapsed, how much had happened. Suddenly Amar felt the poignancy of the moment. Within a matter of weeks all this would be a memory.

The evening moved on amid the arguments, banter, laughter, clink of glasses and general release of tension which characterised a Friday evening. The boisterousness increased in their corner, as the evening advanced. Gary seemed to be doing well with Priscilla, Jane was flirting with a willing Rod, Greg was in the midst of an argument with three others and Amar was regaling Beverly and Dawn with stories about the jungles of India. Two second-year youngsters were deep in what seemed to be an intimate chat. Priscilla kept eying Amar from time to time but he was determined not to respond.

Eventually, Rod raised his voice and said, "Get your glasses filled everybody, there's something I have to say." There were groans. But glasses were filled up.

Rod stood up and there were cries from the group, "Do it sitting, it'll be shorter", "Lying down would be even better", and some more profane utterances. Rod took it all in good humour and finally rapped on the table. "Quiet, you lot! I've tried all the positions you recommend, and I'm not going to tell you which I prefer most." There were shouts of, "Oh, do tell".

Rod held up his hand "For the men who want to know, I'll recommend a good book. For the women, however, I'm available for individual consultations." There were good-natured jeers from the men, and theatrical sighs from the women. "Okay, enough of merriment. Because it's with a certain sadness that I've come here this evening, and I believe you share that with me. We're saying goodbye to somebody who has endeared himself to everybody who has got to know him, and done more for the Fencing Club than anyone of us. Knowing the kind of person he is, I know how embarrassed he feels at any compliments. So I shall spare him too much embarrassment. But I have to say that for warmth, considerateness, humanity and humour he can be an example to all of us. I will not talk of his fencing skills—the full colours are a testimony to them. Personally, I will miss him greatly as a friend—

and the club will miss him equally as a leader. I would like all of you to join me in drinking a toast to our good friend—Amar."

"To Amar," they all said and drank. Amar was dreading this moment because he would have to reply. He got up a little hesitantly. "Upright—kneeling—missionary position … ? What's the form?" There was laughter. Then more seriously, he continued, "Thank you, Rod. Thank you all. I don't have Rod's oratorical skills, so forgive me if I don't try to match him. All I can say is that in spite of the wonderful time we've all had today, I'll walk down the stairs tonight with a heavy heart. I can never forget my three years at the LSE—which were made all the more memorable by being part of this wonderful group. I suspect, that in years to come, when my hair is grey, and my limbs less active, my memories of this club and the wonderful people in it will be one of my abiding recollections of my time at the LSE. I have found companionship, laughter and affection in a larger measure than I ever thought possible. I won't continue further, because I'm finding it difficult to keep my emotions in check. I don't know when I will see you again. But I would like to drink a toast to lasting friendship."

There was applause and everyone drank.

Rod nodded to Beverly and she fumbled in her large bag. She brought out a gift-wrapped package, came over to Amar and handed it to him. "From all of us," she said and then gave Amar a kiss. An emotional Amar sat down, finding it difficult to hold back tears. There was too much welling up inside him. This was more than he had expected and almost more than he could take. Controlling himself, he said in a hoarse voice, "Thank you, thank you all. I just don't know what to say …" After a brief pause he continued, "Not having got over my childhood habits, I'm going to open my present straightaway." He tore off the wrapping, glad that this diverted his attention. They had bought him a beautifully illustrated book on England, and the flyleaf had been signed by each one of them.

Amar took a big gulp of his beer. Conversation resumed all around and he just sat back and let it wash over him. These were not people he knew really well, yet they had managed to make him feel wanted. How much of their warmth was genuine, how much prompted by social conventions, how much by peer pressure—he did not know or want to know. All he knew was that he felt a sense of gratification. Whether this was alcohol induced or reality inspired he was not sure, and he did not really care. He had actually begun to feel a sense of contentment. It was temporary, he knew. It was ephemeral, he knew. But for the moment, it did not matter.

As the evening drew to a close, various toasts were drunk. At one stage Amar staggered up and said he would like to propose a toast to a social cause dear to Indians. This had to do with the abolition of an institution which led to untouchability. "Raise your glasses folks and repeat after me, 'Down with *chaddis*'. You see, *chaddis* lead to untouchability and this applies particularly to women. All together now," and the room resounded to the cry of 'Down with *chaddis*'. Then they all drank. If they had realised what *chaddis* meant, there would have been louder cheers.

❖

The next afternoon a weary and hungover Amar sat drinking black coffee with Pramod.

"I can't believe you dragged a serious subject like untouchability into your drunken conversation and actually made a joke about it."

Amar sat with his head in his hands. Tiredly, he said, "I did not make a joke about untouchability as it exists in our country. My joke just used the literal meaning of untouchability, okay? All I was saying was that panties come in the way of touching women, which even you'll have to accept is a fact. So what's the problem?"

"I won't waste time discussing this subject with you. You're not in a state for any serious discussion, anyway. I would suggest you get yourself some Alka Seltzer and sleep off your hangover."

Angela

Some days later, rummaging disconsolately through the pigeonhole, he came across a note in a handwriting which seemed familiar. Feeling breathless, Amar opened the note from Angela. It was brief to the point of terseness, but said that she could meet him for a short while the next day but it should be outside the LSE. Feverishly Amar tore a page out of his diary and wrote her a note suggesting a coffee house on Kingsway. He left it in her pigeonhole hoping desperately that she would look in there sometime during the day.

He was in a fever of excitement and stood irresolutely wondering what he should do now. He finally decided to go for a walk by the river. It was cool and windy outside but he needed to be out in the fresh air to clear his confused thoughts. He buttoned up his coat as he walked. A few light drops of rain were carried by the wind onto his face but this only soothed him.

He realised that the first thing he needed to do was to curb his racing expectations. Deep down, he knew that nothing would come out of this meeting. All he could do was to try and clear the air. But the heart, unversed in logic, raced ahead with its hopes.

❖

It was a desolate, drizzly morning as Amar made his way up Kingsway the next afternoon. He recalled his first walk down this road three years ago when he had gone for the interview at the LSE. He was probably more nervous today than he had been then. His hands were cold. A steel band of tension seemed to be encircling his head. He still had no idea what he was going to say to Angela. Nor, whether she would be there at all.

He walked into the dimly lit, cosy atmosphere of the coffee house and took off his coat, then found a table from where he could watch the front door. The aroma of fresh coffee was curiously soothing. Yet his hands continued to be cold and his head tight. He watched absently through the large glass windows at the pedestrians walking past. There was no sign of the slim, long-legged figure he was looking for. He kept looking at his watch every few minutes and then decided to ignore the watch. She was already ten minutes behind schedule. The waitress came for an order. He told her that he would order as soon as his friend arrived.

Ten more minutes passed, and he decided that she was not coming. His disappointment was immense and despair engulfed him. A black misery.

Trying to be rational, he told himself that he had not really expected her to come. But it brought no comfort. He once again recognised his failure with relationships. There had to be something very wrong with him. He suddenly felt an immense weariness. He would have liked to put his head down on the table and go to sleep. He saw the waitress approaching again and tiredly thought that this time he would not disappoint her. When she arrived, he apologised for not having placed an order, and asked for a coffee. She smiled and said, "No, I haven't come to ask for an order, sir. There's a young lady sitting over there who asked if you would like to join her."

Amar's heart seemed to stop. He slowly got up and looked at the corner table the waitress was pointing to, with a mounting anger. He walked across and stood looking down coldly at her. She was sitting with her face cradled by her hand trying to suppress a smile. A half-empty cup of coffee lay in front of her. In spite of himself, Amar found his anger melting. He sat down opposite her. "You wicked woman—you watched my anguish for half an hour before sending me a message," he said sternly.

"Anguish? What anguish? You were busy ogling all the women passing by," she said calmly.

"Yes, because I was looking for a special one. While she sat heartlessly here, watching my torment."

"You won't get me to believe you were in any torment. Why should you be anyway?"

He did not answer immediately. The waitress was hovering around and Amar ordered a coffee. "Yes, I suppose you're right to be wary of what I say," he said slowly. "But this I can promise—I did not ever lie to you." At the back of his mind, this sentence seemed to find a resonance. He had heard it not too long ago.

"Yet, you destroyed something in me," she said and then immediately seemed to regret her openness. "Anyway, I don't really want to discuss this. Why did you ask me to meet you today?"

"I don't really know," he said honestly. "All I do know is that I didn't want to leave the country without seeing you again—and trying to explain things."

"What is there to explain? You have a girlfriend in Germany to whom you're committed. End of story."

"No, that is not the end of the story. There is much more, but I won't tax you with the details. It's all a very complicated and messy business which is coming to its chaotic end. But that is not why I wanted to see you."

"Coming to an end?" her voice was now sharp with anger. "So you thought why not settle for second best—Angela is there waiting, panting for me. Let's give it a twirl with her. So I'm to be the replacement from the reserves, since your first preference Fraulein has ditched you. Is that what this is all about?" she said this with a suppressed fury which shook Amar.

"No, no, no. I told you earlier, that has nothing to do with it. I'm not asking for anything from you. All I want is for you to understand that what I said that day at the Embankment was from my heart. Nothing can change that, nothing will. What happened subsequently was a cruel fate unwinding a malicious series of events which left me reeling in confusion and despair. There seemed only one honourable course of action open to me and I took it, irrespective of the price I had to pay. And the price was you. I lost you. I won't go over the torment I went through. But I had no choice, don't you see? Please—please try to understand that ..." his voice broke.

His coffee arrived and gave him respite. He took a sip of the hot liquid to give himself time to recover his equanimity. Her expression seemed to have softened a little, but he put that down to his wishful thinking.

"Angela, I want to repeat again, I'm not asking anything of you. Please believe me. And I'm going against my inclination in this, because I so desperately want to go back to the evening at the Embankment and wipe out all that has happened after that. But that is not possible and the pain that seared both of us will have left an everlasting scar. And don't ever think I've come to you because I faced rejection elsewhere. You have always been first in my heart and will remain so. It's my own timidity and fear of rejection which stopped me from expressing my feeling for you earlier. Anyway, that's all water under the bridge now. All I want from you is your understanding. I leave within the month, and I don't know whether I'll ever see you again. But I would like to leave with the belief that you've at least begun to understand what happened. That's all I can ask of you."

"What's to understand, Am? You've hurt me. I've reacted. All that cannot change."

"No. But what can change is the awareness—the recognition that all that happens is not always within one's control. I'm not seeking an escape route for myself. I'm deeply sorry for the pain I've caused you. All I'm asking you to appreciate is that at that time I had no other course open to me—your understanding and forgiveness is all I ask now."

"But why did you start this whole thing that evening at the Embankment when you knew that you had a girlfriend in Germany?"

"Because the whole thing had wound down. It was near closure. And because I could no longer hold back my feelings for you. Maybe the imminent end of my stay here panicked me.

Maybe the sensible thing would have been to formally end my relationship with her, before I said all that I did to you. But can one always be sensible and reasonable?"

"And now you're asking me to listen to my heart and forget reason?"

"Sadly, I don't know what your heart is saying. I know mine—but I don't want to embarrass you by giving voice to it."

"My reason tells me I should not have come today. Maybe I should have listened to my reason."

Amar's patience was now running thin. His words seemed to have made no difference to her attitude. "Maybe you should have, because I am beginning to feel I'm talking to a blank wall," he said a little sharply.

"And maybe the wall has to be there for protection."

"Why *did* you come today, Angela? To see me grovel?" His voice was angry.

She sighed. "Oh, Am, sometimes you can be so obtuse. Can't you see beyond your nose? Can't you think of any other reason for my coming today?" She put her head down and closed her eyes. He thought he saw the beginnings of a tear.

"Sorry if I sounded harsh, Angela," he said gently and touched her hand. "I've become very hesitant about reading too much in to what is beyond my nose. Besides my nose is too long to allow me to see clearly."

She managed a smile as she rummaged in her bag for a handkerchief. "You *are* a clown," she muttered. She blew her nose in a handkerchief and surreptitiously wiped away the tear. As she replaced the bag and put her hands on the table again, one of her hands touched Amar's. She didn't remove it. The atmospherics seemed to have subtly changed.

"You put up a very tough front—I was quite intimidated," Amar said.

Her voice sounded weary as she replied. "What could I do? I've been badly hurt, and the person who caused this hurt was sitting opposite. I wanted to be as wounding as I could. Unfortunately, I am not good at this sort of thing. As a result, it took a lot out of me and now I feel exhausted."

"You did a good demolition job," he said while absently stroking her finger.

"Oh Am, that is not what I really wanted to do. Being the fool I am, I really wanted the opposite. And again being the fool I am, I'm telling you all this. But what am I to do? You still mean so … much … to me … and you're going away …" She started crying silently while fumbling for her handkerchief again. Amar took out his handkerchief and gave it to her. She took it and held it to her eyes. Through the handkerchief her tearful voice said, "Now you see why I wanted to meet outside the LSE. I was afraid of something like this …"

Amar gave her time to recover, as he was at a loss for words. What was he to say? He had lost everything and now suddenly rediscovered his lost treasure. And like a starving pauper faced with a sumptuous meal he did not know what to do with the riches. He was afraid that it was a mirage. He was frightened that it may not be true. He was terrified that it would end.

She wiped her eyes, blew her nose and then refreshed the lipstick. Amar realised that he was probably seeing her for the first time with lipstick on. He must have looked startled because she smiled wanly and said, "It's the new look."

"So what else is new?"

She looked uncomfortable. She took hold of his hand and opened it out. She stroked it and said, "You know this is the first thing I noticed about you—your beautiful hands."

Amar was flabbergasted. "My hands? What's so special about my hands? Hell, I'd even forgotten I had hands. What about the rest of me, for God's sake?" he exclaimed in dismay.

She giggled in spite of herself and slapped his hand. "Compliments, compliments, compliments—that's all men live for." Then her face clouded once more.

"There's something troubling you, Angela. Do you want to talk about it?"

Tears again appeared in her eyes and she bit her lips and shook her head. Her grip on his hand tightened. Then she screwed her eyes, as if she was in pain, and said in a choked voice "Yes, there's something I have to tell you. I'm getting engaged." The tears now flowed freely and she made no effort to wipe them. "This was after all that happened between us. Maybe it was an act of desperation. Maybe one of retaliation. But there is this boy I've known for a long time. He has been after me to marry him for some time now. I've always laughed it off, because I just wasn't interested enough in him. Then I gave in because I was so disillusioned with life after our break-up. I thought what difference does it make who I marry—all men have feet of clay, anyway. And now we are getting engaged next week ..." Her voice broke into a sob. "Oh, Am, what have we done to each other?"

His hand which had warmly lain in hers suddenly felt lifeless and cold. He slowly withdrew it as she kept crying soundlessly. He closed his eyes. Retribution had caught up. He felt numbed.

"You were quick off the mark, weren't you," he said bitterly.

"You can blame me if you like. But at least try and think of my situation. I have this one evening of joy with the person I had for a long time secretly wished for, and then within a few days, I'm told that it was all over. What do you think it did to me? It left me marooned on a rock with the sea closing in on me. I was struggling for survival and desperately looking for help. Robin was there to help me. And I was weary. I didn't have the energy to think. So I gave in to his pleading. He was at least stable and safe. He may not have been the most interesting of men, but at least he was constant. All I wanted then was security and peace of mind. What option did I have?"

"So, stodgy, steady Robin walks off with the trophy. And you're all set to lead your grey life with a grey man," Amar couldn't restrain his anger.

Angela reacted sharply. "Don't run down a good man. I'm surprised—I didn't expect this from you."

"Nor did I. I'm sorry. I don't even know the man—and I don't have any right to pass judgement on your choice. I allowed my anger to run away. To lose your cherished woman once, is difficult enough. To lose her twice drives you beyond the edges of civilised behaviour. I'm sorry."

"He really is a decent man," she said again, almost as if to convince herself.

"I'm sure he is," Amar paused. "Well, there seems nothing more to talk about. I should be on my way."

She looked up in alarm. "You're going?"

"Yes—I think so. There seems to be little for us to speak about now. You've taken your decision and all I can do is wish you luck."

He called for the bill. She looked stricken. "Why're you doing this, Am?" she asked in a low voice.

"Doing what?"

"Depriving me of a little time with you. This may be the last time we meet," she said quietly, looking at her cup where the coffee looked cold and dead. She seemed to be trying to avoid tears.

"Yes, it may well be. Unfortunately, my staying on is not going to help, however much I may want to—and if I'm honest, I want to. I want to stretch out every minute, every second, to its limit and extract from it all I can get of you. But to what purpose? As I step out of that door, I step into history for you, since you have another life to start. So why prolong the agony?"

She did not say anything but sat with her head in her hands and eyes closed. An occasional tear rolled down her cheek. Finally, she composed herself and opened her eyes and used Amar's handkerchief, which she was still clutching, to wipe her tears away. Her eyes looked dead and defeated.

"Yes, you're saying the wise and sensible thing," she said in a flat voice. Amar wasn't sure whether it was wisdom which dictated what he had said, or a desire to hurt her.

He paid the bill and slowly got up. He was finding it difficult to speak knowing that he would not see her again. "Goodbye, Angela," he said gruffly and turned. She seemed unable to speak but kept looking at him with stricken eyes.

Amar stepped out into the darkening dusk.

The Light Dims

The term drew to a close. The results came out. Amar had got through, but not with flying colours. Pramod on the other hand had done very well and was now assured of financial assistance for his postgraduate studies. Amar's family had left the previous day and he had moved into Pramod's bedsitter at Clapham Common. He would fly to Dusseldorf the next day. Anisha had come over to spend this last evening together. Amar had become quite friendly with this charming, intelligent, petite girl who hid a great sense of humour beneath a bustling exterior.

"Why on earth are you going to Dusseldorf, Amar?" Anisha asked, cuddled up in one corner of the sofa with a glass of wine. She was privy to all that had happened and had been a great source of support for Amar.

"Difficult to say, Ani, if I'm honest. I suppose it's partly guilt, partly a need for reassurance that things are okay there, since Sudipto has a rather mercurial temperament. Partly a response to his appeal that we should not let our old friendship break up. We were very close friends for three years, you know. Almost as close as Pramod and I are," explained Amar, sprawled on the floor with his mug of beer.

"He's chosen a fine way to show his friendship," she said sarcastically. For her, black was black and white was white—intermediate positions did not exist.

"Be fair, Ani—I haven't covered myself with glory, either."

"Maybe—but you got infatuated with this girl after spending time with her. And she was an adult who chose to be intimate with you. Here, he hasn't even met her and yet he lays claim to her!"

"Well, nobody has forced her to do what she is doing, either."

Pramod who was cooking his famous *keema* curry in the little cooking space at one end of the room interjected, "It's no use, Ani. I've tried and given up. He seems to be suffering from sainthood."

"Don't be so critical," Anisha admonished Pramod. "It requires generosity of spirit to be forgiving. And it's not a gift a lot of us have."

Pramod didn't reply, but opened his eyes wide and looked heavenward and grimaced. "Yes ma'am."

"But, Amar, you are carrying this hair shirt thing a bit far." Amar saw Pramod's grimace change to a grin and his hands go through a silent clapping motion behind her back. Amar restrained a smile, but was obviously not entirely successful.

Anisha addressed Pramod without turning around, "All right, kiddo, I know you're clowning around behind my back. Why don't you get back to your cooking and let the adults have a serious conversation?" After a pause she said, "You know you've aged in the last few months, Amar?"

"Good, I'll now appeal to a rich dowager," Amar grinned. "Seriously, though, there is a positive side, Ani, to all this. I've learnt a few things." He paused, and seemed lost in thought. "Or maybe, I've unlearnt a few 'truths'. When you're in the first flush of youth, you grasp eagerly at a lot of ideas and believe them to be ultimate truths. However, as time passes and experience grows, their frailty gets exposed. And I've had my due share of experience."

Anisha looked quizzically at him. "What have you learnt or unlearnt?"

"A number of things," he replied. "But most importantly that we overvalue intellect and undervalue our instincts. That the intellect does not have all the answers—yet we expect it to, and sometimes get the wrong answers."

"Explain."

Amar scratched his head and smiled ruefully. "Now I'm in trouble. I think I'll have to ask Pramod to rescue me from the inquisition."

Anisha was unmoved. "No copout. Explain."

"W-e-l-l, okay, let's take feelings, emotions. Let's take this thing called love. I don't know what it is, though I've felt it. Being new converts to rationalism, to the sovereignty of the intellect, Pramod and I spent hours dissecting this phenomenon. There had to be a logical explanation to it—there had to be a solution to this equation. And we developed all sorts of theories, as most zealots do. We felt we had cracked it, and felt the smugness of the righteous. Yet as events unfolded, I began to realise that I was a child lost in a dark forest. I could feel things, but could not explain them. All our theories failed to explain feelings. How could I feel love towards more than one woman? How could the nature of this love differ in the shades and textures it displayed for each person? How could I choose between these loves—which one was the true one? Were there any common elements in the love between man and woman, the love between parent and child, brother and sister? Was love really an extension of one's ego? … these and a hundred questions assailed me. And, I finally understood that it was all an exercise in futility. How did it matter? If my innermost being felt a deep love, why waste time trying to dissect it? Would I, looking at a beautiful rose, then proceed to take apart its petals to understand how it was made up? I would destroy the beauty that it had and fail to recognise the very essence of this beauty. What would I have gained? So why not let my inner being be sovereign from time to time, and let me enjoy what I had?"

Anisha sat looking out of the window. Finally she asked, "And what about the intellect, the power of reasoning? To be put on the backburner?"

"No, most definitely not. What I'm saying is, we need to understand that the intellect cannot be our guide for everything that happens to us. After a point it can take us into sterile country. There are certain spheres which are not susceptible to scientific explanation. We need to have the courage to follow our instincts in these areas."

"Are you seriously suggesting that we live by intuition?"

"No. You know that's not what I'm saying," Amar responded somewhat impatiently. "What I *am* saying is that we do not always understand what is going on inside us. That—intuition, gut feel, call it what you will—need not always be very different from what we call rationality. Maybe our internal system is being as logical as a rational mind, but it is processing a much larger body of information than our mind has access to, and much faster too. Can you not see that the output would be of a higher quality?"

"But how does the internal system, as you call it, have access to a larger data bank? Surely the mind has equal access?"

"Maybe we're talking of two different levels of mind. There's a deeper level which we are not consciously aware of, which is a repository of greater knowledge. And our conscious mind does not have easy access to this, while our deeper level of consciousness does."

"You're confusing me. On the one hand you say we should depend on intuition and not be overly taken up by logic. On the other, you're implying, yes do this, but remember that intuition also works on logic. Which ultimately means that we are back to the dependence on logic and rationality. So, what's new then?"

"What's new is that it is a better kind of rationality which I'm asking you to refer to. Not the conscious rationality which says two plus two make four. The other rationality might tell you—no. It doesn't always."

Over the burbling of the pan on the gas ring, Pramod finally broke his silence. "He's been reading Orwell, Ani, where two plus two add up to what the State decides. Don't listen to him. He'll persuade you that it is right and proper to drink beer in genteel company, because the State says so." Anisha smiled at this dig at her father. But said in a severe tone, "And he may persuade me to stop going out with you because you don't wear the state-ordained cravat, don't smoke a pipe, and don't drink sherry. Don't read the *Times* either. So belt up, and let me get on with the discussion."

Amar grinned while Pramod scowled. "Let me go back to what I was saying, before I was rudely interrupted by the 'enemy of the state'. There are things which happen inside us which we cannot explain. Immediately after my ultimate conversation with Helga, when her rejection became unequivocally clear, I was beside myself with rage and despair. You know where the anguish almost took me. Then I woke up one morning feeling a serenity I had not known for some time. My anger towards her had been moderated by an understanding of her. How it happened, I don't know. But it had happened. There must have been some churning at the deeper levels of my consciousness. For the first time in months, I felt at peace. Should I have instead sat down and tried to analyse why it happened, and descended once more into darkness? Can you not see how sterile and pointless the exercise would have been?"

"Maybe," she replied, and seemed to be lost in thought. "Yes, maybe. But you've got to be careful, Amar. You can't go on depending on your gut for all decisions."

"Don't misrepresent what I've said, Ani," Amar responded testily. "These debating tricks are unworthy of your intelligence. I don't wake up every morning waiting for a blinding shaft of lightning to say how I should manage the day. You should know that. All I'm saying is that following the conscious logical tree relentlessly does not always provide us the right answer. And I'm merely reflecting what greater minds than mine have said. At the risk of courting Pramod's ire—more Bengal glorification, let me quote what the poet Tagore has said—'A mind all logic is like a knife all blade. It makes the hand bleed that uses it.'"

"You do feel strongly about this, don't you?" Anisha asked.

Amar was gazing over her shoulder at something. "At the moment my friend seems to be feeling even more strongly about something—he's doing the Saint Vitus dance, clutching on to his hand. Let's find out why," Amar struggled up from the floor. Pramod was jumping up and down holding his right hand.

Anisha looked over her shoulder and got up. "Oh, he's just burnt his hand again. He does that whenever he's cooking. Coming, my poor wounded soldier, coming … coming."

Pramod kept prancing in pain but managed to say angrily "I don't need any help—I can manage on my own, thank you."

Anisha put her arms around him and guided him to the tap. "And what are we supposed to do when we get a dry burn? Put it under the tap and let the cold water flow over it. Right?"

Pramod angrily shrugged her away and put his hand under the tap. It seemed to help, because in a quieter, but still angry voice he said, "Don't keep trying to mother me. I'm quite capable of looking after myself."

"Oh, you are, my little chubby bear, you are …" and then she said something affectionate in an undertone, which brought an unwilling smile to Pramod's face.

Amar turned away and walked to the window to give the loving couple some privacy.

He felt a surge of gloom as he looked out at the dark lonely street.

❖

Soon, having had his hand attended to, Pramod announced dinner and bustled around opening a bottle of good wine, a rare luxury.

Dinner was served, and glasses filled. Pramod had done a passable job on the *keema*, *dal* and rice. Conversation, as happens on emotion-ridden occasions, was stilted. They drank a toast to the future.

Anisha had to hurry back after dinner to get the last bus. Amar hugged her and she kissed him on the cheek. "Take care, Amar, keep in touch. And—stay with your instincts."

Amar felt a fleeting moment of panic. All the familiar faces seemed to be fading into the past. As if he was in a dark room with lit photographs which switched off one by one, until—until there was just nothingness.

The Light Flickers and Dies

Amar had persuaded Pramod not to come to the airport. They had parted with a brief hug. Neither could think of something appropriate to say. Amar took the train to Victoria, and travelled to the airport in the coach, drinking in the last sight of the city he was so loath to leave. He had no idea if he would see it again.

At the airport, a childish romantic notion caught him looking around and hoping for Angela. He was embarrassed with himself. Too many B-grade romantic films.

❖

As he waited for his luggage at Dusseldorf airport, he realised that this was the last part of his three-year odyssey. What had happened in these years, he recalled with mixed feelings. What lay ahead in India, he did not know. He was in no man's land.

He took the coach to the city terminal and then a taxi to Helga's apartment. The arrangement was that she would take him to a nearby inexpensive hotel where she had booked him. He paid off the taxi and carried his suitcase up the stairs. His heart was beating fast as he rang the bell. It wasn't just because of the climb.

She opened the door and didn't register any emotion as she saw him, and his heart twisted. "Hello," was all she said. He, too, responded with a cold "Hello". She was wearing a printed frock which flared out from the waist. Amar was looking for a telltale bulge, but was defeated by the dress. Sudipto was sitting at the dining table reading a book and got up. He looked the same except for seeming a little thinner. He smiled and came forward to hug him. "*Kee re? Kaamon achheesh* (How are you, friend)?"Amar could not summon much enthusiasm for the hug, and replied "*Aak rokom* (Okay)."

They chatted desultorily about the flight and the weather. Madelena toddled forward and grabbed hold of Helga's legs as she looked at the newcomer. He wasn't surprised at her not recognising him, though Helga appeared embarrassed. "You will have dinner with us, won't you?" Sudipto asked with enthusiasm. "Helga has cooked up a superb meal," he said, face beaming. Stony-faced, Helga asked him not to exaggerate.

Amar thought it would be ungracious to decline and nodded his acceptance. "Wonderful!" Sudipto exclaimed. "Why don't you let Helga take you to the hotel? You can then freshen up and come back." He had not changed, thought Amar. Always wanting to be in charge.

Helga put on a light raincoat, as it had started to drizzle, and they walked downstairs. She saw Amar pause at the bottom of the stairs and put the suitcase down. "It's heavy? Can I help?" she asked.

"No, thanks, I can manage," Amar replied.

"It's not far," she said, as they crossed the street.

They walked in silence for a while. "I'm sorry Madelena did not recognise you," she said.

"Children have short memories," Amar said. "So do their elders."

She looked at him, and looked away. "Do you have to be so bitter, A-mar?"

Amar laughed mirthlessly. "No, of course, I don't. There is no reason. Is there?"

She shook her head angrily and muttered something in German. They walked in silence after that. At the hotel she spoke in German to the receptionist who got Amar to register and gave him the room key. She took it from him and led him to the lift. At the room she opened the door and let him go in with the suitcase. She then waited at the door, much to Amar's surprise. He put the case down and stood with his hands on his hip, shaking his head. "You're afraid to come in because I may rape you?" he asked angrily.

He suddenly remembered. He slapped his forehead angrily, closed his eyes in anguish and said, "Stupid—stupid—stupid … I'm sorry—that was very thoughtless of me. I'm sorry."

"No, I do not blame you. Men are like that."

"Like what—insensitive? That's what I am?"

She was quiet. And then said in a low voice, not looking at him, "No, A-mar. I think you are the most sensitive man I have met." Having said this she turned her back to him.

Amar didn't know how to respond. Finally, he said gently, "Why don't you go home, Helga, and I'll follow after I freshen up. What you can do is give me the directions to the nearest wine shop, so that I can buy some wine for tonight."

"There is no need. But if you want to …" And then she gave the directions.

"Thanks, I'll be there in the next hour."

❖

Amar bought a couple of bottles of white wine and made his way to the flat. He found that his anger towards Helga had abated. Was that what a stroke to the ego did to you, he wondered. He made up his mind that he would not be aggressive tonight.

Sudipto opened the door. "*Array, tui eh shob ki niye eshechish* (Hey, what's all this you've brought)?" "Helga," he called out "See what this crazy man has brought! We're going to have a great evening!" He exclaimed, rubbing his hands and beaming. His enthusiasm was infectious.

Helga took the wine and said, "I'll put them in the fridge to chill."

"And in the meantime," said Sudipto, "We'll have some of the excellent beer Helga has bought for us."

They sat in one corner of the living room so that they would not disturb Madelena. "You have not changed, Amar, except for your hair," said Sudipto, raising his glass of beer. Amar suddenly realised he no longer used hair oil, and also had a shorter haircut than in India.

"So, what's all the news from Delhi?" Amar asked.

"Nothing very dramatic. The university coffee house continues to attract more students than the classrooms do, the college cafe continues to look as shabby as it always was—though it still serves the best toast in town—the girls in the university are getting bolder than they used to be—the *cholis* are getting shorter and some girls have taken to wearing trousers or slacks or whatever you call them ... Tutu, my wild ex-girlfriend has got married to a God-fearing Bengali government official and has a puja room in her house..." And he continued providing an update on common friends and acquaintances.

Helga listened quietly, sipping her beer. After a while she got up to go to the kitchen.

Amar took the opportunity of Helga's absence to ask the question that had been bothering him, "How're you going to manage financially here, Sudi?"

Sudipto shrugged, a gesture normally foreign to him but which he obviously thought was appropriate in the present milieu. "Well, I had been learning German in Delhi and will need a few weeks to polish it up. I'll be looking for a job with Helga's help. For the moment I'm dependent on her, and I have to admit that financially things are tight just now. But I'm confident I'll be able to start earning soon."

Amar didn't want to dent his confidence, but was certain they were in for a tough ride for some time. "Well—that's good to know."

Sudipto asked about common acquaintances at the LSE. He was amused to hear about the exploits of the "loin of Punjab". "He must have produced a good few illegitimate cubs by now."

"If he has, he's kept them well-hidden," laughed Amar. Just then Helga returned and both realised that this was a subject they needed to keep away from.

"We were talking of old times," Sudipto explained. "We had some crazy people in college. There was one who was studying English Honours. On the night before his paper on Shakespeare he realised that he did not know any of the texts.

So he spent the night reading the Classics Illustrated comics! And he passed!"

"Not only that," Amar added, "He is, today, teaching English!"

Helga realised that they were trying to include her in the conversation, and smiled at the story for their benefit.

The reminiscences continued, as the beer glasses were refilled. Sudipto went to the bathroom and Amar looked out of the living room window at the neon signs flashing on and off across the road. He remembered Helga, after they had made love, propping up her legs against the wall so that the coloured neon lights shone on them. He looked at Helga. She was also looking at the neon signs.

Sudipto returned and broke the spell. "This is good beer," Sudipto said, taking a swig from his glass.

Amar decided to bring Helga into the conversation. She had been uncharacteristically quiet so far. "Helga is the beer expert. So—is this top or bottom fermented?" he asked mischievously. She probably recalled him asking her during their lovemaking whether she was top or bottom fermented. She blushed but didn't reply. Sudipto seemed puzzled.

Amar decided to help her out. "This is all about the process of brewing," he explained to Sudipto. "We were having a beer at one of the beer cellars and I, fancying myself as a beer expert, was telling her about the characteristics of the beer we were drinking. She floored me completely by not only adding further information, but also talking about the brewing process. I was mightily impressed. Until I realised that she was reading out from a write-up which was on the table."

"I was only doing what you had been doing earlier," Helga rejoined.

"No, I wasn't. I was speaking from my own knowledge," protested Amar.

"Yes, which came from the table top," she replied with a smile.

This was her first recognition of a shared past and it gladdened him. He didn't care if Sudipto liked it or not.

"When will women learn to accept male superiority?" he exclaimed wearily with a sigh.

Helga obviously did not think that deserved a reply. She got up to serve dinner. Sudipto followed. Amar was about to offer to help, but then changed his mind. Let Sudipto feel a part of the household he had adopted. He walked across to the window and looked down at the street, letting memories flood back.

His reverie was interrupted by Sudipto. "*Aiee, Amar, eta ki kore khole* (Hey, Amar, how do I open this)?" He asked waving the wine bottle.

Amar asked Helga for the opener and started the process, not being very adept at it himself. Not wanting Sudipto to see his exertions, he asked him to get the wine glasses.

Sudipto watched Amar's struggle with amusement. "*Tui oh amar mothon Bangal, dekhchi* (I see you're as much of a villager as I am)."

They sat down to dinner. She had made pork ribs in mustard, something Amar had enjoyed so much the last time.

"This pig was called Chuck," Amar said, in good spirits after the beer and the wine. Both Sudipto and Helga looked mystified. "You didn't know that the pigs are given American names when they are being bred for the table? That's to make them eat more and become obese," Amar explained solemnly.

"God!" Sudipto groaned. "Do I have to come all the way to Germany to listen to PJ's?"

"PJ's are a time-honoured tradition of our college in Delhi," Amar explained to Helga. "They are the name given to flat jokes. Sudipto was known to have got his doctorate on PJ's."

"Your anti-American feelings seem to have deepened," Sudipto observed.

"Anti-smugness rather than anti-American," said Amar as he took another mouthful of pork. "This really is delicious, Helga."

Helga muttered a "Thank you" and looked up to see if he would refer to the last time he had eaten it. Amar decided to be discreet and didn't.

"Where's my girlfriend, Hilde?" asked Amar about the au pair.

"She had taken time off to be with her boyfriend," answered Helga tersely.

"Fickle woman," muttered Amar determined to enjoy himself. This did not go down well with Helga either. She got up to clear the plates.

Sudipto rose and said, "Let me get the other bottle of wine."

By the time he returned, Helga had regained her composure. She took the wine bottle and the opener from Sudipto. With a few deft movements she uncorked the bottle and handed the bottle back to Sudipto with a straight face.

Amar sighed. "See Sudipto, another awesome example of woman power. We're as powerless in the hands of women as the bottle was." Helga glanced sharply at Amar, as if she was unsure what his real meaning was.

"Why don't you drink the wine instead of spouting philosophy?" she said firmly.

"*Jawol, Fraulein, Jawol.* But I'm not spouting philosophy, just accepting what is. *Muss es sein? Es muss sein!* as Beethoven said. 'Must it be? It must be.' So let's drink to that!"

Helga looked up surprised. "You're quoting in German?"

"Yes ma'am. I've learnt a few words. Forgive my pronunciation," Amar said, taking a sip from his glass.

"It is good. Thank you," Helga said. Her eyes seemed to mist over and she quickly got up muttering she had to make the coffee.

Sudipto looked at her retreating back and said, "She seemed upset."

"Yes. I must be going. Do you mind if I go and apologise?"

Sudipto laughed. "Of course not. Why should I? I don't own her."

Amar got up and walked to the alcove which served as a kitchen. She was measuring out the coffee powder. "Helga, I'm sorry if I've upset you. I had meant to be on my best behaviour today. But sometimes emotions surface without warning, and you say things you had not planned to. I want you to be happy in your future life. Now I must go."

She had been biting her lips. Then burst out in a low voice, "I don't ..." and tears started flowing. She rushed into the bedroom.

Amar, disturbed and unhappy, went across to Sudipto. He had not heard the exchange but had seen her rush out of the room.

"Sudi, I need to go." He opened his wallet and took out most of the money from it. "Look, I don't need this money since I'm flying tomorrow. It's not much, but it may buy both of you some beers," he said trying to smile.

"*Eta ki korchhish* (What are you doing)? You need to keep your money—you're travelling a long way," a discomfited Sudipto said.

"No, I'll be going home. I really don't need this anymore. I've kept enough for incidentals on the way."

"But this is a lot of money, Amar. How can I take it from you?"

"No, no, converted to Indian money it may seem a lot—but you'll see, it won't take you very far here. Just take it, because I don't need it."

Amar picked up his coat and gave Sudipto a hug. "Take care, old friend."

Sudipto looked confused. "You're going? But what about ..."

"Just say goodbye to her on my behalf."

Sudipto seemed to remember something. "Wait." He fished into his pocket and brought out a folded piece of paper. "Read this later."

Amar opened the door and walked out, stuffing the paper into his pocket.

He walked down the stairs knowing he would not see them again. Another set of relationships severed. He was now truly alone. The melancholy, locked up inside, broke its bonds and bubbled up like a fatal toxin. As he walked down, he seemed to be descending into a well of darkness.

There was no one to turn to. His despair deepened with each step that increased the distance from his last set of friends. He began to feel curiously weightless and disembodied. Loneliness seemed to have sucked out everything from him, leaving him like an empty shell. He could see the streetlights and the neon signs, he could hear the traffic sounds—but they all seemed to be at a distance. They were outside him. They did not relate. They meant nothing to him. He was separate, unseen, unheard. Nobody was concerned with him, he was concerned with nobody. Everything was dead inside him, except a fathomless pain. As he crossed the road he could see a bus coming. He did not alter his steps. This would be the best way out. This time he would not flinch.

The brakes of the bus screeched. He winced as he waited for the scrunching crash, and the tearing of flesh and bones. He closed his eyes, while his body screamed for him to run. The bus stopped just a few inches away. He heard the driver shouting angrily at him. He just walked on, aware that in spite of his desire to end it all, he had felt a mind-numbing sense of terror while waiting for the crash.

❖

In the clinical hotel room, with its neutral grey walls, worn carpet, cold neon lights, his depression deepened. He sat on the bed in a kind of stupor. The easy way out had been the bus. But that had failed. Did he have the courage to follow the more painful way? He had a blade in his toilet bag. He got up uncertainly, and felt the rustle of paper in his pocket. He tiredly pulled out the folded sheet Sudipto had given him.

> I don't have the time to write too much, as I don't want Helga to see this. All I wanted you to know is that the pregnancy thing was a false alarm. No, it wasn't deliberate. She really thought she was pregnant.

He sat down. He felt tired. Did this make a difference? Was it true? Or was it just Sudipto trying to make him feel better? He sat hunched on the bed staring at the threadbare carpet. And wearily thought. There was a pattern. Sudipto had seemed to have stage-managed important parts of his life. Preeti, then Helga, then the break … But it no longer mattered. Nothing mattered.

The note at least had the effect of bringing him back to the world around him. He got out of his clothes, dragged on his pyjamas and slumped onto the bed.

❖

The next morning he got on to the coach at the terminal, feeling weary in every part of his body. He had hardly slept, tossing from side to side. He had dropped into an uneasy doze in the early hours of the morning. A shower had not refreshed him and he had needed two cups of strong coffee in the restaurant downstairs, to wake up. He could not face even a croissant at breakfast. He dragged himself to the bus stop staggering under the weight of the suitcase. His strength seemed to have left him.

He checked in at the airport and realised there was still some time left before boarding. He listlessly browsed around in the bookshop and finally picked up an English newspaper. He went back to the lounge, found a seat and opened the paper. But his mind could not focus. Around him lay the detritus of an airport. Crushed paper cups which had missed the bin, remnants of coffee trickling from them; creased newspapers scattered on seats; used baggage tags on the floor. His mind seemed to reflect this—used memories lying crushed, names and faces discarded, the past—a depressing, jaded remembrance.

His left jacket pocket felt heavy and he remembered that as he was leaving Pramod had given him a few papers he had found in Amar's pigeonhole at the LSE. He had stuffed them into his pocket and forgotten about them. He took out the wad. There were a couple of scribbled notes from Fencing Club members wishing him bon voyage. He threw them in the bin next to him. A couple were circulars from societies he was a member of. He chucked these away too. He was left with an envelope with his name printed on it in capital letters. He could not recognise the handwriting and was about to throw it away. But then curiosity got the better of him. He tore it open, and his heart jumped at the familiar handwriting.

> Dear Amar,
>
> I did not know how to contact you. And you didn't seem to have been coming to college. I just wanted you to know that the engagement is off.
>
> Angela

Her phone number was appended.

Amar sat with the note in his hands staring unseeingly at it. Angela was free of her obligation and here he was flying in the opposite direction to her.

He didn't know how long he sat in a daze. The boarding of his flight was announced. He kept sitting. The announcement came again. He slowly got up and made his way to the departure gate.

I have found power in the mysteries of thought,
exaltation in the changing of the Muses;
I have been versed in the reasonings of men;
but Fate is stronger than anything I have known.

—Euripides, *Alcestis,* 438 BC

ACKNOWLEDGEMENTS

I had not realised when I started this, my first book, the kind of demands it would make on me. Writing, I soon realised, is an achingly lonely business and often releases emotions which have lain dormant, making the author a difficult person to be around. For having withstood these periods of stress with fortitude and love, I have to thank my ever patient and ever supportive wife, Niloufer.

For having pushed me along the path when my spirit was flagging, I also have to thank my children – Aaliyah, Rabia and Suhail. As well as my older grandchildren Raisah and Kian who kept asking me for updates. In a different way by the joy they provided with their innocence, my younger grandchildren – Ayesha, Yohan, Taerah and Aryahn provided the stimulant I needed.

My two sisters, as well as many friends have encouraged and helped me. While space constraints do not allow me to mention them by name, my thanks go out all the same.

I have used the internet for information frequently as well as referred to Wikipedia, and am indebted to them for the help provided.

Finally, my thanks to my editors for their patience and advice.